An Irish Hostage

ALSO BY CHARLES TODD

THE BESS CRAWFORD MYSTERIES

THE IAN RUTLEDGE MYSTERIES

OTHER FICTION

An Irish Hostage

A Bess Crawford Mystery

CHARLES TODD

WILLIAM MORROW
An Imprint of HarperCollins*Publishers*

HarperCollins books may be purchased for educational, business, or sales promotional use. For information, please email the Special Markets Department at SPsales@harpercollins.com.

FIRST EDITION

Designed by Kyle O'Brien

Library of Congress Cataloging-in-Publication Data

Names: Todd, Charles, author.
Title: An Irish hostage / Charles Todd.
Description: First edition. | New York, NY : William Morrow, [2021] |
    Series: A Bess Crawford mystery |
Identifiers: LCCN 2021011589 (print) | LCCN 2021011590 (ebook) | ISBN
    9780062859853 (hardcover) | ISBN 9780062859877 (paperback) | ISBN
    9780062859884 (ebook)
Subjects: GSAFD: Mystery fiction.
Classification: LCC PS3570.O37 I75 2021 (print) | LCC PS3570.O37 (ebook)
    | DDC 813/.54—dc23
LC record available at https://lccn.loc.gov/2021011589
LC ebook record available at https://lccn.loc.gov/2021011590

ISBN 978-0-06-285985-3

21 22 23 24 25 LSC 10 9 8 7 6 5 4 3 2 1

Alas, it is never easy to say goodbye to anyone or even a pet who has shared years with us. It was particularly hard to lose Charles Dickens, shortened to Dickens. We got him as a kitten, and he became our "nurse" for anyone ill, the arbitrator of any fight, a protector of all the other cats who came into his life and ours, and he was just plain special. Black with an undercoat of white, he was like all black cats, gentle and very loving. Sometimes even fourteen years isn't long enough. Like all our other treasured friends, losing him left a huge gap in our home.

And there was Muffin, a long-haired tuxedo cat with a plume of a tail, a gentle and loving giant, who could stand by the dining room table with his paws on the top, and eat from his own plate. Kittens looked to him for comfort and protection. And for Fran he was her baby and her friend. Caroline loved him too. He was just always there, always greeting us at the door, filling our world with joy...

An Irish Hostage

CHAPTER ONE

Somerset, June 1919

WE HAD FINISHED our supper and were taking our tea in my mother's morning room.

It's quite a lovely room, the long windows open to a surprisingly mild spring evening, and a bit of a breeze pleasantly lifting the lilac curtains just a little, so that we could hear the nightingale singing in the tree by the garden gate.

The very picture of a happy family enjoying a companionable silence as we listened.

The only thing that spoiled this charming scene were the expressions on our faces.

Simon Brandon, home from whatever it was that had taken him to Scotland while I was in Paris, was trying his best not to look grim.

I had come home from Paris to discover that I was on extended leave while the Queen Alexandra's Imperial Military Nursing Service decided what to do with me. It was especially disappointing to me, because I'd expected to return to one of the clinics for the wounded who were still in our care. But for my parents' sake, I was trying to put a brave face on waiting for news.

My mother, as always sensitive to the feelings of those around her, was doing her best not to look worried.

And my father, on a brief leave from the Peace Talks in Paris, was attempting to hide his frustration with the direction the talks were taking, because he was privy to much of the behind-the-scenes maneuverings—maneuverings he couldn't discuss, bottling them up inside instead. He hadn't even complimented Cook on dinner, a measure of his preoccupation.

Adding to this merry evening was my own mention of the wedding in Ireland that I was to attend in a fortnight's time.

One of the Irish nurses who had been aboard *Britannic* with me when it sank off the Greek coast had nearly died from severe injuries to her legs when we abandoned ship. I had barely managed to pull her into one of the lifeboats and stop the bleeding. Then as we waited for rescue, several of the doctors and I had done our best to save her left leg, and miracle of miracles, we had succeeded. Eileen had been able to walk again after several months of intensive rehabilitation, and she was so grateful that she asked me to be her attendant at her wedding in Ireland when the war ended and both she and her fiancé were free to marry.

My parents and Simon were against my going there.

The problem was the Easter Rising in Ireland in 1916, an attempt to break away from England and set up home rule. It had been put down ruthlessly, and that had only aggravated the situation, hardening the Irish determination to be independent. The English position was that whatever their goals, to openly rebel while Britain was engaged in the Great War was little short of treason, and several of the ringleaders were shot. In 1916, we weren't certain of victory in France, and then on the heels of the Easter Rising, the Somme Offensive in July had dragged on for months, killing thousands of men. The Government wasn't in a mood of clemency.

The Irish, on the other hand, had felt they had waited long enough for independence, and many were tired of promises. There were only about four hundred people involved in the revolt, but it had set a spark alight across the countryside. Those at home, bearing the brunt of Britain's displeasure, turned on their own and considered the Irishmen who were fighting in the trenches as traitors to the Cause, and there had been *incidents* that kept the anger on both sides of the issue very close to the boiling point. Some of the worse attacks had been reported in the British press, and of course my parents had read about them.

I could understand my parents' position. On the other hand, Eileen had told me that I would be safe, and her family's protection would be more than enough for the short time I would be in Ireland. Indeed, her cousin had been one of the defenders at the Post Office in Dublin during the worst of the fighting, and he was looked upon as a hero. What's more, he had written to my father—as if they were equals! Unheard of! After all, the Colonel Sahib, as we called him, was a high-ranking British Army officer and Eileen's cousin had a price on his head—to assure him I would be taken care of. Another English officer would also be present—he was to be the groom's best man—and he would certainly see that I traveled safely to and from Ireland.

We had left the discussion at the supper table and were drinking our tea in a far-from-comfortable silence. But I couldn't leave the matter there. I owed it to Eileen to let her know if I wasn't able to come. Still, considering what I had done in France, on my own, while I was serving there, I was better prepared than most young women to take care of myself in hostile situations.

Our nearest neighbor's daughter, Sara, had never been out of Somerset. I could understand if *her* parents had told her she oughtn't go. I'd have agreed.

And so I said now, offering a compromise, "I won't go as a nursing Sister, in uniform. I'll dress very simply, so as not to attract attention."

"You must cross Ireland, my dear," my father said. "By train. And it isn't a direct connection. You'll change twice. The last ten miles you must travel by motorcar. Or dogcart for all I know. And come back in reverse."

I glanced at Simon, hoping he might suggest that he accompany me. Then I looked away. He would be less safe than I was, with his English accent and his soldier's stride.

"Surely Eileen could have someone meet me in Dublin?" But she hadn't suggested it . . .

I sighed.

Accustomed to making my own decisions for four years, I was finding it hard to be the dutiful daughter I'd been in 1914. Much as I adored my parents, I'd changed.

My mother seemed to grasp that. She said, finding a smile, "There have been several murders lately, darling. Of English travelers. In France, you had the Army's protection—well, umbrella. You were a Sister, an officer. It gave you a standing that everyone understood. That won't exist in Ireland. You will be seen as a target, if someone wishes to make a name for himself by shooting at you. You must see that."

It was a different argument from my father's or Simon's. They had been worried about travel, about finding my way in an unfriendly country, about the difficulties of being a bridesmaid when the English were anathema in most quarters. Everyone at the wedding would know who I was, and while I might not be in trouble *there*, it was possible that between the wedding and the ferry to England, someone might decide to do something rash.

My mother did have a point. I finished my tea and set the cup on the table as I considered what she'd said.

And then I remembered something.

I glanced at Simon, then looked away again. He hadn't been himself since Scotland. The easy friendship that had always been between us had been replaced by a stiffness that had left me to wonder what I'd done to deserve it. And so I hesitated to mention what had just occurred to me.

There had been a flyer in France, while I was in Paris, an American. As I was leaving the country, boarding my ship in Calais, Captain Jackson had asked me to tell Simon hello for him. I'd suspected at the time that the Captain might have been keeping an eye on me at Simon's request. It would have been typical of Simon—then. And much as that annoyed me in hindsight, I'd found the pilot very helpful indeed and couldn't very well complain.

The question now was, how did I bring Captain Jackson into the conversation without letting Simon know what I'd guessed?

I took a deep breath. In for a penny, in for a pound . . .

"I think there's a way we could avoid all the problems of traveling in Ireland. What if I could fly from England to Eileen's village? And back again. I'd be there just for the wedding, and with her family the entire time."

There was a smile on my mother's face as she turned to the Colonel Sahib. But my father's frown had deepened. "I could probably find someone to fly you. But I'm not sure I could do that in time."

"You don't need to find anyone. Simon? Captain Jackson is eager for any opportunity to fly. Do you think he might come to England and take me to Ireland?"

The surprise on Simon's face was quickly covered.

I could see that Captain Jackson hadn't told him that I knew about his friendship with Simon.

"I can ask him," he said. "Certainly."

"Do you think he'll agree? I'll make it worth his while," my father said.

And that's how I got to attend a wedding in Ireland.

CHAPTER TWO

IT WAS LOVELY to see Captain Jackson again. He winked at me as he greeted me, then was introduced to my parents. He was charmed by my mother and got along famously with my father when we met him in London eight days later.

Turning to Simon, he said, as if they hadn't met in some time, "Hello. How are you?"

And Simon shook his hand without a pause. "Good to see you again."

I kept a very straight face.

His aircraft was presently at a private field outside London, and he'd happily agreed to meet us near Bristol on the day in question, and transport me to the wedding, returning for me on Sunday evening after the Saturday ceremony.

We dined in a restaurant in the City, and afterward my father and Simon spent the night at the Colonel Sahib's club while my mother and I went to Mrs. Hennessey's, where I'd kept my lodgings. Mother took Diana's room, but we had a last cup of tea with Mrs. Hennessey before going up.

It was then I told my mother that Simon had asked the Captain to keep an eye on me in Paris.

She laughed. "Why am I not surprised? There was a distinct appearance of having dined on canary about the two of them tonight. There were feathers everywhere, in spite of their efforts."

"You see too much." I hesitated. "Speaking of that. Do you know why Simon was in Scotland recently?"

"He's said nothing to me since he came back to the cottage." Simon lived just through the wood at the bottom of our garden. "I haven't asked. I didn't want him to feel he had to confide in me."

"I must admit I'm curious."

"Yes, darling, so am I. But you know, when he's ready, he'll tell me whatever it is that's troubling him."

"Iris swears it's unrequited love." She had been our housemaid for ages.

Mother laughed again. "I'm sure she does. She asked me as I was packing for London if this Captain Jackson, whoever he might be when he's at home, was your beau."

I could hear the echo of Iris's voice as Mother mimicked her.

"Because he's flying me to Ireland?"

"To her way of thinking, anyone who came all the way from Paris to see you safely to the wedding must be in love with you."

"I don't think Captain Jackson has any intention of carrying me off to New Mexico."

"You know that, and I know that, but Iris is always hopeful."

I found myself wondering if my mother was also hopeful that I would marry soon and settle in a house near my parents. It wasn't likely to happen—most of the eligible young men I'd known before the war, danced with and played tennis with and ridden with, were dead now on the battlefields of France.

I gave her a hug, and we went to bed. But I lay there for some time in the familiar surroundings of my room. How many times had I come here on leave, however brief, and slept the clock round, tired as I was? If I no longer served in the Queen Alexandra's, would I be encouraged to give up my rooms at Mrs. Hennessey's? After all, why would I need to stay here, on increasingly rare visits to London? For I'd really have no excuse to go up, would I?

I wasn't sure I was ready to consider that possibility. Mrs. Hennessey's was a part of my years in France, a home I had come to love nearly as much as the one in which I'd been born in Somerset.

It hadn't been difficult to decide to join the nursing service in 1914, when the war began. I knew without a doubt that it was my duty. I couldn't fight with my father's old regiment, as I might have done as his son. Nursing was the next best thing, using my skills to keep alive as many of the wounded as I could. Looking into the future was far more difficult, as I was discovering even as that future crept closer.

Would they decide to keep me in the Queen Alexandra's, given my experience, or would they choose someone who had fewer resources, and needed the money?

That question was getting ragged around the edges, I'd brought it up to myself so often. And the last thing I wanted was for the Colonel Sahib to use his influence on my behalf.

I fell asleep finally, dreaming I was in one of the forward aid stations as the Germans broke through and we had to evacuate the wounded in a great hurry, carrying stretcher after stretcher to the ambulances and putting the walking wounded on the floor between the two tiers, with only a blanket to ease the rough journey behind the lines. I was in the last ambulance that pulled out as the last of the line covered our retreat.

I awoke in a cold sweat, and lay there quietly, hoping I hadn't disturbed my mother in the next room.

As I discovered, it was absolutely the most beautiful experience imaginable to fly.

We took off from an airfield just outside Bristol, and as the wheels left the ground and we were airborne, I had the oddest feeling of freedom. I'd never felt anything to compare with it before this, a lightness that took my breath away.

And then we were flying across the Severn, over Wales, the mountains and valleys spread out before me like a giant, living map. I could see the black scar of the coal valleys to my right, and thought I could even pick out the Gower peninsula, a blue thread on the horizon to my left. Ahead I could see the narrow channel of water that separated Britain and Ireland.

I could feel the wind in my face, while the heat of the huge motor in front of me kept my feet warm. Behind me, I could just hear Captain Jackson telling me where we were, a calm running commentary. Above me in the distance floated gossamer threads of clouds, dappling the landscape below with light and shadow. I could understand why Captain Jackson loved to fly. Even when people were shooting at him.

He turned north.

"That's Mount Snowdon to your right. And Harlech Castle is down there to your left. Can you see it?" He sideslipped on the wind, and as the wing tilted, I could see the gray square, and the sea beyond, white-capped as it rolled in. I was captivated.

We passed over Caernarvon Castle, and followed a ferry pulling out from Holyhead. And there was the green spread of Ireland ahead.

It was surprisingly beautiful. We were flying at about twenty-five hundred feet, and the day was bright and clear as we crossed the coastline.

Below there was rolling green countryside, the small white cottages of the Irish scattered about the landscape, a village church here and a small lough there, a ruined abbey, a great house with gardens riotous with color, and ruins casting morning shadows across the green grass.

We avoided the sprawling cities, kept to fields where sheep or cattle or even sleek horses grazed. People who heard us approach would come running out, the children waving madly while the adults shielded their eyes to stare up at us. I waved back, but I couldn't tell if they saw me.

I heard Captain Jackson laugh with sheer joy, and I laughed too.

And then I could see the Atlantic Ocean in the distance. We were approaching our destination, which was on the west coast of Ireland, where fingers of land reached out into the water. I wasn't sure which finger was ours. We had just passed over a very large lake that seemed to cut the land in two as we banked slightly for a better view. There he turned slightly south. Soon he was pointing down, and in front of me was the field where we were to land. Beyond it stood a fine upright house of gray stone, with sloping lawns surrounding it, and beyond, on a knoll, a church. A bit farther on, the village of Killeighbeg nestled by the sea, which was blindingly bright in the sunlight. A lane ran from the house to the church, and then continued down to the village proper, and I was glad for my parents' sake, worrying at home, that it appeared I'd never need to go that far. Only to the house and the church.

Arthur did a low flyover of what was supposed to be our landing site, and I could see there were quite a few rocky patches in the green grass, as well as a wall of gray stones flecked with white that enclosed it. Even from here it appeared to be a smaller expanse than I'd pictured.

I heard Captain Jackson swear, and knew he too was expecting something flatter, more level for our landing.

Just as we turned for our final approach, a hare, flushed from cover, darted in a zigzag pattern toward the little copse at the end farthest from the house and outbuildings, and a flight of doves took off from there in panic.

Still, the Captain put us down with such skill that I turned my head and smiled at him.

As we swung around and taxied back toward a break in the rock wall, he shouted, "There is no welcoming throng."

He was right. From my perch in the aircraft coming in, I had seen the house, the lawns, the outbuildings and stable block, even rows of trees that appeared to be an orchard. In a small paddock behind the barn a pair of donkeys grazed, unperturbed by our swooping over their heads as we turned. But they were the only living things in sight. No people. No one busy in the stable yard, no one sitting under the trees that dotted the lawn. No one opening the door and rushing out to greet us. In the gardens to one side of the house there had been a long, ribbon-bedecked table with a good many chairs on either side of it—where had all of their occupants gone?

"Are we early?" I shouted back.

"Not at all. Just on time, actually."

After a moment of hesitation, I said, "Well, we can go over and knock at the house door. They may be inside, with all their guests. I'd like to change before meeting them."

He cut the motor, and there was a sudden silence. In the small spinney of trees behind us, I thought I heard a dove cooing as the birds settled back into the trees.

Climbing into the aircraft, I'd stepped on a particular part of the wing, then a small bit of metal, then swung my leg over into the forward seat, blessing my mother for suggesting that I wear my riding clothes to fly. But getting out of the deep pocket that was my seat and swinging my leg back over the edge so that I could reach the first step down was another matter. I could hear Captain Jackson laughing as I finally got myself on the rim of my seat and made my way to the ground.

Then we started walking toward the stone wall. Instead of a gate, there was actually more of a stile, and as we climbed over, Captain Jackson said uneasily, "I don't like this, Bess."

Neither did I, for in spite of the sound of the aircraft, no one had come to the door of the house. But I said brightly, "For all I know, they've gone to the church, and the service lasted longer than they'd expected."

He didn't answer.

Walking on toward the farmhouse, I listened but couldn't hear voices at all, then the donkeys brayed, and I jumped.

The Captain said, "Let me go first, Bess."

Lengthening his stride, he moved ahead.

The three-story house was rather plain, no ornamentation except for the corners, where stones were inset at different lengths, and a long window with an oval top set inside the flat pillars that created the appearance of a columned porch.

As Arthur reached the house and walked up the graceful steps to the door, he paused.

I noticed it too. No sound of voices from the open windows.

Then he lifted his hand and knocked at the door.

We could hear the knock echoing inside.

And then a window opened above us on the first floor, just to the left of the oval window.

A woman with iron-gray hair poked her head out. I couldn't judge her age. Sixty? Seventy?

"And what is it you're wanting?" she demanded, staring down at us. She was dressed in severest black, and her expression was anything but friendly.

Surely she'd heard the aircraft overhead?

"Hallo," I said with a smile. "I'm Elizabeth Crawford, Eileen's bridesmaid. I've come for the wedding."

"More English!" She slammed down the window and disappeared from our view.

We were left standing there.

"I don't like this at all," Captain Jackson said again in a low voice.

Finally, the door opened, but it wasn't the woman we'd seen just now. Instead it was a young girl of about fourteen, and she stared at us warily. With, I realized, some anxiety in her eyes.

"Hallo," I said again, and repeated what I'd told the woman.

"Nobody's here," the girl said quickly. And then she repeated it. "Nobody."

"Where is Eileen?" I asked as she began to close the door.

"The police station," she replied, casting a glance down the lane, before quickly swinging the door shut in our faces.

"Bess. Let's go back to the aircraft. I've enough fuel to get us back to Bristol. Whatever it is that's wrong here, I think we're wiser to get ourselves out of it."

"I don't even know where the police station is. In the village, I should think. Perhaps we ought to wait. It could just be a formality, something to do with the wedding." We were in Ireland—I had no idea how they managed things. But where was the much-vaunted Irish hospitality?

"We ought to leave," he persisted.

"I've come all this way," I replied quietly. "A few more minutes won't matter—"

I broke off as the door opened again. An Englishman stood there, frowning down at me. He was dressed not in uniform but in casual country attire, but I didn't need a uniform to recognize an officer in the way he carried himself.

He was of medium height, fair, with a kind face. I put his age at thirty-four or -five. But I noticed too that his blue eyes were hard. I'd seen many men, survivors of the trenches, with that same look, as if what they had been through had taken something from them.

"You must be Miss Crawford," he said, holding out his hand. "Ellis Dawson. I was Michael's commanding officer in France. And now his best man. Welcome to Ireland." But there was a wry twist to his mouth as he said the last words, and I was sure he couldn't possibly mean them.

We shook hands, and I presented Captain Jackson.

"I thought I heard an aircraft a few minutes ago. Was that you?" He looked at Captain Jackson's cap and the goggles he'd pushed to the top of his head. I'd left mine in my seat.

"Yes. Sir."

"I don't see how you managed on that meadow. I told Michael that, but I don't think he'd had much experience with landing aircraft." He remembered his manners. "Come in. Please. I know there's cold water in the kitchen. This way."

"Where is everyone?" I asked, still standing on the steps outside. "I had expected to see Eileen—"

Major Dawson took a deep breath. "It's rather complicated. They asked me to stay back. But the truth is, I don't think they wanted to parade me around in front of everyone in the village." He grimaced. "Mind you, I was just as glad to keep out of it."

"Out of what?" Captain Jackson said, remembering suddenly to add, "Sir."

"Michael is missing."

"What?" Captain Jackson demanded. "The *groom*?"

"The groom?" I said at the same time, like an echo.

"Yes. They've gone to the police station, the lot of them. Well, that's what it's called, but I don't think it's more than a room in one of the shops. Michael was here last evening—he's staying at the pub in the village. But he'd come for dinner and then said good night and left. This morning he was to have had breakfast with us. You may have seen the table set out on the back lawn. And he didn't come. By noon, it was decided to send for help. Only there's no telephone. And so they walked down. All of them. To lodge a complaint. I was to stay here in the event he came back. But he hasn't."

We were still standing there, on the steps. Major Dawson opened the door wider. "Best to come in." He looked down the lane that must lead to the village proper and the church. "There's no one here but me, one of the bride's grandmothers upstairs, and the kitchen girl. We can talk inside."

Captain Jackson opened his mouth to refuse but I was already stepping over the threshold. He had no choice but to follow. And as soon as we were clear of it, the Major shut the door.

We followed him into the front room, which appeared to be the family parlor. It was rather plain, a dark blue wallpaper on the walls, dark furnishings, and a painting of the Virgin over the mantel. I realized as I drew closer that it was actually a framed copy from a news cutting. There was a cross over the door we'd come through, and in the corner, oddly enough, an old spinning wheel.

"I'd offer you some refreshment," the Major was saying. "But I don't think the girl would provide it. She's frightened."

"But what has really happened?" I asked. "Where *is* Michael?"

"I've no idea. But according to something I overheard, he's not very popular around here. He was in the English Army, you see. The Irish Guards. And I don't know if it's the Irish who took him or the English." He rubbed his eyes with his hands. "It's been rather tense around here. And not just this morning."

"Why would the English want Michael?" Captain Jackson asked.

"He's been seen in the company of some suspected troublemakers. Irish rebel sympathizers. Two of them are Eileen's cousins, for God's sake, and one of them has come out of hiding for the wedding. I shouldn't be surprised if the English think Michael knows something that could be used to find where the rest of Terrence Flynn's followers can be found. I've been warned to leave, myself. But I came to support Michael, and I won't abandon him now."

"Who warned you?" I asked.

"The old woman upstairs, for one. The bride's grandmother. She's a rabid supporter of the Rising. Her grandson—Flynn—was active in it. How he escaped hanging I don't know. Michael told me he was seriously wounded, and some friends got him out of Dublin before the whole rebellion collapsed. The Army never found him. I've also been told he was going to give the bride away, since her father's dead. That could be what the Army's after—laying their hands on him."

"Is Michael in danger, do you think?" Captain Jackson asked, frowning. "And if he is, can the local police do anything about it? Or will they?"

"God knows. If I were you, I'd get that aircraft out of here and head back to England."

"I can't leave Eileen like this," I said.

"I don't know that you can help her," the Major replied soberly. "Truthfully, your presence could make matters worse."

I turned to the Captain. "You must go. Talk to my father. See if he can find out if the English do have Michael. The wedding invitation is in my desk in the house in Somerset. It has everything you'll need to know—his name, his mother's name."

"I am not about to leave you here," he replied stubbornly. "Your parents would never forgive me."

"The Major is staying. I'll be all right," I told him, just as stubbornly. "And if Eileen's cousin Terrence Flynn is indeed attending the wedding, he'll see to it that I'm safe. He promised."

"Bess—your father—"

He broke off as we heard the front door open, and footsteps into the passage. At the same time a voice from upstairs called down to whoever had arrived. It was loud enough that it reached us clearly, with all its venomous force.

"Well, Missy, and you're seeing what happens to those who turn their backs on their country. You thought it a fine thing to heal the enemy, you brought another traitor into this house, and now you're reaping what you sowed. No, don't look at me like that, your father would be turning in his grave, he would, if only he only knew—"

The front room door was flung wide, someone whirled in and slammed it shut behind her, and then her hands flew to her ears, covering them against the vitriol pouring down the stairs.

It was Eileen. When she turned around, eyes wide in her pale, drawn face, to find witnesses to her shaming, I saw a mere shell of the friendly, laughing shipmate on board *Britannic*.

Her gaze swept over me, then flew back. *"Bess!"*

It was an anguished cry. The next thing I knew she was in my arms, sobbing as if her heart was breaking, and I had a fair idea that it truly was.

Her voice muffled against my shoulder, she said, "I am so grateful you are here—I had nowhere else to turn."

Over her shoulder, I saw Captain Jackson was looking down, doing his best to give us a modicum of privacy in such a small room. The Major was staring hard at the painting of the Virgin, as if he'd never seen it before and found it engrossing.

I soothed her as best I could and soon had her sitting beside me on the bench by the cold hearth. Her hands were gripping mine, as if she feared that should she let them go, I might vanish.

"Tell me," I said. "Quietly and calmly."

And after a struggle to keep her voice steady, she managed it. Falling back into the familiar routine of a nurse reporting to Matron.

"Michael only came home a month ago. We'd set the wedding day while he was still in France, expecting him to be demobbed sooner than most, since he was Irish, but with one thing and another, he was delayed. Then he stayed awhile with his mother and sisters—she's not been well, and he was afraid she'd not be coming to the wedding."

She looked away, embarrassed, and I realized that Michael's mother might not wish to come to a wedding where Eileen's grandmother was present.

I said gently, "Was she proud of her son's service? Or did she feel it was wrong of him to enlist?"

"His mother was a widow—his sisters were still at home. She was grateful for the allowance she received from the British Army. There were many Irish families who depended on that allowance. And they were terrified that the Army would stop it after the Rising. That's another of the problems here, you know—a good many people were against the Rising. Until the court-martials and the firing squads, and others carried off to prison camps in Wales. That changed their point of view. But yes, she was proud of him, and then fearful for him when he came home."

"But he got there safely."

"Yes, thank God." Quickly resuming her account, she said, "All was well at first. He'd been careful, you see, traveling in his own clothes, not his uniform. Who was to know? But *someone* did. He'd not been here a week when the whispers began, and the next thing we knew, my grandmother was telling the world they were true. Wicked old woman that she is. Then on the heels of that, Major Dawson arrived. And the whispers turned dark. There were things said. Coming out of church. In the pub. The shops. You never saw who it was, just a voice. Cowards that they were. He was worried about his mother getting to hear about it and worrying. But you see, we aren't planning to stay here in Ireland. He's already found work. We thought people might forget in a few years, and we could come back again." The last words came as a wail.

The handkerchief I'd given her was soaked with tears, and as she wept again, Captain Jackson quietly handed her another.

I waited, and finally she was able to go on. "I told my family and he told his. We told the priest. Please let us marry, with our friends and family about us, and we'd leave. That's all we asked. Just to the end of the week, and we'd be gone. And all was quiet for two or three days. We should have *known*—we should have seen why they were quiet—they were taking the time they needed to plan. And last night, leaving here after dinner, Michael vanished. Not even his cap left behind, nor a shoe. I watched him out of sight on the lane, but he never reached the pub. When we went to summon the police this morning, someone in the crowd shouted, 'No need for the constabulary. He's dead, darlin', and good *riddance*.'"

Her voice broke again. "He can't be dead, Bess. He can't. We *waited*. Four years apart, and him at risk of dying any day in the trenches. We thought God was with us, because he survived. But my own *grand-mother* hates him and says terrible things about us. There *was* no Rising in 1914 when we went to help England fight the Germans. Michael wasn't the only Irishman who took the King's shilling. We thought it would prove to London that we were willing to die for England. As every good Englishman had done, enlisting. And in the end, London might see that we were worthy of Home Rule."

Hadn't the Suffragettes done much the same, bargaining with London? *We will suspend our fight for the vote and do all we can for the war effort. Afterward, in return, we expect to have the issue of voting rights for women addressed.*

Only, unlike Eileen and Michael, the Irish hadn't waited for the end of the war. In 1916, the hotheads—or heroes, depending on where you stood in the matter—had risen up and fought for what they wanted. And been brutally crushed. There was already talk in London about creating an occupying force, if the Irish didn't settle down. But executing the leaders of the rebellion had turned Irish feelings too bitter to settle down at all.

Eileen was imploring now. "No one wants to search for Michael. No one will help me, because I was willing to marry him—a traitor to Ireland. You must see, Bess, that you're my best hope."

I said, "Eileen, I don't know the countryside—the people who might be involved—anyone I dared to trust."

She shook her head vehemently. "You can learn. I'll help you."

I sighed. Politics could be cruel and heartless. And I was afraid, with the tensions in Ireland, that it could also be deadly. What had my mother said about travelers being killed?

Major Dawson cleared his throat. "Eileen. Let me travel to Dublin and find someone with a cooler head who can get to the bottom of this. It's only Thursday. There's time. Besides, one man's taunt isn't the truth. I refuse to accept that Michael is dead. And so should you."

"Then where is he? Why doesn't he come *home*?"

"You must be brave, for his sake," Major Dawson told her. "Someone must have an answer."

"I'm trying," she said, "but it's awfully hard, when even Father O'Halloran is against us. You'd think God would be impartial." There was anger in her voice now.

"God probably is," Major Dawson answered her wryly. "It's the Church that wants to see Ireland free."

"If we could reach *your* father," Captain Jackson added, avoiding using the Colonel Sahib's name or rank in this household, "he might have better luck. He must know the right people to speak to. Who might help and who wouldn't." It was a polite way of saying that it was less of a risk than for the Major to go to Dublin. He might be brave enough to try, but even if he got there, who would give him honest answers?

"But we *can* reach him," I said, rising. "Captain Jackson, if you leave now, before anyone sees you or tries to stop you, you could be in Bristol tonight."

Eileen turned eagerly to me. "*Could* he help Michael? Bess? Would he listen?"

While in the Queen Alexandra's, I hadn't told many people who my father was, although of course friends and officers from his days with the Regiment knew. For one thing, I didn't want preferential treatment in my training or postings, because of my family. And for another, my father had reminded me that it could make me a target for the Germans. Here in Ireland, that might be doubly true. For the Colonel Sahib as well as for me.

I said, "He'll need all the information we can give him, so that he can reach the proper authorities. Eileen, do you have any idea who might have taken Michael? Or why? Where to start searching?"

She shook her head. "That's just the problem, it might be anyone. What if someone here believed he'd come to spy for England—or to look for traitors? We've heard the rumors, that the English are eager for an excuse to treat us like a conquered nation. And my cousin Terrence has enemies—they might have taken Michael to strike at *him.*"

"If your cousin fought with the rebels, why should he have enemies here?" I asked.

It was Major Dawson who answered. "He wasn't shot or incarcerated with the other leaders. Not for want of searching on the Army's part, I can assure you. Still, there are factions here. And some of them think that dying for the Cause makes a man a better hero."

I heard the Captain say something under his breath. I knew what he was thinking, that the state of affairs here in Ireland was murkier than we'd guessed while sitting around an English dinner table.

But there was something else to consider too. I knew Eileen's temper, and I'd also seen that flare of anger just now. Before very long, if Michael didn't come home, it would soon take over and lead her to do something foolish. Something that might even get Michael killed.

"I'm sure my father would try, if I asked," I told her. "But you mustn't pin your hopes on him. Not yet." Then turning back to Captain Jackson, I added, "My family will be at the house in Somerset for one more night. If you fly back to Bristol now, he'll come and fetch you. And you can travel to London together. It will save a whole day, don't you see? And a day might make all the difference to Michael Sullivan's situation."

"Not without you," Captain Jackson said grimly. "Simon will wring my neck if I leave you here in such circumstances. And God knows what your father might do."

I hadn't heard the Captain's delightful drawl since we'd landed in the meadow and no one from the house had come to greet us. He'd been worried then, and he was even more worried now.

Then how to convince him? Short of leaving with him?

"Better still, I'll bring your father here to talk some sense into you," he went on, certain I'd never allow him to do that—certain I'd come to my senses before I'd risk my father becoming a pawn to exchange for Michael. "You wouldn't care for that, I'm sure, and it will only waste time. You can do more in England to let people see what's happened here."

He must have read my determination in my expression. He added, "With the Major's help, I can put you in that cockpit and tie you there."

I bit my lip as I wondered how I was going to make any headway here at all, and persuade the Captain to leave now while he could. For I really did believe him when he threatened to bundle me into that seat and tie me there. It wasn't an idle threat.

"We're running out of time," I said. "The sooner we find Michael, the sooner they can marry, and then we can *all* go home—"

Someone spoke from the doorway, cutting across my words.

"Miss Crawford will be safe enough. You have my word. But if you want to save Michael, you'll have to speak to London. We don't have him. And I don't know who does."

CHAPTER THREE

THE FOUR OF us turned in surprise.

He must have opened the door quietly, while we were arguing. For I hadn't heard him, nor had the others.

Standing there was the handsomest man I'd ever seen.

I had heard the term Black Irish, most often used in a derogatory tone, referring to the mostly small, poor Irishmen who had come over to England to work building roads, digging subways, and any other jobs to be had. Often the same men who drank and brawled and had a reputation for troublemaking.

This man was taller than the Major, with broad shoulders, thick dark hair like Eileen's but his was just graying at the temples, dark eyes and dark lashes as thick as a girl's. But there was nothing about him that spoke of femininity. Indeed, he could have been a hero in one of Walter Scott's novels. But the poorly healed scar across one cheek and another along his neck, disappearing into his collar, spoke more of *Treasure Island* and pirates. As he moved forward, I noticed that one hand was scarred as well.

I had seen enough wounds like these. He'd been shot several times.

He came farther into the room, and Eileen said, "Can you be sure about that, Terry?"

I realized then that this was the man who'd promised me safe conduct across Ireland. As if he ruled the land and could guarantee it.

"I've passed the word. And I trust the answers."

I couldn't quite be sure whether he was telling the truth about Michael's captors or simply trying to relieve his cousin's fears. And if he had such authority, why couldn't *he* bring Michael back?

What's more, there was something in his expression when he turned to Eileen that I couldn't quite define. But it made me suddenly uneasy.

Still, this man was my best hope of convincing the Captain to let me stay.

I smiled at him, to indicate that I was grateful for his support. "Are you sure? Do you even know that Michael is—safe?" I stopped myself in time, before I'd said *alive.*

I could feel Eileen's gaze on me, even so, and knew she was afraid of Terrence's answer.

"If the English have him, they're questioning him about me. I'm wanted. Sadly for him, he doesn't know I'm here. I've kept my presence quiet, until Eileen's wedding. It was for the best." He turned to his cousin. "I've sent out search parties. They wouldn't go for the Constable, but they agreed for me."

She gave him a grateful look, her face brightening for the first time.

I was sorry to spoil her mood, but I said, "Will the English let him go, once they're satisfied that he doesn't know anything useful?"

He considered me. "You're English. You tell me."

But I couldn't. I certainly had no idea who had taken Michael or why. I'd only just arrived. Still, his question brought me back to Captain Jackson. Turning to him, I said quietly, "You must go, and do what you can in London."

"I won't leave you," he said stubbornly.

I sighed. "I think we should discuss this in private," I said. "My valise is still in your aircraft," I added. When we hadn't seen any sign of welcome, we'd left it there.

Reluctantly the Captain followed me out of the room and then out of the house, as we made our way back to the meadow. No one tried to stop us, but I caught a glimpse of Eileen's anxious face at the front windows as we passed. I gave her an encouraging smile, then walked on.

Once out of earshot of anyone trying to hear our conversation, I said earnestly to Captain Jackson, "Don't you see? The minute I land in England, no one will care about Michael Sullivan. He was demobbed, he returned to his home in Ireland, and that is all London wants to hear about him. If he's disappeared since then, it's an Irish problem, not an English one."

"Have you considered that London might be right? Bess, it's not the same here as it is in England. Look at that man Terrence. He's walking about as if he's king, promising that you'll be safe. And all the while he could very well have taken Michael himself. Just because the man once wore a British uniform. He's not going to want his cousin married to someone he considers to be a traitor. Is he?"

He had a point, one I had to consider. We crossed the stile, and for an instant I wished I'd never come to Ireland. But what about Eileen? She had nearly died as *Britannic* went down. She had served England in its time of need, and afterward had spent months learning to walk again. She had earned her happiness, and so had Michael Sullivan, who had served England honorably until war's end. I knew that for a fact—my mother had told me privately that my father had looked up his military record.

I said, "I must stay. At least until Michael is found—or until I have a better reason for leaving. You know how to find me, you could land here in the dark, couldn't you, if I needed to go in a hurry? Now that you know what the field is like?"

"I could put my aircraft down in the front walk if need be. But that's not the point."

He tried his best to persuade me, but I think he'd already accepted the fact that I was going to stay.

Finally, he looked hard at me and said, "I'll fly close by every night after dark. I can come in from the sea, no one will see or hear me. If there's a white handkerchief on the stile, I'll see it, and not land. If it's not there, I'll come find you. I don't want to be responsible for anything happening to you, Bess. You must promise me you'll do this, or I shall stay as well. I'm an American, after all. They won't dare to touch me."

I wasn't very sure he was right about that.

All the same, it was important for him to reach my father as soon as possible. And so I promised, and I meant that promise.

Someone spoke just behind us, and we turned to see the Major coming toward us.

"Are you leaving?" he asked me.

"No. Not yet. Not today."

He turned to the Captain, his face grim. "I'm not safe here, myself, but I'll do everything in my power to protect her. You can depend upon it."

Handing down my valise, the Captain made one last attempt to persuade me to board the aircraft, then climbed up on the wing and swung himself into the cockpit.

But he waved as he turned into the wind, circling the meadow as he gained altitude.

I had to admit to myself that I felt an odd uneasiness in the pit of my stomach as I watched him lift over the stone wall and climb into the blue sky above me. *Had* I done the right thing?

He dipped his wings a last time in salute, and then turned toward England.

And I walked back to the house with the Major, who was carrying my valise.

I hadn't been afraid in France, even in the midst of a bloody war. After all, I was an officer in His Majesty's Army, and I had the power of England on my side. As my mother had reminded me.

I wasn't entirely sure who was truly on my side in Ireland.

The Major turned to me, his face grave. "I hope you don't have reason to regret staying," he said as we climbed over the stile.

I gave him my best smile. "It will be all right. You'll see. And you stayed. How could I do any less?"

But even as I spoke, I could tell that he didn't believe me.

Chapter Four

WE WALKED THE rest of the way in silence, Major Dawson and I.

We had nearly reached the house when we heard raised voices coming from the front room, and not just one or two. A serious argument was in progress. Major Dawson glanced at me, then walked a little ahead of me toward the door to the house. As we stepped into the front room, there was a sudden silence, and we found ourselves facing at least a dozen men crowded into the small space.

They stared at us. And it wasn't a friendly stare.

By the hearth stood Eileen and her cousin, and from the expression on their faces, I could see that matters weren't going well.

Terrence surged forward, saying as he came toward me, "The search teams I sent out are reporting. No luck."

I had the feeling that the search teams weren't at all what they had been discussing—not from the sounds I'd heard from outside.

No one responded. Terrence came right up to me, and the Major started forward. Then Terrence reached out to put a hand on my shoulder in a comradely fashion, and Dawson stopped.

"She saved our Eileen's life, lads. Do you understand me? And she's kind enough to come over for the wedding. That makes her family."

A short, dark-haired man said with a scowl, "There's have been no need for saving Eileen's life, if she hadn't gone to fight for the English."

"And how did she know we'd rise up and claim for ourselves what we'd been promised for so long? Men went to fight for England in the hope of speeding up that promise. Michael was one of them."

"He didn't come home, did he? When the fighting was *here*?"

Terrence's hand was light on my shoulder in the beginning but was heavier now. I sensed the tension in him.

"What good was a man to us, shot for desertion?"

"Some came home. Thumbed their noses at their officers, and left."

"I didn't see them there at the Post Office when we could have used their guns," Terrence retorted harshly. "A grand gesture doesn't stop the enemy."

The other man looked down, falling silent as he did. But I could see he wasn't convinced.

Someone else spoke then, a man with twisted hands, grimed from heavy work.

"Granny Flynn says *she's* a spy, and up to no good."

"My grandmother sees spies under the bed when she says her prayers."

"And who's to say she's not right?"

Terrence was angry now.

"Since when is my word not good enough for you?"

There was grumbling from behind me—I couldn't see who it was—and then another voice spoke from the doorway.

"Terrence's word is good enough for me. But I say he keeps his eyes on our guests. To be sure, and all."

I turned slightly to see a priest just coming into the room. He was a small man, wearing the traditional black cassock but no hat, his ginger hair mixed with gray, and his forehead heavily lined.

"Fair enough," Terrence said, but I could tell from another change in his grip that he wasn't happy with the priest's comment. Still, the rest of the men in the room murmured agreement with the newcomer.

And I had the sudden feeling that there was something between the priest and Terrence Flynn. Animosity? Mistrust? Then I realized what it was: the priest was engaged with the Rising hero in a battle for power. They were like two dogs circling each other, growling, hackles raised, looking for the best angle for attack. Only, unlike dogs, they had to pretend to a friendship neither man felt.

"And won't you present me to the bride's attendant?" the priest went on.

"Father O'Halloran, this is Elizabeth Crawford. It was she who saved our Eileen's life." He left out the particulars of that. "And she's come to stand up for her at the wedding."

"Now it's odd, don't you think, that with a village full of kinfolk of one kind or another," the priest asked with a smile, "that both Michael and Eileen chose English attendants for their wedding?"

Unexpectedly it was Eileen who answered him. "Not so surprising, Father, when you consider what I owe Bess. It wasn't anyone here who stopped them taking off my limbs as I lay there in that little boat screaming in pain. She gave me back my life, Father, when I despaired of ever seeing Ireland again."

He had the grace to say nothing. And not waiting for anyone else to speak, Terrence said, "The searchers haven't caught a whiff of information about Michael. You'll be keeping him in your prayers, Father?"

"Oh, indeed. I've asked God to keep him safe."

Some of the tension went out of the room. And then the young girl I'd seen earlier opened the door from the kitchen and stepped in. Her voice trembling only a little, she said, "Mrs. Flynn wishes to see Father O'Halloran."

The priest nodded to the room at large and left with her. I could hear their steps on the stairs.

Eileen came to stand beside me as Terrence moved away. "I want you to meet my mother," she said. "She doesn't come down very often.

Granny has browbeaten her since the day Father came home and told his mother he was marrying her."

"She didn't care for the match?" I asked, ignoring the men speaking quietly to Terrence behind me.

"It wasn't the match. She didn't want her son to marry anyone. After all, no one was good enough, you see."

"I've already discovered that she doesn't care for the English in her house."

"No, but I'm so very grateful you stayed. Major Dawson as well. Thank you, Bess!" She embraced me again with such warmth that I knew she saw me as her only anchor just now. As I had been when *Britannic* went down, saving her and then saving her legs.

"Let's hope they find Michael soon," I said bracingly, "and the wedding can go on. Which reminds me. Does your grandmother know you intend to move away? Would that leave her alone, here?" If the Army didn't have Michael and the Irish didn't, I wouldn't put it past Eileen's grandmother to decide that she didn't want Eileen to leave her. And the best way to do that, of course, was to prevent the wedding. In fact, she probably had a much better motive than anyone concerned about Irish politics.

"I tried to tell her, but she wouldn't listen. Still, she hears things, it's as if she has her own spies everywhere. What I haven't told her or anyone else is that I'm determined to take my mother with me. She deserves better than being treated like a scullery maid." We'd been speaking quietly, but now her voice was very low, and I had to bend forward to hear her.

"Could *she* have had anything to do with Michael's disappearance? Your grandmother?" I came right out and asked.

"She never goes out. How could she have arranged it?"

"She must have friends in the village," I said. "And there's the priest."

"I don't want to believe such a thing."

That didn't make it any less true. But I said nothing.

Eileen glanced around the room. "Let's go into the kitchen. We can talk there."

I looked around for Major Dawson. He had moved toward the door to the hall, and my valise was in his hand. He quietly stepped out of the room, and then I heard his footsteps on the treads of the stairs.

I followed her to the small kitchen, where she poured both of us a little wine. "I've never been fond of wine," she said. "But it has got me through this day."

We sat at the kitchen table, and Eileen looked forlorn as she said, "Who could want to hurt Michael? Or me?"

"It may not be personal," I told her. "Or Michael could have enemies of his own. How did his family feel about his serving the English King?"

"His father died in 1912. Typhoid. His older brother was killed at Ypres, and his younger brother is in seminary, to be a priest. His older sister is not happy about his service, but she's married and has three children to care for. It hasn't been easy for them, and Michael has helped her more than once. Money, mostly, but he also put the fear of God into her husband, stopping him from drinking. His younger sister is a nun."

"Does *he* hold a grudge? This brother-in-law?"

Eileen frowned. "I don't know—they live in Belfast, and I've never met him."

I put the question another way. "Is he a staunch Republican?"

"Oh, yes, when he's in his pints, he's a great one for talking about the Cause and down with the English, but when he's sober, he's a mouse."

But sometimes mice can fight viciously if cornered.

Changing the subject, I asked, "Is it possible that Michael had a very good reason for leaving abruptly? Illness or trouble in his family, for instance. And didn't want to alarm you, expecting to be back in a matter of hours?"

"He'd have told me, for fear I'd worry if he was held up. We've been apart for so many years, and now we can't bear to be out of the sight of each other."

I remembered Diana telling me how much she longed for the war to be over, her duty done, so that she didn't have to face separation after separation from the officer she loved so deeply. Diana, who could have had any man she set her cap for, beautiful, accomplished, sophisticated Diana, falling for a man who had barely escaped being tried for a murder he hadn't committed. A lovely man, I had liked him immensely in the end, but I would never have guessed that he would be a match for my flatmate at Mrs. Hennessey's.

I had never felt that kind of love. In 1914, I'd been young, too carefree to think about marriage. There hadn't been time during the war to worry about the future. Now that it was here, my friends were dead. I'd been quite fond of several. And, of course, there was Sergeant Lassiter, the Australian who had proposed to me in France . . .

It struck me suddenly that the man I might have loved and married could very well have died in France or on the sea or in the deserts of the East, before we'd ever met. And that was a very unsettling thought.

Eileen said, "What is it, Bess? You looked as if someone had walked across your grave."

"Not my grave, or that of anyone I know," I managed to say. "No, I was just thinking how fortunate you and Michael have been. Both of you survived the war and found each other afterward. I find myself envying your happiness, and wishing for my own." I smiled, to let her see I wasn't serious about my envy.

She reached out and gripped my hand. "You'll find someone, Bess. What about that lovely man who flew you here?"

I laughed. "I like Captain Jackson very much. But I don't seem to be in danger of falling in love with him. He's an American—and I think he loves flying most of all."

Her eyes twinkled for a brief moment. "There's the Major. He hasn't flown away."

"I'm sure the Major would be shocked to hear you giving away his heart quite so cavalierly." But it was good to see her distracted from her own troubles.

"Well, you can't have Terrence, you know. Not if you want to return to England. He'd be in great danger there."

The handsome Irishman, with the scarred face? The image of him on one knee before me or gravely asking the Colonel Sahib for my hand nearly brought on a fit of laughter that I had some difficulty suppressing.

Eileen asked, almost affronted, "Is it so comic, his danger?"

Sobering quickly, I tried to make amends. "No, of course not—I was just thinking how my mother would face policemen arriving in the midst of my wedding. She's quite formidable when she needs to be, but of course you couldn't know that about her."

"Sadly, my mother would be the first to hide. Caught between my father and my grandmother, she lost any spirit she'd ever possessed."

But I thought she must have possessed quite a lot in the beginning, because she's passed it on to her daughter.

Before I could say anything about that, the door opened, and Terrence came in.

Looking from Eileen to me and back again, he said, "What's wrong?"

"We were talking about my mother."

I was surprised that Eileen had told him what we'd been discussing. If she trusted him that much, it warned me to be careful what I told her.

He said, "She was a different woman as long as your da was alive. It's Granny changed her. God knows, I walked in fear of her myself, even into university. But I came to ask, shall I bring dinner from the inn, for you, your mother, Sister Crawford, and Granny? You'll not feel much like waking up the cooker tonight."

"Could you please? I'd be so grateful. Still, I'll put the kettle on, and we'll have some tea. Have they gone? The searchers?"

"I sent them out again. Eileen, there's one fear I have that you'll have to face. The sea is just there, and if he was put aboard a boat, he could be anywhere by now."

Her face paled. "They wouldn't kill him and throw his body into the sea?"

He took a deep breath. "Until we know why he was taken, there's no certainty about anything. My people don't have him. I'm ready to swear to that."

"But you'll be related to Michael when we marry. They might have taken it on themselves to rid the family of a traitor. To please Granny if not you."

It was almost a growl. "They wouldn't dare."

I had known that feelings had run high in Ireland ever since the Easter Rising had not succeeded. What I hadn't realized is that bitterness and anger and a desire for vengeance had split families and even the countryside into factions that often must be at odds with each other—and therefore dangerous because of their very deep feelings. Feelings that sometimes mattered more than people.

Had Michael Sullivan of Belfast crossed the wrong faction?

How could anyone tell where the lines were? This meant of course that I could take nothing—no one—for granted. Perhaps not even Eileen.

Terrence was saying, "Stay here, make your tea, and keep an eye out for Michael. He could return as quietly as he went. Bess can go with me to help with the parcels."

"My place is here," I said quickly. "In the event Michael is hurt—wounded. I can help him."

"You're to come with me, show your face to the world in my company—protected by me. And you'll keep your ears open for anything said about Michael."

Major Dawson, downstairs once more, wasn't happy about that invitation, when we left the kitchen and started to walk out the front door. Nor was Eileen, who had argued with her cousin for a good ten minutes before I told her that it was all right, I'd be glad to help in any way I could. The Major was not as easily put off, but Terrence was adamant that he should stay at the farmhouse.

"You're a reminder of things best not stirred up," he said bluntly. "Not until we have Michael safe."

And so Terrence and I walked quickly across the lawn to the lane, and followed it into the village.

I'd seen the sea as we came down in preparation to land, but my attention had been on the meadow, and I hadn't realized that the village was actually set at the head of a small harbor of fishing craft. Water came up into what appeared to be a narrow inlet, the mainland to the east, and a broad finger of land between it and the sea to the west.

We came out of the lane onto the dusty road and walked down that for a little distance before we came to the church, set on a slight rise. At the foot of this knoll, whitewashed village houses, most of them no bigger than crofts, were crowded together between church and harbor. Nearer the water were the shops and an inn, all curved around the little port. Half a dozen fishing boats rode at anchor there, moving with the incoming tide, while gulls circled lazily above them, waiting for them to go out again.

"It's a poor village, at best," Terrence was saying, breaking the silence between us. "Granny owns a fair-size property. It came down in the family free and clear, though the story goes that we had an ancestress who slept with an English lord and was given the property when she discovered she was pregnant. I'd not mention that to Granny. She likes to tell a different version, that the land was given to an archer who saved the laird's life in battle. For all I know, he was husband to the lady who served in a different way." He grinned at me, expecting me to be shocked.

I said, "And no one has tried to take the property away from you?"

"Oh, they've tried, but the lady made a good bargain, and passed the parchment down, to prove it."

We had paused to take in the view. "Why is the church here, not in the middle of the village?"

"It was rebuilt here after raiders burned an earlier church close by the water. Where the inn stands now. Twice they did that, and stole the church silver, killed the priests, among other atrocities. Still, you can see this church tower from the sea. A torch on the roof has guided the fishing boats in more times than I can remember, when the night was stormy."

I wasn't sure whether Terrence's tales were just that, or the real history of the village.

Moving on, we followed the single curving street into the heart of the village, and made our way toward the inn. Long before we got there, I could hear the music.

I was also aware of the stares. I'd never had an opportunity to change out of my riding clothes, but that wasn't what drew attention. The searchers must have taken home with them an account of my presence. The women of the village were curious. Dressed mostly in black, with black scarves on their heads, they must have found my dark red habit rather daring, in spite of its sober cut.

Terrence, enjoying the spectacle, was chuckling quietly to himself.

He held the door for me as we reached the inn and walked to the pub entrance. The bar took pride of place, but the tables scattered about it and the hearth were empty. The music I'd heard appeared to be coming from the direction of a short but dark passage on the far side of the bar, and Terrence led me down that into a back room. It was fair-size and filled with men smoking heavily. The air was hardly more than a blue haze. At the far end, a group of musicians was playing violins and those oddly shaped Irish pipes and a small set of drums. A tall, thin man was also holding a violin and singing a ballad. I couldn't understand him, but clearly the rapt audience did. I could tell, though, that the subject matter was tragic from all the long faces in the room.

As soon as he caught sight of me, coming in with Terrence, the singer stopped in midsentence, and the music faded almost as quickly. The spell broken, everyone wheeled to see what was happening. The tension in the room rose, then fell as they saw it was Terrence and not a threat. But the stares my way were decidedly unfriendly.

Terrence grinned at them all, took a violin from one of the players, fitted it under his chin with accustomed ease, and began another tune. It was rowdy, but the mood was slow to change.

I stayed where I was, trying not take note of the intense scrutiny. I was reminded of my early training, trying to dress a wound properly while Matron and the doctor watched with arms crossed.

A man stepped forward out of the crowd and challenged Terrence while he was still playing.

"Why did you bring *her* here?"

"Because, boyo, she's here for my cousin's wedding, and that means she's a guest in my house. She's to be treated as such, or I'll know why."

"There's no wedding without a groom," another man said.

"Ah, but it's only delayed a little. He wandered off, the dear man. He'll find his way home again, I've no doubt of it." He hadn't missed a note, his fingers flying across the neck of the violin as his other hand deftly used the bow.

He sounded so sure that it made me wonder just what he *did* know about Michael's disappearance.

Coming to the end of the tune, he handed the violin back to its owner with a little bow, and then, pointedly ignoring the tall, thin man, he started back toward me.

I happened to catch the expression in the singer's eyes as he watched Terrence, and if looks could kill, Eileen's cousin would be falling down dead on the floor. When he realized I'd seen what he must have been thinking, he quickly looked away. For some reason, I had the feeling that he wasn't sure enough of his own position to challenge Terrence, as if he were an outsider, not a local man.

"And would you like a drink, love?" Terrence was asking, the perfect host. But I could see a spark of anger in his eyes, that he'd been questioned quite so openly. And that had surprised me as well—I'd gathered that he was the local hero and everyone admired him. But twice now, in my presence, he'd been challenged. I wasn't really sure why that had happened, but it could well mean that there was another faction in the town. And that complicated the problem of who had taken Michael.

I was expected to give him an answer. What should a lady drink in an Irish pub, that didn't smack of being English to the core? A sherry was out, as was a cup of tea.

He seemed to sense my uncertainty, and said lightly, "The snug is this way." And he led me back down the dark passage into the pub again, and nodded toward a curtain on the far wall. As he swept that aside, I realized there was a small room behind it. As I went in, he said quietly, so that only I could hear him, "Take a seat in here."

And then he was gone. A few minutes later, he brought me a glass of porter, which he said Irish women drank in their homes.

I said, looking at it, "Is that all you've put in the glass?"

That flash of anger crossed his face again. "You're Eileen's maid of honor. I'd not be getting you drunk in a public house."

Smiling, I tasted it, then set the glass down. He picked it up, drank it slowly, and put it down, empty now. Then he walked out, leaving me sitting there with the glass. When he came back, he was carrying a basket. "We can go now."

And we left the pub.

I hadn't realized until I was outside, walking back up the hill, how tense I had been.

"Do you think it worked? Taking me there?"

"The word will get out. You'll be safe enough for now. All the same, I'd stick close to the house, if I were you. But please God we find Michael soon and see the wedding over and done with. The quicker the lot of you are out of the village and out of Ireland, the better."

He appeared to mean that. And I took it to heart too. I was beginning to understand just how many undercurrents there were in everything that went on here.

Granny was at her window as we came down the lane to the house, and when we were close enough, she called, "I thought we'd seen the last of her."

"I can hardly drown her in the sea."

"I don't see why not," she retorted, and pulled down her window before he could reply.

"Why is she so bitter?" I asked as we came up to the front door.

"You haven't lived under foreign rule, have you. Or you'd know."

And he moved ahead of me to set the basket down before running lightly up the steps and disappearing in what must be the direction of his grandmother's room.

Picking up the heavy basket, I found Eileen in the kitchen, her face anxious.

"What happened?"

Smiling, I said, "I was introduced to the village, I believe. And given a glass of porter. Fortunately Terrence drank it for me. No harm done. And we have our supper."

"You never know with Terrence," she said darkly. "Leave the basket on the table and come away upstairs to my room. You've hardly had time to settle since you got here." As I followed her toward what appeared to be the back stairs, behind a narrow door in the far wall, she added over her shoulder, "No word of Michael, then?"

"None," I said. "Did you expect there to be?"

Ahead of me, she opened a door into a large, comfortable room with windows on two sides. I saw that the Major had left my valise at the foot of the bed.

"This was my parents' room." She nodded to the framed photographs on the wall. "I took it over after my father died. My mother couldn't bear to stay in here, and I gave her my room." There was a brass bedstead against the wall facing the window, and she lifted my valise to set it there so that I could unpack. "Michael and I were to spend our wedding night in this room. And leave the next morning for Dublin. If you don't mind sharing, I think it's best if you stay with me."

"Yes, of course," I said, looking at the wedding gown hanging from a hook between the windows. "It's a lovely gown, Eileen." I walked over to it, admiring the lace.

"It was my mother's wedding dress," she said. "The lace came from Belgium. For a miracle, it fits me. I'm a little taller, but as slim. We had to let out the waist a bit, but that's all." Her eyes filled with tears, and she looked away. "I can't bear to see it now."

Coming back to stand beside her, I lowered my voice. "Father O'Halloran doesn't seem to care for your cousin Terrence. Or for Michael. And there was someone in the pub who questioned Terrence. I thought he was a hero of the Rising, that everyone looked up to him?"

"There are those who feel that what was started in Dublin ought to continue. They weren't there, but they're full of wild talk, and Terrence swears it will do more harm than good, carrying the fight to the English. They don't want to hear him, and they go on stirring people up without a thought to the consequences if someone decides to go out and shoot the wrong person."

I didn't want to ask, but I had to know. "Could it be these people who decided to take Michael? To frighten him," I added quickly as alarm spread across her face.

She sat down on the bed, the springs squeaking a little from the suddenness of it. She didn't look at me, her fingers tracing the pattern on the pretty coverlet. "I don't know. I can't believe they'd kill him for wearing a British uniform. But they *have* done—according to the whispers."

"Surely not."

"A friend's brother, now, he burned his uniform before he left England and claimed to everyone who'd listen that he'd been in prison for the past four years, for attempted desertion. That he'd gone to enlist, but when he thought better of it, they claimed he'd already signed the papers and threw him into prison. He told terrible tales about English prisons, but his mother had got letters from him while he was in France, and there were people who had seen them. So he swore he'd paid someone to post them from France, to keep his mother from worrying about him in English custody."

"What happened to him?"

"She sent him away. For his own good. A ship to America. But the Irish there may feel just the same in Boston as they do here. And she's had no word at all since he landed. He was told not to go to New York, that they hanged Irish workers there. But Terrence says that was a long time ago."

I took a deep breath. "Wouldn't it have made a difference, that you and Michael were planning to leave Ireland?"

"That might only make matters worse. We didn't make a public announcement, no, but word got out. Terrence thought it might be for the best. But Granny says a traitor is a traitor, and running away doesn't change anything." She looked up finally. "I wish I'd never asked you to come here. But I so wanted you to see me walk down to the altar, to be married." She lifted her skirts, and I could tell that the scars were still there. Even in her stockings her legs were slightly misshapen. "Michael said he didn't care. I don't think he did." She dropped her skirts again and sighed. "I should have listened to Father O'Halloran, and gone to England to meet Michael and marry him there. But I wanted to be married in the same church as my mother and my grandmothers and all the Flynn women before me. I wanted to start my marriage in Ireland, not a strange church in England. Was that asking so much?"

"No. Not at all." It was a tangle, and I wasn't sure just who I should believe about Michael's disappearance. I tried to consider what would have happened in Somerset if I'd brought home a German officer and told everyone that I wanted to marry him in the village church. It wasn't quite the same, of course, but there were families in the village who had lost loved ones in the war, and those losses were still fresh and painful.

Letting it go, I took her in my arms and tried to comfort her.

After a bit, she moved away, saying, "And here I am, thinking only of myself, while you've had nothing to eat the whole day! My mother taught me better." She tried to laugh at herself. "There's a bit of roast from last night. I'll make tea, and sandwiches." She suddenly realized I was still wearing my riding clothes. "Change first! I'll bring hot water to wash your face and hands. You'd think the Irish had no hospitality at all."

And she left the room in a hurry, needing to be busy. I closed the door behind her, found one of the plain dresses I'd brought that didn't identify me as a nursing Sister, and by the time she was back with the hot water, I was more presentable.

We ate the sandwiches in the kitchen, after she'd carried a plate up to her grandmother with a pot of tea and a small glass of Irish whiskey, then took another to Major Dawson and the younger Mrs. Flynn.

I couldn't help but wonder why Eileen, the daughter of the house, was preparing tea and sandwiches, carrying trays upstairs. There had been a young girl here when I first arrived, but I hadn't seen her since, nor anyone else who might be staff. It didn't fit with the family's position here or the size of the Flynns' property. It didn't appear to be a matter of money—there was nothing shabby about the house or the grounds. Surely it couldn't be our presence here, the Major's and mine? Even that thought made me uneasy. But of course I couldn't ask. It would be rude.

Eileen's cheeks were flushed when she came back, and I took it that the older woman had been ungrateful and rather nasty. But Eileen said nothing, and nor did I.

There was nothing we could do about her grandmother.

Warm air, a slight breeze that lifted the curtains at the open window, and a buzzing of bees somewhere in the tall bushes just outside lulled me into wishing for a nap. It had been an eventful day so far, and the Captain and I had risen before dawn to begin our flight.

And then Terrence came into the kitchen, banging the door wide open against the wall, saying angrily, "If that woman had been at the Post Office, no one would have dared to surrender."

The Post Office in Dublin had been the scene of much of the action in the Rising. I gathered he meant his grandmother.

Eileen didn't smile. He poured himself a cup of tea, and as she rose and began to make more sandwiches, he reached for the bottle on the shelf and added whiskey to his cup. But when she had prepared them, he shook his head. "No. I'm not hungry." Then he said, as if suddenly aware of who was not there, "Where's the Major?"

"In his room. I took up a tray."

He nodded. "Best place for him." He finished his tea, then poured more whiskey into the empty cup. "He ought to leave. You as well," he said, gesturing toward me with the cup.

This was a change in attitude.

"Are you saying there won't be a wedding?" Eileen asked in a small voice.

"God, no. But having English attendants at a wedding of an English nursing Sister and a former English soldier is not the best decision you could have made."

"But that's just it. It's *my* wedding. I wanted it to be happy. Joyful. And Michael's brother died in France. He would very likely have chosen *him*, if he'd lived."

"It doesn't sound right, somehow. An officer coming all this way to stand up for his Sergeant." He stared into the contents of his cup. "There's talk that the Major was glad of the excuse. That he's an English spy."

"That's ridiculous, and you know it. You've talked to him often enough. And what is he spying on, here at the edge of the world? The fish in the nets? The number of gulls flying over the harbor? If he was a spy, he'd be in Dublin."

"What if he's after me? London wouldn't mind seeing me hang. Or shot. Even this long after events. Still. Both should go, and you should find a nice Irish girl to stand up with you, and I'll stand up with Michael."

"But I thought—you were to give me away? As my eldest cousin."

He turned on her. "Eileen. You're living in a pretty dream, and this is Ireland in 1919. Don't you see? Your stubbornness has put everyone on edge. You're as bad as your grandmother, in your own way. She sees everything in the blackest possible way, and you see only what you want to see."

Her face flared red. "Do you remember how my legs were when I first came home? I couldn't even put one foot in front of the other! Someone had to carry me up and down the stairs, I was in constant pain, and I wanted to die before Michael saw me that way. Helpless, ugly—I had to do my exercises even when I couldn't *bear* it. And you were in hiding, and Granny was awful, even Father O'Halloran had something to say. Punishment, he called it, punishment for deserting my own people in their time of need."

He stared at her. "You made your choices, Eileen. Against all advice. You went to London to train. Your *choice!*"

"I went to London because Michael had enlisted. I wanted to be in France, closer to him. I wanted to be there if he was killed. Don't you understand? I had to wait four years to know if he was going to live or die. Four *years.* It isn't too much to ask to be married in the church that buried my father and my little brother—where I was christened and confirmed. *My* church, not a stranger's church."

She had used the same words to me. And I could see that Eileen was still Irish, no matter where she'd trained or where she'd been posted during the war. Or where she might be going to spend the rest of her life with the man she loved.

But her family couldn't see that. Only her apparent desertion. I wondered how many held that against her.

CHAPTER FIVE

THE EVENING MEAL was late. Together Eileen and I took it from the basket and warmed it in the oven, and we had no idea how many we would be serving.

As it happened, there were six of us at the table. And we prepared a tray for her mother.

Eileen, her grandmother, her cousin Terrence, the Major, and I. Just as we were sitting down, another man came in, nodded to Granny, and sat down. Without a word Eileen set another place for him.

I learned he was another cousin, Niall. I could see the likeness, the dark curling hair, the long dark lashes, the straight nose, and the dark eyes. But there the resemblance ended. This man was shorter, slimmer, his chin less square, and without the power of personality that marked Terrence. But without that comparison, he would have been considered a handsome young man in his own right. I had a feeling that he must have stood in Terrence's shadow all his life. It was there in the diffidence he showed his older brother, sometimes edged with a sharpness.

He seemed to be fond of Eileen, he was polite to me and the Major, and he gave me the impression he was afraid of his grandmother.

That was no surprise. She was tall and dark, a woman to be reckoned with, in spite of the gray in her hair. I was reminded of one of the Maharani's friends: strong-minded, opinionated, and rude.

Granny had glared at me as she sat down, as if she wished she could order me from the table. Then she ignored me. The Major seemed to interest her, although she was short and insulting with him. In fact, I thought she was enjoying having a British Army Major to bully. And Major Dawson was politely distant in his turn.

Eileen was clearly put out with her grandmother, but there was little she could say or do. It was Granny's house, after all.

And so, the meal was unpleasant enough to give us all indigestion.

We were nearly finished when there was a banging at the front door, and Terrence rose quickly, moving toward the passage to answer the summons. As he went he motioned to Niall to stay seated.

The table was silent as we all tried to listen to whatever was being said at the door. There had been an ominous sound to that banging.

Just then Major Dawson rose and went to stand in the doorway to the back stairs, where he had a better view of the passage. He too had heard more than just someone pounding on the paneling.

Terrence came racing back down the passage, beckoned to me, and said, "Do you have your kit with you?"

I didn't, but Eileen said, half-rising, "Mine is in the cupboard in my room."

"No, stay, I'll fetch it. Sister?"

And he was gone, his feet pounding on the treads of the stairs, going up and then down again by the time I'd reached the door. He'd borrowed one of Eileen's coats as well, for me to wear.

"This way." He set out toward the village, almost running, and I was hard-pressed to keep up. There was a chill in the air, now, coming off the water.

We passed the church, dark against the sky as the long day was beginning to fade into the last few minutes of sunset. I kept pace, even though his legs were longer than mine, but I was nearly out of breath by the time we'd reached the little harbor. The gulls had disappeared for the night, resting out on the water somewhere.

Five or six dogs lay at the approach to it, staring at us, knowing at once that we were strangers. I heard one growl, a huge and handsome Irish Wolf Hound with a great many large teeth, but Terrence snapped his fingers at it, and it subsided as we moved on.

I loved dogs, but hadn't been able to keep one because we never knew when or where my father might be posted abroad.

A cluster of men stood on the mole, staring down at something at their feet. I couldn't really see past the forest of dark trouser legs. And then Terrence was pushing them aside, and I could see the body lying there.

A man. He was dressed in dark clothing, like most of the men I'd seen that day, but he had reddish-brown hair. The pale freckled skin was marred by a large scrape down one side of his face.

I knelt quickly beside the body, but I could tell without touching him that he was dead. Half-closed hazel eyes stared blankly back at the deep lavender sky overhead, and there was a slackness in his limbs that was unnatural in life.

Above my head, someone was saying to Terrence, his voice still edged with shock and apology, "I was out fishing. And there he was. In the water. I thought it must be Michael. I don't know how I got him into the rowing boat. But that wound—it was *there*, I never touched him."

I had never seen Michael, I didn't know what he looked like. Was this the missing man? I felt my stomach turn over—how was I to tell her?

"I'm sorry. There's nothing I can do," I said, looking up at Terrence. "He's dead, very likely has been even before he was pulled from the water."

"How do you know that?" It was the barkeep.

"The body is very cold." I turned back to Terrence, and saw that he was frowning. "And there is no pulse, no heartbeat."

"Who is he? Do you know?" another man put in.

"He's an artist living in one of the other villages down the coast," someone else replied. "He came to paint the sea. And stayed on."

I felt intense relief sweep through me that it wasn't Michael lying here.

I went on with my examination. And apparently the poor man had been in the water for some time, because the puddle under him, draining from his soaked clothing, was widening as we talked. I moved slightly, out of its reach.

"What killed him?" Another voice, this time one I recognized. And Father O'Halloran was pushing me aside and kneeling in my place to give last rites. He seemed oblivious of the water making its way toward him.

"The blow on the head?" I said. It was nasty enough to have fractured his skull. "It must have been something large and very heavy to do such damage."

But the priest ignored me. And Terrence said, "Well, then. That tells us he didn't take his own life. A fall, do you think? There are rocks along the water up and down the coast." He turned toward the fisherman. "Ewen. Any rocks near where you found him?"

"It was dark. I can't be sure."

Or didn't wish to be?

The priest went on with what he was doing. The onlookers had stepped back, giving him room, shadows on their faces as they crossed themselves.

"Was he Catholic?" I quietly asked Terrence, who seemed to be the only one taking charge. If the dead man hadn't been local, he might not be.

"He was. He'd been in Dublin that April. 1916. And afterward painted what he saw by the Post Office and down by the bridge. The dead, the dying. And there were some who weren't happy about that. The English didn't want the dead to become martyrs."

I looked at the long pale fingers lying lax against the sun-bleached wood on which he lay. There was a dark blue stain on two of them. Paint. He must have been painting earlier in the day.

"What was he working on?" I asked quietly.

Terrence shrugged. "Portraits of the dead, last time I was there."

Apparently, no one wanted him to paint those either. No one being the English, of course.

The priest finished and rose, looking down at the body. "A pity," he said softly. And then he glanced at Terrence, who nodded once in an unspoken reply to whatever it was the priest was asking.

"Take him up," Terrence said, "and carry him to the pub."

I watched several men lift the body, its clothing still dripping sea-water, and start forward with it. The last of the light had faded, and it was dark. As the men moved on, I could hear the lapping of the tide and the rowboat gently nudging the pilings where it was tied up.

We followed the sad little procession. I said, "Is there a doctor in the village?"

"No."

"A policeman?"

"No. But one will have to be sent for."

"I want to look at the wound again."

"Why?"

"Because I'm a nurse," I said shortly.

He glanced at me, then walked on. I was left to carry Eileen's kit.

At the inn, they laid the body out on a table in the bar, hands by his sides, eyes closed. Someone had put pennies on the lids.

"Was he married? A family?" the barkeep was asking.

Again the men looked at Terrence. He shrugged. "I don't know. I never saw a wife. Or children."

I wondered if the dead man had painted the living too. Like Terrence. That might explain how he'd come to know the artist.

I stayed in the background while the men moved restlessly around, then began to leave, with a nod to the priest.

Finally, when there were only four or five left in the room, among them the priest and the barkeep and Terrence, he turned and motioned me forward. From somewhere the barkeep produced a torch, and I took a longer look at the wound.

It was deep, and it was my opinion that the jaw, the eye socket, and the cheekbones were broken. The skull as well, surely. If he'd been alive when he was put into the sea, he would have been unconscious and unable to fend for himself. But I kept that to myself. And no one asked.

There was nothing in the wound to tell me what had caused that much damage. And I couldn't think of a weapon that would inflict that much damage with one blow. Yet there were no signs of more than one blow.

"I'll send for the Constabulary," Father O'Halloran said, finally. Then to Terrence, "You'd best be least in sight for a while."

"I didn't kill him," Terrence said.

"No, but they'll be looking for you, without making it plain that they are."

"Send for them then."

With a jerk of his head in my direction, Terrence started for the door, and I followed.

Outside, there were men in small groups talking quietly together, and a few women in dark shawls, come to see what was happening. There were other women in doorways as we walked back up the hill.

"Where are the children?" I asked Terrence. I hadn't seen any.

"They've been kept indoors since Michael vanished. Safer for them if there's unexpected trouble."

"Who would cause that trouble?"

"Damn it, I don't know. I wish to hell I did." It was full dark now, and I couldn't see his face. He sounded as if he meant it, but there was something of the actor about Terrence. And so once more I couldn't be sure.

As we were passing the church I said, "You were afraid it was Michael lying there, weren't you? When that man came to the door."

"There are a dozen men it might have been, lying there on the mole. That fool Michael is only one of them." He swore, shaking his head. "If he'd had a bit of sense, now, he'd have told Eileen that they'd marry in England, and never come home."

"Alone, in a strange church, no one to stand up for them," I said. "It's not the way she'd hoped to marry."

But he didn't answer that.

We could see the lights from the house windows now, squares of brightness in the dark, growing larger as we kept walking, picking up our pace now on the flat lane.

"What will you tell the others?" I asked.

"The truth. They didn't know the man at first. But it wasn't Michael. We are certain of that." He stopped so suddenly I nearly thundered into him. "It was an accident. Leave it at that. You'll be safer. And so will I."

"The truth is, I couldn't tell."

He didn't say anything for a moment, then he touched my shoulder in the darkness. "When they've gone up to bed, I want to have a look at that man's house. I want you to come with me."

Wary, I said, "I'm in Eileen's room. I can't just walk out without a word."

"Don't be a fool, woman, I've got a good reason to want you along. I'd take the Major, for choice, but I don't trust him."

"Why not?"

"I've told you. It's damned odd that he's here—what is he really about?" He started walking again. "Tell Eileen I want to talk to you.

Then come down." He glanced toward me. "Wear something dark. Can you ride? You were wearing that fancy habit."

"I had to climb into the Captain's aircraft. Difficult to do in skirts."

But he wasn't listening. "*Can* you ride?"

"Yes." I almost added that I'd learned in India, with the Army. And stopped myself.

We had reached the house. "Go in, then. Tell them it was a stranger. They'll learn his name soon enough. Tonight all they'll want to know is that it wasn't Michael," Terrance said.

And he was gone, disappearing into the darkness as he walked around the corner of the house. I went inside, to be met by the Major, Eileen, and Niall, their faces anxious or fearful. Eileen reached out to me, her hands trembling. I took them, and they were cold.

"It isn't Michael," I said at once. "A stranger. He was pulled out of the water by one of the fishermen."

She closed her eyes, and for a moment I thought she was about to faint. Then she pulled me into the passage, down toward the kitchen.

"Drowned?" It was the Major.

"No. I don't think so."

They followed me into the kitchen. The table had been cleared, and Granny was nowhere in sight. I told them what I could, but they still had a good many questions.

"Who was he?" It was the Major again. "Did you hear his name?"

"No one told me his name." That was true. But for some reason, I didn't mention that Terrence had known the dead man, and that he'd been an artist. I was learning very quickly that there were minefields everywhere, in this part of the world. The less said, the less to regret later.

Finally, after I'd gone over and over what little information I had, they were satisfied.

But after Eileen had gone up to her room, and Niall had stepped outside for a smoke, the Major nodded to me, and I followed him into the front room.

He said, keeping his voice low, "You're quite sure it wasn't Michael? You weren't being kind?"

"Actually, it was the man who pulled him out of the water who thought at first it could be Michael. And then we realized that it wasn't. The priest was there, I don't think the fisherman was lying for my benefit."

"You never know," the Major said with a sigh. "He was killed, do you think? The dead man?"

"Yes. There was a blow to the head. It must have killed him straightaway. Or within a very few minutes. Then he was put into the water."

His gaze on my face sharpened. It was an appraising look. "You're very certain."

"I dealt with war wounds, Major. Even the doctors couldn't have saved him. If the blow itself didn't kill him, he'd have drowned, helpless to do anything to save himself."

Nodding, he said, "Yes, I see. Is the death being reported?"

"I was told it would be."

"And he wasn't a local man?"

"I gather he wasn't. Some of the local men didn't know him."

"Why did Terrence take you with him, and not Eileen?"

"I expect he was afraid it might be Michael. Would you have risked it, in his place?" I wasn't actually defending Terrence, but I thought it was true, although it served two purposes, keeping me under his eye as well as protecting his cousin.

"No, of course not." He paced away from me, then came back. "My given name is Ellis. If we're to get out of this business in one piece, we'll need to trust each other. May I call you Bess?"

There was no reason why he shouldn't, and so I told him it was all right.

"I knew Ireland was in turmoil. But the Sergeant saved my life in a situation where he could have easily left me to die in the middle of No Man's Land. And when he asked me to come for his wedding, I imagined three or four days at the most."

"How did you come here?"

"By sea, actually. A friend with a boat brought me to the village. Just as you came by air. It seemed to be—a great deal safer."

"Is he coming back for you?"

"No. I'll make my own way back through Holyhead. Anglesey."

I knew that ferries from Ireland came into Holyhead, in northern Wales. I'd considered taking that one myself, or possibly closer still to where I lived, perhaps going out through southern Wales. But I merely nodded.

He added, "You should have left with the Captain. I don't like what's happening here."

"Nor do I, but I gave my promise. As you must have done," I told him frankly. "If my parents knew what I've learned since I arrived, they'd be more than worried."

"I'm lucky. I have no family to worry about me. Only my Colonel." He smiled, but it faded as he added, "My parents are dead, and my fiancée died in the influenza epidemic." He shrugged. "The Army is my life now. I've decided to stay in the Guards."

My father and Simon had made the Army their lives as well. And so I understood what he was saying. It was a family, in a sense, although my father had had us as well. I'd often wondered why Simon hadn't decided to stay with the Regiment. But he'd resigned when my father did, and didn't seem to regret it. I'd been glad to have him nearby, and hadn't questioned his choice too closely.

But I said lightly, "We may well need the Guards before this is over."

"If they can find Michael before Saturday and the wedding, we'll be in the clear."

"I'd better go up. Eileen will be waiting for me. Good night, Ellis."

"Good night."

I left him there, and went upstairs. Eileen's eyes were red from crying, and I said at once, "You mustn't, my dear. He's not dead. If he were, we'd have his body by now." That was rather brusque, but it was the only way I could think of to comfort her. As long as we hadn't found Michael's body, there was hope, and it was better for Eileen to hope as long as possible.

"I know. But I was so frightened when Terrence asked for my kit. I knew then he was afraid. *Someone* had been hurt, and he wasn't sure who it could be."

"It's true, he wanted to spare you. If it *had* been Michael, I would have done everything possible for him. Everything you could have done."

"Still, I'd have wanted to be there if—if he was dying."

"I didn't know that you had no doctor here," I said, trying to change the subject.

"We're too small for such luxuries as doctors or policemen. We don't even have an undertaker. I did what I could in emergencies. Once I was fully recovered." She smiled a little. "I've done a bit of everything, come to that. From sewing up wounds from a fight to saving the lives of women in childbirth. That's why I can't understand why anyone would harm Michael. If only for my sake."

"Eileen. Was Michael in any way active in the Rising?" She was about to protest when I put up a hand to stop her. "No, I realize he was in France that Easter. I mean, did he support anyone—a cause—give money—write letters—anything?"

"Of course not. Michael was never political. He wanted to see Ireland freed from the English Parliament, yes, but he thought it could be done peacefully. That in the long run, it would be for the best."

But that attitude surely hadn't been popular among the hotheads bent on revolution. And the fact that there was a Rising in the middle of a war when we were fighting for our lives in France and elsewhere, the Army spread thin across the Empire and the Navy not much better at sea, had cost a lot of sympathy for the Irish cause among the British. Especially among those who knew that the Germans had attempted to supply arms for the Rising. These had been intercepted, but they could have turned the tide of the Rising if they had got through. Who could be sure?

I said nothing about any of that. I'd heard my father talk about it, and I thought it best not to speak of anything that might cause trouble for me or anyone else.

Eileen began to undress and prepare for bed, and when I didn't, she asked, "Do you mind sharing a room?"

"Of course not. But I'd promised to put a marker on the stile for Captain Jackson. And I haven't done it. I think I'll change into something dark and slip out to the meadow. He might even land with news. So don't worry if I'm not back straightaway."

She tried to persuade me not to go out, then insisted she should come with me, but after a bit, I succeeded in convincing her that two people would draw more attention than one.

"I won't go to sleep," she told me.

"Of course you should," I said, smiling. "And if I learn anything at all, I promise to wake you at once."

In the end, she got into bed, we turned out the lights, and I waited until I heard the Major and then Niall come up and go into their rooms. By that time Eileen was breathing quietly, and when I softly spoke her name, she didn't stir.

I gave the men half an hour before pulling on my habit again, slipping down the back stairs and into the kitchen. It was dark, and I had to feel my way around the unfamiliar room, for fear of knocking into something and waking the household.

I went out the kitchen door to the yard, not wanting Granny to spot me walking out the front, and ran lightly toward the meadow and the stile. I left my handkerchief there, in plain view from anyone flying overhead, and then got back to the house just as Terrence came out the door, searching for me.

"Where have you been?" he demanded in an angry whisper.

"Well, you didn't tell me where to meet you, and I didn't want your grandmother to see me coming out at this hour."

Mollified, he said, "The horses are down the lane. This way."

We circled the house at a distance, and for a moment I thought we might be going by the stile, but he stayed at the edge of some trees bordering the wall. The horses were waiting, and he helped me mount, then led the way down the lane, keeping to the grass.

When we were safely away from the house and the village, he picked up speed, and we made good time to the cottage where the painter had lived.

It was set on the outskirts of what appeared to be another small village farther down the coast, yet well away from nearest cottages and actually cut off from them by an inlet, a tiny rocky finger of water that ran out toward the open sea. On our side of the inlet, close to the water and facing it, there was a long single-story white dwelling, ghostly in what little light there was. Looking at it, I realized that someone had taken an old tenant farmstead, where once two or three families had lived in adjoining cottages, and converted these to his own use. I'd seen something quite like it in Scotland.

As he drew rein before the single door, Terrence said, "They either died or fled to America during the potato famine. The people who once lived here. And the British did nothing to help them. My grandfather told me stories about those days. There were dead everywhere, and those who could scrape together passage left. Most of them never came home again."

As I was about to dismount as well, Terrence stopped me.

"You're to stay with the horses. That's why I brought you."

I could barely see his face, a pale square in the darkness. The moon hadn't come up, and there was only starlight.

"You brought me here as a witness," I said, realizing how I had been used.

"Nevertheless, stay where you are."

He disappeared through the door that served the middle of the three cottages, and I saw the torch he was carrying flick on. In the ensuing silence, I could hear the whisper of the sea in the little inlet as the tide came in, and found myself thinking that for an artist who loved the sea, this was a perfect setting. Then I pulled my attention back to the house.

Terrence must have found a lamp, lit it, and begun to look around him. Through the nearest window I could see the orange glow as he moved about.

I dismounted, tied the reins together, and slipped up to the window, looking in.

The artist had opened up the interior and improved it with a hearth, more windows back and front, and other amenities the former owners could never have imagined. This was clearly the main room, with a small alcove for a cooker and above it, two small cupboards, very likely one for dishes and the other for tea and sugar and tins of food.

I could see all this even though the room was a shambles. What must have been a bachelor's quarters, rather plain but pleasant enough, had been tossed about without a thought to anything but what someone had been looking for. I could hear Terrence swearing as he righted chairs, set up a table again, and pushed his way through the papers and broken crockery littering the floor. At first I thought there was a body among the debris, and I caught my breath. Looking again I saw that it was only a dark red carpet that had been tossed aside in a heap.

This was what must have been a sitting room. The next window to my right as I followed Terrence's lamplight was a bedroom. It too was wrecked, even the pictures on the wall broken out of their frames and then discarded, clothes from the cupboard thrown about, the bed overturned and the linens stripped, the mattress slashed.

I wasn't certain now whether someone had been searching for something—or was maliciously intent on destroying what was left of a man's life. As if his death wasn't satisfying enough.

Terrence went back through the middle room and to our left, which looked to be the studio where the dead man worked. For there were windows in the far wall to let in light, where the bedroom at the other end had had a solid wall in the same place.

There were canvases scattered everywhere, and I watched as Terrence righted them. Paints were scattered on the floor too, and some stepped on as whoever had been here searched. I could see an occasional work, one of what must have been the Post Office building in Dublin, for I recognized it from newspaper accounts of the Rising.

There were others of men's faces, and more of the sea in all its moods, from moonrise to sunset.

From what I could judge, the dead man was quite good, talented and with an eye to the use of color. My mother, who loved seascapes, would most certainly have admired these.

What a shame, I thought, looking at the devastation bared by Terrence's lamp.

But Terrence was still looking at each of the canvases, intent and very angry. I couldn't tell whether he was in search of his own portrait, or something else. He opened a cupboard, dragging out the remaining clean canvases, empty frames, rags, and other things a painter collected, and then he stopped short.

Reaching in, he pulled out what appeared to be an old sheet, and wrapped up in it was a small square, perhaps twelve by fourteen inches, smaller than the other canvases scattered about. He gently removed the sheet and looked at what it held.

I couldn't see the canvas, only the sticks onto which it had been stretched. And then as he reached again for the sheet, this time to cover it, I saw what it was.

Nothing that I had expected.

It was a woman's face, and behind it was the sea, glinting in the sun, a deep green flecked by whitecaps and the sun's reflection. The woman's dark hair was loose and caught by the wind, but I couldn't quite see her features.

But I could guess. I'd seen Eileen brushing out her dark hair before going to bed, long strokes that gave it a black sheen.

Satisfied, he gave one last look around, shook his head at the destruction, tucked sheet and painting under his free arm before making his way back through the house.

I ran back to the horses, nearly stumbling on the rough ground. I was holding both reins and stroking the white blaze on the nose of my mount when the light went out in the cottage, the door opened, and Terrence stepped over the threshold, closing the door behind him.

"I told you to stay on your horse," he said roughly.

"I was tired of sitting in the saddle. Besides, it was easier to keep them quiet."

He looked around us in every direction. There didn't appear to be anything to worry him, but I thought it had become second nature for him to be sure there was no threat. He helped me mount, then stowed his burden in the leather bag behind his saddle.

"What is that?" I asked him, gesturing toward the bag. "What did you take?"

"That's none of your affair, woman."

"It is if you took it from a murder scene. That makes me an accessory. And so I have a right to know."

He hesitated, then answered me. "It is something that belongs to me. It has nothing to do with that man's death. I just didn't want the police to find it and draw the wrong conclusions. We're always the villains, we Irish. Wait and see. The Constabulary will turn out every shed, barn, and household in the days to come. And use whatever they find however it seems best to them. Never mind Fergus's murder." Swinging himself into his saddle, he touched his horse with his heel and we moved off.

"Is that his name? Fergus?"

"Fergus Kennedy. His mother was English, she died when he was eighteen. Before he came to live here."

"You seem to know him fairly well."

"I did. I liked him."

He couldn't have killed Fergus Kennedy, could he? Surely if he had, and thrown the body into the sea, he'd have collected that painting before leaving here. But then I couldn't be sure just *when* the man had been killed and put into the sea. And for that matter, they could have met somewhere closer by.

We fell silent. Traveling through the night, sometimes near the sea, more often inland. Ten miles? Twenty? I couldn't be certain how far away that cottage was, because we'd never ridden in a straight line, the coast here was so irregular. My instinct said closer to twenty.

I was thinking about why Terrence had taken me into the village, had insisted that I accompany him to the harbor, and now had made certain I was with him tonight. It was most certainly not the pleasure of my company that he wanted. Was he just trying to make certain nothing more happened to mar Eileen's wedding?

Or was I simply there to help him cover his tracks, as Captain Jackson would have described it?

CHAPTER SIX

WE DIDN'T SPEAK the rest of the way to Eileen's house. And when we reached the place where he'd kept the horses earlier, he said only, "Get down and go in. I'll see you safe to the door before taking these to the barn."

"Thank you. Good night." I began to walk briskly toward the house, once more turning toward the rear and the kitchen door before I reached the point where Granny might see me. All was quiet, and I slipped into the kitchen, carefully shutting the door behind me.

A voice in the darkness spoke, and I nearly leaped out of my shoes. "Bess?"

It was Major Dawson, and judging where his voice was coming from, he was sitting at the table.

Collecting my wits, I said softly, "You couldn't sleep, either?"

"No. Niall is next door to me, and he snores loud enough to wake the banshees, whatever they may be."

I smothered a laugh, but he was continuing in a more serious tone. "You shouldn't be wandering about alone in the dark. You don't know the grounds. You only just got here today—yesterday."

"I walked down to the meadow. Where I'd landed. I needed to think, and I didn't wish to keep Eileen awake."

"The priest—O'Halloran—came looking for Terrence. The last of the searchers had reported in. Still no sign of Michael. I heard the knock and came down. The priest has called it off for tonight. The men are weary, he said, and need rest."

"Do you believe him? That there was no sign of Michael?"

His voice was tired as he said, "We have no reason to doubt O'Halloran. But then we have no way of knowing where he stands in regard to Michael serving in the British Army."

"I don't think he approves of it. I wonder—is Eileen's grandmother someone Father O'Halloran wouldn't particularly wish to cross? Is it like England here, and the living is in the hands of the squire or someone else of importance in the village?"

I could hear his sigh. "I have no idea how that works here. As for crossing her, I'm already in her black books simply for being English, and that's unpleasant enough." There was the slight scrape of his chair as he rose, adding, "We ought to be in bed. You might wish to go up the back stairs. Two of us using the main staircase might cause talk."

"Good night." I opened the door and started up the steps in the dark, feeling my way. He waited, and then closed the door when he thought I was safely at the top. I slipped into Eileen's room, which was almost at the head of the back stairs, undressed in the dark, and got quietly into bed beside her. Only then did I hear the Major's door shut softly.

It was nearly half an hour later when I barely heard the distant sound of an aircraft, riding high in the night sky. I was just falling asleep, but I'd been half listening for it.

I woke early, a little after sunrise, and dressed quietly. Eileen was deeply asleep, a reaction, I thought, to the stress of yesterday.

Closing the door gently, I went down the back stairs with my boots in my hand, and in the kitchen quickly pulled them on and did up the laces. Then I let myself out the back door.

The morning was cool, and there had been a heavy dew. I had to hold up my skirts so that it didn't wet my hems as I walked close to the house and then cut across the lawns down to the stile.

My handkerchief lay where I'd left it last night, and with my back to the house, I hurriedly stuffed it into my pocket. Standing there, looking out across the meadow, I could see a scattering of wildflowers, some of which I recognized. And beyond, the stand of trees. The grasses were still flattened where the Captain had landed and taken off again. And I noticed something lying there that seemed a bit out of place.

Without hurrying, I walked across the meadow, listening to the early birdsong, seeing a flash of color here and there where the birds were feeding on the seeds.

I was near enough now to realize that I hadn't been wrong. There *was* something just ten paces farther on, half hidden where it had fallen.

I was still more or less strolling along, and when I reached the spot, I stopped, as if only just seeing what was there.

It was a bit of paper wrapped around a stone, the ends twisted together and tied off with a length of twine.

I bent down, picked it up, dropped it in my pocket, and kept walking, finally turning and heading back toward the house.

I was halfway back to the stile when I saw that someone was standing in the shadows by the side of the house, watching me.

It was Terrence.

He started toward me, and for an instant I considered dropping the paper and stone under the stile as I went over it. But how long had he been watching? If he'd seen me pick it up—and I didn't have it with me when he questioned me—what then?

I had to trust that whoever had written the message had taken into account the possibility that it might be found by someone else.

And so I left it where it was.

And wondered, as I kept walking toward him, if Terrance too had heard the aircraft in the night.

We met on the lawns beside the house, and he simply held out his hand.

I reached into my pocket and pulled out the stone and paper.

Terrence smiled, then started to take it from me.

I snatched my hand away and said crossly, "It's mine. I'll read it first." Without waiting for an answer, I struggled with the knot in the twine. Impatient, he pulled out a pocketknife and, reaching out, cut it.

I unfolded the paper, dropped the stone by my foot, and began to scan what was written there.

"Aloud," Terrence ordered.

Giving him as angry a look as I could muster, I began to read.

Dearest Bess,

Has Michael been found? Do you need rescue? I can only hope that all is well and that you aren't already repenting your decision to stay on. If you need help, you know I'll do everything I can to get you safely out of there.

Yours always,
Arthur

"Who," Terrence was asking, "is Arthur?"

"Captain Jackson, of course! The pilot who brought me here." I'd already seen the signature before I'd begun to read, and I was ready for his suspicions. "We met in Paris. During the war." That was true, actually: the peace treaty hadn't been agreed upon, much less signed. I looked up, meeting his intent gaze. "He thinks he's in love with me." I hoped Arthur would forgive the lie.

"And are you in love with him?"

I shook my head. "He's a good friend. I like him immensely. But no. I'm not in love with him. He's an American. He'll soon be going back to his home." I was fairly sure that the Captain's accent had been noted. I was still on safe ground.

He held out his hand, reading the note for himself, to see that there was nothing I'd left out—or changed. No hidden message, no secret code.

Giving it back to me, he said, "And do you need rescue?"

"I don't know," I challenged him. "Do I?"

He laughed. And started back to the house. Turning slightly, he waited for me to walk with him.

"He can drop all the love letters he wishes," Terrence said as we walked on. "That's the thing about an aircraft. It can drop—but it can't pick up, can it?"

"It can land," I replied.

"Yes. So it can. I'm famished. Have you had your breakfast?"

"No. I needed a walk to clear my head. And I saw the message. Did *you* hear an aircraft last night? It must have flown over while we were at Fergus's house."

"I expect it did." He held the kitchen door wide for me, and I went inside.

Although I had offered to make breakfast, Terrence pointed to a pot on the cooker. "Porridge," he said, and set about heating it up and serving it to me.

Eileen came down while we were eating, and I could see how much worry had already changed her face. It was drawn, thin, and what little color she had left came from crying. I expect that not finding me beside her in the bed we shared had frightened her.

"There you are! Any news?" she asked, looking from one to the other of us.

"They were out at first light. The searchers. There hasn't been time for them to be reporting in," her cousin told her. "You must trust them to do their work."

"Where could they have taken Michael? And *why*?"

"My darling girl," he said gently, "if I knew the answer to that, he'd be sitting here having a wedding breakfast with you. I've tried all my sources. So far, there's nothing." He glanced at me, then turned back to her. "If it's the English, they've kept very quiet about it."

"But why would they want Michael?" she asked. "He's got nothing they want. He wasn't even here in '16. And if it's to draw *you* out, surely they'd know where to find you by now. Someone would tell them, even if Michael didn't."

"Someone would betray your cousin?" I asked Eileen, surprised.

"There're factions." It was Terrence who answered. "Some I don't hold with. They're out for blood. They'd betray their own mothers, if it advanced the Cause."

"Then you aren't safe here? How can you protect us?" I demanded.

"Because they won't defy me openly. Not yet. But I too have spies. I'll hear, if there's to be trouble." His face was suddenly grim.

He and Eileen began discussing where the searchers had been, and where they were looking today. "And there's the Constabulary coming," she added, reminding him.

"True enough. Bess here can tell them she was there when the body was pulled from the water, that I'd taken her to the village in the hope that she could help the poor man. She can tell them that I was here at breakfast, but left to join the search for Michael. All she can tell them, being a stranger here herself, is that I was heading north. She saw me leave. Which she'll be doing in ten minutes' time."

And that was precisely what happened. I saw him walk off toward the stables and outbuilding, and then ride out, toward the north. At least that was the direction he was going, when he trotted steadily toward a small orchard. After that, of course, I couldn't have said . . .

I went upstairs while Eileen took breakfast to her mother and grandmother, and I put the message away in my kit. Where anyone who searched my belongings could easily find it. My love letter from the pilot who had brought me here.

Only, though it was signed *Arthur*, I had recognized the handwriting. And it wasn't Captain Jackson's. Simon Brandon had written that note for him.

The only "code," I thought, was in that last line: *If you need help, you know I'll do everything I can to get you safely out of there.*

I also detected the Colonel Sahib's hand in the writing of that letter—it was there in the word *repenting*. When we were in India, it was sometimes a code word for *searching*. Was my father already trying to discover if the Army had taken Michael?

But how Simon, who was very English, was going to be there to get me out of Ireland, I couldn't imagine.

It was more likely that he would find himself in as much trouble as I might be in. And that wouldn't do at all. It would mean my father would have to send in the cavalry, and I wasn't about to let that happen.

Still, the thought was comforting.

That done, I went downstairs to await developments. I had a feeling that the quiet of the morning wasn't going to last.

I was right.

It was a little after ten when someone pounded on the house door.

Eileen and I were in the front room. She had been showing me some of the things in her trousseau, and she looked up expectantly, but I put out my hand. "If it was news, they would knock, not hammer at the door. Go and answer it. They might have come for Terrence."

Casting a frightened glance at me, she straightened her shoulders and went through to the entrance. I shut the parlor door and stood close enough to the crack to hear what was happening.

Eileen said, "Good morning—"

A harsh voice demanded, "Terrence Flynn, if you please."

But before Eileen could answer, Granny spoke from the stairs. "My grandson isn't here. You can search wherever you like. It won't do you any good, I can tell you that now."

"This is in reference to a dead man pulled out of the sea close by the harbor."

"I know about the dead man. He had nothing to do with us. My grandson has gone to search for my granddaughter's missing fiancé. Half the village is out looking for him."

"Mrs. Flynn—"

"I've said what I wished to say. Good day to you."

"Mrs. Flynn, we've also come to speak to your house guest. A young woman from England," the man pressed on doggedly.

"She's no guest of mine."

I heard a door slam somewhere upstairs, and then after a moment's hesitation, Eileen must have allowed the Constable to step into the entry.

There was nothing for it. I had to admit him. There was no time to do anything but find a chair and sit down in it.

He came through the door and nodded to me, but Eileen didn't follow him into the room. She shut the door quietly, and I thought I heard her going up the stairs.

The Constable's deep voice had indicated a larger man. Instead he was only of medium build, with brown hair and cold hazel eyes that focused on me and didn't leave my face. As if I'd vanish when he blinked. I gestured to a chair on the other side of the room and then said, "My name is Elizabeth Crawford."

He took out his notebook and wrote something in it.

I knew very little about the Royal Constabulary. Only that they were mostly Catholic, in a primarily Catholic land, and the Law outside Dublin. It and a few other large towns had their own police force.

But what the Constabulary's politics were, which side they had taken in the recent political upheavals, I didn't know. And therefore, I would have to walk carefully.

"You have come to Ireland for a wedding, as I understand."

"I have." I didn't know what resources he might have, and so I was afraid to lie. But it was imperative to keep him or anyone else away from my father's connection with the Army.

"Where is it you live?" He was writing my answers down in his notebook.

"I have a small flat in London."

"How do you make a living?"

"I was told I was too strong-minded to be a teacher. And so I became a nursing Sister. I'm presently on leave from a clinic for the long-term wounded."

"English soldiers?"

"Welsh—Scottish—English. I treat patients, not their countries."

"Where do you come from? What part of England."

"A cousin lives in Kent, and I go to her on holidays and the like."

He looked up. "Your parents are deceased?"

"Retired." I could see where this was going, and so I added, "He was a civil servant in India. When that dreadful outbreak of cholera occurred in Lahore, he took his retirement and brought his family home. He thought I would have better opportunities there."

"You aren't married?"

There. He was distracted from my father. "Sadly, no."

He considered me, clearly weighing up my value in the marriage market and the fact that I was still single. I felt my face warm, as if I'd flushed. But it was anger, no maidenly blush at my failure to find a husband. I quickly looked down at my hands, folded in my lap, so that he wouldn't take note of whatever spark might have been there in my eyes. And so I didn't see what conclusions he might have drawn about my eligibility.

"Religious affiliation?"

Frowning, I said, "I expect it would be Protestant. I don't often have the opportunity to attend services. Of course we do have a chaplain in the clinic."

I was beginning to heartily dislike this rude man.

And I now had a file in the records of the Irish police.

Apparently satisfied about me, he asked, "Tell me about this dead man."

"There's little to tell. I'd only just arrived that morning, and except for Miss Flynn, I knew no one here. I'd never seen the man before. When I reached the mole, I could tell that he was dead, beyond my help. And then Father O'Halloran was there and gave him last rites before he was moved to the pub."

"I've been told that Terrence Flynn identified him."

"The name he gave meant nothing to me, I'm afraid."

"Were they friends, Flynn and this dead man?"

Careful, Bess, I warned myself. "I have no idea."

"Did the man drown?"

"I couldn't say. It's always possible that he hit his head, fell into the water, and was unable to save himself. It's also possible that he was dead from the injury, before he fell in. It would depend on what his lungs could tell us. Unfortunately, I couldn't look at them."

"Why did you decide to go down to the harbor? A stranger, as you said?"

"I was asked to. I learned afterward that there's no doctor in the village."

"But you went to the pub, when the body was taken there."

"The light was fading. I was hoping to learn more when I could see him better. Sadly, a closer look didn't tell me anything new. And so I came back to the house, leaving the men who had gathered there to see to the body."

He considered me again, as if hoping to find a flaw my statement. Then he closed his notebook, put away his pencil.

"How long will you be in Ireland?"

"I was only given enough leave to come to a wedding. When that is over, I'm expected to return to my duties."

"Without a bridegroom, it isn't likely that there *will* be a wedding."

"I'm told there are men still searching for him."

"Did you know the groom in France?"

"As far as I know, I've never encountered him there. But then I won't be able to tell until I meet him. I've treated hundreds of men, you see, and after a while, their faces are a blur. All I really notice is the wound before me on the table, and what I can do about it."

"Did you come to Ireland under cover of the wedding, to see Mr. Kennedy? Is that why he was killed, before you could meet him?"

I replied as coldly as I could, "I came for a wedding. I know nothing about Irish affairs, nor do I wish to know. Nursing Sisters are not used as spies."

He retorted, "I believe Nurse Cavell was shot by the Germans for spying."

I stared him in the face. "You are misinformed, sir. Edith Cavell was shot for helping English prisoners of war escape. To my knowledge there are no English prisoners of war in Killeighbeg."

Immediately I wished I'd held my tongue.

But he rose and said, "It would be best if you stayed in Ireland as long as these matters are unresolved. You may be needed to give your evidence at an inquest."

It was a warning.

"Yes, of course," I answered, and he left me sitting there in the parlor. I heard his footsteps on the stairs.

Eileen slipped quietly into the room from the kitchen, glancing anxiously over her shoulder as she carefully shut the door.

Crossing to where I was sitting, she asked, "What did he say to you, Bess? Anything at all about Michael? Does he know where Michael is?"

"Should he?" I wasn't sure just how the Constabulary worked. If they had been called in officially or if his disappearance was still being treated as a local matter. Even though there wasn't a village Constable.

"Oh, God, *someone* must know."

"He only asked questions about the man who had drowned. And why I had come to Ireland."

Absently biting her lip, she considered that. "Terrence didn't want to bring Michael to the attention of anyone outside Killeighbeg."

I didn't have the heart to tell her that someone had already told the Constable about the missing man.

A little after lunch, Eileen said, "My mother would like to meet you. She doesn't come downstairs very often. Would you mind going up to her room?"

"I would be happy to go to her. Of course I would."

But we climbed the back stairs, as if to keep our visit from Granny.

Mrs. Flynn's room was on the back of the house, the opposite corner from Eileen's. It was smaller, got the afternoon sun instead of the morning, and was crowded with furnishings. I gathered she had brought a lot of her favorite pieces with her when she had changed rooms with Eileen after her husband's death. They shone with love and polish.

I don't know quite what I'd expected—a quiet mouse, someone thoroughly intimidated by the elder Mrs. Flynn. A reclusive woman living in the past . . .

The woman who rose from her chair by the window was very attractive still, her dark hair drawn back to the nape of her neck, showing off an almost cameo-like profile—straight nose, lovely cheekbones, and a firm chin. She was wearing the black of widowhood, but the dress was beautifully made, with black lace at her wrists and throat.

Holding out a slim hand, she said in a pleasant voice, "It's lovely to meet you at last, Sister Crawford! I owe you my daughter's life and happiness. It is a debt I can never fully repay."

"She would have done as much for me, Mrs. Flynn. The Sisters aboard *Britannic* were well trained."

"Nevertheless, Bess—may I call you Bess?—nevertheless, I shall keep you in my prayers. Now come and sit by me, and tell me about yourself."

I did as she asked, skimming lightly over my past, keeping to the account I'd given the Constabulary.

"Was the training as rigorous as Eileen told us?" She smiled at her daughter.

We talked about that and about France, and dealing with ugly wounds, and then about Michael, and how much she hoped the wedding would take place as planned.

"Because I can't think why such a thing happened. It's cruel. I've told Terrence that I'll hold him personally responsible if Michael isn't back in time."

That was the first sign that she was out of touch with what was going on around us here in this divided house.

"I'm sure he's doing everything he possibly can," I assured her, not needing the frown of warning I'd got from Eileen.

We talked a little longer, and I could see that Mrs. Flynn was tiring.

Eileen rose, saying, "It's time to be thinking about Granny's afternoon tea. I'll bring Bess to visit again soon, shall I?"

"Yes, darling, please do." She gave me her hand again, and I told her how happy I was to meet her. And then we were on our way down the stairs.

"She's lived in Granny's shadow for so long, it's taken a toll," Eileen was saying. But I wondered if it was more than that. And couldn't ask.

I wandered outside for a bit while Eileen was busy with her grandmother, going as far as the barn to look in at the goats and horses and a sad little donkey who came at once to have his ears scratched. I was just turning back toward the house when I heard Eileen calling urgently to me.

I hurried to the kitchen, but she wasn't there, and when I stepped into the front room I could see why.

The Constabulary had returned, and wanted to ask me more questions.

"Do you ride?" It was blunt and to the point.

"Ride? Horses?" I repeated, as if taken aback. But my mind was racing. In spite of Terrence's precautions, had someone seen us last night?

"Yes."

"Well, of course I do."

That seemed to put him off, as if he hadn't expected me to be so open.

"When did you last ride?"

"I expect it was the last time I visited my cousin in Kent. I can't keep a horse in London, it's too expensive. And so I must wait until I go down there."

"I'm told you were wearing a riding habit when you went into the village earlier in the day, yesterday."

"Oh," I said, smiling, "yes, I do see. A friend from France brought me over to Ireland in his aircraft. And I had the most awful time getting into the cockpit. Fortunately my mother had suggested that I wear riding clothes, for the sake of modesty. And I hadn't had an opportunity to change."

"When did you change?"

"It was just after I got back from the pub visit, I believe. Eileen—Miss Flynn—was just going down to make sandwiches for our lunch."

I waited for the next question.

He was busy writing in his little notebook. Without stopping, he asked, "You didn't change again, after dinner?"

"I was rather tired, and we went up to bed."

"Thank you." He snapped the little book shut and with a nod turned to go. But at the door, he stopped. "Where is Terrence Flynn?"

"I'm sorry. I don't know."

"He keeps horses here, does he not?"

"I have no idea." I started forward. "Shall I take you up to speak to the elder Mrs. Flynn? She might be able to help you."

"Good day, Miss Crawford."

And he was gone. I watched from a window as he mounted his bicycle and pedaled away.

I found myself thinking that I was as grateful not to have to beard the dragon in her den as he appeared to be.

There was a sound behind me, and I whirled.

"What was that all about?" Eileen asked, coming to join me at the window.

I said, "People in the village were staring at me. I gather someone told him I'd been out riding. I don't think he knew about the flight—why I'd worn riding clothes."

"Does he think *you* might have killed that poor man?"

"I can't see why he should. I didn't know the dead man or where he lived. How could I have harmed him? And who has been saying he was murdered? Even I couldn't tell how he died." Not quite true, but the less I appeared to know, the better. "Besides, I haven't been alone since I landed here."

"Niall says that rumors are making the rounds, that it must have been murder." She shook her head. "It's just that he makes me nervous, that Constable. He's like a weasel, waiting for his chance."

She went back to the kitchen, but I watched the man out of sight.

The only thing I could think of to explain that odd conversation was not very reassuring. We'd been very careful, Terrence and I, to leave no trace of our presence the previous night. But what if one of the horses had left droppings behind, close by the cottage? We hadn't considered that.

And I needed to warn Terrence as soon as I could.

Weddings were happy affairs as a rule. People coming and going as all the preparations were made, house guests and gifts arriving, an air of festivity and excitement surrounding the event, the house and the church decorated with flowers and ribbons and candles.

There were no guests, except for the Major and me, the mood was anything but festive, and if there were candles or flowers or ribbons about, I hadn't seen them. There wasn't enough food in the pantry for our dinner tonight, much less a wedding feast.

It was like a German fairy tale, where everything had vanished with the groom, cursed by the wicked witch.

As Mrs. Flynn pounded on the floor above with her cane, I realized that we most certainly had the resident witch.

Eileen was putting the finishing touches on her grandmother's tea tray, and I was helping by arranging the dishes on her mother's.

Then I held the door while she carried the first tray upstairs.

Major Dawson came down them just afterward, greeting me. I hadn't seen him since last evening, and it was nearer dinner than breakfast.

"Did you have breakfast? Or lunch?" I asked him. I hadn't seen any indication that he had.

"I helped myself to the porridge and the bread this morning. And washed up afterward. I could do with some tea now." Smiling at my surprise, he said, "I got accustomed to fending for myself in France. And I thought it best not to be underfoot, since there's so little I can do to help just now." The smile faded. "The Constable was back again."

"Yes. More questions. Apparently they haven't interviewed Terrence yet."

"Not surprising, if he doesn't want to be found."

"Where is he staying? The pub?"

"I suspect he's been staying in the barn."

We had moved into the kitchen and were talking quietly.

I said, "I wish I knew what to think about Michael's disappearance. Those men go out and search the surrounding countryside, then come back with nothing to report for their efforts, no luck, no new information. How many hiding places can there be?"

"If you want the truth, my view is that they go out to please Terrence. And he sends them to give Eileen the feeling that something is being done."

"Michael is out of the Army now, Dublin wouldn't be too keen on coming all the way out here to look for him. But you're still a serving officer, aren't you? Would they come if you asked?"

"I'd already thought about that. My Colonel wasn't too pleased when I requested leave to attend the wedding. He thought Ireland was still too unsettled unless I was posted here and had a garrison at my back. The trouble is, there's no way to find out. And if I leave, chances are I couldn't make it back." He shook his head. "Those who have the most to gain—preventing the traitor Michael from marrying into the family—are suspect, of course, but Michael isn't easily frightened off, and they'd have to kill him to stop him. I'm not fully convinced that they'd go that far."

"If it isn't Terrence—or Father O'Halloran—or Mrs. Flynn, Senior—who else could be behind this abduction?"

"It's rather far-fetched, but there could even be something in Michael's past that we don't know about. And this is the first chance some-one has had to deal in a little revenge. On the other hand, there's a man in the village. I've seen him walking on the lane several times, as if reconnoitering, and I don't like the look of him. It's one of the reasons I stay out of sight. He might think killing an English officer would put him in good odor in certain quarters. What's more, he doesn't appear to be local. I asked Niall who he was, and Niall didn't know. And like Cassius, the man has a lean and hungry look."

It was a quote from Shakespeare's *Julius Caesar*, a description of one of the men who would join Brutus in stabbing Caesar.

And I was at once reminded of a man I'd seen on my first visit to the pub. The tall, thin man singing and playing the violin as we came through the passage from the bar into the back room. I'd seen too the way he'd stared at Terrence.

"I agree, I don't believe he's local, either. And Terrence doesn't care for him. There's something between them. There were two other men at the pub as well who questioned Terrence openly. As if trying to stir up trouble. But when he spoke to them, they fell silent. Looking back on that visit, it was almost as if the singer left it to them to confront us, rather than take on Terrence directly. It made for a very tense moment."

The Major looked sharply at me.

"You've seen him, then? You believe this man you call the singer is the one I've watched?"

Before I could do more than nod, I could hear someone on the stairs.

Ellis Dawson leaned forward. "One more thing. Don't trust Niall," he added quickly in a whisper, and by the time Eileen stepped into the kitchen, he was cutting more slices of bread while I was finding plates in the cupboard.

CHAPTER SEVEN

EILEEN STEPPED INTO the kitchen, the most forlorn expression on her face, as if as the day wore on, and there was no sign of Michael, her faith in his swift return was slipping away.

Then, seeing the Major, she forced a bright smile, greeted him, and when he asked how she was holding up, she replied, "I keep telling myself that all will be well. But I know it isn't true. I don't know where to turn or what to do. Granny told me just now that she believed Michael had realized how impossible it was for us to marry, and that he'd done the proper thing by just walking away. That's why the searchers haven't found any trace of him. He doesn't *intend* to be found."

Ellis swore under his breath as I said bracingly, "Well, that's to be expected from your grandmother, darling. She wants you to believe that."

"But what if it's true, what if he really did think he was doing the best thing for us both?"

"If he felt the wedding couldn't take place here in Killeighbeg, he'd have come to you, asked you to pack what you needed, and left Ireland. With you." I'd never met Michael, but I remembered how wonderful his letters to Eileen had been, when they were separated by the war. How she had cherished them, and how she had talked about him. He hadn't seemed then to be the sort of man who would cut and run after all of this time, leaving Eileen to wonder and grieve.

She clung to my words, as if they were a lifeline.

And Major Dawson said, "He never let his men down in France. I refuse to believe he would turn his back on you."

Just then Niall came down the steps and into the kitchen.

For an instant, remembering the warning about him, I wondered if he'd been listening from the top of the stairs.

But he said cheerfully, "Any word?" And went to pour himself a cup of tea. It was probably strong enough to dissolve the spoon, but he drank it down.

Eileen said, "Nothing new. Niall, where have they searched? Do you know? What if they've not looked in the right *places*?"

He came across the room to put an arm around her shoulders. "You know they have. They've lived here all their lives. How could they not?"

"He can't have vanished," she replied. "And yet it's like something in the old tales."

"Gone with the fairies? Fallen in love with a mermaid and followed her into the sea?" he asked in mock horror. "I don't see Michael doing either of those mad things. You're his mermaid, his fairy queen. What does he need with anyone else?"

She smiled, and he squeezed her shoulders affectionately as he let her go. "That's my cousin," he said, nodding. "If you don't keep your heart up, love, how can the searchers?"

"I know. I know. But it's wearing, just the same."

"Come and help me muck out the stables. Exercise is what you need. You know what Granny says. Idle hands do the devil's work. And worry is the devil's work."

She hesitated, then said, "Let me fetch my boots."

She went into the hall and came back with a jacket and boots. "Do you mind?" she asked us, following Niall to the door. "With the two of us, it will be short work."

"Go," I said, smiling. "Give the donkey a pat for me."

And she was hurrying across the back garden to the outbuildings. They were set off from the lawns and the gardens by a tall hedge of fuchsia, the lovely pink and purple flowers dancing in the slight breeze like ballerinas. I remembered just such a hedge in the south of Wales, marking the stairs down to the sea. Here there was an arch in the center, of the same gray stone as the house.

"Best thing for her," Ellis said, watching her go.

"I always thought she might marry Niall," a voice said from the open door into the passage.

We turned, surprised to find Eileen's mother standing there. I'd been under the impression that she never left her room.

"He's such a handsome lad. They'd make a fine pair," she went on.

"Good afternoon, Mrs. Flynn," we said almost in unison, and I added, "Would you care for a cup of tea? I was just about to put the kettle on and make a fresh pot."

"That would be lovely. I came down to see if there were any of those little iced cakes left. Cook used to make them especially for me."

I didn't recall seeing any cakes, iced or not. "I'll have a look." Had someone brought them for the wedding?

Setting the kettle on the cooker, I went into the pantry, but just as I'd thought, there were no cakes to be found. Stepping back into the kitchen, I said, "I'm afraid someone has finished them. Perhaps Eileen can be persuaded to make more. Shall I ask her?"

"Would you, dear?" She walked to the door, looking across toward the stables. "We had horses when I was young. Beautiful ones. My father raced them, and I loved to watch them run."

"Where did you live when you were young?" the Major asked, joining her at the door.

"My father was Harry FitzGerald. We had a house in Dublin for the Season, but we loved the country—the house in Connemara. There were ducks and geese in the pond during the winter, and even a peacock that roamed the lawns. I was terrified of it. Mama told me she'd bought it to remind my father that even the proud peacock had ugly feet." She laughed, a silvery sound. "She kept him in line, Mama did."

"Did the peacock have a name?"

"Dandy. We called him Dandy. I remember when he lost a feather, Papa gave it to me for my hat. I always called that one Dandy's hat."

"Tell me about Eileen's father," I asked.

"You have only to look at Niall to see how handsome my Eamon was. There's a strong family resemblance. I fell in love at first sight. My mother didn't want me to marry him, but I wore her down in the end. She told me I'd rue the day. And sadly I did. He died far too young. I was left with a daughter and a mother-in-law who hated me. I was Anglo-Irish, you see. Dirt beneath her feet, she called us. Bog Irish, I called her. But not to her face, of course."

The kettle boiled, and I went to make the tea. I didn't like questioning her in this way, but she seemed more comfortable in the past than in the present. And I was frankly curious about her. She seemed so out of place here. And I was aware that the circumstances under which she'd lived could have affected her mind more than a little. I couldn't help but wonder how she had fared when Eileen was away training in England and then posted to France, leaving her to the none-too-tender mercies of Mrs. Flynn the elder.

As if my thoughts had conjured her up, there was a pounding on the floor upstairs, and the angry voice of Granny came down to us.

"Where are my slippers? What have you done with them, you goose of a girl?"

Eileen's mother turned, alarmed.

The Major said quickly, "It's all right. She won't come down. Bess?"

"The tea," I said, leaving him to finish what I was doing, and then taking a deep breath, I started up the stairs, preparing myself to meet the dragon in her own den.

She was standing in the doorway to her rooms. Her black clothing was well made, but with her hair threaded with iron gray, and her dark angry eyes, there was a harshness about her that spoke to me of disappointments and sorrows that she hadn't been able to accept.

"Where's Eileen?"

"She is helping Niall in the stables."

That didn't please her. "That's not work she should be doing. Niall is lazy, he'd get out of breathing if he could find someone else to do it for him. And what use you will be, finding my slippers, I don't know."

"I can but try," I said, giving her what I hoped was a cheery smile.

"Don't gape at me, woman," she said, and turned back into the room. I hesitated, then decided she wanted her slippers more than she disliked me, and so I followed.

I realized as I stepped inside the room that she had taken over most of this wing of the house. We were standing in the sitting room, and through the other door was her bedroom. Not only that, but she had taken most of the fine furniture for her own use. There was a dark green patterned carpet on the floorboards, a fine settee and a matching pair of chairs facing the hearth, and from what I could tell, the tile surrounds were Delph, that particular shade of blue, with Dutch scenes of water life and villages. The drapes at the windows were velveteen. And surely that pretty little desk and the matching cabinet had come from Italy? I had seen an olive wood desk in Cousin Melinda's house that was very similar.

This then had been the master bedroom, and she hadn't given it up to her son when he married and brought home his bride.

It was odd, I thought, that both the Mrs. Flynns had collected their favorite pieces of furniture and left the rest of the house rather bare and plain. And then both had retired to their suites, as each tried to ignore the presence of the other.

It was as if they had set up separate camps, and expected family loyalties to choose between them. Only Eileen belonged to her mother's camp, as far as I could tell. And it was not surprising that she wanted to rescue her mother from this stalemate existence.

"Don't stand there gawking, girl! Find my slippers."

I said, "Where did you last see them?"

"In my bedroom, ninny. Where else would they be?"

I went through to the other room and began to search. The slippers weren't under the bed, nor were they under the chair with the polished cotton skirts.

From the doorway, Mrs. Flynn said in a very different voice, "You know you are only making trouble for my granddaughter by staying here. Nobody wants you."

I straightened, and faced her. "Eileen does. And I have come for her sake. I am sorry if I have displeased you by having to stay in this house, but I made a promise, and I keep my word." I'd dealt with wounded officers who were far more aggressive than Mrs. Flynn, men accustomed to having their own way and not caring who was standing between them and whatever it was they wanted. It had helped tremendously that I'd grown up in the world of the Army, and over the years I had seen how my father had dealt with such arrogance.

Unaccustomed to being crossed, she stamped the floor with her cane. "You, Miss, are impertinent."

"I am only telling the truth."

"What's between you and my grandson?"

Aha! I thought. This is why she asked me to find her slippers. She must surely have seen Eileen running across the back lawns, following Niall.

I said, deliberately misinterpreting her question, "Niall? I've hardly spoken a dozen words to him. He seems very nice."

"Not Niall. He knows his place in this house. Terrence is protecting you. Why?"

"If he's protecting me at all, it's for Eileen's sake. Not mine. He wants to see her happy."

"More fool he." She considered me. "He's a very attractive man. I can't imagine what he sees in *you*."

Once more I could feel the hot blood rising in my face. But it was anger this time too, not embarrassment.

I said, "I am a guest in your house, Mrs. Flynn. I can't defend myself without being rude. And so I'll find your slippers, if I may, and leave you in peace." I turned to look again at the handsome bedroom, with its mahogany bed and tall armoire—

Crossing the room, I opened its ornate door and saw her slippers sitting just where she must usually keep them, in the space at the bottom where my mother kept her own slippers and shoes.

"There you are," I said, making myself smile. "They aren't lost after all."

She was standing in the doorway, between me and escape. I couldn't leave.

And she was as angry with me as I was with her. I could see her right hand fingering the black thorn cane as if she would like nothing better than to strike me with it.

I braced myself, not knowing what was going to happen next. Or what to do if she did attack me. If I tried to defend myself, I could easily injure her—even a light push or a fall could easily break a bone—

Just then I heard footsteps on the stairs, and Father O'Halloran walked into the sitting room. "Good afternoon—" he began, and then saw me standing in the bedroom.

"Am I interrupting?"

"Not at all, Father. I was just going downstairs." I started toward Mrs. Flynn, not sure what she would do.

But she moved out of my way and let me pass. I nodded to the priest and gently pulled the sitting room door shut as I left.

My knees were trembling as I went down the stairs. Mrs. Flynn, I knew now, was capable of anything. Including removing her granddaughter's fiancé from the scene to disrupt a wedding she didn't want to happen.

If she had attacked him there in her rooms, would Niall or Terrence remove Michael's body and bury it—or toss it into the sea?

Was that why Terrence had taken me with him to see the body—fearing it was Michael, come back to haunt them? And not wanting Eileen to find him that way?

How had she managed it? Who had been a willing tool? There must have been more than enough willing hands. But *would* she go so far as to have him killed?

It was a disturbing thought.

It was late in the afternoon when the Irish Constabulary returned. Eileen had gone up to our room to rest. The stress of not knowing anything about Michael was taking a heavy toll on her spirits, and I thought perhaps she just wanted to escape from all the conjecture and questions. We'd had a half dozen visitors during the afternoon, all wanting to know if the wedding was still on. One or two of them struck me as morbid curiosity-seekers, because their questions hinted at what she would do if Michael didn't come back at all.

I was sitting in the front room alone when the Constable knocked heavily at the door. It was as if he intended to frighten the occupants of the house.

Since there was no one else about—Major Dawson had gone for a walk, and I hadn't seen Niall since breakfast—I went to answer the summons.

The Constable nodded. "Miss Crawford. I have a few more questions, if you please."

"Of course." I led him into the front room and sat down. He remained standing, looking at his notebook, as if deciding what to ask me first. Another technique to frighten miscreants, I thought, watching him.

Finally, he looked directly at me and said, "Did you come to Ireland to meet Fergus Kennedy?"

"I have told you. I came for Eileen Flynn's wedding. To my knowledge the first time I saw Mr. Kennedy, he was lying dead on the mole in the village. I didn't even know his name or where he was from. Only that he'd been brought in by a fisherman who found him floating in the water. I was asked if there was any hope of saving him, but sadly it was too late."

"By declaring straightaway that he was dead, you prevented any further medical assistance being given to him at that time. Ensuring that he would die of his injuries."

"I assure you, Mr. Kennedy was dead when he was brought ashore. Had been dead for some time. Nothing I could do—or not do—would change that."

"One of the men who helped to carry him to the pub swears Mr. Kennedy tried to speak."

I stared at him. So this was why he'd come. Someone was making trouble. Keeping my wits about me, I replied, "And the others? Did they also hear this attempt to speak?"

He referred to his notebook. "They did not."

"Before he was taken to the pub, did Father O'Halloran hear Mr. Kennedy try to speak, while giving him last rites?"

Again he referred to the notebook, although I was certain he knew the answer. "He did not."

"There you are, then. But I should like to know who it is who believes Mr. Kennedy tried to speak—what medical training he might have had."

"He's a musician, I believe." Back to the notebook. "Shawn Fahy."

Careful, I warned myself.

Shaking my head, I said, "I'm sorry, I don't believe I know who that is."

The Constable considered my answer, then asked, "Did you know that Mr. Kennedy was painting a series of portraits of the men involved in the 1916 Rising? In some quarters this would be considered inflammatory. Most particularly to the English. They wouldn't care for martyrdom."

Oh, dear! I was going to have to lie. Or else involve Terrence.

"There were quite a few people milling about. Talking. I didn't hear everything they said, I was too busy examining the poor man's body. I do recall that someone asked if he had any family close by. No one seemed to know if he did or not."

There. I had managed to tell the truth and avoid the question.

Sitting there, my hands folded lightly in my lap, I made myself think of Matron—any of the women who had held that post, all of them formidable. One didn't lie to them, one took responsibility for one's actions and either apologized or learned a lesson. I hoped I conveyed that same impression here, that I was being helpful.

His next question nearly caught me off guard.

"Major Dawson. How long have you known him?"

"Since my arrival, yesterday. I hadn't met him before."

"Are you sure of this?"

"As sure as I can be."

"Did he know Fergus Kennedy?"

"I have no reason to believe he did, he never spoke of the man to me. But, of course, you must ask him. I was under the impression that like me, he'd never been to Ireland before."

We were going around in circles, it seemed to me, while the Constable fished for information. Which seemed to indicate he had no real information of his own to be going on with.

Based on that feeling, I tried something.

"We both came here for a wedding. I can't speak for the Major, but I think it is probably true to say that neither of us would do anything that would upset our hosts, the Flynns. We want to see Eileen happily married and starting her new life, and then return to our own, in England. I am so sorry that your Mr. Kennedy is dead, but my concern is for Michael Sullivan. Unless he returns by Saturday, there will be no wedding, and I don't know how poor Eileen will face that. Or what we are supposed to do then. Stay and support her? Return to England until Michael is found? I wish I knew what to do, how to help. It is worrying."

The Constable listened politely. Then he asked, "Could Michael Sullivan have disappeared because he was going to kill Fergus Kennedy, and there would be less suspicion falling on him, if he was already thought to be in trouble of his own?"

I opened my mouth to answer, shut it smartly, and then said, "I haven't met Michael Sullivan, but he has waited four years to marry the woman he loves. Do you really think he would have done anything that would stop this wedding? If he planned to commit murder, he'd at least be sure Eileen was safely out of it."

"What is it you were about to say—and thought better of?"

Careful, Bess! I scolded myself. Don't underestimate this man!

"I was going to ask if you'd ever been deeply in love. But that would have been rude of me."

He regarded me for a moment, then nodded and snapped his note-book shut. "I should like to speak to Major Dawson, please."

"I believe he went for a walk. I don't think he went very far. Shall I call him?"

"No, thank you. I prefer to find him myself."

And catch him unawares? But I made certain I showed no concern. Instead, I rose and escorted him to the door like a proper hostess, even though it wasn't my house.

He crossed the threshold and started down the steps to the lawn, but I waited until he had taken ten more strides, being polite—but also scanning the grounds for any sign of Ellis—before I closed the door.

"Now you're in the thick of it, young woman," Granny said from the top of the stairs after she made sure the Constable couldn't hear us. "Once the Constabulary is after you, there's no way back."

"He only wished to know if I'd ever met Mr. Kennedy when he was alive. But of course I hadn't. I've only just arrived, and the only times I've left the house, I was in the company of your grandson, at his re-quest." I looked up the stairs at her gaunt, crow-like figure. "Did you know him?" I asked innocently. "I just learned he was a painter. Do you have any of his work?"

"Mind your own business, girl." And she turned, disappearing back into her lair. A very handsome lair, but still definitely just that.

Eileen's door opened, and she stepped out into the passage. "I thought I heard voices. Any news?"

"How I wish I could say yes. It was only just the Constable asking for information about the dead man."

"I thought you didn't know him."

"I didn't." I waited until she'd come down the stairs and we were in the front room with the door closed. "I was told he was a painter. Why would anyone wish to kill an artist?"

"I don't know. And truthfully? I don't care about him. I just want this waiting to be over. And for Michael to come back safely."

"I know, love," I said sympathetically. "You've met this man? This Mr. Kennedy?" I tried to sound merely curious.

"He came to the village from time to time. He told me not long ago that he'd like to paint me. I thought he was trying to flirt with me, and I was short with him. After that, he left me alone."

Was that because Terrence had asked him to paint Eileen?

I smiled. "Perhaps Michael had put him up to it, to have a portrait of you for a wedding gift."

"It's not something Michael would do," she told me shortly. "We aren't likely to have a settled home for some years." She was restlessly pacing now, back and forth, back and forth. "What would we do with a painting?"

"What did—does Michael like? I've never met him, you know. But I thought his letters were lovely."

"He didn't want to be a soldier. But we all thought—or at least many of us did—that if we helped the English win the war, they'd give us Home Rule in gratitude, as they'd promised. But of course the Rising changed everything. And I was called a traitor, and so was Michael. They were foolish men, to try to force the English. Oh, I know what Terrence and the others believe, that the English only dangled that hope in order to convince us to help. Or to keep us quiet until they'd finished the Germans. Or both. Take your pick." She took a deep breath. "Michael wanted to raise fine horses. A racing stable. That was probably wishful thinking as well, but his uncle was a fine horseman, and he'd taught Michael to ride and to care for horses. And he had inherited some money. With that and what he could learn working for someone else for a time, he'd have a fine start. I was willing to let him try." She gave me sad smile. "The Irish love horses. It's a madness we have." Then she stopped pacing and strode to the window, looking out. "I thought I heard something?"

"The policeman went to find Major Dawson. He's probably just now leaving."

"Why can't he help find Michael? I fail to understand it." She was agitated again, and I cast about for something—anything—to distract her.

"I think we've been penned up here long enough," I said brightly. "It's taking a toll on us. Would you like to go for a walk? Would that help? I haven't seen very much of the countryside."

I'd hardly finished when her fist pounded the window frame angrily, and I realized too late that I'd made a mistake.

"Nothing helps." It was more a wail than a statement.

"I know," I said again.

She whirled around. "No, you don't, you've never been in love, not like this. You can't even imagine what I've been through."

I swallowed the answer I was about to offer. "Perhaps you're right."

"I don't trust any of those searchers. I need to be out there myself, *looking*. But everyone tells me I must stay at the house in the event there's news. Well, there's been *no* news, and I am at my wits' end." She looked at me. "Can you ride? Will you go with me, while I search?"

"Do you think that's wise—"

"No. Don't talk to me about wise. I'll go myself." She started for the back stairs, not willing to encounter her grandmother on the front stairs.

"Of course I'm coming with you, Eileen," I told her, against my better judgment—and wishing Terrence were here to calm her down and tell her she mustn't do this.

"There's still a good deal of light. Let's change." And she was through the kitchen and up the stairs, wings on her feet now that she'd made her decision.

It took all of five minutes to change. And then we were hurrying out to the stables. I found myself being given the same horse I'd ridden when I'd gone with Terrence to Fergus Kennedy's house. I said nothing about that, but the horse nearly betrayed me by nudging me as if we were old friends. I was glad Eileen was too busy to notice. We saddled them, mounted at the block, and set out.

Even with her scarred legs, Eileen was a superb horsewoman. I could see why Michael felt that she would join him in his dream of raising fine horses. We didn't set off toward the front of the house, instead taking a path by the stables that led through a small orchard and then to another path that skirted fields and soon came out on a slight rise that overlooked the distant sea.

"The Flynns were sea captains in the old days," she said, patting her horse's neck as she stared out toward the water. "Merchants who sailed as far north as the Orkneys and Iceland, even to the coast of Norway. I have a little carving of a Viking boat that someone once brought back—my father gave it to me, an heirloom, he said. I thought about that when we first went aboard *Britannic*. That here was a Flynn back at sea at long last. But of course that didn't end well either, did it?"

"No." Beyond a few stunted trees and a wasteland of tall grasses, the water was a deep blue, waves whitecapped as they moved ashore. I couldn't quite hear them, or the gulls riding high above us, but there was a lark singing somewhere in the fields behind us. I wondered if Mr. Kennedy, the painter, had ever sat in a place like this, and watched the sea coming in. Or if he'd worked closer to home.

Eileen turned her horse. "There's an old barn not far from here. Half fallen in. Let's have a look." But the barn was empty—what's more, it didn't appear to have been used by anyone for ages. I saw a long-eared owl high in the rafters, staring down at us and blinking even in the dim light.

We moved on from there, quartering the fields, looking everywhere.

The sun moved with us, heading west, and after a while it was sinking toward the sea.

I said, "We've had no luck so far. Perhaps we should turn back and start fresh in the morning."

But Eileen wouldn't hear of it. We came to a pasture where horses and several small donkeys were quietly grazing. We crossed that, and came to a field where there were the ruins of an ancient barrow. Eileen got down to look it over carefully, her face grim, as if she half expected to find Michael's body stuffed in there. We walked our horses for a time after that, passing a number of crofts and small holdings, white-washed and quiet at this hour. All of them had seen better days.

I said, "They must be having a late supper."

Shaking her head, Eileen told me, "They left during the famine. The people who lived here. They walked to Dublin and found ships to take them away. I've heard the stories, but no one knew whether they'd ever reached Dublin or not, much less anywhere else."

She scoured the cottages, startling bats in one and a small mouse in another.

It was well after dusk when we finally started back toward the house.

I said, "Given what I've seen today, the search parties would have had no better luck."

"Still, I had to be *sure*. They could have ridden by the cottages. Or that barrow. They're a superstitious lot, some of them in the village, and God knows, some of those places might have been haunted. Ireland has had a good deal of sadness, you see. It's a wonder there aren't ghosts crowding us out everywhere we go."

It was dark now, the last of the light sunk beneath the western waves, and I felt a sudden surge of sadness that I couldn't explain. I wasn't prone to melancholy, and yet just now I found myself wondering what lay ahead in my own life. What did I really want?

Eileen had fallen silent, lost in her own thoughts, and there was only the sound of our horses' hooves covering the dry ground.

I was suddenly reminded of that shelled village and the house where we'd brought the wounded—where Sergeant Lassiter had proposed to me. And I had turned him down as gently as I could.

I hadn't been in love with him, although I cared for him in a very different way. We'd shared so much, he'd saved my life and I his. There was a bond between us, there always would be, forged in a bloody war. But it wasn't the bond of love.

Afterward, he'd asked me a question, and I'd laughed at the idea. And he'd said, "Well, then, there's still hope for me."

I'd laughed . . . But it had stayed in my memory, that question, even though I'd tried to shut the door on it. And I had been quite successful in the beginning, the war and its aftermath keeping me occupied with duty. Of late, something behind that door was starting to scratch at it, trying to get out. And I was doing my best still to ignore it.

It was better, shut away. Less painful, I told myself. But here in the darkness, in the quietness, I could hear that scratching more loudly than ever.

Taking a deep breath, I made myself look across at the woman riding several feet away from me. It was Eileen I should be thinking about. And how on earth I was to help her find Michael, so that she could be married. So that I could go home.

I looked away, up at the bowl of sky above me. In the darkness, so different from London, the stars were brilliant, thousands of them. A thin layer of clouds was spreading across them, but I could pick out familiar constellations with ease.

We were passing the place where we'd stopped to look out at the sea, when there was a loud report that startled both of us and the horses.

Eileen said, "What on earth—"

But I knew what it was. A rifle shot. God knew, I'd heard enough of them in France to recognize them in my sleep!

"I think it's best to get back to the house," I said. "Now." And without waiting for an answer, I put my heel into the horse's flank. It moved forward with a jerk, then fell into a trot then a gallop. Eileen was just behind me.

A moving target was harder to hit. I kept telling myself that even as I listened for another shot.

Leaning forward, low on my horse's neck, I kept my profile as indistinguishable from the mare's as possible. Soon enough we'd reached the orchard, and we were forced to slow.

"The horses were already tired—why did you press them into a gallop?" Eileen asked, irritation in her voice.

"I didn't care to be out there at night while someone was wandering around with a rifle. It's the war, I expect—"

"They weren't shooting at us."

"Nevertheless."

I didn't tell her—then or later—that I'd heard the distinctive sound of an angry bee as the bullet sped past my head. Whether it had been intended to hit me or was intended for someone else who might have been riding with Eileen, I didn't know. But I didn't want to linger long enough to find out.

Chapter Eight

I think Eileen was still put out with me as we silently wiped down the horses, fed and watered them, and walked back to the house.

"Heat lightning," she said as we reached the lawn. "Out at sea. There might be a storm tonight."

I could just see the distant flicker of light, and when I looked up, I could tell that the thin layer of clouds I'd seen earlier had thickened. Only the brightest stars were visible now.

I expected her to take me to task again about pressing the horses, when we went up to our room to change, but Terrence was in the kitchen doorway as we reached the steps, saying angrily, "And where the hell have you been? It's dark, and no time to be out wandering about. Have you no sense?"

I wondered then if he'd heard the rifle shot. I had no idea where he'd been most of the day. For all I knew, he had been out looking for Michael himself.

And then I wondered if *he* still had the rifle he'd used at the Post Office during the Rising. And how many others had theirs, hidden under the hay in the barn or under the floorboards in their houses.

"I was looking for Michael," she told him furiously, turning toward him, her pent-up anger with me spilling over on him.

"Nevertheless," he snapped. "It's not safe, and you know it. Good

God, woman, you are as much a target as Sullivan. You were a nurse in the British service."

"I've lived here all my life, for one thing, and for another, Granny wouldn't let anyone touch me."

"Don't be so sure of that. She's an old woman. There may be someone not willing to wait for her to die—" He broke off, as if suddenly aware that I was standing to one side, listening.

I realized two things as he turned toward me. That Mrs. Flynn had even more power than I'd understood, and that very likely the reason she'd questioned me about Terrence was her fear that any entanglement with an Englishwoman would put paid to his chance to take her place when the time came. There was already a cloud of sorts over his head . . .

He was saying, "You should have stopped her from being so foolish."

"I'm sorry. I didn't know we would ride so far."

"That's the problem. You don't know anything about this part of Ireland. You could have got yourselves into trouble," he went on, still angry. "The fact that someone has taken Michael should have warned you to be more careful."

"I thought it best not to let her go alone," I replied, defending myself. "And you weren't here."

He opened his mouth to say something more, and thought better of it. "Go and change. There's dinner from the pub. It's already cold."

We did as we were told. Supper at this hour was a tense affair, all the same. The two Mrs. Flynns had already dined, and that left Terrence, Eileen, and me to sit in the kitchen. Niall wasn't there, and no one mentioned him. I didn't know where the Major was, and I didn't want to ask.

By the time we'd finished clearing away the table and seeing to the dishes, it was already thundering, a low rumble to the east of us.

Terrence asked, "You saw to the horses?"

"Of course," Eileen told him. "I always do."

He nodded, and then took himself into the front room. Eileen watched him go. "He's in a mood," she said. "I'd prefer to go up."

"I think that's what I should do as well," I told her, and we turned out the lamp and went up to her room.

I was drawing the curtains at one window while she was seeing to the other when a flicker of lightning caught two figures out by the barn. It was too far away to be sure who they were, but one was quite tall, and I was reminded of the singer at the pub. Just then the first gusts of wind and rain came sweeping across toward the house. The taller man ducked into the barn, but the other one ran toward the house. I heard the kitchen door slam shut.

If Terrence was in the front room—was that Niall then, who had been talking to the enemy, so to speak?

I quickly pulled the curtains just as I heard footsteps clattering up the back stairs and then someone opened and closed the door to one of the other bedrooms.

Looking toward Eileen, I realized that she was occupied with her own thoughts and hadn't paid any heed to the sounds outside in the passage. She was brushing her hair, and when she turned in my direction, I saw tears glistening in her eyes.

"All Terrence and my grandmother think about is Ireland, Ireland, Ireland. Not one of them even considers how I feel—how much I love Michael. Or he'd have been found by now."

Her last words were almost lost in a crash of thunder, and I could hear the rain beating against the windows.

"I'm so sorry," I said, and I meant it. "I wish I knew how to help."

"I'm glad you are here, Bess. Truly I am. I don't feel so alone. I just wish I knew if he was alive or dead. If there was any hope at all."

I went to her and put my arm around her shoulders. "No one has found his body," I told her for a second time. "And that's something to hold on to."

"You can't be sure—what if they don't *want* his body to be found?"

Her logic was sound. But I said slowly, as if taking her seriously, "Of course that's possible. But I should think whoever took Michael would much rather make an example of him, by letting him be found."

That cheered her a little. "It's the English then, who have him. God knows why, but the last thing they'd want is a martyr."

She began to ready herself for bed. Our supper, on top of that long ride, had left us more than a little drowsy. And the sound of the rain on the roof and blowing against the windows had us yawning. I had to fight to stay awake after we'd turned out the lamps. But the storm seemed to circle around, intent on staying, and I dared not go out in it, even to leave my handkerchief on the stile.

It moved away at last, and I got up from the bed without waking her, dressed, and started down the back stairs.

Then stopped, as voices floated up to me. Terrence and Niall, I thought, talking about something—no—arguing, their voices rising as they grew more heated. I realized, listening, that it had to do with something Niall must have said to Major Dawson.

"He's a guest under our roof," Terrence said. "And you'll remember that or leave. I wonder sometimes if you have anything in your head but what's happening in Dublin. Well, I can tell you, it's more likely that you'll bring disgrace on this family than come out of it a hero."

Niall swore with some force. "You went off to play the hero, and look where it's got you. Granny's right, it would have been better if you'd died with the other martyrs or were shot with the leaders. At least we'd know where you stood."

A chair scraped across the floor as someone got up.

"When *you've* stood for what's right in this world, you can use that tone with me, boyo. For now, you're a member of this family and you'll do as you're told!"

"We'll see what Granny has to say about that!" Niall must have risen as well, for I heard his boots coming toward the back stairs.

I hastily got myself back into the bedroom, shutting the door before he reached the upstairs passage.

A voice just behind me startled me.

"Eavesdropping, are you?"

I turned. Eileen was standing in the middle of the dark room, wide awake.

"I've a little indigestion from the meal tonight. I was going down for a glass of water. I didn't feel I could interrupt them, heated as they were."

"And so you listened?"

I stood my own ground, then. "I was afraid they would come to blows. I don't know what is wrong, Eileen. If you wish me to leave, I'll go."

She came forward and put out a hand. "Oh, Bess, no. I'm so sorry—tomorrow's my wedding day—I can't seem to think of anything else. And I lash out because I'm so frightened, so worried—and there's nowhere to turn for answers. I close my eyes and all I see is Michael's body, and I'm not there to comfort him—I think I hear him crying my name, and when I listen, there's only silence. Please, don't *go*."

We sat there in the darkness for what seemed like hours, and she told me how she'd met Michael, and how he'd decided it was his duty to enlist—how she felt she had no other choice but train as a nurse, to be closer to him there in France. Then, at last, she felt she could sleep.

There was nothing else to do. I undressed, found my gown, and got back into bed. But I could tell by her breathing that she wasn't asleep. I couldn't see her face, but I was ready to wager that she was lying there, staring up at the ceiling, pretending for my sake.

And I was pretending too, in the hope that *she* would finally sleep.

It must have been close to three in the morning when I heard the faint sound of an aircraft passing high overhead, delayed by the storm.

And the pilot would be looking down with field glasses, hoping to see the small white square of my handkerchief on the stile.

My signal that all was well.

Would the Captain believe that the storm had kept me inside? Or would he be more likely to fly back to Bristol and tell my family that I was in trouble? He had been worried enough about leaving me here.

I bit my lip. There was nothing I could do about it. Nothing.

I tried to sleep then. But I was still awake with worries of my own when the first faint glow of dawn brightened the room.

I looked at the figure beside me. She was finally asleep herself.

I felt like swearing.

Damn!

It didn't help.

The rain had cleared the air, and the day was fresh and bright.

I came down quite early to breakfast. Niall was sitting at the kitchen table with his head in his hands, looking like a man with a hangover. When he glanced up at me, I was sure of it, for his eyes were bloodshot and he was clearly still in a temper.

I said good morning as neutrally as I could, making certain it didn't ring with cheerfulness. I was hardly in the mood for cheerfulness myself.

As I began to put the kettle on for a fresh pot of tea, Niall said, "Where's that English soldier, then?"

"The Major? I don't know. I haven't seen him this morning." There were porridge dishes and a cup in the dry sink, but I couldn't tell whether they were his or Terrence's. "Sometimes he takes early morning walks."

"Meeting his spymasters, is he? Aye, well, that's not very smart of him. Best way to come to grief."

"We came here for a wedding. And we haven't been exactly welcomed. I don't blame him for leaving this house as often as he can."

"And if he finds himself shot, that's on him." He sounded now as if he was serious.

I reached in the cupboard for cups and saucers. "Eileen told me that your family once owned a merchant ship. That it sailed north to Iceland and Scandinavia." I was trying to change the subject, but it didn't appear to be working.

"The trouble is, men like Dawson can't be trusted. He's a high-ranking officer, and yet he takes the time to come over to Ireland for the likes of Sergeant Michael Sullivan's wedding. I ask you, does he think we're that stupid, we'd believe that was true?"

The kettle was boiling and I took it off. "Michael saved his life. And he was grateful." I'd rinsed the pot and added the leaves, and so I poured in the hot water. "Why would anyone kidnap him? What had Michael done to be taken away like that?"

"He licked the boots of the English."

"I was told he thought he was helping Ireland. And he wasn't the only one who believed that. You can't kill them all."

Niall gave a short bark of a laugh. "Can't we, now?"

Disgusted, I didn't even take any of the porridge. Instead, I turned, and with cup in hand, walked out toward the barn. The horses were better company than Niall Flynn.

I found Terrence there, looking at the hoof of the mare Eileen had been riding last night.

"Is she all right?"

"Stepped on a stone. But she'll be fine." He let the hoof go and stood up, giving the mare a pat on her sleek neck.

I said, "Is Michael going to come home today? For the wedding?"

Terrence sighed. "I don't know. I wish I did."

"Do you know who took him?"

He shook his head.

"You're in love with her, aren't you? Is that why Michael was kidnapped?"

Terrence swore then. "Stay out of it, Sister." He strode toward the door of the barn, but when he reached it, he turned and said, "I heard an aircraft flying over, after the storm. Quite high up. But the first pass he made, he cut his motor, gliding low over the meadow. Who was he looking for? The Major?"

I laughed. "Hardly. It's the flyer who brought me to Ireland. Arthur. He's worried about me. He'll probably come to collect me tomorrow."

Terrence considered me. "He's courting you, is he?"

"He's a friend. I told you, I knew him in France."

"Ah." But it didn't sound as if he believed me before or believed me now.

I took a risk, then, and asked Terrence, "Did you know the men, the leaders of the Rising, who were court-martialed and shot?"

He stared at me, something in his face I couldn't quite read.

"They were heroes to us," he said finally.

"Misguided, if they really intended to free Ireland. They should have known, in the middle of a war we thought we might very well be losing, that any Rising in Ireland would be viewed as a stab in the back. Almost literally. Easter, only months before the Somme? And whispers that the Germans were behind it all? It's not a surprise that the English would deal harshly with those involved. If for no other reason than to prevent another such Rising." I had heard the Colonel Sahib discuss what was happening in Ireland. I had a fairly good idea of what had occurred in the aftermath. "Anyone whose name was on the Proclamation they posted before the Rising. Was yours on it?"

"No," Terrance said slowly. "I wasn't there to sign. But you have to understand how Ireland has suffered for a very long time. You haven't been treated as if you didn't have a right to be in your own country. What did England do when we were dying, in the potato famine? Did they even care? I don't think they did."

"It was still the wrong time to try."

He looked out the door, across the lawns and the hedge, toward the house. "It took remarkable courage. Right or wrong. They shouldn't have been executed. Even some of the English believed that. They were patriots, not traitors."

He believed that. I could hear it in his voice, see it in his face.

Now was the time to ask the most pressing question. "*Will* we find Michael before it's time for the wedding? Even at the last minute? I have to know, I have to be able to comfort her."

"I've told you," he said, angry now, "that I don't know where he is. Or why. Don't you understand? I couldn't marry her, not with a price on my head. Michael can take her out of the country, where she'll be safe. That's what I want. And whether you believe me or not, I've done my damnedest to make certain that happens."

He turned on his heel and walked away, his words echoing in my ears.

I stayed in the cool stillness of the barn, listening to the soft shuffle and sounds of the horses moving about in their stalls. I felt the same way—although shut into a larger space—the house—but no less confined.

What would Captain Jackson do, when he didn't find the handkerchief on the stile? More to the point, what would my father do?

My cup of tea was cold. With a sigh, I walked back to the house, hoping that Niall had gone away.

He wasn't there.

I took breakfast up to Eileen, but she shook her head. "I can't. Not today."

I said, "Today is your wedding day, I know. But there's this to consider, Eileen. It's only a day. You can choose any other day you like, once Michael is home again. This isn't going to be your only day to be married."

But it didn't do much good. I was about to leave her when the younger Mrs. Flynn came in and said quietly, "I'll sit with her for a while."

I was ashamed of myself for feeling a flood of relief. While my heart went out to Eileen, while I knew how she must feel, I was at a loss for words of comfort. In truth, what comfort *was* there? Perhaps, I thought, her mother could find the words I hadn't.

I took the tray back to the kitchen—and found Major Dawson there, scraping the last of the porridge out of the saucepan and into a dish.

I smiled, so very glad to see him. But where had he been last night—and again this morning?

"Shall I make you more porridge?" I asked.

"This will do, until lunch," he said, and reached for the pitcher to pour milk into the dish. "Did you know, there's a little pond on the far side of the wood at the end of the meadow? I found a flat stone and sat there, watching the water. There was a brown frog on the bank, and he was an expert at catching insects. I didn't realize their tongues were so long. Out it came, then back it went."

He sounded more cheerful than he had been in several days.

"If there's no wedding today, will you leave?" I asked.

He sat down, staring into the dish. "That was one of the questions I put to the frog. He had no better answers than I did."

I laughed, because it was expected of me, and then he looked up, saying, "I don't know. You?"

I shook my head. "It seems awfully unkind. But I expect we ought to consider what's to be done."

"We can't stay forever. Waiting."

"There's that." Remembering, I asked, "Did the Constabulary ask you questions about that poor man's death?"

"He did. I couldn't tell whether he preferred to think of you or of me as the murderer. I'm serious, Bess, he was asking questions that pointed in that direction."

"I know. He spoke to me first."

"Who was this man, Bess?" He looked up from his porridge. "I was told he was some sort of artist. Who was likely to have wanted him dead?"

I knew what Terrence had told me, but I was reluctant to share that, even with the Major. "That's all I've heard, as well. I don't think he was terribly well known—people at the mole weren't sure who he was, when he was brought in. I heard them say so when I was examining him."

"Was he Irish?"

That was trickier. "He lived here. I expect he must have been."

"I'd as soon leave the country before the police are serious about pointing to us. *Was* it murder, do you think?"

I moved closer to where he was sitting so that my voice wouldn't carry. "It could easily have been. Something—someone—had smashed in the side of his face. It could have been a fall—" I stopped. I'd almost said there were rocks close by where he lived, but I quickly changed that to, "—and he struck his head on something, rocks or even part of a boat as he went down. I couldn't tell. But if someone had hit him with something hard, the damage would have been the same. He'd been in the water, I couldn't find anything in the wound that helped me."

And then I remembered last night, and being shot at. Because I had examined the dead man? But surely the Constabulary had seen just what I had seen? And drawn the same conclusions? They were the police, they had examined bodies before . . .

The difference was, of course, that I had medical training. And there was no doctor in Killeighbeg. I might well have seen something that the police had missed, something a village doctor would have recognized.

Was *that* why the dead man had been brought here? To this village? Because it had neither police nor doctor?

"What is it, Bess? What do you remember?"

I shook my head. "I was trying to recall what I'd seen, that's all. But it's true, I couldn't have sworn to either, an accident or a crime."

"Just as well."

Terrence had said the same thing. Only, he'd suspected the Major.

I looked at Ellis Dawson. "They can't understand why a man of your rank would bother to come to a wedding for a man in the ranks."

"I've told you. And them. He saved my life when he didn't have to. At great risk. I owe him. I even put him up for a medal, but so soon after the Rising, the Army was reluctant to give one to an Irish soldier. But you'll keep that last to yourself."

"I've never asked you what regiment that was." I'd never seen him in uniform.

"Irish Guards. I was sent over with reinforcements while the First Battalion was at a rest-camp in Hornoy. That was the autumn of '16. I was wounded later, outside Arras. That was when Sullivan came out and got me, brought me back to the lines and kept me from bleeding to death until the stretcher bearers could get me to the closest aid station." And then he added wryly, "And all the while I kept telling myself that it was a damn—a shame to die so close to the end of the war."

The Irish Guards had been formed by Queen Victoria after the Second Boer War, where the Irish had served so faithfully.

"Was he wounded as well?"

"Oh yes. In the arm, the hip, the calf. One of my sergeants told me later that he 'was bleeding like a blo—like a veritable spigot.' How he got me back is still a wonder."

I walked over to the door to the stairs, opened it quietly, and when I saw no one there, listening, I came back to him.

"Terrence was wounded in the Rising, wasn't he?"

"He was. It was Michael who told me. It was his men who got him away and found a doctor. Or else the English would have had him."

And as if conjured up by use of his name, Terrence came through from the front room, stepping into the kitchen and frowning.

"Where's Eileen?"

"Still in her room," I said. "What can I do?"

"Someone from the pub is here, wanting to know what to do about the wedding breakfast. And O'Halloran has sent to ask about decorating the church."

Oh, dear!

I said, "I don't know what to tell you. What if Michael arrives just in time, and nothing is ready?"

Terrence swore, ladies present or not. It was quite colorful.

"Here!" the Major reminded him sharply.

"I'm sorry. But I'm at my wits' end. Granny is all for sending them packing, and my aunt is weeping—" His gaze was on me.

I wanted to say, *Don't look at me!* But for four years I'd been trained to think in any crisis, and so I replied, "Tell them to come back in an hour. And I'll speak to Eileen."

He nodded, grateful, and I went up the stairs as he left to pass on the message.

I found that in my absence, Eileen had bathed and was dressing in her lacy silk undergarments, as if the wedding was going on as planned.

"Ah," I said, rapidly rethinking what I was about to ask her. "The inn is asking about the wedding breakfast—"

"I've looked. It's fair outside. Tell them to decorate the tables out there."

"And the church?"

"That should already be done," she said crossly. "I thought my mother was attending to that."

"I'll be sure," I told her soothingly. "Can I bring you something from the kitchen—"

"It's a Nuptial Mass. I can't eat until afterward."

Of course. This was a Catholic wedding. I bit my tongue, then said, "I didn't know if a cup of tea was allowed." But she ignored me, asking me to do up the laces in the back. I did that, while she reminded me that I must hurry, if I wished to be ready on time.

"Let me speak to your mother, to see if I can move things along, and I'll be back."

I found Mrs. Flynn wringing her hands. "I don't quite know what to do—" she told me anxiously as I entered her room.

"I've spoken to Eileen," I said soothingly. "She wants to go on with plans for the wedding. I'll be happy to help in any way I can."

"I must bathe—dress—" She looked around distractedly, as if to find answers somewhere just out of sight.

It was up to me, then.

"Don't worry—I'll see to everything," I promised, and left to find Terrence, taking the front stairs in my hurry, never mind Granny in her lair.

Terrence was still trying to work with the people who had come to the door. He turned quickly, as he heard someone coming out, and I watched the hope flaring in his face change to a frown when he saw that it was not Eileen.

Quickly scanning the faces turning toward me, I looked for the tall singer and the two other men, but they were not among the men from the pub or the ladies from the church.

"Good morning," I said brightly, hoping that everyone spoke English. "I am so sorry for the confusion. I've just spoken to Mrs. Flynn"—I didn't mention which one—"and to the bride. We're to go forward as planned, please. If there is any way in which Mr. Flynn here or I can assist you, do speak up. We'll be very happy to help."

They stared at me. I didn't know whether it was a language problem—this was a Gaelic-speaking area—or something else. And then I realized that I had no authority here. They were turning to Terrence to have my words confirmed.

He shot me a glance that I couldn't read, and then he said, "You have heard what my cousin's wishes are."

"There's no groom," someone from the pub said.

"We have every hope that he will be here by noon," I said. Glancing at my little watch, pinned to my dress now, not my apron, I saw that it was already nearly ten. There wasn't much time left . . .

"You heard the lady," Terrence said. "What my cousin wants, she shall have."

And he turned away, as if finished.

The ladies from the church moved off, whispering among themselves, and the people from the pub began to pull covered dishes from the cart they'd brought with them.

I started for the door, following Terrence.

And glanced up to see Granny at her window.

If looks could kill, I'd have been struck dead on the spot.

Chapter Nine

It was a close-run thing.

By the time I had hurried down to the church to approve the arrangements there, and rushed back to look again at the festive tables on the back lawn, it was nearly eleven-thirty.

I ran up the steps, bathed as quickly as I could, and began to dress. Eileen had told me long ago what it was she wanted me to wear, and my mother, bless her, had had it made up for me. It was rather pretty, with lace at the throat and wrists, and inset in a square at the bosom, with tiny sprigs of white flowers tied in white ribbons embroidered all over the skirt. The pale green of their leaves offered the only color, except for a matching pale green ribbon around the hem. My hair was piled on top of my head, with white and green ribbons entwined in it.

I nearly failed to pin it up properly!

Eileen had already gone down, wanting to see the tables herself. They had white linen tablecloths, with bunches of silk flowers looped together with green ribbons and white china with pale green napkins.

She was calling to me as I put finishing touches to my rebellious hair, and I hurried down to meet her.

She was lovely, her hair beautifully put up and covered by a long white veil, her gown of French silk with Belgian lace. I had never seen her so elegant.

We smiled at each other, and then Terrence came out of the front room, followed by the Major. Both wore dress clothes, and while the Major carried off his as a man accustomed to evening clothes, Terrence looked absolutely rakish, more like someone about to run off with the bride than to give her away.

He saw my expression, and scowled at me.

Behind him, the Major quickly suppressed a smile.

Mrs. Flynn came down the stairs just then, dressed in stylish black silk and lace, still in mourning.

Granny was nowhere in sight.

Terrence stepped forward, said something to Eileen that made her smile—it was a watery one, but a smile nonetheless—then took her arm and led her out the door.

I was surprised to find an ancient carriage, polished within an inch of its life and pulled by matched black horses, waiting for the ladies. I learned later that they had been borrowed from the undertaker in the next town, since the family's were bay and brown. I recognized the carriage from the barn, polished handsomely and decorated with flowers.

The three of us were handed in, while Terrence and the Major followed behind us on foot.

It must have been quite a handsome procession toward the church.

All that was missing was the groom.

When we reached the church, I could see people waiting. Many of them were villagers, come to watch, while others were friends and neighbors who were invited. There were more than I'd expected—some twenty or thirty of them—and all dressed for the occasion.

The guests filed into the church, and I could hear the organ playing from where we sat. Father O'Halloran was waiting by the church door, speaking to the guests as they passed him, then he turned toward us.

I suddenly remembered that I hadn't seen Niall—

The coachman spoke to the horses, and they brought the carriage closer to the church door. Terrence was there to give the bride a hand down, while the Major came forward to assist first Mrs. Flynn and then me.

I could hear the murmurs and comments as the onlookers saw our dresses, and then we were stepping into the cool, dim interior of the church. Candles gleamed from tall stands and greenery mixed with white lace and ribbons decorated the ends of pews where the guests had been seated.

The organ was playing music that Eileen and Michael must have chosen, and then Eileen moved a little on Terrence's arm. As she did, I could see the front of the church, where Major Dawson now stood alone, except for the priest. I realized he must have left us and gone around to the outer aisles to find his place. He had on his parade face, completely blank of expression.

Eileen stood there, waiting for the music to change, and the guests had all turned our way.

She was already holding a pretty bouquet, and now someone handed one to Mrs. Flynn, and to me. I realized that Niall was there to walk Eileen's mother down the aisle to her seat. Her face white and set, she took his arm and they proceeded to the front of the church, where she took her place.

Niall said something to her and then walked over to stand beside the Major.

The organist kept playing the chosen selections, but he hadn't begun the music for me to walk ahead of Eileen down the aisle. Indeed, she stood there, just behind me, and I couldn't see her expression.

Terrence's arm tightened, bringing her arm closer to his side, and he spoke to her, but I couldn't hear. Her chin went up.

And then the organ music changed, as if someone had given the signal, and Terrence said softly, "Go on."

I moved ahead of Eileen and began my slow walk down the aisle. The smile on my face felt pasted there, but I kept my eyes on the Major, never looking to one side or the other.

I could sense that Eileen was now coming down behind me, because I saw the priest's eyes shift toward something behind me.

I reached the three men standing there, and stepped to one side, as I was supposed to do. When I could look back, I saw that Eileen's veil had been pulled down over her face, as was proper, but it also made it impossible for anyone to read her expression.

She reached the priest, just as I had done, and stopped. I could see how white her fingers were, clenched on Terrence's arm. He looked like a man facing the hangman.

He glanced up, his gaze moving toward me, and I could read the anger that was boiling up in him.

The organ finally fell silent.

We stood there like figures in a tableau, not moving, and the church was silent too.

How long that continued, I didn't know. And then I heard the ripple of sound spreading through the gathered guests.

It was a gasp, and I looked quickly toward Terrence, thinking that they must surely have begun to understand that no matter how much Eileen had wanted Michael to be there for his wedding, he wasn't coming.

I felt such a wave of sympathy for her, for the courage that had brought her this far, and I wanted to shout at someone, tell whoever it was who held Michael Sullivan what I thought of them.

And then the nature of the gasps reached me. People were looking toward the pulpit, an ornate affair just behind the Major and Niall.

I quickly glanced that way, thinking that Granny had decided to come after all, and make a scene. It would be just like her!

But out of the shadows of the pulpit came a shambling figure, his clothes torn, bloody, his face a mask of dried blood and perspiration.

I knew at once that this must be Michael.

He was moving like someone in a daze.

The Major had seen my reaction, and he wheeled to look behind him. Taking in the situation with a swiftness that came of long experience in dangerous situations, he rushed forward and took Michael's outstretched hand.

Eileen had seen him now too, and with a cry she started forward, but Terrence kept his grip on her arm, stopping her.

"Let me *go*," she cried, struggling against his hold. Niall had stepped out of the way as Ellis Dawson gently led the bloody scarecrow that was Michael Sullivan toward the priest, almost holding him up on his feet, his arm supporting the injured man, heedless of his clothes.

Eileen stopped struggling, turning toward Father O'Halloran. "Marry us," she whispered fiercely, her voice almost a hiss.

"The Mass—" he began, but she repeated her demand, louder now.

Terrence moved slightly, then was still.

The Major had brought Michael forward, and he looked worse in the light filtering through the church windows. I could see that a good deal of the blood was fresh as well as dried, and his eyes were glazed, as if he had forced himself this far by will alone.

The Major was supporting him as Michael looked up at the priest. Something in the man's face reached the priest, for after a momentary hesitation, he began the service of marriage.

I heard him ask who giveth this woman, and Terrence answered, but didn't step back to sit down, as was usual. Instead he was holding on to Eileen, who had reached out to take Michael's bloody hand, making him wince from her touch.

She looked on the point of collapse herself.

The ceremony continued, with more haste than solemnity.

The church was hushed when Father O'Halloran asked if there was any impediment to this marriage. I could almost hear my own heart thudding in the stillness.

What would happen if the elder Mrs. Flynn spoke now?

But there was only silence. I hadn't realized until then how I was holding my breath.

Major Dawson fumbled in his pocket and brought out the ring for Eileen's finger.

Close as I was, I could barely hear Michael's responses, but I did hear the Major's as he whispered to the broken man beside him.

And then it was over. They were pronounced husband and wife.

Eileen's veil still covered her face. She reached out with one hand and began to lift it.

And Michael Sullivan quietly sank to his knees and then fell forward in spite of the Major's grip, until he was sprawled untidily at Father O'Halloran's feet.

With a cry of despair, Eileen broke free from Terrence's hold and threw herself across the body of the man lying so still I was sure he was dead.

Chapter Ten

Half the church was on its feet, everyone talking at once.

I was already on my knees, trying to reach around Eileen to find a pulse, as Michael didn't move. I couldn't even be certain he was breathing.

Beside me, Terrence and the Major were also kneeling, trying to persuade Eileen to let me examine Michael.

Precious minutes passed as she refused to let him go, weeping as if her heart would break.

At the edge of my vision, Mrs. Flynn, her face white as the white ribbons on the pew beside her, was weeping.

I looked around, found Niall, and said sharply, "Comfort your aunt."

He seemed as stunned as anyone else, but after a second or two he seemed to hear me, and nodded.

By that time Terrence had pulled Eileen aside, holding her in his arms and telling her over and over again that she must let me tend to Michael.

The Major, his expression grim, was trying to turn him over.

Reaching out, I managed to find his wrist. His pulse was slow and erratic.

"We must get him to the house, where he can be looked after," I said quietly. "Otherwise I can't be sure he'll make it."

The Major struggled to gather Michael in his arms and lift him. Terrence saw what he was about, and came quickly to help.

Mrs. Flynn reached out to Eileen and gathered her into her arms, just as Terrence had done.

There was no sign of the priest, and half the guests had already left the church, while the rest were collected just beyond Mrs. Flynn, staring at the wedding party.

No one else came forward to help, but I rose and began to make a path through the onlookers as the Major and Terrence carried the inert body of Eileen's husband up the aisle and out the door to the waiting carriage.

Eileen broke away from her mother, and followed them. I left Niall to collect Mrs. Flynn and kept going, summoning the carriage to come closer, for it had moved away, expecting the Mass to go on for some time.

The two men got Michael into the carriage, and then turned to let Eileen and then me step in beside him.

Terrence leaped to the empty place behind the coachman, and whatever he'd said to the man, the horses were turned and then urged into as swift a pace as possible given the state of the lane.

And then we were in front of the house, and Terrence was leaping down to help us.

There was blood all over Eileen's white gown, and I realized I too was covered in it.

There was no hope of getting Michael up the stairs to Eileen's room. The Major had arrived on the run, and between them the two men got Michael into the house and through the door into the front room, lowering him to the carpet. The two women who had come to help serve the wedding breakfast stood in the kitchen doorway, their expressions shocked. I looked up at them.

"Bedding. Towels. Hot water. *Hurry!*"

Terrence had already gone up for Eileen's kit, while she sank to the floor beside Michael and held his hand between both of hers. She wasn't crying now, but I was afraid she might faint from the shock and stress.

Major Dawson came back with a basin of water and some cloths from the kitchen, and I began to clean Michael's face. It was so bruised and battered that I could hardly tell what he actually looked like. His eyes were puffy, nearly shut, his lip was split and swollen, there were cuts across his nose and cheeks, and one ear was bleeding.

I couldn't remember seeing anyone beaten this savagely since I'd left my training in the London hospital. He very likely had a concussion.

I began to feel his limbs, and while they were bruised and cut, I didn't think they were broken. But it was impossible to judge internal injuries.

He had been unconscious since we'd got him into the carriage, but as I began to feel his chest, he groaned in pain.

Not a good sign, and his breathing was ragged.

I turned to the Major as the two women brought bedding down and began to make up a pallet on the floor. "See if you can put the kettle on. I'd like strong, sweet tea in something other than a cup—a bottle? And if there is a hot water bottle, fill that too."

Eileen, her own training finally coming to the fore, was reaching for a blanket and a pillow, cushioning Michael's head and covering him against shock.

The Major did as he was asked, and I was very grateful for his support. Terrence was looking for bandages and ointments, and then Mrs. Flynn was there, an apron over her dress, cutting away what was left of Michael's shirt.

Terrence said quietly in my ear, "Will he live?"

"I don't know. But we must keep him quiet. Can you lift him to that pallet?"

Terrence and the Major managed it quite efficiently, and the injured man was quickly made as warm and comfortable as possible.

I managed with Eileen's help and a spoon to get some of the tea between his lips, and he swallowed reflexively. That done, I began to deal with the worst of his cuts, and Eileen worked beside me.

Busy with what needed to be done, I hadn't heard the elder Mrs. Flynn come down the stairs and enter the front room.

When she spoke, I realized that she was standing over us as we worked, Eileen and I. "He looks to be at death's door. It's for the best, of course. Not much of a wedding night."

I felt Eileen stiffen beside me. "Get out. He's my husband now, and you'll keep a guard on your tongue."

The tone of her voice matched her grandmother's perfectly, the same contempt, the same cold, harsh, callousness. But under it was a seething anger.

Shocked, Mrs. Flynn took a step backward. I don't know that anyone had ever spoken to her like that. And then she turned and went out of the room. In the silence, we could hear Michael's rough breathing and Granny's footsteps on the stairs.

It was indeed a long night. We kept Michael warm, saw to it that he drank as much tea or water as he could, then added warm milk to that just before dawn.

I'd taken a few minutes to go up and change, insisting that Eileen come with me. She refused at first, short with me for even suggesting it. But then she rose and followed me. We were both better off with practical clothing, since we intended to sit up with the patient. What's more, Terrence stayed with us until around midnight, and then he left, his face grim. Major Dawson changed as well, then sat with us, ready to run any errand we might need.

Someone—I thought it was Niall—brought us sandwiches several times, with wine from the untouched wedding feast. I remembered eating but couldn't have said what it was I'd swallowed.

Eileen's mother had gone up around nine in the evening, clearly exhausted. I took one of the extra blankets and sat in one of the chairs, finally drifting into a light sleep around ten o'clock, but still attuned to my patient.

Michael had not spoken, although I thought he drifted in and out of consciousness as he lay there on the made-up bed. At one point, Eileen lay down beside him, speaking to him in whispers, and I think he knew somehow that she was there because he seemed quieter with her by his side.

I heard the Captain's aircraft fly over just after midnight, and came awake with a start when I realized I hadn't put out my handkerchief a second night in a row.

But there was nothing I could do about that now.

By morning Michael was no better, but no worse.

Where he'd been—who had beaten him so severely—and how he'd got back to the church were questions on everyone's minds. But there was no possibility of questioning him. For one thing he simply stared at us when we spoke, as if he heard us but didn't quite understand what we were asking him. For another, Eileen had become a fierce guard, warning us not to tire him or press him too hard.

"It's not important now. He's *here*. He's safe. Everything else can wait. I won't lose him, not to you nor to anyone else. When he's well enough, then we'll see what he can tell us."

Major Dawson told me quietly, "She's probably right. He looks as if he's at death's door this morning."

He did, but his heart rate was improving, and his color—what I could see of it—was better, and most of all, his body was taking this opportunity to heal, which was a good thing. He needed a doctor, but I had no idea where we might find one, and when I asked Terrence, he just shook his head.

"Best not. We have no idea who we can trust."

By late afternoon, Michael was able to manage a little porridge thinned with milk to make a gruel he could swallow. But I thought it was like feeding a child. When the spoon was presented to him, he opened his mouth and accepted it until he was too tired to go on.

And that worried me most of all. Was there brain damage from the repeated blows to the head?

It seemed he hadn't been fed or given water from the time he was taken, and I thought the tea was helping replace lost fluids.

Quite early I'd heard Mrs. Flynn come thumping down the stairs, making no effort to be quiet, her cane vigorously striking every step. Apparently she was on her way to Mass, for when I looked out the window I could see that she was properly dressed, with a broad hat to shade her face, gloves, and handbag. Niall was waiting to walk with her.

The four of us—Terrence, Major Dawson, Eileen, and I—had had almost no rest, even though we'd managed to drop into a restless sleep off and on. I'd have loved to crawl back under my blanket for another hour. Terrence, disappearing into the kitchen, came back in a few minutes with a tray and four cups of tea, which the rest of us accepted gratefully. No one expressed any objection to the spoonful of whiskey he'd added to each one.

And that was how we passed our Sunday . . .

At breakfast on Monday morning, Michael appeared to have more appetite, for he ate his porridge with Eileen's help, finishing the bowl.

Then he dropped into one of those deep sleeps of exhaustion, as if even eating was still too much for him. But by Monday afternoon late, he spoke Eileen's name, and she came rushing to him, holding his hand and brushing at relieved tears.

I had to wait until I was in the front room alone, when everyone went to the kitchen to eat. Food was plentiful—all the meats and puddings and other dishes prepared for the wedding feast. But Eileen had insisted that the wedding cake must not be touched, and it now rested in lonely splendor on a shelf in the pantry.

I had volunteered to sit with the patient while they ate, as we had been taking turns going for meals or a brief nap.

Waiting until I could hear the clatter of utensils and dishes, I dropped to my knees beside Michael, and watched until his eyes opened. They were a little more focused this evening, I thought, and I said quietly, "You don't know me—I'm Bess Crawford. I'd come for the wedding."

There was a pitiful attempt at a smile. "Bess. *Britannic*."

His voice was only a croak, but I was afraid Eileen might hear it and come running.

"Glad," he added.

I returned his smile. "I am also glad I was here," I told him.

He closed his eyes for a moment, then opened them again, as if it had taken more strength that he possessed to raise the swollen lids.

"Who did this to you?" I asked softly.

He tried to shake his head in alarm, wincing as he did. "No. Mustn't know."

"Who mustn't know?" I persisted. When he didn't answer immediately, I added, "Eileen? Terrence? The elder Mrs. Flynn?"

He managed a brief nod. "All."

"But why?"

"Must get her away. Quickly." His good hand fumbled for mine and gripped it with such strength he hurt my fingers. "Do it. For me."

"I must know why—" I stopped, thinking fast, then went on, "I must know who to trust."

"Nobody." His whisper was urgent now. "Just—go."

"*Why* were you taken? Where is the danger coming from?"

But before he could answer, the door to the kitchen opened, and Eileen walked in.

"Is he awake? Michael—" She rushed to his side, and pushed me away to reach him, bent over him, taking his hand and kissing him. "Oh, my darling—"

"He's not out of the woods, yet, Eileen."

Heedless, she was assuring him that she loved him, asking him if he remembered their marriage, pouring out all her love and fear and worry, struggling to keep him awake and with her.

But he had used up all his strength. He spoke her name, then drifted away into that half world where he'd spent the last two days.

She called his name again, but this time he didn't respond.

Turning on me, she said, "You were talking to him—what did he say? *Tell* me?"

I lied. "When I noticed that he was awake, I asked him what he might care to eat. I told him there was ham and chicken—"

"You should have called me. He's my husband, not yours."

"Eileen!" I said sharply, losing all patience with her, seeing an unpleasant reflection of her grandmother in her behavior. Were they really that much alike? Or had Eileen lived too long under her spell?

She was at once contrite. "I'm sorry, Bess, truly. I'm sick with worry, I want to be there whenever he's awake. I'm jealous of every minute I have to be away from him."

"I know," I replied, reining in what I'd have liked to say.

After that, we couldn't persuade her to leave him at all, and although I thought several times that he was awake, there was no opportunity to speak to him. And I had a feeling that he might already be regretting what he'd told me.

The trouble was, it wasn't enough. He was afraid that something would happen to her, if Eileen stayed in Ireland.

I needed to think. And once I was sure that Michael was stable and that it was safe to leave him, I slipped away and left my handkerchief on the stile. It was early, but I couldn't take another chance of missing the Captain's flight. Then I went up to Eileen's room. A handful of bees outside her open window were taking advantage of the fading light as I lay down without changing my clothes. But their whispering, as tired as I was, sent me into a deep sleep. It was rest I needed desperately, although my concern about what Michael was trying to tell me produced uneasy dreams.

It was dark when I woke up, and the house was quiet. I sat up, surprised to realize how late it must be. Not waiting until I'd collected myself, I hurried to the stand to bathe my face in cool water. It was then that I heard something outside. The sound was familiar, somehow, but I couldn't quite place it.

I hadn't lit the lamp, and curious, I crossed to the window to peer out, knowing I couldn't be seen.

There it was again—the soft call of a dove.

I smiled, about to turn away, remembering that I'd seen doves in the spinney just beyond the meadow where Arthur had landed. It was a comforting sound.

But it was dark outside—birds would be nesting for the night, wouldn't they?

Suddenly alert, I hastily dried my face and hands, then quietly went down the back stairs and stepped into the front room.

But all was well.

Eileen was lying on the bedding beside Michael, one hand on his shoulder, and Terrence was asleep on the sofa. In the dim light of the covered lamp on the tea table, I couldn't see Major Dawson, and I thought he had probably gone up to bed, as tired as I'd been.

I went back upstairs, relieved. If someone had come after Michael, we were all too vulnerable.

I climbed into bed once more, drew up the coverlet against the night's chill, and let myself drift into sleep.

The window was still open, and I heard the dove again. As drowsy as I was, I thought of the birds I'd watched come and go from the dove-cote at the bottom of our garden in Somerset. It stood by the path that led through the wood to Simon's cottage.

Flinging back the coverlet, I was fumbling for my shoes when I heard the kitchen door into the garden bang back on its hinges. A drink-slurred voice demanded loudly, "What the hell are you doing on this property?"

I thought it was Niall, but I couldn't be sure. There was a second voice, quite gruff, but I couldn't hear the reply. Then Niall said roughly, "Be off with you, or I'll set the dogs on you!"

The door slammed. And I heard a horse and cart pull away, pots and pans and harness rattling.

Irish gypsies, by the sound of it. I'd heard they were no more popular here than they were in Britain. Stories of their horse thieving, child abduction, and trickery were legend.

As I got into bed a second time, I heard Granny's querulous voice on the stairs, and Niall's reply as he came up them. "I'll not have them camping on our property."

I lay awake for some time afterward. How did an Irish Traveler know the sound of doves in a Somerset garden?

Michael was quite feverish the next morning when I hurried back to the house after retrieving my handkerchief, and I was concerned. Eyes too bright in a flushed face, he tried weakly to reassure Eileen, but as I wasn't in love with him, I took a different view of his situation. I rummaged through Eileen's bag, but over the years many of the contents must have been used and not replaced.

After breakfast, while Terrence and I were clearing away, I mentioned my concern. "If there's no doctor," I finished, "and he's going to rely on my care, I'll need to find an apothecary somewhere and replenish our supplies."

"I'm not happy, appearing in the village just now, not so soon after Michael's miraculous reappearance. There will be questions—bound to be—and a good deal of suspicion. God knows what the guests have told the world and its brother. Can you not wait a day or two?"

I couldn't—or rather I didn't think Michael could.

"I'll do my best," I answered. "But he's running a fever. That's never a good sign. I'm worried."

"Tomorrow, then." He sounded relieved.

Keeping a close eye on the patient, I did what I could for his fever, changed the bandages, and tried not to worry Eileen.

She, on the other hand, seemed oblivious to what was happening. In her relief to have Michael home again and the wedding over, she doted on him, trying to find something that he might care to eat, bringing cups of tea and cool water, never letting him out of her sight except finally to change her clothes. Refusing to see what any good nurse would have noticed first thing in the morning.

I realized that she couldn't face his needing care. She had nearly lost him once, and she wouldn't hear of a second threat to his life. She told me several times in the course of the day that I was hovering, and I held my tongue.

But by three o'clock even she had to take notice of the change in him. Anxious, she came into the kitchen where I was making a list of what I would need from the chemist's and said, "He's far too feverish. I thought—I put it down to all he'd endured to get back for the wedding. Exhaustion—his wounds. But it's more than that, isn't it? He's having chills, Bess. That's not just a slight fever."

"No. I've tried to reduce it, but it's climbing. And we need supplies. More bandages, ointments, something for his fever—"

"He needs a doctor! But Terrence won't hear of it. I got quite cross with him just now. He said *tomorrow*. Bess, I haven't got Michael back only to lose him now. Help me!"

I smiled, for her sake. "As I have been doing all day. I don't think Terrence wants everyone to know how—how much Michael's been through."

"Well, they could see that in the church, couldn't they? If they had eyes at all, they would know he's suffered terribly."

"Yes, of course—"

But she couldn't listen. "Does Terrence think that they'll come for him again? Is that why he doesn't want us to bring in a doctor? He didn't think I'd seen, but he has his revolver with him now. It was under his pillow last night."

"Let's worry about the moment, Eileen. I was about to make tea. Why don't you ask your mother if she has a little aspirin we could borrow? There isn't any more in your kit."

This gave her something to occupy her, even though I didn't expect Mrs. Flynn the younger to have them.

But she did, and I breathed a sigh of relief myself.

We took turns watching Michael, and just after midnight, I managed to take my handkerchief out to the stile again.

Michael's fever broke at two in the morning, covering him in sweat. We bathed him by a roaring fire, gave him clean nightclothes and sheets, and I took Terrence's place on the couch, to help watch over the sick man.

I noticed that Terrence had taken his revolver with him. I had mine, of course, a replacement for the one I'd lost to the authorities in France. It was now in my pocket.

Pale and exhausted, Michael slept until ten the next morning. He wasn't out of the woods, by any means, but this was a good sign.

All the same, I reminded Terrence that we must find a chemist. If not in our village, then another one.

He was still reluctant, and I wondered for a moment if he was hoping Michael might die.

It was nearly noon when Terrence and I set out for the village. There was a small chemist's corner in the general store, but it wasn't at all what I needed.

Terrence said, "Are you certain this isn't sufficient? I'm looking at it myself, and I don't know what's lacking."

"I'm the nurse," I reminded him. "The ointments I need aren't here, and if I take those bottles of aspirin, there won't be any left for the rest of the villagers. I need more bandages, and you can see for yourself how few they have."

I went on with my list, and he said, raising his hands in defeat, "All right. Enough. We needn't embarrass Mrs. O'Grady. There's a larger village some miles away. We'll need the horses."

I bought what the shop could spare, and we left. We were starting back toward the house when we heard bursts of laughter from the pub yard. I could see people clustered around a gaudy red and yellow Romany caravan, its patient horse feeding from a nose bag.

"We ought to see what's happening," I told Terrence, and started in that direction.

"Bess—no—wait."

Just then there was a burst of music from a violin, and I glimpsed the thin man who had played before, standing on the steps of the pub, violin in hand.

I kept going, and Terrence came after me. It appeared that the singer had brought in reinforcements, and that was worrying. What was he up to? And what did a gypsy have to do with the singer? What's more, why hadn't Terrence told me this was happening?

"It's best to stay away from there. Bess—"

But short of physically restraining me, he had no choice but to follow me.

I wasn't foolish. I stayed well clear of that cluster of men, standing back where a handful of women were also watching. But I didn't have a clear view. And then someone shifted.

Suddenly I saw what was causing the uproar. There was a large green parrot in a cage, and I thought surely he must have been owned by someone who had sailed just about everywhere, for the parrot had a vocabulary that would make even a sailor blush, sitting there brandishing what looked like the fried leg of a chicken that someone had given him, eating it and talking at the same time.

When the violinist started playing, the parrot squawked in sympathy, and people were bent double with laughter.

Beside me Terrence was saying, "That must be the Romany who stopped by last night to ask permission to camp in our meadow. Niall told him to get out."

"Yes, I expect you're right," I said absently. Someone was on the far side of the caravan, and whatever he was doing competed with the parrot for attention.

"Bess—you've seen enough. We need to move on."

"Not yet," I said. Why had the owner of the caravan asked to camp in the meadow, so close to the house? To spy on us? Or was it to do with Michael?

He put his hand on my arm, intent on pulling me away.

And then the Traveler came round the corner of the caravan, to remove the feed bag from the horse, and offer it a bucket of water.

He was tall and had on the most flamboyant clothes, a bit of this or that, more like a mountebank than a Romany, with a hat that would have made a cavalier proud, broadbrimmed and with a feather that swept from the crown with such a graceful flourish that it nearly concealed his face.

I recognize the hat and the plume. We'd used it dozens of times when I was a child for dressing up and all sorts of theatrics.

My heart stopped in my throat.

And then the tall man by the side of the horse lifted his head and said something in a foreign language that sounded like a string of curses that matched the parrot's.

And I had all I could do to keep from showing my shock. For the "curses" were intelligible—but only to me!

"Well, it's about time you noticed the commotion and came up to find out what it was all about."

The words were almost drowned out by another burst of laughter at the apparent inventiveness of the curses, but they were actually Urdu, one of the languages we'd learned in India.

And he smiled, a flash of white teeth in a very familiar face. For the tall man in the cavalier's hat was Simon Brandon, looking like anything but an English Sergeant-Major.

He didn't appear to be looking directly at me, but I knew he had picked me out of the throng of laughing people.

Just then the handsome scarred Irishman beside me put his arm around my shoulders and made me turn away.

And I barely caught Simon's expression as he watched . . .

Chapter Eleven

As soon as I was safely away from the pub and the crowd applauding some new trick, Terrence withdrew his arm.

"You should never have gone near there. Did you see how he was staring at you?"

For a wild moment, I thought he meant Simon, but I quickly collected my scattered wits and replied, "Who was staring? I was looking at that very odd parrot."

Where on earth had Simon found him? Or had he come with the caravan?

I was glad I'd been careful because Terrence snapped, "The man with the violin. He's dangerous, Bess. Stay clear of him, do you understand me?"

"I think I've seen him somewhere before . . ."

"It was the evening we went to the village to fetch our dinner." We were passing the church when he finally went on. "I don't trust him. He tried to court Eileen when she was able to walk again, and he was an eager part of the Rising. Only he and others like him wish to carry on, and make it a far bloodier business. In 1916, only those involved in the Rising fought and died, and they did it openly, with a Proclamation and weapons. He and his like want to begin a campaign of attrition, wearing the English down until they're glad to be rid of us. I want no part of that, and I don't think those who signed the Proclamation would have wanted it any more than I do."

That was his *public* viewpoint, I thought. But there was more to it. There was bad blood between these two men, and it was very personal. Was it Eileen?

"I was told when I was considering whether or not to come over, that the Irish were splintered now into many groups, all of them advocating for different responses to what happened in the Rising."

"There was great disappointment when it failed. Some are afraid to try again, while most of us want to find a new way. Not everyone wants what the fiddler wants. But we'll have independence in the end. If we must try all of the ways, one after the other."

"Was the artist—Fergus Kennedy—pushing for any particular way?"

"I don't know why he was killed." We had reached the drive up to the house.

"Go in and change, if you want to find that chemist's shop." And he walked on, carrying the things we'd bought, leaving me to follow.

And I would have dearly loved to run back to the village and ask Simon what he was doing here, and if my father was with him.

In the end we found the chemist's shop in a larger village closer to the mainland. We were met with stares. An Englishwoman in the company of an Irishman was not the usual sight even here, and a handful of young boys followed us as we rode down the high street in search of our goal. I wished I'd brought my mother's dark blue riding dress, far less conspicuous than my own dark red one.

Terrence stayed with the horses while I went in to place my order for medical supplies. The owner was clearly of a mind not to help me until I said, "I've been sent by Mrs. Flynn of Killeighbeg. She won't be very happy if I'm not served."

Apparently her name carried weight even here.

"And how is the dear woman?" the owner asked, moving to find the things I needed. "Not under the weather, I hope?"

"Not at all," I said, as if I were her spokeswoman. "She asked me to see to her medical cabinet and I was shocked at the state it had got into."

He frowned as he plucked items off the shelves. "There's requests here that could deal with major wounds."

Oh, dear, I've overplayed my hand, I thought.

"Falling out of a barn can do as much damage as you like," I said aloud.

"True, true. Mattie Byrnes's brother broke his neck coming out of the hay door headfirst."

I had no idea who Mattie Byrnes was, but I commiserated. When we finally had my order tied up in a parcel I could carry, and I had paid for it all with money Terrence Flynn had given me, the shop owner said, "Rumor has it that Mrs. Flynn's granddaughter's wedding was quite the shock."

Rumor had run quite far.

"Mrs. Flynn hasn't told me," I said and wished him a good day.

Terrence took my purchases as I came out the shop door, and something in my expression must have told him how things had gone inside. He put the parcel across his saddle and then gave me a leg up. I noticed that our little escort had gone away. As we turned back toward Killeighbeg, I said, "He asked—indirectly—about the wedding. Apparently word has spread."

"Several of the guests came from here," he told me. "Old friends of my grandmother's."

"Does that put Michael in greater danger? I don't know if he escaped or was allowed to go. He won't talk about what happened. I don't even know who it was who took him."

"Nor do I," Terrence replied. "Whether he likes it or not, we have to know. How long before he can travel safely?"

"Several more days. And then it should depend on how he'll travel."

"Too bad that aircraft of yours can't take the lot of you. We'd all be better off."

I looked across at him. "I need to know more about Fergus Kennedy. Is he in any way connected to Michael's disappearance?"

He didn't answer, urging his mount forward, making conversation more difficult. And this wasn't a topic that ought to be shouted about, for anyone to hear. We'd just passed through another small hamlet, and there was a scattering of other houses just ahead.

I caught him up. "You think it doesn't matter if I know or not. But it does. I don't think Eileen is aware of anything at the moment but Michael's condition. And Major Dawson is all but a prisoner here, now the wedding is over. As am I. The younger Mrs. Flynn isn't able to fend for herself, much less help me. I don't trust Niall. And the Constabulary is questioning both the Major and me. I feel surrounded by something I don't understand, and it's not a pleasant feeling."

"Then send for your flyer, and leave."

"I can't. Not for a few days. Not until Michael is recovering."

"Then keep out of it, Bess Crawford. Or you'll wish you hadn't."

"Are you threatening me?"

"No. It's a warning, woman. There's a difference."

And those were the last words he spoke to me all the rest of the way to the house.

I walked into the house through the door by the kitchen and started up the stairs to change out of my riding dress.

Major Dawson met me on his way down. I took his arm, leading him into the pantry, where we couldn't be overheard.

"Have you spoken to Michael?" I asked quietly.

"I've tried, but Eileen seldom leaves his side. You?"

"Once, briefly. And then it was only to beg me to take Eileen out of the country. I wish we knew more."

"Did you find the medicines you were after? The sooner he's well enough to talk the better."

"Yes—"

I heard someone starting down the staircase and we stepped quickly into the kitchen. I had the presence of mind to hand him the milk pitcher while I caught up the board holding the bread.

But it was just Mrs. Flynn the younger.

"Good morning, Mrs. Flynn—" I began.

She put a hand on my arm. "Will you call me Maeve? I was proud of the name Flynn once, but now I hate it. Because of *her*."

Her mother-in-law.

"I—yes, of course—"

She smiled. "Does it seem so awkward to use my name?"

"A little," I confessed. "But I will become used to it."

She turned to the Major. "How is Michael this morning? I can barely squeeze a word out of my daughter."

"Improving slowly."

"I looked in on them in the middle of the night. He's been roughly handled."

Surprised, I said nothing. Had I been that deeply asleep? But then she moved like a wraith, sometimes, although in theory this was her house, not Granny's.

"He has," Ellis was replying. "We still don't know who held him. Or why."

She drew a deep breath. "I think it has to do with what is being planned. We're so far from Dublin, you see. What better place to have secret meetings?"

She rarely left her room. How could she know what was happening?

As if she'd heard the thought, she said quietly, "My room is across from hers. And she can be very loud when she's displeased."

"Did she know what had become of Michael?" I asked quickly.

"I tried, but there was never anything said about him that I could hear. I did wonder—Father O'Halloran is very much a rebel. He'd have been in Dublin himself if he'd known what was to happen. There are a lot of them who want to make up for not being there. But the leaders of the Rising knew how to choose men who could be trusted."

That was enlightening. "How do you know?"

"My father knew most of the leaders. Over the years, when I was a child, I saw them come and go."

"Was he involved in the Rising?" Major Dawson asked.

"He was far too old. He was eighty-five when he died in 1913, but he'd hoped to see the day, I think." She gestured toward the cooker. "I came down to find a cup of tea . . ."

It was clearly a change in subject, and I set about making tea while the Major looked in on Eileen. The front room had become a sickroom for the moment. It would have been impossible to carry Michael up the narrow stairs, and besides, I was sleeping in Eileen's room just now.

In her letters, Eileen had talked about leaving after the ceremony and reception, spending their first night in Galway, then traveling on to Dublin before taking a ferry from Dunleavy. I still wasn't certain Michael would be traveling at all this week.

I could hear the Major speaking to Eileen, and then once, a hoarse response from Michael. Setting the tea on the table and finding some biscuits for Mrs.—Maeve—I went to find where Terrence had put my parcels from the chemist's.

He had left them in the front room, and with the warm water left in the kettle from making tea, I washed my patient's wounds, covered them with ointment, then bandaged them. I'd given him aspirin before we left, and it was time for more. All the while he lay there with his eyes closed, but I wasn't sure whether that was from his weakness or his refusal to answer questions.

Busy as my hands were—riding with Terrence, talking to Ellis and

Mrs. F—Maeve—in the kitchen, even working with Michael—I was trying to think of a way to reach Simon.

I was washing up the pan I'd used to bathe Michael's wounds when there was a knock at the kitchen door.

I hadn't seen the girl who sometimes worked in the kitchen—she seemed to come and go at will. I thought this might well be her and was just going to answer the knock when Maeve came into the kitchen.

I smiled at her, went into the passage, and opened the door.

There stood Simon. Without the parrot. He'd changed from the flamboyant clothing he'd worn when he first came to the village. Now he was dressed like so many Irishmen, in a dark suit of clothes and a white shirt without a collar. On his head he wore the flat-billed cap that so many men favored here.

He raised his eyebrows, and I gave a slight shake of my head to let him know that we could be overheard.

He asked in an accent that was neither Irish nor English if we had any pots or pans that might need mending.

"Who is it, Bess? Is that Molly?"

Simon brushed past me, stepped into the kitchen, swept off his cap, and gave Mrs. Flynn a bow that Louis XIV would have envied.

She turned pink.

"The lady of the house," he said in that same accent. "I have come to ask, are there pots and pans to be mended? Yes? I am remarkably good at this."

Behind him I smothered a laugh with a cough.

Maeve Flynn collected herself. "I have no pots or pans. But there is a chair in my room that has an arm that is loose. Could you repair that?"

"Indeed, Madame. You have only to ask."

She turned and led him up the stairs. I followed. And as I did, Simon's hand came back toward me, a slip of paper in it.

The Stile. Midnight.

I dropped it in my pocket and kept going.

There was indeed a chair with an arm that was loose. Simon picked it up, looked it over, and quoted her an outrageous price to repair it.

To my surprise, she said, "When you return with the chair mended, I will pay you."

He grinned audaciously, gave her another bow, and set out for the door, chair in hand. I just prayed he didn't run into Terrence or Niall on his way.

Maeve said, "After him, Bess. He's likely to help himself to the silver if you don't see him out."

I did, but there was no chance to speak to him. He marched off with the chair, and I breathed again.

I went back up to Maeve's rooms, to ask her if it was wise to trust him to mend the chair and not sell it instead of returning it.

"I don't know. Or care. I only did it to annoy *her.*"

"But how will she know? I don't think anyone else saw him." I hoped not, at any rate.

"That's the chair she prefers to sit in, whenever she visits. I think she deliberately weakened the arm to annoy *me.* I shall have the pleasure of telling her how it was repaired."

I was beginning to see that the younger Mrs. Flynn wasn't quite the invalid that her daughter feared she was. It was a useful act, in this household.

Major Dawson wasn't there for tea, nor did he come for supper, and I asked if anyone had seen him since I'd come back from my travels with Terrence.

And no one had.

Eileen said, "I think I saw him walking down to the meadow shortly after we'd settled Michael. He's restless. The wedding's over. He wants to leave but feels he can't until Michael is a little stronger."

Terrence said, "I'm here. He can leave whenever he likes."

But I knew that Ellis wouldn't leave until he was sure I could as well.

I said, "It's still light. He may come in shortly."

"It's not safe to go wandering about alone. An English officer? Fair game, to many people. He should know that by now," Niall put in.

Still, as soon as the meal was over, I left Eileen and her mother to see to the dishes and quietly went out to look for the Major.

I remembered the place he said he went to, to speak to the frog in the pond. Crossing the meadow, I started through the spinney, scanning among the trees without any sign of him. And so it took me several minutes to reach the far side. I wasn't sure whether the pond was to my right or my left, and so I had to cast about before I saw it some thirty yards away. It was larger than I'd expected.

Ellis wasn't there, either.

I was beginning to be glad I'd brought my little revolver with me. There was something about the silence. No birds were calling or moving about, as if there had been trouble here and they were keeping out of sight.

Still, I kept going until I was close enough to notice the bruised grass on the side of the pond nearest me. There was a large stone just to one side, and I thought it might be where Ellis sat while he was here. Ahead, in the water, two black eyes rose as I got nearer, then vanished from sight. The frog.

I turned toward the large stone. It was shaped like a rough U, and I realized that it was actually two stones so close together they appeared to be one. Where they joined was a small plaster shrine, the Virgin Mary's blue gown faded, the edges of the plaster surrounding her chipped. As if it had been set here a long time ago and forgotten.

And at the far end of the stone, I saw something dark.

I went over to it, put out my fingers, and touched it. Dark there, perhaps, but when I looked at my fingers, the smear was a rusty red.

Blood.

And by the looks of it, whatever had taken place here had happened some hours ago. Four? Five? Longer?

Just like Michael, Major Dawson had gone missing.

I quickly turned, looking all around. Was there someone out there, watching? Or waiting . . . ?

Shoving my left hand in my pocket, I felt for the cool metal of the little weapon. I dipped my other fingers in the pond water to clean away the blood, then I dried them on my handkerchief. I could just see the frog's long legs pushing itself deeper into the shadows at the bottom. And then it was gone.

Moving as if undisturbed, I went back the way I'd come and counted my steps until I could reach the spinney and some semblance of safety.

I tried to tell myself that no one was out there, and yet the sense of being watched was so strong I dared not ignore it.

I didn't realize that my teeth were clenched until I stepped into the shelter of the first tree. But there was still some way to go—through the spinney—that little wood that now seemed to stretch on forever—then cross the meadow and over the lawns to the house.

Concentrating on that, I walked deeper into the cool shade of the trees. I'd taken no more than half a dozen steps when I caught movement out of the corner of my eye.

I stopped short with my back against the nearest tree. I could feel the rough bark through the cloth of my dress.

"Whoever you are," I called harshly, "I'm armed, and I know how to shoot."

A shadowy figure stepped out into my line of sight, and I had already brought up my revolver when he said, "Well, I damned well hope you do. I taught you, after all."

It was Simon.

I felt like shooting him anyway. But I put the revolver back into my pocket and went toward him.

He was dressed the same as he had been earlier, but there was a subtle difference about him now.

The soldier, not the Traveler, I thought. And something else I couldn't define.

He said, "I'm to alert Arthur to pick you up tonight. Where's the Major? He and I can make our way home by boat. I only persuaded the owner of that bl—that caravan to lend it to me for a week."

"I can't leave yet," I told him. "For one thing, Michael was badly hurt and he's still not well enough for me to go."

"I heard about the wedding. At the pub last night. But Eileen is trained, is she not? She will manage."

"She's too shaken to be of any use. Even to Michael. And we can't move him yet. Besides, there's another problem. The Major is missing. Just now. He had a place he went to sit, to get away from the house for a bit, but today he was away far longer than usual. I went to look for him. There was a fight, I think, and I found a little blood on one of the stones. I can't swear that it's his, but I have a feeling it must be. You didn't see anything while you were lurking here?"

"I wasn't lurking. I'd hoped you might be able to leave the house to look for me."

"What did you do with Mrs. Flynn's chair?"

"Eileen's mother? It's safe enough. And I can mend it."

"Couldn't you have dressed a bit less noticeably?"

"I could have done. But I'd be spotted as soon as I came down the road. I don't think they care much for gypsies in this corner of Ireland. Making a spectacle of myself, making the village laugh, was the best way of insuring I could stay here a day or two . Who took Michael? And do the same people have Dawson?"

"I can't tell you. Michael won't talk about what happened to him, and so I'm not sure why he disappeared. There's something going on, Simon. Have you met the tall thin man with the violin?"

"I have. A nasty one, that. Do you think he's behind all that's happened?"

"I don't know. Possibly. And then there's Niall, Terrence's younger brother. I don't trust him, either."

"And the—" He didn't finish what he was about to say. He broke off and suddenly went still. Then he said, "Go, quickly."

In the same instant I heard someone shouting my name.

"Terrence. You saw him with me in the village. I must stop him."

He shouted again.

Abandoning Simon there, I ran through the trees, trying not to stumble over what might be lying beneath the rotting cover of winter leaves. Anything to prevent Terrence from coming to meet me.

I saw him as I reached where the trees were thinning. He had already moved away, starting back across the meadow. I called to him, and he turned.

"I've told you about wandering off!" he replied, coming back for me.

I didn't want to shout what I knew, but when he was closer, he got his news in first.

"Give me your hand, we've no time to waste. The Constabulary has come to question Michael."

Together we ran back across the meadow. I wondered what Simon was thinking as he watched.

Already out of breath, I broke free at the stile, saying, "No, let me follow you."

He climbed over, reaching back for me, but I managed quite well on my own.

I could see the Constable's bicycle leaning against the side of the house.

"Eileen is doing her best to put him off. Of all the times for you to go wandering!"

We were halfway across the lawns now, and I managed to say, "You need to know something—"

"There isn't time."

"But there is." I stopped, midstride, but he carried on, and I had to catch him up. We walked in the front door, and I glimpsed Mrs. Flynn's face at her window as we passed under it. Without pausing we went into the front room.

The Constable and Eileen were standing on either side of Michael's bedding. She was flushed, and he was clearly adamant about something.

I said with my best Matron's voice, "What are you doing, disturbing my patient?"

Out of the corner of my eye I saw that Michael had his firmly shut.

"I need to question him. I've put it off, allowing him to recover, but now I must do my duty."

And Eileen, almost overriding his words, was saying, "He's not well enough!"

I said, ignoring her, "He's had a terrible beating, and so far he has not been conscious. I believe he knows where he is, that he's under our care, but the only word he's spoken to us is his wife's name. And I am not even certain that wasn't in delirium. His fever is high from his wounds."

It was true, that was what all the others had heard, except for the usual medical questions about his wounds and seeing to his needs, but I wasn't about to tell this man what Michael had whispered to me. I couldn't be sure where his allegiances lay, and if there was any chance at all of getting both Eileen and Michael out of here safely, it was best to let the world think he was very ill and unable to tell us anything.

The Constable dropped to his knees, touching Michael's shoulder, calling his name. Eileen flew around the bed and tried to stop him. And Michael rose—figuratively speaking—to the occasion, groaning and muttering "No—no—" as if he expected to be struck again, pulling away. His face was still ugly with bruising and half-healed cuts, he certainly looked the part of a very ill man.

The Constable, uncertain whether he was being played, called his name again, but there was no response.

The worst of Michael's fever had fallen, but he was still warm to the touch, and I was sure the Constable had felt it through his shirt as he put a hand on Michael's shoulder.

He remained unconvinced, but he could hardly take hold of the poor man, pull him up, blankets and all, and force him to speak. Still, I bit my tongue to stop me from giving him a piece of my mind.

Finally, to save face, the Constable nodded his head, and got to his feet. Looking toward me, he asked, "How soon will he have recovered sufficiently to be interviewed?"

"I can't tell you that. Only a doctor could."

He considered me for several minutes, then asked, "Where have you been?"

"I walked for a little while in the meadow. As you can understand, I don't get much sleep just now. And I must keep a clear head."

He nodded again, then said, "And you never treated him, during the war?"

"As far as I know, the first time I saw this man was in the church on Saturday. I knew who he was only when the bride cried out his name."

He'd asked me that before. I was beginning to think he believed that somehow Michael Sullivan and I had been in collusion in some fashion. But why? As British spies? What could be going on out in this spit of land jutting into the Atlantic that would attract even one British spy, much less two? Or three, counting the Major.

But then they had been in the Irish Guards, hadn't they?

I wished him away, but he lingered, speaking to Terrence about Fergus Kennedy, telling him that the man's brother was coming over to see to the body.

Finally he was finished and out the door, still questioning Terrence. Eileen was biting her lip, still on edge, staring out the window.

I looked down at Michael just then, and I saw that his eyes were open, and he was staring at me, trying to convey some urgent message. Clearly, he couldn't speak while Eileen was there, and I couldn't lean down to hear a whisper.

I nodded, and had just looked away when Eileen turned back into the room. "I heartily dislike that man," she said. "He's cruel."

"Has he gone?"

"Yes, I saw him mount his bicycle and ride off."

"Then I must speak to Terrence. See to Michael, he may wish to have a little milk or some tea." I didn't want her to follow me.

But Terrence wasn't in the passage, as I'd expected him to be, and the last thing I wanted to do was go to his room. I wasn't even sure which was which, and I could just as easily knock at Niall's door.

Angry with him, I went through the house and out to the barn, where I discovered him looking in on the horses. He was abrupt when I called to him.

"The man's gone. Thank God. You should have been within call."

I didn't waste my breath. "They've taken the Major. Whoever they are. It wasn't easy. There's blood, so we know he put up a fight."

"*What?*"

I had his full attention now.

"What do you mean, *taken?*"

"Just that. He wasn't there for his meals—and he could hardly decide to dine at the pub. So I went to a place he'd mentioned—"

He cut across my words. "Where? Show me."

I hoped Simon had moved on. I was sure he'd have a look at the pond before leaving the spinney, and would search for anything I might have missed. I'd been more concerned about not finding myself taken as well, before I could tell Terrence what I'd seen. But what if he'd encountered the Constable somewhere on his way back to the village? I couldn't worry about that—it was the Major who needed our help now.

We went back to the meadow, into the little wood, and we hurried on to the pond. I showed Terrence what I'd noticed, the bruised grass and the blood on the stone.

"If he'd slipped and fallen, even if he'd hit his head, he'd still be here. Or he'd have found his way home. I might even have stumbled across him in the meadow or among those trees. But he's gone. Without a trace."

Terrence was casting about, looking for any indication that he'd been taken. "You can see here," he said after several minutes, pointing to another patch of bruised grass. "He was dragged. No sign of a horse. They couldn't have risked that. But they purposely dragged him, then picked him up and carried him off. In that direction."

The ground was rough here, stones just showing in places, nettles and other sour land growth. Dragging the Major must have been paying him back for fiercely resisting. And once he was unconscious or too dazed to fight on, his attackers made greater speed by lifting him.

Terrence dropped into a squat, studying something, and I felt a frisson of fear that he'd found a print left by Simon. But a Regimental Sergeant-Major would be far too experienced to make a mistake like that.

"Look here," Terrence was saying, and I hurried forward to see what he'd discovered.

It wasn't a footprint. His carriers had put the Major down for a time, because we could see blood on the bent stems and low-growing weeds where his head must have rested.

I looked back. We'd come some distance from the pond. It appeared that the Major's attackers had set him down, and while one watched, the other had gone to another small stand of trees just ahead, to fetch a horse.

For just ahead, some thirty paces, there were droppings.

Terrence saw them as well. "It must have grown tiresome, carrying a dead weight between them."

I didn't care for the words *dead weight*.

I said, "If he was dead, they'd have left him. I don't think they intended to kill him, just to render him manageable while they took him away."

Terrence regarded me for a moment. "Killing an Englishman would be a badge of honor in some quarters."

"Yes, I'm sure. But I'd rather believe that they wanted him for other reasons."

He was still watching me closely. "What has Michael been saying?"

"Mostly Eileen," I retorted. "And groaning." I turned the question back at him. "What did you think he might be saying?"

"Well, for one thing, it would be damned helpful to know who had taken him, why, and how he got himself free."

"That's three things."

He shook his head, angry. "Don't play games with me, Bess Crawford."

"I'm not. But you know this part of Ireland far better than I do. You know the people here. You know which causes they support. Why can't you think of a good reason for taking first Michael and now the Major?" It was in a way a taunt. "Or are you afraid that your brother is involved—or your grandmother for all I know—and in that case blood is thicker than water. As they say."

"Damn it, woman! I don't have any ties to Major Dawson. But I do to my cousin. And she was bent on marrying the man. And that was the best thing for her. So why would I abduct the groom and stop the wedding?"

"But it wasn't stopped," I replied, standing my ground. "He got free—or was released somehow. That's the only reason it went on."

"If I'd been behind it, I'd have killed the man and been done with it!" he said roughly, and turned back toward the house.

"Aren't you going to track the horse?" I asked.

"I know where it was going. I live here, as you said. On the other side of those trees is a farm lane, disused now, but once it led to a road."

"How could they transport a bleeding man thrown over the back of a horse down a well-traveled road?"

He turned. "I didn't say it was well traveled. But they could have had a cart or a wagon or even a caravan waiting. Covered with straw or sacks, even behind a crate of chickens, who would guess a man was hidden there? A better use of my time is collecting a search party."

He had a very good point.

I set out after him, and by the time we came to the spinney, he had stopped to wait for me to catch him up.

His head to one side, the late sun on his face, making it hard for me to read, he said, "Have you not given a thought to the fact that both Michael Sullivan and Major Dawson are Army men? *British* Army men? Whether they call themselves the Irish Guards or not, they pledged their allegiance to the Crown when they signed on. And what better way to start a new and bloody Rising than by attacking that hated symbol of our oppression?"

Chapter Twelve

I HAD TO admit that Terrence was right. It made sense. What better preparation than to question two military men—one from the ranks and the other an officer. About such things as where to find uniforms, where the point of an attack ought to be focused, even how to behave as soldiers, look like them, until they were ready to act.

As soon as Michael had told someone—anyone, even Eileen's grandmother or the priest—that he was pleased to have his commanding officer to stand with him at his wedding, the planning must have started. A godsend to men looking for any opportunity to cause trouble.

And they had left Terrence out of it, because he was related to the bride and might not be trusted to spoil her wedding.

Terrence was saying, "I see it hadn't occurred to you."

"I'd been considering a more personal level."

"So like a woman!"

We had come out of the spinney and were crossing the meadow now, wasting no time returning to the house.

I said, "Actually, I thought stopping the wedding might be more to your grandmother's taste then defeating the British. I can see that I was wrong."

To my surprise he laughed. But it wasn't with amusement. "She's capable of many things, my grandmother."

"What will you tell her? That's he's been taken, like Michael?"

"That we can't find Dawson and we're sending out a search party."

And then we were approaching the door. I looked up to see Mrs. Flynn at her window.

Terrence must have seen her as well. He caught my hand, pulled me to him, and kissed me. And then let me go.

Wanting nothing more than to slap his face, I went after him into the hall. But he turned as soon as we were out of Granny's sight, looked at me with nothing like a lover's expression, and said softly, "Don't take it personally, my dear. I wanted to give her something more to worry about than the Major's disappearance."

He was already on his way through to the kitchen, heading toward the stables.

I was starting after him when the door to the front room was swung open, and at the same time, I heard the door to Granny's room open as well, the angry thump of her cane heading for the top of the stairs.

Both Eileen and her grandmother rounded on me as if I'd committed an unpardonable sin. I was ready to kill Terrence as Eileen said, "I saw that. What have you been doing behind our backs?"

And Mrs. Flynn, staring down at me with daggers in her gaze, was saying, "I asked you once what was between you and my grandson, and you lied to me—you are little more than a whore."

Anger changed to fury. I seldom lose my temper—really lose it. I took after my mother in that respect. But I was beginning to see what Terrence Flynn had been up to. If I was suddenly made unwelcome in this house, I'd have no choice but to go. And the quickest way to make that happen was to appear to be dallying—for want of a better word—with the son of the house.

He wanted me gone—for my own safety? Or his?

I looked from one to the other and said with what came out as contempt, not shame, "Oh, do shut up, both of you. There are more things on my mind than your precious Terrence. For one, something has happened to Major Dawson, and I need help, not recriminations. And for another, I wouldn't marry that Irishman for any amount of money you could offer me. If you feel like lecturing someone for what just happened, I suggest you speak to him."

I left them with their mouths wide open in shock and hurried out to the stables, but Terrence had already saddled the mare and was mounting as I came through the wide doors.

"Not now," he said, and pointed the mare toward the door. I moved as quickly as I could, but her flanks brushed me as she set out.

Dusk was already falling, the sky a lurid red in the distance, somewhere out to sea. Overhead it was lavender now, fading from pink.

I marched back to the house and went from the kitchen into the front room.

Eileen was standing in the middle of the floor, clearly uncertain what to say to me.

I ignored her, kneeling by Michael and saying, "Major Dawson has just gone missing. As you'd done, last week. I need to know everything you can tell me—everything you remember—"

Eileen was on her knees on his other side. "Don't do this—"

Michael's eyes were open, and if not completely lucid, he was capable of understanding me.

Still ignoring her, I said, "You're well enough. Talk to me. Where can I find him? Where were you taken?"

He cleared his throat. Eileen cried, "Please, leave him alone. Don't do this."

"I don't have any choice."

Michael's voice was still rough as he said, "I don't remember much. A-a boat, rocking. The smell of the sea. Not—not a river. There were four of them. I-I was blindfolded, I couldn't see their faces. They all—all but dragged me ashore. I was held between two of them, stumbling with them. From—from the shore, then grass. There was a horse. I was put in the saddle then. We walked for a-a long time—climbing. I had a-a terrible headache. They must have drugged me. And several times I-I was quite sick, the motion of the horse, whatever I'd been given. Then we were—I could feel the wind blowing. Somewhere high. I was kept there."

"In the open? And still blindfolded?"

"Blindfolded, yes. But they had put up canvas, we were cold at night, but dry. The stone was—was warm during the day."

Small wonder the searchers had had no luck in finding Michael. He'd been taken away in a boat. In this part of Ireland, that could mean anywhere. There were cliffs and fingers of land—I'd seen the map in my father's study—and even caves.

Eileen was crying now, clutching his hand. She didn't want to know any of this. Her imagination had already seen enough in his wounds.

"What did they do to you? And why?"

His gaze moved to the top of Eileen's head. "They wanted information. I refused. In the end, I lied. They told me there—there—there were other ways to hurt me."

I knew what he was saying. That if he didn't talk to his captors, they would bring Eileen and torture *her*. And they had taken the Major to confirm what Michael had told them.

"Who were they?"

"I was blindfolded."

Yet I thought he must know a little—perhaps he'd recognized a voice, glimpsed a face. This was not the time to push him.

"How did you escape?"

"When they were satisfied, they told me they would let me go. I knew they wouldn't. They just didn't want to kill me there. But they made a show of untying my hands and feet, although I was still wearing the blindfold. I could barely walk by then, and the horse was brought up, I—I didn't give them any trouble, even promised I'd say nothing, in exchange for my life. I was taken back to the boat, and when I thought they were occupied with the rowing, I stood up and jumped into the sea."

I said, "That was dangerous."

"They searched the sea for me, then decided I'd drowned. But I've always been a strong swimmer. I made it to shore, found a place among some reeds, and slept for a time. I don't know how long. But it was dark when I woke up, and I moved on. Without the blindfold, I could see the sky. I headed north, praying that was the right direction. Walked all night, part of the next day. I wasn't sure what day it was. But when I saw the carriages all around the church, I slipped inside. My mind wasn't functioning well, it could have been Sunday. But I willed it to be my wedding day, and willed Eileen to be there. And she was."

His strength was seeping away with every sentence. Closing his eyes, his mouth a tight line, the split lip still raw.

I said, "Michael—"

But he shook his head.

And I realized that he was slipping into sleep again.

Eileen turned and pushed me away. "Leave him alone. Do you understand me? And if you tell anyone what you heard just now, I'll swear you are making it up." She brushed back strands of hair that had fallen across her face. Then she said earnestly, pleading with me. "Bess, I owe you more than I can ever repay. But you don't live here, you don't know the undercurrents left by the failure of the Rising. Some of us, like Michael and me, just want to see this country free. We don't *want* more trouble. You'll be leaving us in a few days. Please don't stir up something that we'll be left to deal with!"

I understood her. And I also understood that for the Major's sake,

Michael had told me as much as he dared. But the *why* was still unanswered, and the question of what they'd wanted as well. I had a fair idea. But it was still just a possibility. I also understood that the less Eileen knew, the safer she was. But in order to make Michael talk, those men had threatened to hurt her. I could just imagine what ugly fears Michael must have had, to relent and tell them what they wanted to know. Even if it was all lies.

Who would they threaten to harm if the Major refused to talk?

Someone else who was also English?

I felt a little shiver of uneasiness.

Was that why Terrence wanted me out of Ireland as soon as possible?

He'd been interrogated after the Rising. He must have known . . .

Chapter Thirteen

I GOT UP then, walking into the kitchen, leaving Eileen to watch over Michael.

I also recognized that he was a very brave man. A good man.

Leaning against the table, I considered all the possibilities, and they weren't very pleasant.

I needed to talk to Simon, but it was too early to slip down to the meadow.

Did Niall have anything to do with Michael's abduction? Was that why Michael had urged me to get Eileen away as soon as possible? Why he refused to tell us what he'd been asked? Who better to watch him and decide what needed to be done, than a member of his own household?

Come to that, where was Niall?

I heard the thump of a cane on the stairs, and heavy footsteps. With a sign of resignation, I realized that I had one more confrontation ahead.

Straightening my back, making certain that she found me strong and still angry, I waited.

And then she was at the foot of the steps and coming through the door.

I'd expected her to tear into me about Terrence, but she said, "What is this about the Major? What's happened?"

"I don't know. He's been missing for some hours, now. I've looked, Terrence has looked. And he hasn't just wandered off. The Major is not that sort of man."

"I thought you hadn't met him before you came here. And now you know what he will and won't do?"

"He's an English officer. That's all I need to know."

She flushed, angered by my response. "Well, Miss. English officers are fair game in this country. I've no doubt he's been killed. And when the body is found, let it be a warning to you."

"It's odd, Mrs. Flynn, that two men who have lived even briefly under your roof—under the protection of this house and the Flynn family—should have been taken away under your very nose. I can't think how Michael survived. He could easily have died of what was a very savage beating. I'm sure the Major is enduring much the same treatment. He may not be as fortunate."

She didn't like that, either.

"And while this English officer is suffering, you have nothing better to do than flirt with my grandson."

"Indeed. You know him better than I do. Could an English nursing Sister find it so easy to turn his head?"

Giving up that line of attack, she returned to the missing house guest.

"Why should anyone want the Major?"

"You said it yourself. To kill him, for Ireland."

"Stop talking nonsense, girl!" She was contradicting her own pronouncement, but I didn't argue. "We aren't savages. He was an officer in the Irish Guards, commanding traitors to this country. I know that. What I'm asking is whether or not he could be held for ransom. If his family is wealthy or important enough for London to step in on his behalf?"

"I don't know. We never talked about such things." But Simon might well know. He and my father wouldn't have overlooked that possibility.

"It should be considered." And with that she turned and went back up the stairs to her room.

With searchers out, scouring the countryside, I had to be careful going down to the meadow so late at night. And Simon might have had just as much trouble getting to it.

I'd heard men on foot, torches flashing this way and that, going down toward the spinney, while others headed up through the orchard behind the stables. How far they'd go and how soon they'd be coming back, I couldn't guess. Would they continue to search all night?

If Michael was right, and he'd been taken away in a boat, searchers on foot around Killeighbeg were not going to find Major Dawson, unless they could track his captors to some quiet inlet where they had left a boat.

I had been standing at a window, looking out across the dark lawns, wishing I had a view down to the stile, when I was struck with a horrible thought.

Was this why Fergus Kennedy was killed? There were inlets near his house—Terrence had said he loved painting the sea in all its many moods. Had he seen a small boat putting out late one evening as he was working, and later discovered what it was?

From everything Terrence had told me about the man, he was a patriotic Irishman, regardless of his background. He was even painting the portraits of the men who had fought and died for Ireland. For the day when Ireland was free and could build a memorial to them? Terrence had said the English weren't very happy with what he was doing. But perhaps that's what his killers wanted us to think.

There are rogues in every Cause. People who were either so intensely loyal they couldn't see beyond their faith in it, or were hungry for the power any change would give them. And they could do more damage to that Cause, even betray what it had stood for in the beginning, by their actions. I'd seen it happen elsewhere.

Was that what was going on here? A pocket of angry men who couldn't see that they were only going to make the English Parliament more resolute in bringing Ireland to heel?

It was all the more important to speak to Simon, to warn him what might be happening. I didn't want to bring more trouble on Eileen and her family. I just hoped that Mrs. Flynn wasn't so deeply involved that any trouble others brought to this house would touch Eileen or her mother.

Even so, his captors might not be as careful with the Major. God alone knew what they might do to him. And the sea was as good as any place to rid them of a body. Fergus Kennedy had gone into the sea, and it was likely that the same fate awaited Michael. I had no idea if the Major could swim.

Watching the hands of the tall case clock in the front room go round and round, I sat with Michael and his wife for over an hour, then Eileen asked if I'd stay a bit longer while she went up to her room for some of her things. But first I had to swear not to question him.

She came back some twenty minutes later, and we moved into the kitchen.

"My mother had seen the search party going through the orchard. She was worried about us. I had to tell her about the Major." Shaking her head, she said, "I love Ireland, but I can't wait to leave. Isn't that sad? When can Michael travel?"

"I think he's much stronger today. By the weekend, surely. But how do you expect to go? There are horses in the barn, but your carriage won't hold all of us, not if we find the Major in time. And Michael can't walk as far as the next village. A boat? Does Terrence own a boat?"

"We were planning to use the horses. Terrence was going to take us as far as possible, to somewhere we could find transportation to Dublin, then bring the horses home. I wish your aircraft could take three people, not two." She sighed. "And Michael won't leave without the Major. I wish you'd never told him—we could have lied, told Michael he'd already left."

"He wouldn't go without saying goodbye. Michael would know that."

"I expect you're right." She shook her head in despair. "I wish I knew what to do."

"I'm going up to bed. While the house is quiet, you should try to sleep as well. I have a feeling tomorrow might be a difficult day for all of us."

I wished her a good night and went up the stairs and into our room. She had taken a change of clothes and other things for tomorrow, but even to do that she had been afraid to leave Michael unattended. As if he might vanish while her back was turned.

It was sad. I felt for her. This wasn't a wedding she would ever wish to recall with happiness.

It was a little after midnight when I heard the aircraft flying overhead.

I waited but didn't hear it land. Simon must have waved it off, somehow.

No one else was awakened by the sound, as far as I could tell. And drawing on a dark coat, to make me less visible, I quietly went down the stairs and out the kitchen door. Keeping close to the house as far as I could, I struck out across the lawns and prayed that no one had seen me.

I climbed the stile, and as I started down the other side, Simon seemed to materialize out of the darkness to give me a hand.

"Was that Captain Jackson?" I asked quietly.

"Yes. I used your signal that all was well. This way."

And taking my hand again, he led me to a corner of the meadow where a clump of what looked like hawthorn trees had grown up, forming a little space where we could stand, protected from view if the searchers came back. Even so, we had to be very careful of the trees' sharp thorns.

"Any news of the Major?" Simon asked. He was standing close to me. But in the darkness I couldn't see his face.

I told him then everything I knew, including what I'd thought about Fergus Kennedy's death.

"By boat, you say? There are islands off the coast out here, but they might have gone anywhere by water, even to another village. He was blindfolded, he wouldn't know."

"He was lucky to have got away, Simon. He really believed they were going to kill him, throw him into the sea. He didn't know it of course, but if I'm right, that's just what they did to Fergus Kennedy."

"Only the currents brought him to where a fisherman spotted him. And that was a bit of bad luck. It might have been days—longer—before anyone realized that Kennedy was missing. And even then, unless someone came to the house looking, they would have no idea where he might have gone to paint. If his killers searched the house, they were looking for any sketches he might have made of a boat that the police or some of the villages might recognize."

"Eileen wants to leave as soon as possible, taking her mother with them. But she's right, Michael won't go until he knows the Major is safe. What if he's never found? Oh—"

A hare broke cover and went zigzagging across the meadow, startling both of us.

When the night was quiet again and we were sure the hare hadn't heard sounds we'd missed while talking, Simon told me, "I'll have to report him missing to the nearest garrison. The Army will take over the search. And they'll have a better idea of where to look, given Michael's experience. But are you sure that these people, whoever they are, mean to try an attack on the Army somewhere nearby?"

"I have no idea. But that's the only reason I can think of for them to have taken Michael *and* the Major. If they simply wanted to kill an Englishman, a sniper in the orchard or across the lane could have done it with far less trouble."

"But shooting either one of them would have brought the Army here, posthaste. If they simply go missing, and there's no body, it's harder to convince the Army to step in. Much less persuade them that this is a prelude to an attack. Whatever is being planned, it's cleverly done." He was quiet for a moment, then said, "Who in that house or the village has military training, other than Michael?"

"Terrence took part in the Rising. He was in Dublin. But military? I can't think of anyone. But you don't need to be in the Army in order to be a good strategist."

"True."

He was silent, thinking again. I waited. Letting him work out what I'd already had time to consider. "You're right, it must be a garrison they're after. The problem is, if we alert the Army, they'll come roaring in, and the ringleaders will disappear into the countryside. Free to plan something else, somewhere else. Arthur has already made his pass for tonight, but I'll want you on tomorrow's flight—"

Before I could tell Simon what I thought about that plan, he stiffened, then put a hand on my arm. Out of the corner of my eye, I saw the briefest flash of light, then it was gone. And then it was followed by another.

The searchers were in the spinney, on their way to the meadow. And the last thing we wanted was for them to stumble across the Traveler and the English Sister lurking behind the hawthorn clump.

Simon moved his hand to my shoulder, and both of us slowly

dropped into a crouch. I turned my face into his dark coat, and he lowered his head as well.

We could hear voices now, talking together as they came out of the spinney and started to cross the meadow. From the tone of the voices, they hadn't had any luck finding traces of the Major's captors. Had they really tried their best? For an English officer? But perhaps they would for Terrence.

They were tired, they hadn't been successful, and they were eager to reach their homes. None of them expected to find anything or anyone this close to the house. But they flashed their torches ahead of them as they walked, and for a breath-stopping moment, one beam swept over us—and passed on.

I felt Simon tense, then relax as we faded back into darkness. And then the searchers were climbing the stile and moving on toward the lane in front of the Flynn house. It was dark, quiet, and they stopped talking. Soon their footsteps faded away.

We stayed where we were, in the event there was a straggler or two still coming through the spinney. But the night belonged to us now, and to an owl, calling plaintively from somewhere among the trees.

And then I realized it wasn't an owl at all, but a signal. Two men materialized at the edge of the trees and stood there for several minutes. They had no torches, or if they had them, they didn't use them.

It occurred to me that they had been watching the search party. Very likely keeping an eye on their progress.

Simon whispered in my ear, "Recognize either of them?"

I had. I couldn't miss the tall one, the violinist. But the other was turned so that I could only see one shoulder and his back. Another of his friends? Or perhaps a better word was *co-conspirator*.

Finally they turned and went back the way they'd come.

"Interesting," Simon said in my ear. "If I'd had to name someone behind this, he'd have been my first choice."

Again we waited. When all was quiet, we got to our feet. My knees were stiff from crouching.

"Do you think the Army—someone—has a file about him? He's said to have been at the Rising," I asked.

"If he signed the Proclamation, there will be an order for his arrest on sight." He laughed, deep in his chest. "I have a duty to report the presence of Terrence Flynn."

"Will you?" I asked.

"Do you want me to do my duty?"

It was an odd question.

"Terrence is an annoying man. But he has kept his word, to protect me. I think he did everything he could to find Michael. That could well be why Michael wasn't killed where he'd been kept. Terrence would have known—guessed—who was behind the abduction. But if he fell out of the boat on their way back to the mainland, who would know for certain? They untied Michael. I think to be sure there would be no bonds if he was found by a fisherman. As Fergus was."

Simon took a deep breath. "Quietly pack your kit. When Arthur comes tomorrow night, he'll land. I'll disappear, once that's done, and report what we've learned."

"No. I won't go."

"Bess. You must. Don't you see that you're in danger? Your father was adamant. My first duty was to get you safely out of Ireland. They're married. Michael and Eileen. It's what you came for."

"I've got a duty to them—and to Ellis Dawson. The Major. I think if Eileen and her husband try to leave, they'll be killed as soon as they're on the road, away from Terrence and the house. And if no one tries to help him, the Major will be killed."

"I will deal with it—"

"You can't. Not alone. We'll need a boat, for one thing. There's a place beyond the orchard where we could meet it. If you could signal

Arthur, ask him to speak to the Colonel Sahib, have him arrange for a boat, if he could. There will be Eileen and Michael, of course. The Major, if he's still alive. And Eileen's mother. Five of us. You. Too many for Arthur to come for, it would take too long."

"Why are there no dogs in the house?" Simon asked suddenly.

"I—I hadn't really thought about it—"

"You've managed to come and go quietly. Is there someone who comes and goes in that house, without rousing the hounds?"

"Niall comes and goes," I said. "And so does Terrence. If anyone comes to visit Mrs. Flynn—if she's part of the conspiracy—they could do so quite easily. She sits by her window, watching everything. She could signal someone when it was safe to slip into the house. The stairs are just there, and her rooms are in the front of the house." I remembered something. "The Major told me not to trust Niall."

"I'll bear that in mind."

"Please don't ask Arthur to land tomorrow night. It's a risk, and for nothing. Can you signal him? In code?"

"You can't stay, Bess."

"I won't go," I replied stubbornly.

"You can't save the world."

"I can stop three—possibly four—murders. Terrence will help me get his family out of danger. And I'll ask him where they might have taken Michael. He knows the countryside. He may help us find the Major."

"You're damned trusting. He's a wanted man, Bess."

"There's a very good reason why he'll help me. And that's all that matters."

There was a change in Simon. He said, "If you say so." He began to move out of the shelter of the clump of trees. "It's late. You should go back to the house."

"I'll meet you here tomorrow night. And, Simon? That man, the one I call the violinist or the singer. If that *was* him tonight, at the edge of the spinney—and I'm certain it was—be careful, please. I don't think he has any scruples about killing. I have my little revolver. Do you need it?"

"I brought my own."

"I'm glad."

He couldn't see me back to the house. But he kept watch from the stile until I was safely back in the shadow of the house. The moon was just rising.

I wondered if the Major was watching it from wherever he was, and despairing of rescue.

I got into the house, up the stairs, and into the room I shared with Eileen, without being seen or disturbing anyone. Or so I thought until I heard a door shut, and footsteps on the stairs.

It was not Niall's door, or Terrence's. It sounded like the Major's—his was farthest along the passage, a guest room.

I raced to the window, but all I could see was a dark figure disappearing into the deeper shadows by the house wall.

If the Major had escaped, he'd have stayed in his room, not left it! Then who was in his room just now, when the house was quiet?

I hadn't lit the lamp in my room. And I knew where my own torch was. I reached for it, found it at once, then opened my door and stepped out into the silent passage. Moving carefully, keeping to the wall where the floorboards were less likely to squeak, I made my way to the Major's door.

I'd heard snoring as I passed the first bedroom, nearest mine, deep and rhythmic, impossible to mimic. I knew—how many wounded men had pretended to be asleep, when they hadn't wanted to have a wound dressed or be given more medicines? One giant Scot had had a stage snore that rattled the walls.

There was no sound from the next room. Was it occupied, someone alert and listening? It was possible that Terrence might be out meeting with the returning searchers.

I was at what I hoped was the Major's door. I reached for the knob, then pushed it gently open.

Keeping my torch beam low, so that it wouldn't flash across the windows, I scanned the room.

It was neat, a soldier's quarters. Everything in its place.

What were they after?

I kept looking. But nothing *appeared* to have been changed or moved or even touched. Nothing disturbed the tidiness. I'd lived in a soldier's world, where order mattered.

Frowning, I moved to the tall chest. On top, in front of the mirror, there were his brushes, nothing else.

In the top drawer were his shaving gear, the straight razor with an ivory handle, handkerchiefs, and other personal items. Although he hadn't worn his uniform, he would have carried his Army identification, but it wasn't there. A small silver double frame, like a book, with velvet backing lay in the back of the drawer, as if shoved there in haste. I drew it out. It was the sort a man might carry with him on his travels, with space for two photographs, one on each side. My father had one much like it, with my mother and me as a child inside.

In the left-hand frame there was a photograph of a handsome woman, straight-backed, her fair hair becomingly arranged, dressed in a pale green gown of the sort worn a generation ago to a dinner party. Three feathers, held together in a diamond pin, adorned her hair, and the other jewelry—elegant pearl necklaces and an ornate silver chain, several rings on her hands—looked like family heirlooms, worn for a special occasion. I knew, because my mother wore her mother's jewelry in the same way.

Someone with the skill to do it properly had tinted the photograph, giving life to the figure. And the woman's smile reminded me of the Major's. His mother, very likely.

There was nothing in the other frame.

His father? His fiancée, who had died in the influenza epidemic? We hadn't exchanged more than the briefest of family histories, the Major and I. I had wondered if he knew who my father was and had chosen not to bring it up. For which I was grateful. But now I had no idea who might have been in the other frame.

Why was that wanted?

I could understand taking the Major's military identification. It might prove useful. But why the other photograph?

Or had there ever been a photograph in that frame?

I was jumping to conclusions without any evidence to support them.

Going around the room, I looked in other drawers, bringing them out carefully in the small desk and in the armoire so that they made no noise. This wasn't the time to be fastidious about prying, I needed to know what was missing, if possible.

I came up with nothing else that might have been taken.

Making certain that the room was just as I'd found it, I turned off my torch and opened the door.

And Terrence Flynn was standing just outside of it, a frown on his face.

"I was just about to come in. I heard a noise."

But he couldn't have done. I had been very careful.

Before I could answer, he went on. "What were you looking for?"

"I think someone had been here, searching. I couldn't imagine what he was after. I wanted to see if anything was missing."

He looked me up and down. "You're fully dressed. At this hour."

I gave him an exasperated look in response. "I hardly wished to go exploring in my nightgown. Anyone could be lurking in the passage."

"What's missing?"

"I'm not really sure," I hedged. "Would he carry his military identi-fication, if he wasn't going out?"

"I don't know. I didn't know him that well."

Didn't. Past tense, used for the dead. I felt cold suddenly.

"Well. Either whoever it was got what he came for, or he didn't. Ei-ther way, it doesn't help us very much, searching for the Major," I said, still cross with Terrence.

"Are you certain someone was in the house?"

"I was awake, worrying, hoping there was some news. At first I thought it might be you coming in. Instead, it was someone going out. I glimpsed him for a moment."

Oh dear, that wasn't very wise of you, Bess!

I shook my head. "I assume it was a man. Just a fleeting glimpse doesn't tell you very much. And the house doors are never locked."

He said, "Go to bed. There's nothing more to be done tonight."

And he waited, watching while I went back to my room, went in, and shut the door.

I slipped to the window, to see if Terrence had gone out to verify my story.

He hadn't, even though I stood there, well hidden by the curtains, for half an hour.

Unable to sleep, I lay there, staring at the ceiling until the gray light of dawn crept in the window. I found it hard to read Terrence. He was accustomed to being circumspect, and there must have been times when his life depended on his ability to hide what he was thinking or feeling.

What's more, Simon wasn't himself. I couldn't pinpoint it, but ever since he had come home from Scotland, he'd been—different. The only spark of the Simon I knew—thought I knew so well—had been some-thing he'd said to me in the spinney, when I'd threatened whoever was coming toward me with my revolver, boldly claiming I knew how to use it. Which was of course the truth.

He'd replied, *Well, I damned well hope you do. I taught you, after all.*

Had he proposed to someone there—it was what our maid Iris had claimed was the reason he'd gone off to Scotland in the first place—and been turned down?

Somehow I couldn't believe it was a broken heart.

Like my father, Simon never took out on those around him whatever it was that he was feeling. I'd seen the Colonel Sahib return from a hard-fought battle where there were casualties on both sides, and speak to the house staff as if nothing had happened. Even though we'd lost good men. It was locked up inside. He'd already told the survivors what he felt—that they had served King and Country well, and that he was proud of them—and that he mourned their fallen comrades just as they did. It was where such things ought to be said.

Then what had Simon locked up inside?

Did my mother know? He'd have given his life for her if asked. I knew that much about him. I didn't know why, but she always turned my questions aside.

Perhaps she'd guessed what was troubling him. And said nothing.

Tossing and turning, I finally got up, dressed for the day, and went downstairs to put the kettle on.

A cup of tea couldn't provide any answers, but it could provide solace.

As I waited for the kettle to boil, I found myself thinking that Simon had always treated me like his little sister. Argued with me, ordered me about, protected me, and was in many ways my best friend. I'd always thought I was his.

Then what was it he couldn't confide in me?

CHAPTER FOURTEEN

WHEN I LOOKED in on Eileen and Michael, they were asleep. From what I could see of his face, he was better—less feverish, the cuts and bruises beginning to fade. That was a good sign, if we were to walk as far as the sea and a waiting boat. But I would have to make certain he got on his feet soon. The hidden damage, the blows to his body, his legs, had begun to heal as well, or so I hoped. Now he needed to regain his strength.

Closing the door quietly, I set about making the porridge, and taking one of the eggs in the pantry to cook for myself. I had been in Ireland a week—I'd arrived on a Thursday, and here it was Thursday once more. Eileen hadn't been married then, and now she was, but I was still in Ireland . . .

I was just finishing my breakfast when the outer door opened, and the young girl who helped in the kitchen when she could slipped in and stopped short when she saw me.

"Oh. Ma told me to come half an hour ago, but I dawdled. I'm sorry, Miss."

"I can fend for myself," I told her with a smile. "I was just about to start breakfast for the Mrs. Flynns."

"I'll see to it," she said, taking down the apron from its hook by the door. Then lowering her voice, she said, "If you please—is it true that the English Major has been taken? Like Mr. Sullivan was?"

When I didn't answer at once, she said quickly, "It's the talk of the village, Miss."

I could imagine that it was.

"What are they saying?" I asked, trying to sound merely curious.

She shrugged. "I dunno. But Madame won't like it, she never wishes to be talked about. She told me that when first I came here. And it's not like I took the Major away myself, is it?"

"I can't imagine where he's being hidden. Or who took him. Or why. It's a great mystery to me. I mean to say, I understand that no one cares for the English. But I thought he and I had been very careful not to upset anyone with our presence. After all, we wouldn't have come if Eileen Flynn hadn't asked us."

"Is it true you were with her on that ship that went down?"

"I was."

"Ma remembers when she was let out of hospital and was brought home. She said her limbs looked something terrible, and nobody thought she'd ever walk again. Mr. Terrence took such great care of her, in spite of being hunted. Night and day he was with her. He made her walk, it's what the doctor said she must do. Back and forth, up and down. She'd cry, begging him to stop, but he wouldn't. 'Six more lengths,' he'd say. 'You must try.' And soon she could do it without his arm, but he was there, close to her, fearful that she would fall. My mother was Cook for the house, she saw it."

He'd been in love with her even then.

Bringing her back to the subject, I said, "With Michael, they sent out search parties, but they never found him. Yet he walked home. How could they have missed him?"

"I don't know, Miss. I don't think anybody does."

She set about preparing trays for the Mrs. Flynns, and I took my cup of tea out to the stables, on the chance that Terrence was there. But it was Niall who was mucking out.

He looked up when he heard me speak to one of the mares—the one I had ridden—and said, "If you are looking for your Major, he isn't here."

I left without answering him.

When I started back to the house after walking as far as the stile, Mrs. Flynn the Elder was talking to someone, clearly angry. I veered away from the front door, because I could see the priest, Father O'Halloran, standing in the entry at the foot of the stairs, looking up, presumably feeling the brunt of her temper. As I was about to round the corner of the house, I heard him say, "I tell you, this is not a reflection on you—"

"Then you're a fool," she said—I could hear the contempt in her voice.

I lingered for a moment, just out of sight, for she was continuing to give him a piece of her mind. "He should have been dealt with as soon as he showed his face out here."

"It was too dangerous. *He's* dangerous."

"Of course he is. That's why he should never have been allowed to show his face in this house."

I heard a door slam somewhere in the house. I wasn't sure whether it was Mrs. Flynn ending the conversation with a pointed show of disgust—or the priest leaving, letting her see that her behavior toward him was unacceptable.

Who were they talking about? The Major? Because they believed he had the authority of the Army behind him? But he didn't—he'd told me as much.

But now someone needed him, if I was right, to confirm what Michael had told them.

I was already around the far corner of the house and halfway to the kitchen door when Niall stepped out.

I stopped, and he said sharply, "Where have you been?"

"Walking," I told him, continuing toward him. "I need the exercise."

"Stay close," he said. "You know what happens to people who stray about."

And he walked on to the stable yard.

I didn't take that as a kindness. Or grave concern for my welfare. It was a warning.

Had Niall been the other man speaking to the violinist in the dark, at the edge of the spinney?

I couldn't be sure, his outline hadn't been as clear, standing closer to the trees than his companion.

I watched him go, then went inside. The girl Molly seemed tense as I came into the kitchen, glancing nervously at me, as if expecting the devil himself to come through the door.

Not surprising, given the shouting match between the priest and Mrs. Flynn. Or possibly the presence of Niall, who always seemed to be cross in the mornings, had disturbed her.

I said cheerfully, "Fresh air is a lovely way to begin the day."

But she just agreed with me and seemed very happy when I went on up the stairs instead of staying in the kitchen.

I could hardly wait for nightfall, to speak to Simon. I looked in on Eileen and Michael several times—she had changed his bandages, and I didn't stay. I looked in on Mrs. Flynn the Younger to bring her a dinner tray, and managed to avoided Terrence when I heard his voice from the stairs. Mrs. Flynn the Elder was in a black mood. She glimpsed me in passing and glowered. I was sure she would be delighted to see the back of me.

No word about the Major in the morning or later in the afternoon. I'd even resorted to asking Molly if she had heard any news, before she went home between dinner and supper.

Looking frightened, she shook her head. "They've searched along the coast, and the fishermen know to watch for a body. But there's a whisper going about that he slipped away in the night, to return to England."

"That can't be true. For one thing, his clothes and personal items are still in his room. So I've been told by Terrence," I quickly amended. "Why would he leave without his belongings?"

Still, I could see too that such a rumor was useful in casting doubt on whether or not he was truly missing.

And certainly Molly was unconvinced. "That's to throw us off," she suggested. "He's an English officer, he can buy what he needs in London."

I didn't say anything about the bloodstain on the stone or the marks where he must have been dragged to where a horse was waiting.

"Well, I refuse to believe such a story. And you shouldn't, either. After all, you've met the Major. Do you really think he would do such a thing, and not say goodbye?"

Nothing I could say seemed to change her mind, and I let it go. But when Terrence came in an hour later, looking tired and more than a little cross, I told him what Molly had told me.

"There was much the same rumor about Michael. That he'd changed his mind about the wedding and slipped away, rather than face it like a man and tell us the marriage was off. Another rumor had it that my grandmother and Michael had had words, and she frightened him off. I think half the guests at the wedding had come to see how Eileen would take the disappointment of the groom not appearing."

And instead they had seen him for themselves. Bloody wounds and all.

"Who's behind this sort of talk?" I asked him. "It must be someone who doesn't wish the family well."

"I don't know," he said, angry and trying to conceal it. "There are those who claim that after the Rising failed—after the leaders were condemned or sentenced—we didn't do enough to avenge them. God knows we wanted to, but the English had us under their heel. The bloodshed would have been far worse, the next time."

"The war is over, the treaty has been signed—not by everyone, of course, but by enough to make it valid. We can concentrate on Ireland now. Don't the hotheads realize that England can bring all its might down on them, if they aren't careful? Don't they think England will?"

"God knows." He shook his head. "I doubt it. And the northern counties have stronger ties to England. They're mostly Protestant, and they want nothing to do with an Irish and Catholic state. It's a sticking point. But Ireland won't be satisfied with half measures. Wait and see." He started toward the stairs. "We go out again at first light. But don't hold your breath. We never found Michael. He found himself."

After saying good night to Michael and Eileen, I went up to my room and mended the hem of one of Eileen's aprons, for lack of anything else to do until it was late enough to meet Simon. And finally, however much I'd willed them to move faster, the hands on my little watch pointed to half an hour after midnight.

Changing to my own dark dress, I slipped out of my room, down the steps, and out of the house.

The night was quiet. I kept to the shadows as much as I could, and then faced that long walk across the lawns to the stile. I'd just climbed over it and was about to turn toward the meadow when something made a sound behind me.

My heart leaped into my throat, and I stopped short just as something heavy pushed me hard in the middle of my back, nearly knocking me off my feet.

I knew what it was almost at once, but that didn't stop the shock quickly enough. I clamped my jaw shut, cutting off a cry.

And the mare that I'd ridden several times blew, in greeting.

They had moved the horses to this meadow, allowing them to stay out and graze.

As I reached up and patted her soft nose, I wondered if they had been put here to prevent the Captain from landing and taking any of us away before whatever they were planning took place. Or was I being too imaginative? It was possible that it was only a matter of moving the horses here to graze in fresh grass.

I gently pushed her aside, started to leave a handkerchief on the stile, saw that Simon had done it for me, and then hurried toward the clump of hawthorn trees.

Simon came forward to greet me.

"You weren't followed?"

"No. But the horses startled me. Terrence didn't say anything about moving them."

"I hadn't expected them, but they were on the far side of the meadow earlier. Are you up to walking?"

"Yes."

"I want to see where this boat could come in."

"I think I can find it again."

We set out, not speaking until we'd made our way across the meadow, and by a roundabout way that couldn't be seen from the house or outbuildings, we reached the orchard and moved on beyond.

When it was safe to speak, Simon told me about last night.

"When I left you, I went to the house that belonged to Fergus Kennedy. I was able to verify that part of Sergeant Sullivan's account. There are several inlets where a small boat could come and go without bringing attention to it. Or its cargo. But where it went after reaching the sea, I don't know. There are small islands out there, a number of them. I don't know how many are occupied."

"Did you look into the Kennedy house?"

"I did. He was a fine artist. It's a shame to see what has been done to his paintings. There was anger at work there. Even though the intent must have been to find out if he'd sketched the boat the night they must have taken Michael out. Most likely, he'd only seen it, and there hadn't been time for him to sketch."

"He was doing a series of portraits of the heroes of the Rising. For the day when a museum or memorial could be built."

"I recognized several faces in spite of the torn canvases. From newspaper accounts of the Rising and the trials."

The sound of the sea came to us, and the distinctive scent of salt water. Around us, the reeds whispered and clicked together in the light wind. Cresting a slight rise, we could see the white line of waves rolling in. It was quite beautiful, in a way. We stopped, to look at it.

And then we had to be practical. There was the long walk back to be considered.

A low roar reached us, growing louder. Looking up, I saw that it was Arthur, flying over us, high above. We waved, but I didn't think he saw us—or perhaps didn't know who we were. But it was heartening to see him there, a fleeting reminder of home, where all this began, around the dining room table . . .

Turning back to me, Simon pointed. "The sea is a little rough here to bring in a boat. Is there an inlet nearby? We have to take into account that it might have to wait or that the weather turns."

"Or even if we are delayed," I said thoughtfully. I'd come here on horseback. It was far longer on foot—or so it seemed. Getting Michael this far might be a problem.

As if he'd read my mind, he said, "I saw donkeys in a paddock behind the barn. We could put Michael on one of them, if necessary."

That was the old Simon I knew, the friend who could share my thoughts as I shared his.

But I said only, "A good idea. I'll go out there and make certain they know me. I think there are some carrots in the pantry."

"Yes, we don't want them braying in alarm. Let's find that inlet."

And we did, not much farther along. A finger of the sea that had cut into the land. I'd seen the map. The west coast of Ireland was threaded with these inlets, like a piece of cloth that had frayed with wear. Here it was the Atlantic that had eaten away the land, except where rocky cliffs held it off as long as possible.

This one wasn't very deep—we explored it for less than a mile. There was a farmhouse at the end of it, the roof long swept away by the winds, leaving jagged edges where the storms had eaten at the walls. A windbreak of trees protected it, bent by the wind. The windows were a dark space indicating neither light inside nor people. Even the door was gone. Another victim of the potato famine that had killed so many and driven so many more to leave Ireland for any country that would take them in?

I felt a wave of sadness. The Irish had very good reasons for hating us, and the famine was one of them. We could have helped—and didn't.

"What is it?" Simon asked, trying to read my expression.

I didn't tell him. Once I might have done, but now I said only, "I was wondering if Michael had been held in such a place as this old ruin? Or the Major, now. Do you think they took him to the same place? Or found a new hideaway?"

"If they're clever, they'll find a new one. But this house might provide shelter for us."

Where the end of the inlet was clogged now with reeds and grasses, there were signs where a boat had once been drawn up. Simon studied it carefully. "I can bring a boat in here, and hide it. The problem is, we'll need strong rowers when we reach the sea, to keep us from capsizing in the waves. God knows what condition Dawson will be in."

"That leaves you and me, possibly Eileen."

"Yes. I don't know if that will be enough to keep us afloat." He didn't seem to be very taken with my idea of a boat. But how else were we going to get everyone out?

Thinking aloud, I said, "I wish Terrence would come with us. He would be able to row."

Simon turned to me. If he hadn't been able to read my face earlier in this light, I couldn't read his either.

"Do you want him to come?"

Nor could I quite decipher his tone of voice. In anyone but Simon I might have thought it was simple jealousy. Perhaps he didn't trust Terrence and was in a roundabout way asking if I did.

And so I answered with what I thought was amusement. "Well, I don't know what we'd do with him, once we were safely away. You could always turn him in to the Army. There might even be a reward."

If I had struck him, he wouldn't have been as shocked.

He turned and strode away, leaving me standing there.

I realized I'd hurt him somehow—hurt him deeply. But I didn't know what it was I'd said. Or worse, how to mend it.

I felt frightened suddenly.

Simon had always been there—well, so it had seemed to me. When my parents had taken him in hand, a tall anger-ridden recruit, he and I had become fast friends. I couldn't have had a brother who was closer. Always there, sometimes chiding me—sometimes outright scolding me—but always protecting me. Teaching me how to ride and how to shoot. We'd lived in a hostile country for some years, and yet I'd always felt safe. The Colonel Sahib and Simon were always there. I knew my father cared for him like the son he'd never had. The bond between them was as strong as any blood tie. And I thought that Simon too had felt as if he were part of our family. We'd been angry with each other many times, but it had not been hurtful. Both of us were strong-willed. I was as stubborn as he was. But he had never frightened me the way he had just now. As if I'd cut to the quick, and worse still, meant to.

My mouth was dry as I hurried after him. What could I say? I didn't even know how, because I didn't know why I had to say something.

When I caught him up, along a bit of strand between the reeds and the tide line, I said, "Simon, what is it? What have I done?"

He kept walking, but he might as well have been miles away, and I was here alone. I felt cold, lost.

I reached out and touched his arm, forcing him to stop.

"Please. What's wrong?" I could feel tears thickening my voice.

He looked down at me. "It's very late," he said after a moment. "I hadn't realized how late."

For some reason I didn't think he was talking about the hands of the clock.

And then he added, in the tone of voice I was so used to, "Come along. It's a long walk back to the house."

Instead of feeling reassured, I was even more perplexed. But I smiled and turned. We walked most of the way in what passed for a companionable silence until we had reached the orchard. There he stopped.

"Can you make your way from here? It's not safe for you to be seen with me. It isn't done."

I knew he was right. I shouldn't be consorting with a Traveler. Matron would have an apoplexy. But I didn't want to leave with things unsettled between us.

There were clouds overhead, but in the east there was the faintest lightening of the sky. And as I looked up at him, for the first time I saw the bruise high on his cheekbone.

"You've been in a fight."

"The singer—violinist as you call him. His name is Padriac Murphy. Paddy to you. For some reason he took a dislike to the parrot. We had words. It turned physical. My impression was, he was showing off for the onlookers. If I hadn't fought him, they would have run me out of town."

"Be careful. The Major called him Cassius."

"I'd agree there. And he would have stabbed Caesar in the back."

"Watch yours."

He nodded, and was gone. But I knew he'd keep watch until I reached the house.

I walked on through the high grass in the orchard and was soon at the end of the stable block. The donkeys were grazing in the paddock. They looked up as I passed. But I had no sugar lumps or carrots to offer them just now. Moving on, I was just passing the stables when a shadow moved out of deeper shadows and spoke.

I thought at first that it must be Niall, or Terrence.

"Where have you been?"

It was Granny—the senior Mrs. Flynn.

And she had her cane with her. I wouldn't put it past her to use it.

"I could ask you the same thing."

"Don't be pert. It doesn't become you."

I sighed, trying to draw her away from the stable—and by extension, the orchard—and closer to the house.

"I couldn't sleep. I'm worried about the Major—when you see what was done to Michael, there's very good reason to fear for him."

She cut me short. "I heard voices."

I laughed. "I was talking to the donkeys. But they wouldn't come to be petted."

"Why the orchard?"

"I intended to go to the meadow, but the horses are there. I didn't want to disturb them."

"Afraid of horses, are you?" It was a typical taunt.

"Certainly not—" I began, then realized that she was trying to draw me away from the question about why she herself was out at this hour. In the growing light, color was still washed out, but I could see that she was dressed in dark clothing, and her hair was pinned up, as if she were joining us for dinner or planning to go into the village. And so I said, turning as if I were planning to go to the stalls, "—I'm sorry, is there a horse needing medical attention? I don't know much about animal illnesses—"

"Oh, do stop," she broke in. "I heard a noise in the stables. A fox, as it turned out."

She marched off toward the house and the kitchen garden door, cane thumping. I walked just a little behind her.

Who had she been meeting in the stable block? It couldn't have been Niall or Terrence, because they would have come to her room if she wished to speak privately with them. And was he still there, waiting for us to go away?

I was impatient now to reach my room and look out, in time to see who was leaving. But she couldn't walk as fast as I could. And I couldn't hurry past her to reach the house sooner.

All I could do, then, was to hope that Simon had been near enough to hear what had passed between Mrs. Flynn and me, and that he would watch the stables to see who it was.

We finally reached the house, and it occurred to me that perhaps whoever she had met might have left before I got to the stables, and her confrontation was to keep me from seeing him on the lane, on his way back to the village.

It couldn't have been her grandsons—she had had words with the priest—I couldn't imagine her having anything in common with that man Paddy Murphy.

Who had come to the house in the dead of night?

The thought followed me up the stairs and into my room, as Mrs. Flynn shut her door with more force than was necessary.

I hurried to my window, but the light was growing, and even though I watched for half an hour, no one came out of the stables or across the lawns.

Giving up, I went to bed, but not to rest. I watched the sunrise fill my window with a golden glow.

What had changed Simon so much?

What had I done to hurt him as I did?

I went over and over it, and couldn't find the trigger. Yet it had been there, I hadn't imagined it.

When I finally began to slip into a light sleep, the house was waking up.

I wouldn't see Simon again until tonight.

Chapter Fifteen

Habit brought me out of a restless sleep at seven o'clock. I got ready for the day, all the while hoping it would bring us news of Ellis Dawson's whereabouts. Both for his sake and for ours. I was ready to leave Killeighbeg. The wedding was over, and that was what had brought me here. But I couldn't leave him to his fate, whatever that might be. Michael had lived, through his own efforts. The intent had been to kill him, once the boat was far enough out to sea. Just as they'd done with Fergus Kennedy.

Breakfast passed without event, but when I looked in on Michael, Eileen told me anxiously that his fever had risen in the night. Not terribly high, but enough for concern.

I suspected that one of the deeper cuts had become infected. That was always a risk with wounds, however they might have occurred.

It was on his shoulder, the edges red and puffy, and I tried to drain it, but that didn't seem to help.

"He needs to see a doctor, Eileen. Neither my skills nor yours seem to be making a difference."

"You were a surgical Sister, Bess. I was only a ward Sister. Surely you can do more for him? At least as much as a country doctor. Besides, the nearest one is miles away."

"Yes, I know. He really should have a surgeon look at that wound.

In Dublin or perhaps in Cork." I was about to suggest London as well, but at the last minute changed my mind. It was best not even to hint at escape.

We continued to argue. I understood Eileen's fear. A deep infection could kill. And she had only just begun to feel that Michael was safe.

He'd been listening all the while as we discussed his care.

Now he said, the weakness in his voice a reflection of the weakness in his body, "She's right, Eileen. We need to leave here. As soon as possible."

"I don't see how. Not until you're stronger. And now this—I wish I'd never insisted on being wed in Ireland. I wish I'd agreed to marry in London as soon as you left the Army."

"I know," he said, comforting her. "But that's past history now, my love. It's the future, not the past, we need to consider. Let's make our plans and go. The shoulder is fine, it's only a minor setback."

Eileen bit her lip. "What about my mother? And there's Major Dawson—you said you couldn't leave without him."

"Yes, I did say that. But they'll find him any day now. I got away. He's a clever man, the Major. He'll make it as well." But there wasn't the ring of certainty in his voice.

"Did you tell him anything about your own capture?" I asked.

Michael shook his head. "I should have tried. God knows. But I didn't think anyone would dare touch him. I just didn't *think*."

He was sitting up, and it was wearing down his strength.

I touched Eileen's arm. "Let's not worry him about the future just now. Has he had his breakfast?"

"Yes, an hour ago. I prepared it. Molly hadn't come." She plumped the pillows at his back. "Is there any more aspirin? That might help?"

During the war, many doctors had been very liberal with their use of aspirin, but some patients had had problems with it, and other doctors had cut back on doses.

But I thought it wouldn't do any harm to give him a bit this morning, and see if it would break his fever. Still, in the back of my mind was the memory from the war, where shrapnel and bullets often carried a bit of filthy uniform cloth or metal fragments deep into a wound. And it would seem to heal on the surface, only to fester from infection we couldn't see. Nothing short of surgery could reach it. Michael might well have the same deep infection, only from the boat, sleeping rough, even from the horse, and it too could spread if it wasn't treated. I wasn't about to attempt surgery here on the front room carpet.

"He needs a regular bed," Eileen was saying. "Where he can sleep properly, and people aren't coming in and out, waking him."

I'd been wondering when she would remember that I was staying in her room. The married couple would have been off on their honeymoon—the trip across to England—as soon as the wedding breakfast was over and they'd changed into their traveling clothes. I wouldn't have been in the way, as I was now . . .

"I'm not up to climbing the stairs," Michael put in, glancing at me before turning to his wife. "That leg is still hurting. I don't think it's a good idea yet."

She was all concern.

And then her mother knocked at the door, and came in to see how the patient was faring.

I used that as an excuse to go and fetch the aspirin.

Terrence stopped me on the stairs. "The search this morning hasn't found anything. I don't know where else to look."

I replied, "You've looked everywhere?"

"We have." He said it tersely, as if I'd doubted his honesty.

"Then perhaps the Major's not out here, on this bit of land that Killeighbeg sits on. Perhaps they've taken him somewhere else."

"Where else?"

"I don't know. How many fingers jut out into the sea, just like this one? There must be a dozen? More? Aren't there islands offshore? Couldn't they have taken him farther away, knowing how thoroughly you'd be searching? After all, they must have known you'd turn this part of the county upside down to find Michael."

Slightly mollified, he said, "There are people on the larger islands. You can't simply arrive with a prisoner in your midst and ask for houseroom to hold him in."

"What about the smaller ones, that aren't inhabited?"

"There's no shelter on most of them. Birds nest there. That's about it."

"How do you reach them?"

"There's a small boat that makes the journey on an irregular basis. Taking mail—such as there is—and goods out, bringing back the ill, if need be."

"It was a thought," I told him. "He can't just have vanished. He has to be somewhere. And how long has it been? What are they doing to him? If they were holding him for ransom, to pay for their wild schemes, surely we'd have heard by now?" And the Captain would have dropped another note, if the Guards had been contacted with demands. My father would have heard about it. "Why else did they take him?" I waited to see how he would answer me.

"I don't know." But I believed he had a fairly decent idea. Terrence Flynn was nobody's fool.

"What does Michael say about where he was taken? I've asked any number of times, and he tells me he has no recollection. Is he lying to me?"

"Why should he?" I countered.

He swore in Gaelic.

"I can't fight an unseen enemy," he said. "I did my damnedest to bring Michael back, and I failed. I'm still not convinced that anyone in the village had a hand in it. I know most of them. I know where they stand on— matters."

I took a chance then. "The man who was singing when you took me to the pub that first day. I didn't care for him then, and neither did you. Does he live here in the village?"

"No, he claims he's from County Mayo. He says there's a price on his head. That he escaped from Dublin as the Rising collapsed. But I knew most of those who were with us. And I don't remember him at all." He hesitated, then said, "I'm told he's not well. Will you have a look at him? It can't hurt."

He'd looked well enough when Simon and I saw him at the edge of the spinney. But since then he'd tangled with Simon.

"What seems to be the trouble?"

"He was in a fight with that Traveler. And got the worst of it," Terrence said pensively. "I might just offer the services of Michael's nursing Sister. Do you have the courage to go with me if he agrees?"

Simon wouldn't care for it. Nor my father. But I said, "I will, yes."

"I was going up to sleep for an hour. Instead, I'll go back to the village. Be ready, in case."

And then he was gone, down the stairs with what appeared to be renewed energy.

Sometimes something to do was the best medicine for hopelessness.

I waited in my room for Terrence to come back. I heard the kitchen door open and Molly's voice as she spoke to someone inside. Niall went out to the stables. And I saw Eileen walking in the kitchen garden, her mind clearly on anything but the vegetables growing in their tidy beds. Who took care of these beds? At home, in Somerset, we had a gardener who saw to the gardens, under my mother's watchful eye.

Molly seemed to be the only servant in the house. I'd ask Terrence about that again, when—if—he came for me.

And then he was tapping on my door, just when I was tired of waiting and was about to go back down the stairs.

"He's agreeable."

I collected Eileen's kit—it was often in my room, and I suddenly remembered that I was to give Michael an aspirin.

"I must stop in the kitchen for a moment," I told Terrence. "It's best if you wait for me outside."

He turned and left. I followed, filled a glass with water from the pitcher, and took the aspirin and water in to the patient.

Eileen was asleep on the sofa against the wall, her breathing deep and regular. But Michael hadn't been asleep, and when he looked up at me there was something in his expression that had nothing to do with his wounds. He turned his head away quickly, hoping that I hadn't seen it.

Making certain that Eileen was really asleep, I knelt beside the pallet.

"What is it?" I whispered, bending toward him.

"What is what?" He offered me a smile, but it looked more like a grimace.

"If there is something on your mind—you won't heal, Michael, until you can rest. Body and spirit."

He closed his eyes. "I-I can't be certain—it was probably only a dream."

"Tell me. Let me decide."

I expected him to say that he hadn't held out against his captors' questions as strongly as he'd let us believe, and he was ashamed. But I was wrong.

"As they were—they pushed me into the boat, my head struck the thwart. But I remember—there was someone on the slight rise a little distance away. The moon was just setting out at sea. We must have been silhouetted against it. They—they were worried about the man, that he'd seen us. My head was swimming, but I tried to shout to him, and they hit me again. When I came to my senses, they were arguing—one said something about waiting, the other said they couldn't chance it, that he would have to die. I thought at first they meant me, but then the other man added, 'I know who he is. When I've left you, I'll take care of it myself. He will trust me.'" He lifted an arm to cover his eyes. "They were talking about the man on the rise. And when I tried to shout for help, I put his life at risk. He must have seen us, Bess. And if they killed him, it was my fault. Mine—but I was desperate, I didn't *think*—"

In that dark room, curtains tightly drawn against the bright sunlight, hearing his account in broken whispers, I could almost picture the scene as two men manhandled a third into a boat. And another man stood on the rise, uncertain what it meant. "Did you hear a name? Anything to identify him?"

"No—yes." He took his arm away from his face and clutched at my hand. "The first man laughed and said something like I never liked his work, anyway."

And the next evening, Fergus Kennedy was found floating in the sea. He'd seen Michael being shoved into the boat—at that distance he couldn't have possibly recognized anyone. Still, tomorrow the world would be searching for Michael, and the man on the rise would start to think about what he'd witnessed, and wonder. Would he have come into Killeighbeg and told someone, if he'd lived? There was no answer to that. But the men who had abducted Michael couldn't be sure . . .

It fit. All too well. Fergus Kennedy standing there—watching the moon set, possibly even doing sketches for a painting later—just in the wrong place. A danger to the men in the boat, all the same. Had ransacking the croft only been to cover up the real reason?

I couldn't tell Michael what I believed. But it made sense, it was what we'd suspected—and it was proof that Fergus Kennedy had been murdered.

Instead I shook my head, and whispered, "Even if it really happened, even if you didn't dream it, you couldn't possibly have been responsible. If they believed he'd seen them—even if you'd never cried out, don't you see?—his fate was already sealed. Besides, you can't even be sure he heard you. But he saw *them*. And if he'd tried the next day to go to the Constabulary or to tell someone what he'd seen, they'd have cut their losses and killed you too."

"I can't be sure!" The strain in his voice was still there. "But what you're saying—it makes sense. Now I don't know what to believe."

"There's nothing you can do until you're stronger. Let it go. I'll see what I can discover. Meanwhile, you must rest."

"Yes. All right," he agreed, reluctantly. "I'm grateful, Bess."

"Here's the aspirin. It will help a little. I have to be careful how much laudanum I give you, until I'm sure what is hurt. I'll leave it beside you, shall I?" He nodded, and I whispered as I got to my feet, "Don't say anything to Eileen. It will only worry her."

"No." He caught my hand again. "In the war we always knew we could talk to the Sisters. No matter what. You must know that."

I smiled, for his sake, and slipped out.

There was no time even to think about what he'd just told me.

Terrence was waiting impatiently.

We walked on toward the village, and as we were passing the church, I asked Terrence what had become of the staff at the house.

"You and Niall work in the stables, we take turns making meals or you bring something from the pub. Molly does the washing up, and the kitchen garden is tidy, apparently without the touch of human hands."

"They tolerated Eileen, even though she was a nursing Sister for the

English. But when Michael came, the staff left. Except for Molly, whose mother needs the money she earns."

"Will they come back, once Michael is gone?"

"God knows."

We were walking down the lane toward the village and its tiny harbor. I'd expected to be taken to the pub, where I thought Paddy Murphy was staying. Instead we stopped at a cottage on the edge of the village. Detached from it, as was the custom, given the risk of fire, stood the small blacksmith shop. One of Paddy Murphy's friends was working the bellows, the orange flames shooting up as the smith was frowning over something. The clang of hammer on metal was loud.

Terrence said, "A distant cousin of the Murphys. And not the happiest of men to take in the likes of Padriac."

We came up to the door and it opened.

An older woman dressed all in black glared at me, but allowed the two of us to enter. I was surprised to find us in a large kitchen, a table to one side, and a dresser against the back wall. I glimpsed doorways at either end of the room, possibly bedrooms. I expected her to point to one of them. Instead she gestured toward a set of steps leading up from the left-hand wall.

"In the loft," she said, and turned her back on us.

We climbed rickety stairs up to the loft, and there was Paddy Murphy, lying on a bed of none-too-clean blankets.

He looked terrible, his face so pale it looked gray under the growth of beard. And it wasn't the marks of his fight with Simon that were affecting him, although I could clearly see bruising and cuts on his face, while his knuckles were beginning to heal a bit.

Simon would never hurt a man deliberately, not even to stay in Killeighbeg a few days longer, for my sake. He was tall, strong, had a long reach, and had fought hand to hand in India and the trenches. He would know when enough was enough. Broken ribs, damaged spleen, head injury, bruised kidneys—I could ignore the possibility of any of those.

Paddy Murphy still had the strength to glare at me as I came across the loft to kneel by him.

"What seems to be the trouble?"

"That damned Romany has poisoned me."

"What?" It was the last thing I'd expected.

"They're good at it." His mouth twisted.

"How did he do it? And where is this Romany?"

"It had to be the drink. He bought me a brandy when it was over." He grimaced, whether in pain or in anger, I couldn't tell. "I'll kill him, see if I don't, when I'm on my feet again. Bury him with that damned parrot in his mouth."

"What are your symptoms?" I persisted. Because whatever was wrong, it was imperative that I find out—if he died, whatever the reason, Simon would be blamed.

"I vomited as if my very gut was coming up into my throat. I've never felt anything like it. Now I can't keep anything down."

"Any other symptoms?"

"Damn it, woman, isn't that enough?" He stirred restlessly.

In my kit was an emetic, to be used only in emergencies. But I didn't have my kit. And I'd used what little I carried while I was in Paris during the Peace Talks.

I opened Eileen's kit, and there was a small bottle in one of the pockets. I held it up, trying to judge what was left in it.

It was nearly empty. But when I opened the cap, I could see that it was wet inside, not dried up from long disuse.

Of course I couldn't be sure. But there were labels on every vial and bottle in my kit. And in Eileen's. No one could mistake a bottle for anything but what was written on the label.

Who else would have such a thing as an emetic? I didn't know if a

Traveler's caravan contained herbs and other remedies. Including a few that weren't in a doctor's kit. But if this man died . . .

I said bracingly, "You've eaten something you shouldn't. Fish—shellfish—chicken—they can make you very ill if they're off. And being sick is the way you know."

I wasn't at all sure what was troubling him. I had no way to test anything. Sisters worked in hospitals or aid stations. We had access to whatever we needed. Not out here, on the very edge of the continent. But for Simon's sake, I had to take away the very idea of poison.

"I ate a fish in sauce . . ." He gagged at the very thought of it. "It tasted fine."

"Yes, it often does, but the meat is starting to spoil. Perhaps," I suggested, "it had already begun to go, and that's why the cook added a sauce."

"It was the drink, I tell you."

"One can't get food poisoning from brandy. Too much and you're ill for quite another reason entirely. How much did you drink?"

"The one glass."

"Well, if you wish to blame the brandy rather than the fish, I have no objection. But it's medically impossible, and anyone who knows that will laugh at you."

He looked up at Terrence, standing just behind me. "This was a waste of time. Take her away."

"You will feel as if you are dying," I said. "It comes with the bad fish. But you aren't, you know," I told him frankly. "You'll be able to hold food by tonight. Meanwhile, you must drink a little tea from time to time. Your body needs fluids. No milk, a little sugar if they have it here. And dry toast to dip in it. Every hour. You won't take much at first, but your stomach will begin to accept it after a while. Nothing else until tomorrow morning. Even then, you mustn't eat too much for several days."

He turned his face away. I thought, he wants to cause trouble for the Traveler.

"If you don't listen to what I'm telling you, you won't get your strength back anytime soon. I've seen men weak as babies, lying on their cots weeping, because they didn't do as they were told." That wasn't quite true. But the sooner he was back to himself, the sooner the rumors of poison would fade away.

I rose and handed Eileen's kit to Terrence, then preceded him down the stairs and out the door, without seeing anyone else.

"He was found on the road last night, too weak to stand. He was already vomiting a little blood, or so I'm told. The old woman didn't want to take him in, but his friends insisted, afraid he would die before they got him back to the pub."

"It was a wild goose chase," I told him flatly. "It was the fish, nothing else."

"I hadn't heard of anyone else taken as ill as he was."

"Still." The church was just ahead of us. "Why did you want me to look in on him? Were you afraid you'd be blamed if anything happened to him?"

"Better the Gypsy than me," he said trenchantly. And then he looked at me, looked away again. "If it was anyone, it was Eileen who did this."

"She never leaves the house, how could she possibly give that man anything that would make him ill?" I stopped, staring at him.

"The girl. Molly. She sometimes works in the pub kitchen. I've told you. Her mother isn't well, there isn't a father in sight, and she's the sole wage earner."

"Would she put something in the dish being served to him? If anyone found out, what would they do to her?"

"I don't know. To both questions."

"Why would Eileen wish to do him harm?"

"He had made some rather foul remarks about Michael. She was convinced Padriac had something to do with Michael's disappearance. Because of Michael's service with the British Army. Padriac had also claimed that there ought to be a bounty on Michael's head."

Was Eileen capable of that? If Molly had been in a hurry or afraid for herself, if she hadn't measured, if she'd emptied most of the bottle into Padriac's food, he would have been terribly ill.

Terrence was saying, "What was that bottle you took out of the kit, then put back after looking at it? *Was* it something to settle his stomach? Or a poison he'd somehow rid himself of, by vomiting so fiercely?"

He was quick. I had to hand him that.

But he'd also told me why he had been so concerned about a man he disliked. For Eileen's sake, Terrence hadn't wanted the man to die. An investigation might open up suspicion . . .

For a moment I wondered if that was why Granny was in the stable yard, if she'd been waiting for Molly to slip away and tell her what had happened. But why would she want harm to come to Padriac? Because he was a risk to Terrence? Eileen's kit was kept in her room, anyone could have had access to it.

"It wasn't a poison. We don't carry such things in our kit." Still, emetics had medical uses, and dosage mattered. Then I added, "I was thinking it might help with the pain he was experiencing, but there wasn't enough left in the bottle. I told you before, Eileen hasn't kept up her kit. That's why we had to find a chemist for Michael." I didn't care to lie, but it was the only way out of this.

There was another way. "I'd like to have a look at that caravan. The Traveler's. I'd like to see if he has anything in it that might have been used to make Mr. Murphy ill."

"There's no need."

"But there is. Why should an innocent man, Traveler or not, be punished when he'd done nothing? And Padriac is just such a one to cause trouble in that direction. You heard him. The last thing we need is more of the Constabulary brought in here."

"I'm not taking you into the village—"

We'd walked on as we talked, and were in the lane that led to the house. From behind us we heard the sounds of harness jangling. I glanced over my shoulder. It was the caravan coming up the rise near the church. My heart sank. The last thing I needed was to encounter Simon just now. And not just because of last night.

"Speak of the devil," Terrence said, and he wasn't very happy about it either.

I stopped to wait for it to catch us up, and Terrence perforce had to wait as well. I could hear the parrot now, with its foul vocabulary. I wondered what it had called Paddy Murphy that started the fight. Or was it going to happen regardless of the poor bird? The marvel was, there hadn't been a fight between Terrence and the man.

Simon was holding the reins, talking back to the parrot in Urdu. What was the bird's owner going to think when the parrot had learned to swear in Urdu and Hindi?

He had surely seen us waiting, but he took his time reaching us.

"Good day," he said affably.

"Good day to you. I'm a nursing Sister. Can you tell me if you have any medical remedies that I might buy from you?"

"What, the silly man who says his brandy was poisoned? See for yourself, I only mend, I don't treat."

He went around and lowered the steps to the rear door. I followed, and he said softly, "Poison?"

"Emetic," I replied, and crossed my fingers where he could see them. Terrence had stopped to look over the horse. It was a handsome one, a black mare with white shanks, and its coat was sleek.

But by the time I'd climbed into the caravan, Terrence was right behind me.

This was my first visit to a Traveler's caravan. I wasn't sure precisely what to expect. It was fitted out with a bed in the far end, a small stove in the middle, connected to a chimney, all manner of seats atop chests, and even a rather handsome carpet. There was even an oil lamp in a bracket above my head. I'd heard that the interiors were often extraordinarily ornate, yet the caravan would be burned during the funeral of the owner. This one was a rich dark red inside, with gilt carvings, although not as many as I'd expected, given what I'd been told. The roof was bow shaped, but I didn't think it was high enough for anyone as tall as Simon.

If he'd cracked his head on the roof any number of times, it might explain his moodiness . . .

There was a chair in the middle of the floor, and I recognized it. The Traveler had promised to mend it for Mrs. Flynn the Younger.

Terrence recognized it as well.

"Here!" he said, turning on Simon. "When did you steal this?"

"He didn't. Eileen's mother had asked him to mend it for her."

Simon picked it up, turning the chair around so that he could point out the mend.

It was perfect, much to my surprise. And the arm was no longer loose, as he demonstrated after he set it down again.

"When did he come to the house?" Terrence demanded of me.

"I don't know—a few days ago? Ask Mrs. Flynn."

The caravan was a little crowded with the three of us and the chair. I turned to go, and both men had to step out to let me escape.

I said to Terrence, "If he has medicines, it would take most of the day to search for them."

Simon stepped in, took out a small drawer belonging to one of the chests, and brought it out to me.

Looking at it, I could see that it was nothing more than the usual remedies any good housewife might keep for use in her family and any staff. But I picked among the bottles and looked at labels, then shook my head. "Nothing here that would make anyone terribly ill." Glancing at Simon, I added, "I'm sorry. That man you fought thought you'd poisoned him. My view is that it was a bit of fish that had gone off."

"I didn't need to poison him. After all, I won the fight," Simon replied calmly.

It was all I could do to keep a straight face, but the parrot had begun another string of foul language, and I said to Terrence, "Take me home, please, I can't listen to any more of this."

Terrence, about to say something, was at least enough of a gentleman to agree, and he said to the Traveler, "Bring the chair on to the house."

And then he took my arm and led me away from the caravan.

Mrs. Flynn was quite pleased with the work that Simon had done, told Terrence that he should pay the man for the work, and shut her door on both of them. I was standing in the doorway of my room—out of their way.

But as they went down the stairs I heard Simon blandly ask if there was any other mending to be done for the ladies. He seemed determined to cause trouble with Terrence. Of course, he knew that the man was wanted for his part in the Rising. That appeared to be reason enough.

I shut my door and went to sit at the window.

I was still concerned about what had happened to Padriac Murphy. I'd been rather shocked to hear Terrence admit that Eileen might be responsible. *Could* she have done such a thing? Without a word to anyone? Yes, she'd seen how terribly Michael had suffered, how severely he'd been beaten to make him answer questions. I could understand how helpless she might have felt, how she must have wanted to punish whoever had done that, even in a small way.

But why did she believe that it was *Paddy* who was responsible? Unless—unless she believed that his earlier comments about Michael had paved the way for someone to take them to heart?

By the same token, why was her grandmother out at the stable yard in the middle of the night? Had she been expecting to meet with Padriac, and he hadn't appeared? She'd have had no way of knowing what had happened to him, and his friends were too busy keeping him alive to come in his place. She was ready to give him the rough edge of her tongue, for keeping her waiting.

Yet I couldn't understand why she was meeting with a man her grandson didn't trust. A man even I knew was Terrence's enemy.

There seemed to be no answers any way I looked. But then I was the outsider, the Flynn family could meet and discuss and arrange anything it cared to do, and I would be the last person to know. There could be whole conspiracies swirling around my head, for that matter.

The only other person who was in a similar position to mine was Eileen's mother. But she had lived in this house for many years, as wife and mother and widow. She might have a surprising knowledge of what the family did or believed or tried to hide.

And she might be persuaded to confide in me, as one woman to another, even if I was a stranger. She must know that I was trying to help Eileen and Michael. That I'd come all this way because I was glad that her daughter was well and on the verge of happiness.

Only, it hadn't turned out quite that way, had it?

All the more reason for Mrs. Flynn the Younger to take a very different view of what was going on in this house.

When everything was quiet again, no one on the stairs or in the kitchen, I walked quietly down the passage and tapped lightly at her door.

Chapter Sixteen

She didn't answer straightaway.

And then the door opened so quietly my hand was raised to tap again.

She smiled. "Bess. Come in, do."

I stepped into the room, and closed the door behind me, just as quietly.

"I wondered if you were pleased with the work mending your chair."

"I was, to my surprise. I only asked that man to do it to annoy my mother-in-law. She doesn't care for Travelers. Nor do I for that matter, but he was clean and polite. I thought it would do no harm." She gestured to a chair—not the recently mended one—and I sat down. "I do wish I had a way to offer you tea," she went on. "I try to stay away from the others as much as possible."

"Shall I go down to the kitchen and make a cup for you?" I asked.

"No, no. Although a lemonade would be pleasant. My father would bring lemons from Dublin, and the well provided deliciously cool water, even on the warmest day. Ah, well, those days are behind me. But I had a lovely childhood."

She must have done. It was there in her manners and her conduct.

I said, "Was it possible for you to return to your home, when you were widowed?"

"I couldn't leave Eileen. And my mother-in-law wouldn't hear of me taking her away. It was stay or abandon my child." Changing the subject, she asked, "How is Michael? Truly? Do you see improvement? I can't bear to think of what was done to him."

"There is a daily change," I replied, "but not as fast as I'd like. I'd prefer to see him up, on his feet, walking around the room for a bit." He needed to strengthen that leg if he was going to walk to the boat.

"Eileen is so worried. And he won't tell her what happened. He says he doesn't remember much of it. I wonder if that's true."

"I don't know," I said carefully. "I only speak to him in Eileen's presence, and he doesn't wish to worry her."

"He's a good man, Michael Sullivan," she said, nodding. "I'm pleased with her choice."

"Even though he fought for England?"

"He did what he believed was right at the time. But time has a way of changing. He couldn't have foreseen the Rising or how serving with the English would be viewed afterward. I've wondered, the last few years— since Eileen came home so badly injured—if Terrence wasn't in love with her. But he seems to have accepted Michael, and I'm very glad for that. I didn't want her to marry her cousin. Her grandmother would have made her life wretched." And then, catching me completely off guard, she asked, "What was my mother-in-law doing in the stables at all hours of the night?"

"I have no idea—"

"Was she waiting for someone? Looking for someone?" Her eyes held mine.

"Does she go out after dark, very often?" I countered.

"I've never seen her do such a thing. I heard Terrence come up to his room rather late. She couldn't have been looking for him."

Had she seen me come out of the orchard? She wasn't asking, but that didn't mean she hadn't.

"How involved is she with the people who seem to be keeping the country on edge with their plots and troublemaking?"

"She wants to see Ireland free in her lifetime. But it will be a bloody affair. Those who are urging violence, like Michael Collins, will get their way, and then the British will retaliate, and there will be civil war. Even promoting the idea of independence carries the death penalty, did you know? The English are quite serious about not letting us go." There was sadness in her voice. "If you return to England and talk about what you've seen or heard here, they will come for her. My advice is to go quickly, and say nothing when you are safely back in England."

This was something I hadn't considered, that my actions could cause a great deal of trouble for the people I'd met here. Small wonder my father had been against my coming to Ireland, even for something as simple as a wedding.

"I came as a friend of Eileen's. Not to spy."

"The question will be, what Major Dawson will do, if he survives?"

And I didn't know the answer to that.

"Do you think the Traveler would spirit you away from here, if you offered him enough money?" she asked. "It's the only way I can think of to get you out of Killeighbeg before my mother-in-law decides it would be unwise for you to go at all."

I could have told her that the "Traveler" would be delighted to spirit me out of Ireland. But I said only, "I can't believe she would do such a thing."

"You don't know her as well as I do. I've been afraid of her for a very long time."

Which explained why Maeve Flynn had seemed almost reclusive and possibly even a little slow when I'd first met her. An act to protect herself and her daughter . . . No wonder Eileen wanted to take her mother with her when she left.

———

In the afternoon, the search for Major Dawson was called off. Most of the men worked, and there was only so much they were willing to give up for someone who didn't belong to the village. I was in the kitchen when the news came.

Terrence said, explaining this to Eileen, "We don't know where to look that we haven't searched already."

"Then he's in someone's loft or cellar, hidden away on a boat—"

"He isn't, I can swear to it."

"Well, Michael won't leave without him. What if he's already dead? And we go on waiting? I don't want to spend the rest of my marriage sitting here until the poor man is found. You ought to know who had taken him, Terrence. You're thick with the rebels. *Do* something!"

"Love," he said gently, "it isn't my lot who have him. If they did, I'd have had Michael home before they'd laid a hand to him."

"I want to go," she said stubbornly. "I want to leave Ireland and never look back. It's going to tear itself apart—or the English will do it for us."

He started to say something, then thought better of it. Instead he asked, "Let me talk to Michael. I know this part of the country better than he does, and I might just make sense of what he tells me. There must be something he recalls that would help us."

They argued over this as well. Eileen was adamant, she didn't want to know what Michael had been through. Terrence said, "You can't have it both ways, Eileen. If you can't bear to hear what he's suffered, step outside while we talk."

"But he doesn't remember anything. You'll just be wearing down his strength for nothing."

He crossed the room and rested his hands on her shoulders. "Eileen.

Hear me. We've got no choice. Much longer and the Major will be dead. And trust me, I know that there is going to be more trouble, before this is done. The sooner you go, the happier I'll be."

She looked at him. "You've always loved Ireland more than you've loved any of us. When I was young, I thought you were the most wonderful man in the world. The handsomest, the strongest, the bravest, the best at everything. I wanted to marry you. Did you know that? No, of course not—because you were never home long enough to care about us. I fell in love with Michael because he knew I was there, he loved *me*. I was first, Ireland second. Nothing will come between Michael and me. Not even you."

There was such bitterness in her voice that I was taken aback.

Terrence stepped back, as if he'd been stung by the truth in her words.

I knew how much he cared for her. I knew how much she had just hurt him.

Without a word, he turned and left the kitchen. I heard the outer door slam, and a few minutes later, the sound of hooves. He'd taken one of the horses.

There was a silence in the kitchen that I didn't care to break. I knew as well that she was listening to where he'd gone, what he was doing.

Then she turned to me. I thought she was going to apologize for involving me in what was a family matter—in many ways a lover's quarrel.

"You'll say nothing of this to Michael. Do you hear me?"

Without waiting for an answer, she went into the front room and shut the door with a slam of her own.

Wild horses couldn't have dragged what I'd just witnessed out of me. Not to Michael, not to anyone. It was far too painful and private.

In the late afternoon the Constable was back. I heard his fist pounding on the door and his voice calling someone's name.

I slipped quietly out of the kitchen and up the back stairs, careful neither to be seen nor heard. I shut the door of the bedroom as softly as I could.

I could hear the argument downstairs. Not the words, of course, but the sound of raised voices, harsh and angry.

It was very likely that the Constable got his way this time and questioned Michael, but I didn't think he got much satisfaction in that quarter. Then there were footsteps on the stairs, and Eileen was coming through the bedroom door, her face flushed with fury and worry.

"He wants to speak to you. That Constable."

"I'll come with you," I said, and followed her down the front stairs, into the room where a very pallid Michael lay on his pallet, his gaze on the ceiling.

The Constable glared at me, but said civilly enough, "I'm told the searchers have found no sign of the Englishman. Where is Terrence Flynn?"

"I truly don't know. He was in the kitchen earlier, but I can't tell you where he could have gone from there." It was the absolute truth.

The man nodded. "At least you've been honest with me. I've called in reinforcements. One man dead. Two abducted. It doesn't speak well for law and order in this village." I noticed he made no mention of a fourth man poisoned. But he sounded irritated with us, as if we'd done these things deliberately, to put him out.

"I'm sorry. I wish I could say I knew what was happening here. All I do know is that my patient is not progressing as quickly as I'd like. His fever went up this morning—never a good sign. And I'm fearful that if we don't find the Major soon, he could die. It's only a miracle that Michael Sullivan didn't."

He wasn't very pleased with that response. But I knew how important it was to keep looking for Major Dawson. And if there were reinforcements, they might have better luck finding him. Depending as always on where they stood in the Irish situation. The Constabulary was supposed to be independent of politics, but several had been ambushed and killed in Ireland in the past six or seven months. It had been in the London papers. By the Irish rebels, or so it was suspected. But that should spur the Constables on to try to keep the peace.

He nodded and left. Standing in the doorway, watching him walk away, I didn't hold out much hope that he would make any more progress than the searchers had done. Not if the Major, like Michael, had been taken away by boat.

Should I have told him that? I bit my lip as I considered my decision. The thing was, the only person I was sure I could trust was Simon.

Terrence Flynn spoke behind me, standing in the shadows of the staircase.

I turned. "I didn't know you were here."

"I was down in the cellar. Amazing what you can hear through the floorboards. You don't trust him?"

"Should I?"

"In theory, you should. He's what passes for the police here. But he doesn't seem to do anything but interview people."

He came down to stand beside me. The Constable was far enough away that even if he turned he couldn't see Terrence there in the doorway with me.

"I think you know more than you've said."

I raised my eyebrows. "I should like to know just how that's possible."

"Michael trusts you, I think. He can't trust Eileen, she's too emotional at the moment. But you keep a clear head, and I think he's told you where he was kept."

He was far too observant!

"Do you think I'd keep that to myself, if I knew? Wouldn't I be trying to rescue that poor man? They intended to kill Michael, you know. I don't think they'll have any qualms about killing the Major. Besides—if there's to be trouble, I don't want to find myself taken up in the middle of it on some trumped-up charge."

"There's something between you and that Romany tinker."

"What?" My response sounded quite genuine, because it was. I stared at him, meeting his gaze.

"He's only come to *this* house to ask about mending pot and pans," he pointed out.

"This is the only house where he can be sure of the money to pay him."

"There's that," he agreed, glancing over his shoulder at the staircase behind us. We'd kept our voices low, so as not to be overheard. Granny had the hearing of a hawk. "But bear this in mind. I couldn't have survived this long without having my wits about me."

And he walked off, down the passage toward the kitchen. I heard the outer door open and close.

Was that an offer to help?

But why should he help an English officer? He'd been actively involved in the rebellion against England, and he had the scars to prove it.

The only reason I could think of for his volunteering was Eileen. Terrence must know that when the Major and I left, Eileen and Michael would go with us. I wasn't sure he knew anything about Eileen's mother's part in all of this. But he wanted Eileen out of Ireland. And there I thought perhaps I could trust him. He loved her enough to want to see her safe.

He must be a lonely man, I realized suddenly. A price on his head, uncertain with the growing factions in Ireland intent on breaking free from England just where he could place his own trust. Yet he'd stayed in Killeighbeg to see his cousin married to another man, one who had served England in the war. Risking much for a love that couldn't be returned.

He'd promised me safe passage, in order to make her happy. He'd done all he could to find Michael for the same reason.

Even using his authority and his contacts to find him. Doing the same for a man who might well turn him in, as he was bound by his Army oath to do, because again Eileen's husband wouldn't leave without Dawson.

I found myself feeling a new respect for the Irishman. And however much my own country might see him as a traitor, his country saw him as a patriot.

I'd never given much thought to the Irish Problem as it was sometimes called. The Irish soldiers and nurses I'd met in the war hadn't had much time to give to arguing for the Irish cause. We'd been too busy trying to stop the German advance and end the stalemate in the trenches, the only way to push the enemy out of France and Belgium.

A few men had deserted and gone home to support the Rising in 1916, but for the most part soldiers and nurses had gone about their duties and never talked about what they must have felt when it began and when it ended. Or when the leaders had been caught and shot.

Perhaps it was just as well to open my eyes and at least try to understand their side of the problem, even though my own side had suffered too.

If the Germans had conquered England, would they have hanged the prime minister and his cabinet for opposing the invasion? Or closer to home, men like my father and Simon who would have fought on, in any way they could, rather than accept their new conquerors?

I jumped as someone spoke outside, and I looked up to see Father O'Halloran saying something to Mrs. Flynn, who was at her window.

Trying to disappear gracefully before he saw me was impossible. And I braced myself as he came up the steps and greeted me.

"How is the patient today?"

"Slowly improving," I responded. "Although his fever has risen today. That's always worrying at this stage. It should be going down."

"He should come out into the fresh air. It will do wonders for him."

"I hope he will do just that very soon." There was no need to be disagreeable, even though I couldn't stand the man.

There had been a young Irish priest at one of the base hospitals, a kind and caring man who attended anyone who needed his care, whatever their faith. Very different from this Father.

"And is there any word on the Major?"

"Sadly, there has not been."

From the top of the stairs, the elder Mrs. Flynn called, "You are keeping me waiting." I remembered that they hadn't been on the best of terms lately.

"Good day, Father," I said, and walked on down the passage, allowing him to climb the stairs to Mrs. Flynn.

But I heard her say when he was about halfway up, "Any word on Padriac? Was he poisoned?"

And the priest's reply. "They are saying the fish had gone off. I ate it myself that evening, and as you can see, I'm—"

The door to her rooms shut, and I couldn't hear any more.

I walked out under the trees on the back lawns, not wanting to encounter the priest as he left.

The gardens were in their best bloom—roses and lilies and iris vying for attention, smaller plants filling in between. I saw lavender and verbena and other plants I recognized. Like England, Ireland got the rain flowers loved, without the heat.

While the coastal trees were shaped by the wind, inland they fared much better, offering shelter from the sun on the warmest days. I found a stone bench under one of them and sat down there, looking at the house. I hadn't been in half the rooms, I thought. Without the staff to keep them up, we lived in only a few. Making a mental note to explore them when the house was quiet, I turned my thoughts toward the Major. What awful agonies was he enduring while I sat here in peace and comfort?

Almost on the heels of that thought, I heard a whistle. Those doves again, I realized as it was repeated.

Rising without haste, I walked along the borders and then strolled past the stables and into the orchard. Moving through the high grass I listened again for the dove's call to guide me.

I didn't need it. Simon stepped out from behind the gnarled trunk of one of the oldest trees, saying quietly, "Were you followed?"

"No. I don't think so."

"Let's move on, just in case."

And so we did. When we had a better view behind us, Simon stopped.

I noticed that he was deeply tanned.

"You've been on the water," I said.

"Yes. I borrowed a boat and I've been exploring the nearby islands. Searching for Dawson. Most of them are either deserted or have small settlements on them. I thought the deserted ones were a more likely choice for his captors, but they don't offer much in the way of shelter. I went as far as Inishmore. It's inhabited, but it's not an island I'd choose to live on in the winter storms. There's a large prehistoric hill fort up on the cliffs, and you can get there without alerting the village. Dún Aonghasa. It's a damnable climb for a wounded man, but it fits Sullivan's description of his way down to the tiny harbor and the boat. I got as near the top as I could without being seen, and someone is up there. It has to be Dawson's captors—there's no reason for anyone else to be in the ruins. No trees for firewood, no forage for animals. And it's large enough to give anyone there fair warning of trouble coming."

"Would they use the same place a second time?"

"You've given everyone to believe that Sullivan hasn't talked about where he was or who had taken him. Apparently, Dawson's captors felt safe enough to use it again."

"That means we don't have much time."

"I'm afraid so. Bess, I can't take it alone, and there's no time to bring Arthur or anyone else out here. Do you trust Terrence enough to ask for his help?"

"I don't trust him at all. Still, he's worried about Eileen, he wants all of us to leave as soon as we can. But Michael refuses to leave until the Major is safe. That alone might persuade him to help."

Simon looked away, thinking it through. "We have no idea how many people are up there."

"Michael only had three, I think. And one stayed with the boat, from what I can gather. But that's not certain."

"The difficulty is, if we attack, they might not leave Dawson alive to talk to us. That cliff is high, they only need to shove him over. I've gone around to the sea side to see if there was another way up. And there isn't." His gaze moved on to the stables. Watchful.

"Let me find Terrence and talk to him. But how do I tell him that the other man is the Romany?"

"You'll find a way."

I said, working it out, "How large is the boat? There will be three of us, four if we manage to get Ellis out—"

He turned back to me. "No. Absolutely not. You aren't going."

"You didn't see Michael after he escaped. How he got to the church is beyond my comprehension—he was moving on will alone. He should have died right there at the altar, but he went through with the ceremony before he collapsed. Ellis can't be much better, and may be in a worse state."

"It's going to be difficult enough to get in there before we're seen, and I can't be watching out for you."

"I spent the war years in France, within hearing of the guns—my position was overrun—" I began, incensed.

"The Colonel Sahib would have my head if I even gave five minutes' thought about taking you with us—"

"The Colonel Sahib is not here to review the situation—"

"Precisely my point. The blame falls on me—"

"It does not. He would trust me to know what is best—that's how he brought me up—"

We were talking across each other, angry and refusing to give in.

And I suddenly realized that this argument was about much more than whether I went with Terrence and Simon to the island. It went far deeper, and I was suddenly frightened.

I turned and walked swiftly back through the orchard, knowing that Simon wouldn't—couldn't—follow me. He had to stay free to get all of us safely out of here.

I came to the stable yard, and as I walked on, I heard Terrence call to me. But I didn't stop. I kept going, and when I got to the house, I went up to my room and sat down heavily on the bed.

Before I could even untangle my thoughts, there was a tap at the door.

I was sure it was Terrence, wanting to know what had brought me all but running out of the orchard.

I was in no mood to answer him, even though my better judgment was telling me that this was probably my safest opportunity to ask his help. Here, where no one could interrupt.

"I'm busy. Come back later."

I hardly recognized my own voice.

"Bess. It's me, Eileen. The Constable is here again. He wants to see you. He says it's urgent."

My first impulse was to tell her to send him packing, but in one corner of my mind the word *urgent* registered. It could have meant word of Ellis. And that they needed my services.

A flood of relief swept through me.

If the Constabulary had found the Major, it would mean we could all go home. We could leave Ireland and that fort on the island and everything else behind. We were safe. I was safe.

I rose and went to the door.

Eileen looked at me and frowned. "Are you all right, Bess? You're quite flushed—you aren't coming down with Michael's fever—"

"Um, no, no, of course not. I was out walking in the sun without my hat—"

I followed her down the stairs and into the front hall, where the Constable was waiting.

Over his shoulder I could see another man leading an extra horse, but it didn't occur to me that that was troubling.

"How can I help you?" I asked, expecting him to tell me that the Major was safe and I was needed.

Instead, he began the formal words of taking a suspect into custody.

I came out of my daze with a jolt, interrupting him.

"What—are you? On what grounds are you taking me into custody?"

"We have reason to believe that you are responsible for the death of one Fergus Andrew Kennedy, and I have here a warrant to search this house."

He took it out of his pocket and unfolded it for me to see. I couldn't tell if it was a legal document or not, only that it appeared to be legitimate.

"You may search my room, if you like. I have nothing to hide. But please refrain from disturbing my patient or the other residents."

He asked directions to my room, and I told him how to find it.

I stayed there in the entrance hall while he went. I expected him to return in a matter of minutes, because there was nothing to find.

In the shadows of the kitchen doorway, I saw Eileen watching, her face pale with alarm.

Overhead we could hear the Constable moving about. And I suddenly realized that the man with the extra horse was now standing just below the steps, the horses waiting with dropped reins for him to return.

Above us the door to my room closed. And the Constable came to the top of the stairs with something in his left hand.

I couldn't tell what it was, but I forced myself to look up at him, not what he was carrying. Whatever it was, I knew I mustn't show any interest, any sign of recognition.

Eileen had moved out into the passage, and she was looking up too as he clattered down the steps.

I said nothing until he reached the foot of the stairs.

"May I see what it is you are taking from my room? I share it with Mrs. Sullivan, who is currently staying with her husband on the evening watch. I wish to be sure what you have is not hers."

There was something in his face, something hard and malicious as he silently took what he was holding and unrolled it for me.

And I stared in shock at what he was showing me.

Two canvases, and I recognized them almost at once. I'd seen them in Fergus Kennedy's cottage as I watched Terrence search it.

Only this time, it wasn't a portrait of Eileen.

These were paintings that were a part of the series I'd been told that Fergus Kennedy had been working on. These were smaller studies, just the faces of two men, to be the pattern for the larger work he was doing.

One was Michael Collins, the other Padraig Pearse. I recognized them from the newspapers I'd seen about the Rising and its aftermath.

They were beautifully painted, each man given both human and heroic treatment, the sort of thing that had taken great skill on the part of the artist, bringing them to life on the canvas. Eye-catching. The sort of thing that would be part of a grand mural or a fine memorial.

Only these weren't going to be a part of anything, anymore.

Someone had taken a knife to the faces, stabbing them in the throat and eyes.

Behind me, Eileen gasped.

The Constable was grinning maliciously.

"There were found in your valise. Do you recognize them?"

"I have never seen them before," I said forcefully, and this time there was no trouble with my voice. I heard it, firm and certain and most certainly mine. "They do not belong to me, and never have."

"You took them from the late Fergus Kennedy's studio. After you had killed him." He was ushering me out the door.

"I have never been in his studio. How could I have taken them? More to the point, why should I have killed a man I'd never met?" There must have been the ring of truth in my voice, but he ignored it.

I was led out the door with the Constable's grip on my arm with his free hand, and the spare horse was being brought up by his fellow officer.

Behind me Eileen stood in the shadows of the passage, looking stricken.

And as I mounted, over our heads a window opened, and I heard Mrs. Flynn's voice clearly as she called, "Good riddance. I always said she was trouble."

The window came shut with a bang as she watched me being led away.

Chapter Seventeen

As we rode down the drive to the lane, I couldn't remember when I'd felt so alone.

I knew nothing about Irish law or what rights I might have.

Nor could I be sure that Eileen would find Terrence and tell him what had just happened.

Surely Simon would find out what had happened—but what could he do? I didn't think Travelers had any rights before the law.

I said, keeping my voice steady, "Why would anyone in his right mind think I would kill a man I'd never met?"

"Because he was working on the memorial, and he had to be stopped. Who would suspect a British Sister of working for the British Government?"

"I came here for a wedding, as you well know."

"For a woman you hadn't seen in how many years? Yes, that was good thinking. No one would suspect you."

"Your time would be better spent on finding the people who abducted and nearly killed Michael Sullivan. Who presently have Major Dawson, for that matter. Don't you care about them?"

"We are searching."

I wanted to comment on that as well, but I had to be careful. I was his prisoner. And I didn't wish to disappear . . . Did prisoners disappear out here in the last fringes of Ireland? Far from Dublin and anyone's watchful eye?

And who had put those damaged portraits in my valise? I hadn't looked in it for a day or so, my clothes were hanging up and Eileen's medical kit at hand, in the event Michael needed something. It could have been anyone. Even the priest, who had visited the house today—while I had gone out to the gardens, offering him a perfect opportunity.

There was a whole host of possibilities. The priest, Niall, Mrs. Flynn the Elder. And although I didn't want to think it, even Terrence himself.

All that was put aside as I noticed we hadn't turned to the right as we reached the lane that led into the village. Instead, we'd turned left, away even from the main road, keeping to the lane in the other direction.

I'd expected to find myself in a cell in Killeighbeg. But, of course, I remembered too late that there was no police station in the village.

Where were we heading? I felt a sweep of cold fear running down my spine.

"Where are we going?" I asked my escorts, keeping any note of panic out of my voice. I didn't trust this man.

But he shook his head.

"I have a right to know where I'm being taken," I demanded more sharply.

"Next village."

It must have been only eight or nine miles away, as it turned out, but it stretched out like an eternity. I wasn't dressed for riding and I had trouble keeping my skirts decently spread around my ankles. Occasionally at first I glimpsed the sea to my right, or was it an inlet? The grass was scrubby and overgrown, no farms or meadows, as if the sea came up often enough into this stretch to keep the land sour. It wasn't that far from the spinney and the pond where the Major was taken. I wondered if this was where they'd brought up their boat—if the land was firm enough to walk across or to pull one up.

On my left, there was a farmhouse in the distance, low and white-washed. As we waded across a little stream, I could just see four or five brown cows asleep under a tree.

We hadn't taken the road that Terrence and I had traveled to find a chemist and buy medicine for Michael. This was more a country lane. But the village, when we came to it, was hardly larger than Killeighbeg. Still, it had a tiny police station and a single cell in the back of it.

I had tried not to be nervous, but when I dismounted and was taken inside the station, I was beginning to feel anxious. Eileen might tell her cousin I'd been taken, but who would know where I was? Surely this wasn't the usual place to take prisoners? This tiny station?

While I waited with his silent companion, the Constable conferred with his opposite number there, a small dark-haired man, and I was led back to that single cell.

It smelled of urine, stale sweat, and cigarette smoke, among other things I tried not to identify, and when I sat down on the single cot as the heavy door was swung shut, the blanket smelled of horses. I tried to ignore the bucket in the corner of the opposite wall. There were no windows, the only light coming from the small grille in the cell door. I didn't mind the dark, but this meant I wouldn't know what time of night or day it might be, unless I asked.

Resigning myself to the inevitable, I tried to think positively, and tell myself that someone would get me out of here. Eileen—Terrence—even Maeve Flynn, perhaps. Surely they would have a solicitor. Unless of course he was in Dublin and had to be sent for. That could take longer. At least someone other than Mrs. Flynn Senior had seen me taken away. I wasn't sure she would say a word. But Eileen would. Surely . . .

Time passed.

The day had been warm enough, and sunny. But suddenly the world around me shook as a clap of thunder seemed to break just overhead. And I discovered that the cell leaked. A rivulet of water soon came trickling in one corner. It reminded me of something. I remembered reading Dumas's *The Count of Monte Cristo* when my governess wasn't looking. Edmond Dantès had dug his way into the next cell. That wasn't possible here, even as the puddle of water spread across the floor. I didn't want to, but I brought my feet up under me on the cot, to keep them dry.

There was another clap of thunder, not as close this time, and the storm must have moved away. The trickle soon stopped but the water stayed. And it was rather chilly in here now as the temperature dropped with the storm. I hadn't brought a wrap with me.

I refused to let my spirits droop. I could just see scratches on the walls, as if other residents had counted the days of their incarceration. Surely they'd take me to Dublin tomorrow. I wouldn't be left here for very long. And I was English, surely that would make a difference.

I was beginning to feel drowsy. It must be fairly late.

And then the light from the Constable's desk went out, and I was plunged into darkness. The building was quiet around me.

What were a Constable's hours? Eight to eight? Or was it later? I remembered our Constable in Somerset making evening rounds before he turned in, walking the village streets to be sure that all the doors were safely locked. But did he come back to the station afterward—or go on to his home?

I hadn't eaten, and no dinner had been brought, although the very thought of eating in here turned my stomach. I'd have been happy for a cup of tea, however.

The night grew even quieter, and I found myself dozing. I didn't want to put my head down on the blanket—sitting on it was disturbing enough—and I was afraid to lean it against the wall, not knowing what else lived in my cell. Lice, spiders, other insects. Instead I cradled it on my knees.

Sometime later, a light bloomed in the square that was my cell doorway, nearly blinding me, and I heard raised voices, but not what they were saying.

This went on for several minutes, and then footsteps approached my cell. Had they remembered my meal? I'd be grateful for that tea. It was one thing the English and Irish shared, tea.

The key turned in the door, and it swung open. The Constable stood there, scowling. "It seems you're to be released."

"Am I?" I said, quite surprised.

"The rightful killer has been found."

He didn't seem to be very pleased about it.

My thoughts were already running ahead. Had Terrence been arrested in my stead?

And then a second thought pushed the first from my mind.

Had arresting me been a ruse to bring Terrence out of hiding? He'd promised me protection, and he might well have come forward because he'd given his word. Even if he wasn't guilty.

Would they jail and try a National Hero?

He had enemies who would be happy to see it. And there were the English.

He'd been safe enough in Killeighbeg—for a long while. But now the jackals were gathering . . .

I followed the Constable down the short passage to the main room, and was shown to the door.

I stepped out into darkness, smelling of fresh rain.

As my eyes readjusted, I saw that the man holding a pair of horses was Terrence, and a wave of relief swept me.

"I'm so very glad to see you," I said, smiling. "I don't know how you managed this, but I am grateful."

He moved forward and helped me mount, then handed me a coat. As I pulled it on, I was thankful for the warmth. It wasn't mine, but it didn't smell of the odors I'd come to know all too well in that cell.

I was about to ask him more about how he'd managed this miracle, but he shook his head.

"Not now."

I suddenly realized my jailer hadn't known who he was. In the darkness, his hat pulled low, he could pass as Niall.

We turned our mounts west and passed out of the village in silence, and it wasn't until we were well away from there that I felt I could speak. Even so, I kept my voice low.

"The Constable told me the killer had been found. I was afraid it might be you they'd caught, using me as bait to bring you out of hiding."

"No. Not from lack of trying, all the same. I didn't come forward. Instead I passed the word through someone else."

I was about to say I was glad to hear it—and then tired as I was, the penny dropped.

"You knew who the killer is? But how? Who?"

He was short with me. "I was in a very tight corner."

"I'm sorry. But for my own safety, I ought to know who killed Fergus Kennedy. After all, I've been in a cell, accused of just that murder."

"It's best if you stay out of this affair. Let it go."

I did. For now.

It was late when we reached the stable yard and I dismounted. Terrence looked at me sharply. "Are you all right?"

"Tired. Hungry. Grateful to be safely home. I'll be fine."

"There's cold chicken in the pantry."

"Thank you. I'll look for it."

I said good night and walked quietly toward the kitchen door to the house, hoping to slip in and go directly to bed after a quick raid in the pantry.

The chicken was there. Even though it was close on three in the morning, I found a knife and put some slices on a plate, with slices of bread and a little cheese. Filling a glass with water, I took my meal back to the kitchen and was just sitting down when Niall came in.

He stopped short. "I didn't think to see you tonight."

I had a mouth full of roast chicken. Swallowing, I said, "I expect they were tired of my company."

"No, I mean, I didn't think the news could travel that fast."

"What news?"

He sat down, reached over, and helped himself to a slice of chicken from my plate. "Sorry, I didn't get my dinner, either. No, really, you haven't heard?"

"Heard *what*?" I didn't mean to snap but I was tired and cross with everyone.

"There's been a lot of excitement in the village tonight. Or is that last night?" He shook his head. "Whatever. The Constable came racing into town, and word got out that he'd made a mistake in arresting you. He was looking for Kennedy's killer, and as mad as a nest of hornets. Not the sort of man to enjoy playing the fool. He was so certain you were his killer."

"Well, I'm not his killer—or anyone else's. I'd never even heard of Fergus Kennedy until someone identified him when his body was brought in." I was tempted to tell him what I thought of the Constable, then bit my tongue. Niall wasn't to be trusted . . .

The Major had told me that. And I'd believed him.

Niall helped himself to another slice of chicken and the last piece of the cheese. "Why didn't you put the kettle on? Both of us could do with a cup of tea." He reached into his pocket and took out a flask. "There's even a little whiskey for it."

"I'm a nursing Sister, not a cook."

"No." He sighed. "More's the pity." Wiping his fingers on the tea towel that had been folded neatly and left on the table, he got up.

"You haven't told me your news," I said.

"I've told you. The village was in an uproar. The Constable was mad as hell and turning the place inside out."

"If he was looking for the singer, he's recovering from being so ill. Are you telling me *he* killed Kennedy? I'm not surprised. He's what Si— what Terrence would call a nasty piece of work."

Niall shook his head as he walked to the door leading to the back stairs. "Either you aren't listening, or prison has addled your brain. They were turning the village inside out searching for that damned tinker. You'd think that gaudy caravan of his would be easy to find."

I nearly choked on the sip of water I'd taken. "The Traveler? I don't understand. Why would he kill an artist?"

Niall shrugged. "I have no idea. Terrence put him on to the man. Informed the Constable that he'd been in the house twice and could easily have hidden evidence in your room. I never liked him, I thought he was far too handy with his fists for a Traveler. They're usually sly, going for you when your back is turned."

"Did—did they catch him?" It was difficult to keep my voice steady. I was so very tired, and this on top of everything else, was such a shock.

"Not yet. But they will. And when they do, I hope they knock him about for a bit. Teach him a few manners while they're at it." He turned and ran lightly up the stairs.

I sat there.

I had to do something. I had to find Simon before anyone else did, and warn him. There was no time to wash my face or sleep for an hour—

I got to my feet and started for the door, my hand was actually on the latch when it occurred to me. Or perhaps it was a sound from the back stairs. I didn't know.

If I go out to search for Simon, knowing him as well as I did, I'd very likely find him.

And lead them straight to him.

How do they know I know him? I asked myself.

It didn't matter. If I left this house tonight, Niall would follow me, or Terrence, to see where I was going.

I opened the door, stepped out for a few seconds, looking up at the sky and taking deep breaths of the cool night air. Then turned around again, and stepped back in the kitchen.

Niall was standing in the doorway to the stairs.

"I thought you might have decided to put the kettle on."

"No," I said quietly. "I can still smell that awful cell. I need to breathe a little clean air. Then I was going to look in on Michael and Eileen."

I shut the door, then walked to the door into the front room. But when I opened it, I could hear the normal breathing of the two people lying on the pallet on the floor. I shut the door again, softly.

"They're all right. I was worried," I said. Then I crossed the room and waited for him to step aside.

"Good night," I told him. And went up the stairs to my room.

But not to sleep. To sit on the edge of Eileen's bed and wait for the dawn. To listen for the soft call of a Somerset dove that never came.

I washed off the smell and feel of that cell in cold water, put on clean clothing, and went down for breakfast.

Except for Molly, the kitchen was empty.

She stared at me as if I'd grown a second head overnight, and I smiled. She blushed to the roots of her hair, and turned away.

"I'm all right," I said. "A little tired but none the worse for wear. And I am not guilty of murdering anyone." I let her absorb that and then asked, "What's the gossip in the village?"

She was busying herself pouring me a cup of tea. "I don't listen to gossip."

"Of course you do. Everyone does. What are they saying about the turn of events? That the English nurse was arrested, and then let go?"

"Yes, Sister. And that the tinker was taken up in your place."

As casually as I could, I asked, "And was he taken up?"

"I don't think so. They found his caravan, but not him."

It was difficult to hide that gaudy caravan. And such a relief to know Simon was still free.

"Do people believe that he's guilty?"

"Some are glad of it. Others aren't as certain."

That was a surprise.

"Why are they uncertain?"

"They liked him. And his parrot." She brought my teacup and the jug of milk and set it down in front of me.

"Where is the parrot now?"

"At the pub. But he is quiet now. He doesn't talk very much. They did ask it where his master was."

I hadn't thought of that possibility.

"And where did it tell them to look?"

"It kept saying, 'in hell, in hell, in hell.'"

I had to smile. I could picture Simon teaching it just that.

I ate my breakfast, then looked in on Eileen and Michael—to my surprise, he was sitting propped up against his pillows, his back to a chair. He looked terrible still, but his eyes were clear, not bright with fever.

They were glad to see me, asked me questions, and then let me go.

I could tell that Michael was concerned for me, because he frowned, studying my face. "It can't have been easy. Being arrested," he said just as I rose to leave.

"No. I'm grateful to be set free. And I'm very happy to find you looking stronger."

"Two nurses. I'm a lucky man."

I smiled and left then. And ran right into Maeve Flynn, Eileen's mother.

"I'm told they arrested that Traveler in your place," she said quietly. "Is it true? Did he kill Fergus Kennedy?"

"I don't know," I said warily. "I'd rather believe he didn't."

"And why is that?"

"I can't imagine why he would do such a thing. In England, the Travelers don't have much to say about politics. They mind their own business."

She nodded. "And so they do here as well. I simply can't picture one being a British spy. And what's more, I didn't know Fergus Kennedy, but I find it difficult to believe London would send a spy to kill him just because of his paintings. Any memorial to the Rising will be a long time in coming. Surely he was no threat to peace."

"Then why *was* he killed?" I asked.

"I don't know," she said thoughtfully. "It might have been personal."

I couldn't tell her what I knew. That Fergus Kennedy had seen Michael being taken away by boat.

We were standing in the back hall, speaking quietly. When Mrs. Flynn began to pound on the floor with her cane, Maeve glanced upward, then said, "I must go. Take care, Bess."

Glad to be free at last, I walked out to the stables, looking for Terrence.

I wasn't certain what I was going to say to him. But now that I couldn't be sure where Simon was or how safe he was, I was going to have to depend on Terrence. The problem was, I had to tell him what I knew and who had told me. And even that would depend on what his mood was.

It was going to take a lot of diplomacy, either way. I didn't find him in the barn or in the stables, and it was my turn to start to panic. We'd lost another day, we couldn't afford to lose another—the Major could already be dead, for all I knew.

Then I heard one of the donkeys braying, and Terrence's laugh. It was the first time I'd heard him really relax enough to laugh that way.

I hurried around the stable yard to the paddock where the donkeys were kept, and there Terrence was, his elbows leaning on the top of the fence, talking to the animals, and actually scratching one behind the ears.

"I wasn't sure they were friendly," I said, joining him at the fence.

"They generally are not. But I've known these since they were born." He moved a little, and I reached out to scratch the rough coat, just behind the ear.

The donkey jerked his head away. And Terrence laughed again.

"He knows you're English."

"He can't possibly," I retorted, laughing too as the donkey turned his back. But the worry that was driving me must have come through, because it didn't quite ring true.

Terrence turned to me. "Is it last night? Is that what's troubling you?"

Here was my chance, and I wasn't sure just what to say.

"Out with it. You'll be better for it."

But it wasn't last night . . .

I told myself that I could face Matron and the doctors when I believed that a patient needed something more to keep him alive. How was this any different from trying to save the Major?

I said, "I've come into some information, Terrence. And I need help. I don't know where else to turn."

He considered me for a moment, then took my arm and led me to the far end of the paddock where we wouldn't be overheard.

"The Major," he said. "Do you know where he is? Did Michael tell you?"

I was afraid to put Michael in the middle. "I have to be careful about what I know. I shouldn't have that information, you see."

Rubbing his chin, he said, "All right."

"I think he's in the prehistoric fort of Dún Aonghasa. On Inishmore."

His eyebrows went up. "Is he indeed?" Then he nodded. "That's damned clever, in fact. We've searched miles in every direction. I even took a boat to the nearest islands. That explains why we've had no luck."

"It may already be too late—still, I want to try to rescue him. I should have gone last night, but that was impossible—and I can't go alone. I know how to use a revolver. I won't be any trouble. But I need someone's help. I'm not sure I could manage a boat alone, even if I could navigate it to this island."

His mouth twisted in a grimace. "He's the English army. Do you know what they did, after the Rising? The executions, the innocent people caught up and transported to England, the atrocities—"

"It wasn't Major Dawson who took part in that," I said staunchly. "You can't blame him for what others did."

He took a deep breath. "At the wedding Eileen had to have an English nurse, and Michael had to have an English officer. Fools! Both of them. None of this would have happened if she had had one of the local girls stand up with her. And he'd chosen Niall. Or someone from the village." There was a savagery in his voice. "Is there no end to this?"

"Michael won't go without the Major. But if we can bring him home, we can leave."

"You do realize that it's suicidal for the two of us to try this?"

"I was hoping I could find someone else. The Traveler, perhaps. He's not a part of whatever is going—"

Terrence cut me short. "He's being hunted as a murderer."

"Yes, because you set the police on him."

"I did it to get you out of that cell."

We were beginning to shout at each other. I lowered my voice.

"Please, Terrence, will you help me? I can't manage a boat across to the island—I don't know the currents, I don't know where to land it without betraying my presence. I don't mind facing the men holding the Major, but it's useless to try if I am going to fail straightaway."

"Oh, bloody hell," he said under his breath, but I heard him.

I knew what he was thinking, that the last thing he wanted to do was find himself involved in something that would draw attention to him. He'd risked coming home, he'd stayed for the wedding because of Eileen, and now I was asking him to take action that might well find him caught and tried and executed.

"We can't let him die," I said quietly. "I don't want that on my conscience."

"Do you have any idea where that mad Traveler might be?"

"I don't," I said honestly. "If I did, I wouldn't have had to come to you."

"We can't trust Niall. We need another man."

Simon had said the same thing—we needed someone else.

"I don't know who to trust," I replied. "But time is running out."

"Yes, all right. We'll go tonight. The nights are short, we'll have to make it fast."

"Do you know how to get to that island?"

"I used to sail over there. It's an isolated place, they have their own ways. But a boy bent on trouble doesn't think twice. Not that I did any harm. I'd walk up to the fort and eat my lunch there, knowing my mother didn't have any idea where I was. I thought it clever of me."

There was a sadness in his voice. A regret.

Shrugging it off, he said, "All right. Go back to the house. I'll follow in a bit. And I'll need to find a boat."

I nodded, and walked back to the stables and then to the lawns. I wasn't convinced that he would help, once he'd thought it over. It was rather crackbrained. Just as well my father didn't know what I was planning. But I wished for Arthur and his aircraft. Another man.

For a moment I toyed with the possibility of asking Eileen to help, then discarded that idea almost immediately. She wasn't used to getting herself out of trouble.

With a sigh, I stepped into the house and went up to my room.

I'd been honest with Terrence. I couldn't simply leave the Major to his fate. I couldn't have his death on my conscience. I had to try.

CHAPTER EIGHTEEN

I WENT THROUGH my wardrobe to see what I might wear tonight other than skirts.

I needn't have wondered.

When I came back from having lunch with the others, hoping to appear as normal as possible, I found a boy's trousers, a heavy dark shirt and heavier jumper lying on the bed. There was even a flat cap, the kind so many Irishmen wore.

They were clean. I had no idea where Terrence had found them or what excuse he might have given for borrowing them. Or perhaps they were from trunks of his own outgrown clothes.

Locking my bedroom door, I tucked them out of sight and then sat down to clean my little revolver.

My only concern was that I didn't have many bullets for it. I would have to be judicious in how I used them.

It wasn't much in firepower, it was given to me for self-protection, not a battle. But I knew how to use it, and I could hit what I aimed for.

That done, I considered another problem.

If Terrence and I left and—God forbid—anything went wrong, someone ought to know.

But who to trust?

I considered leaving a note for Arthur, but if he couldn't land, it did no good. And if someone else found it, that could cause considerable trouble.

I considered Eileen but again worried that she might not be able to keep such a secret if Michael was put in any danger. I considered Michael, as well, but he would do his best to talk me out of such a mad idea, and I didn't want to risk another fever.

Maeve? Did I trust her? She didn't share her mother-in-law's rabid belief in the independence of Ireland at any cost. She wanted freedom from London as much as anyone, I thought, but she had a more sensible approach to achieving it.

I wasn't certain at this stage that independence or even Home Rule was going to happen anytime soon, but I had a very troubling feeling that matters were going to escalate rather than slow down. London would take only so much disorder, and then send in more troops to enforce peace, and there was very likely to be worse bloodshed this time.

But turning my thoughts back to Maeve, I decided that she was the only real choice I had. She hated her mother-in-law too much to betray us, and she seemed to like me. How far she would go in protecting me was another question.

With a sigh, I got up, put my weapon away where it wouldn't be easily discovered by someone coming into my room—Eileen's room— either to search or to make more trouble for me. Even the Constable probably hadn't bothered to look in one of Eileen's hatboxes on the top of the armoire. Besides, I had a feeling he'd known exactly where to search.

I still didn't know who had put those damaged paintings in my kit, but they had served their purpose with the police.

I went quietly out into the passage and to Maeve's door, tapping lightly.

After a moment or two she answered.

"Bess," she said, smiling. "I was just about to have a lie-down."

"Oh—" I said, not expecting to find her busy. "I'll come back later."

"Of course not. Come in." And she stepped aside. "Have you quite recovered from your ordeal, my dear? You look—distressed."

I followed her into her sitting room and took the chair she offered me. I wasn't ready to tell her why I had come, and so I said, "To be honest, I'm concerned for the Traveler, I do understand why Terrence told the Constable that he was to blame. Still, another innocent person in jail isn't going to solve that murder."

"He's Irish, my dear, he knows the country. He's probably in Dublin by now."

But I didn't think he was in Dublin. Simon wouldn't leave me. Still, I could hardly tell Maeve Flynn that.

"I expect so," I replied, but I could hear the doubt in my own voice, and I was sure she heard it as well.

"But it wasn't the Traveler you came to talk to me about. What's worrying you, Bess? Is it Michael? I thought he was looking much better this morning."

"Actually, it's the Major. He's still missing. I—" I broke off. "Tonight, Terrence and I are going to take a boat and sail over to that island, Inishmore. I wanted someone to know, in the event something goes wrong. And I didn't wish to worry Eileen."

She looked horrified. "Bess—what do you mean, you and Terrence are going over? Is the Major there? Are you going to try to rescue him? My dear, it's the height of folly. Promise me you'll do no such thing!"

"There's no one else to go. And I don't trust that Constable. And I can't just do nothing and let Ellis die."

"You don't believe that whoever is holding him will kill him?"

"Look what they did to Michael. He should have died. I think it's because he wanted so much to marry Eileen that he survived. Why else would he come staggering into the church as he did? To find her?"

"And you feel that way about Ellis?"

"No, of course not. But Michael won't leave without him, and he's English, and I feel responsible somehow." I remembered what I'd said to Terrence. "It's a matter of conscience."

"Yes, I do see that, but you can't possibly hope—it's madness!"

"I have to try."

"But where did you get this information? How do you even know it's accurate?"

I took a deep breath. "I can't tell you how I know. And I don't know if it's accurate, but I must do *something*."

"Go to the English garrison—"

"I was planning to go last night, and I was taken into custody instead. By the time I can convince someone that I know where Ellis is, another night will have passed. Can you imagine what he must be enduring? And when they are tired of that, they will kill him. I don't like to think of him hoping help will come, and then, no help ever arrives."

"I know you were in France during the worst of the war, Bess, but I still think you ought to speak to the authorities."

I shook my head. "There isn't time." And then to lessen her worry, I added, "You do realize that Terrence and I might well discover that he's been moved—or was never there? That this information is just rumor."

She considered me. "How did you manage to convince Terrence to do this?"

"He promised my family to keep me safe, if I'd come for the wedding. I expect he never bargained for this sort of thing. But I must give him credit. As much as he didn't like it, he didn't want me to go alone. I'd have tried. The problem is, I don't know the currents, or how to reach the best landing place on the island. And if the Major has been badly hurt, I can't bring him back to the boat alone. I'd hoped to have someone else along, but there's no one I could ask."

Maeve said with resignation, "All right. Tell me what I need to know. And I'll keep your secret. It's imperative that *someone* knows."

And so I told her. "Terrence is finding a boat. I have a boy's clothing to wear. And we'll have to go as soon as it's dark. I shall have to cry headache and go up early. Then slip out as soon as I can. I don't know where I'm to meet Terrence, but he'll let me know."

"He's an honorable man, Terrence. Very like his father. If he says he'll take you, then he'll do everything in his power to bring you back safely." She was silent for a moment. "He went to Trinity, you know."

I didn't. But Trinity College in Dublin was the premier university in Ireland.

"What did he read?"

"The classics. I think he was hoping to become a lawyer. He'd have been a good one. Another life changed forever by the need to free Ireland."

I rose. "Thank you for listening to me. And thank you for keeping my secret. I feel much better about going now."

"I wish I could discourage you. I urge you to consider what you're about to do, Bess. I'd be sick with worry if it were Eileen planning such a thing. And I worry about you as well."

"I know. That's why I felt I could trust you. Have your nap. I'm sorry to interrupt."

"On the contrary. I shan't sleep now or tonight. Will you let me know you are safe? I don't care how late it is—just tap at my door. I'll hear it."

"I promise." As she rose to walk with me to the door, I turned and put my arms around her. "My mother would have liked to meet you," I said.

"Perhaps one day, I'll meet her. Under happier circumstances."

I left her then, and went out to walk under the trees.

I didn't think I'd lose my courage. I wasn't my father's daughter for nothing. But I had to be realistic with myself. I wasn't sure just what was going to happen.

Later, I looked in on Michael, sat and talked with Eileen even after he'd dropped into a light sleep.

"He wants to walk outside tomorrow," she told me. "He says he's strong enough."

"That's good," I told her. "He needs the fresh air. And a little exercise will help his appetite."

It hadn't been very good, although he made every effort to finish his food.

As I rose to go, I said, "I need to check your kit. To see what I need to ask Terrence to find for me. Michael is so much better, he won't need it tonight."

She was a little reluctant to let it go out of her sight. In her fear and worry for Michael, it had been a lifeline.

Lowering my voice so that no one else could hear me, I said, "Eileen. I need to make certain it's got everything we'll need when we leave. The journey is going to be hard on Michael, even with a little exercise now. And there is Ellis to think about, if the searchers find him."

"He won't leave without the Major." She glanced at her sleeping husband. "We'll have to drug him, Bess. That's the only way we'll make him go."

"What about the Major?"

"I can't worry about him. I have Michael to think about. And getting him safely away. I'm sorry if that sounds heartless. But I overheard Granny talking with Father O'Halloran. And she told him bluntly that with you in jail, the Major gone, all she had to think about was ridding the family of Michael. I heard her, Bess, and she said, 'The marriage can be annulled.'"

Surprised, I said, "You can't believe that she would harm Michael?

Or that she had anything to do with the Major's disappearance or my going to that jail?"

She shook her head slightly. "I don't know what she's capable of. I used to love her, but you can't imagine how the Rising changed her. She's always said she wanted to see Ireland free in her lifetime. Now, it's as if nothing else matters. No one else matters. It's like a sacred duty. I don't think she would worry about her own soul, if she could free the country."

I'd wondered about that myself, but to hear it from Eileen was rather unsettling.

"What about Niall?" I asked. "Does he feel the same way?"

"He does now. She's been after him to join one of the groups planning things. I sometimes think she's sorry Terrence wasn't one of the martyrs."

"He's still fighting for Ireland," I pointed out. "Doesn't that count?"

"I don't know. I wish I did."

I took the kit with me when I left.

What would happen to Mrs. Flynn when her daughter-in-law and her granddaughter deserted Ireland? Because that was most certainly how she would view their leaving . . .

I claimed a headache at supper, and begged a cold cloth from Molly before I was sent up to lie down in a dark room.

Everyone offered their sympathy. Mrs. Flynn had taken her meal upstairs, and Niall wasn't at home.

I thanked them, and went up the back stairs. When supper was over, Eileen looked in on me, as I thought she might. I said, the cloth covering my eyes, "I'll be fine in the morning. But if I can't get to sleep soon, I'll not come down for breakfast."

"No, don't even consider it." Then she said, "Has Michael told you much about what happened to him?"

Oh, dear.

"I haven't had much opportunity to talk to him—I mean in the sense of really speaking with him. Has he told you anything?"

"No. That's just it. He refuses. That's partly my fault—at first I couldn't bear to think of what he'd suffered. I didn't want to know anything. But when you opened that door, when he told you—I realized then that I'd been selfish. Only, now when I ask, he shakes his head."

"I shouldn't worry about it. Let him heal first. Physically and emotionally. It was a terrible ordeal, Eileen." There was a hint of jealousy here. That I'd shared something that she as his wife should have been asking about all along, and hadn't. It didn't matter that I was trying to find Ellis. To her it appeared that Michael had confided in me, and not in her.

"Then you believe he'll tell me? I've begun to feel so left out—it's always there between us, every time I look at his bandages. I'm his wife, I should be strong enough to share what he suffered. And yet I couldn't bear to know what they did . . ."

"I'm sure of it. But in his own good time, Eileen. Don't force a confidence. He'll hold nothing back when he's ready to face it again. That will be better for you both."

She came over to the bed and kissed me on the forehead.

"I don't know what I'd have done without you here, Bess. I'm just sorry that it has turned out this way. I hope when you marry it will be a joyous time. You deserve it."

I didn't know quite how to answer her. "I'm glad I was here. I seem to be making a habit of rescuing this family."

She laughed, wished me good night, and left.

I lay there quietly until I was certain she wouldn't come back. Or Maeve might come and try again to persuade me to give up my plan.

As it happened, no one else came to my door.

And as soon as it was completely dark, and the house had grown quiet, I got up, dressed, made sure of my revolver and Eileen's kit. And then I slipped down the stairs and out the kitchen door, my heart in my mouth for fear someone would spot me.

It would be difficult indeed to explain why I was dressed like a boy, my hair pinned up under the flat cap, a revolver in my pocket and Eileen's kit in my hands.

I veered toward the trees there on the lawn, then made my way to where the donkeys were penned.

Terrence hadn't come in to dinner, and there had been no message about where to meet him. I had to assume that this was where he'd expect to find me.

And there he was, leaning on the top of the fence, as he had been this morning.

I said a quick prayer that all would be well this night.

Moving out of the shadows of the stable block, I went quietly toward him.

He wheeled, suddenly alert as he heard my footsteps.

And I gasped, realizing all at once that it wasn't Terrence standing there.

It was Simon Brandon.

I ran the rest of the way. "You can't imagine how glad I am to see you! But what are you doing here—I've been so worried—"

He relaxed as he heard my voice, almost a whisper, but recognizable even in the dark.

"You make a very fine boy," he said. "I didn't know you at first."

"A loan from Terrence. Skirts and boats don't deal well together. Simon, he's going to take me to Inishmore. I didn't know where you were, I had to ask him. Will you come? Is that why you're here?" I realized I was talking too much. "Is it safe for you to be here?"

"Hush, someone will hear you," he replied, quickly scanning the shadows.

I stopped myself from saying more. But he couldn't imagine how happy I was to see him. Instead, I went to stand beside him. And together we waited in silence. I could hear him breathing, and so I could feel when he tensed again, shoving me behind him.

It was Terrence, coming not from the house but from the orchard. He had a large pack on his back, giving him a hunchbacked shape.

"Who is this?" he demanded, stopping short and glaring at Simon, hard to see in the dark in his plain dark clothing.

"The Traveler," I said. "He's come to help." Although I realized that Simon hadn't said anything about going with us.

"How did he know?"

"I—I think it was because I asked him before."

"And how did you manage that?"

Simon answered for me. "It was before the Constable came. I was sleeping under one of the trees in the churchyard. She nearly stepped on me."

"What were you doing in the churchyard?" Terrance asked, turning to me.

"Escaping from the house for a bit," I retorted. "Can we please go? The night is slipping away—"

Terrence turned, and we followed him. He was heading, I realized after a bit, for the strand I'd seen when I was out with Eileen, searching for Michael.

Over his shoulder, he said, keeping his voice low, "The island is longer than it's wide. I've been there. The side where the fort is located rises up three hundred feet or more. Over time part of the fort has already collapsed into the sea. Eventually it will all be gone. But now it's a semicircular plan, three concentric walls opening toward the cliffs over the sea, and behind the walls, a stretch of stones designed to deter cavalry. Or even infantry, come to that. No idea who they were afraid of, but there you are. And anyone in the fort can see us coming for miles."

Simon said nothing—he'd already been there—but I found it useful information. I asked, "There aren't any villages where you intend to land?"

"That's right. Too shallow for most boats. Puts us a little farther away than I'd like, but we need to be sure the currach is there when we come back. It's a rough climb," he warned me. "Watch your feet. In the dark you can easily break an ankle."

If we come back, I thought to myself. It was already seeming to be even more of a fool's errand.

When we got to the strand, I saw a long, dark outline of what appeared to be a shipwreck drawn up out of reach of the tide. It hadn't been there earlier. Surely this wasn't—

I turned to Terrence. "I thought—a rowing boat?"

"It is. A currach. Hide stretched on a wood frame. It was mine as a boy. I found it in the barn loft."

"Is it seaworthy?" It looked more like a small beached whale, barely large enough for two.

"Yes. I tried it after Niall went into town."

We had reached the dark shape, and it looked as impossible as it had at a distance.

It was lying upside down on the strand, and as Terrence and Simon turned it over, Terrence was saying, "If someone sees this out in the water, they'll take no notice. The islanders use it to fish. And when it's drawn up, and someone comes across it while we're searching, it won't raise any alarms."

He handed Simon a pair of oars. "Sit in front," he said. "I prefer you where I can see you."

They took the currach down to the water and shoved it into the sea.

I started after them, intending to wade out as they were doing, but Simon turned, scooped me up, and set me dry shod amidships as it were. Then he got in the bow, while Terrence held her steady, and then he climbed aboard in his turn.

She was amazingly easy to handle, this little currach. And larger inside than she'd appeared. We took the waves at a slant, rather than head on, and were very quickly in open water.

It was then I noticed dark clouds on the horizon. I turned slightly and pointed them out to Terrence.

"Then we'll just have to hurry," he called back.

They were rowing smoothly, in rhythm. I was surprised to see them working so well as a team. But then Simon had always known how to match his companions. It was what made him such a good leader. I watched him handling the oars, getting the most out of every stroke, yet without tiring himself. I turned, and saw that Terrence was doing the same. Long pulls, using the sea and not fighting it. Men accustomed to the water.

When had Simon learned to row?

Ahead of us loomed a darker shape, and I thought it must be Inishmore. Just then beside me something rose out of the water, a white thing that startled me, so intent on what lay ahead that I hadn't noticed the sleeping gull floating on the sea. Smothering a gasp that quickly turned into a smothered laugh, I watched it fly away.

But that reinforced what Terrence had said—this little boat attracted very little attention, the oars dipping in and out of the water quietly.

I'd expected to feel the little craft turn toward the dark shape, but it kept straight on its course. One of the other islands in this group? I hadn't seen a map.

Again I turned to glance at Terrence.

He shook his head, then nodded toward something he knew was out there but I couldn't see yet.

Finally, when it seemed that we'd been out on this sea for hours, the slight movement of the water picked up a little. And ahead there was another shape looming out of the sea. I thought at first it was two islands, but we stayed beside it for some time, and I saw that it was actually one island, and several miles long. Inishmore, then?

Terrence said, "Fort's on the far end. Too far to walk."

We were moving parallel with the land, still out at sea. I couldn't tell whether Terrence was looking for the right place to land, or knew where he wished to put in. Then he was pointing, and we turned toward the shoreline. Very soon I could pick it out.

It wasn't a tidy strand, like the one we'd left behind. I saw grasses coming right down to the water, and tiny inlets half hidden by them. Terrence found the one he wanted, and we shot over the waves and into it so quickly I was afraid we'd run aground.

But as the currach went in, it filled the tiny space, coming to a halt where water stopped and land began.

Terrence said quietly, "There are houses not far from here."

It was slightly boggy as they shipped oars and then Simon and Terrence got out. I could hear their boots making a *squishing* sound. I followed them, handing Simon my kit as I did, then nearly slipping before catching my footing. Another step along, I could feel the firmness of land under me.

We moved in silence toward the rising ground, and soon we were on the loose scree of a rough path. It reminded me of the fells in the Lake District.

In the starlight I could see it stretching ahead of us, rising up to the dark shapes that must be the edges of the cliff. There were no trees, just rough stone walls that seemed to enclose pasture or crops, but even they finally stopped.

We stayed on that track until we came to a vast range of slanted and upright stones that protected the fort. It was a formidable sight, reminding me of the medieval stakes that protected infantry from cavalry attack. I couldn't imagine how we were to get beyond them—it would be daylight by then. But Terrence turned to one side, where we weren't quite so visible against the sky at our backs, leading us to a thick stone wall forming an enclosure of grass and rubble. We quickly found our way around it into that enclosure, only to be faced by another wall with an enclosure beyond it.

Behind me, Simon asked softly, "Are you all right?"

I nodded, staying behind Terrence, and watching his every move.

We got around that second wall into the next enclosure, but ahead was a formidable platform partly surrounded by a very thick wall. I couldn't see a way into it. It wasn't something we could climb, either.

Terrence stopped, listening, then he took out a flask from the pack he'd carried with him. We squatted in the lee of the second wall while Terrence passed me the flask. I had the first drink, expecting water, but it was whiskey. My eyes watering, I passed it back to Simon. Terrence took his, then capped it and returned it to the pack.

I could feel the fire spreading through me, giving my muscles new life.

All was quiet as we crossed the enclosure, making our way toward what appeared to be an insurmountable obstacle. I still didn't see the way up and inside it.

We'd made it this far without attracting attention. The wind was rising, covering our progress toward the top, but I was starting to wonder if there was no one up here but ourselves. Perhaps we'd been wrong about the Major being kept here. I took a quick look back at the way we'd come. If anyone was awake in the houses by the harbor, no light showed to mark it. And then in the far distance, out at sea, lightning flickered in the clouds.

Terrence touched my shoulder, pointing, and I followed him. He'd played here as a boy. He'd know where to look. This entire fort was amazing. The walls must have been much higher when it was new, hundreds of years ago, and I couldn't imagine how prehistoric people had dragged stones up here to create this place. A *massive* undertaking.

Terrence stopped, and I could see the way up to the wide platform. He leaned forward to say in my ear, "Stay here. Can you find your way back to the currach? If you have to? If not, keep going until you find a house. They'll help you get back to Killeighbeg."

"I can find my way," I told him. "But I'm going with you."

He started to argue with me, but Simon cut in. "Let her stay close. We may need to leave in a hurry." He passed my kit to me.

And I remembered that Simon had got this far on his own without being caught. Peering up the steps I could just see grass and stone, and then a smaller flatter platform by the edge, overlooking the sea. Leaning forward a little more, I was surprised to see that the thick, steep wall we'd crept around, although nothing like what it must have been, still offered shallow shelter on the seaward side. And in a small hollow there was the flicker of a flame. A fire.

The wind must have blown the smell of smoke out to sea.

A shadow moved across the light, and Simon pulled me back, out of sight.

A rough voice carried to us—just the sound, the words indistinguishable. But I thought whoever it was must be shouting.

Out of the corner of my eye, I saw Simon and Terrance adjusting scarves over their faces.

"Stay here," Terrence said again and crept up the steps, Simon at his heels. They had drawn their weapons, moving in the shadow of the wall toward the fire.

I stretched forward, my own revolver in my hand, to keep watch, and was just in time to see what appeared to be two men dragging a third toward the precipice and the sea.

I wanted to cry out, to stop them, and then I heard Simon shout something. He and Terrence came out of the shadows, racing toward the two men, who dropped their burden and faced the unexpected attack.

There was no way of following what happened next. I heard a gunshot, and someone fell, crying out. Another shadow broke away from the fight, racing toward the stairs, where I was watching.

I held my breath.

He hadn't seen me—

Let him go? Or stop him?

I rose up out of my crouch and brought up my revolver.

I'd forgot that I looked like a boy, not a woman. He slid to a stop on the loose chippings that littered the platform, and I'd have sworn this was one of the men I'd seen with the singer. He made up his mind, even as I watched, and rushed toward me. I brought the revolver to bear, and it didn't waver.

He veered then, leaping down, nearly falling. He got to his feet and ran on.

I'd lost whatever was happening on the platform, and as I turned back, there was silence.

Three men lay on the ground. Only one was standing, looming over them, a black shape against the dark clouds behind him.

Friend—or foe?

Chapter Nineteen

I MADE CERTAIN that the fleeing man hadn't circled around the enclosure, intending to come back and deal with me, then, keeping my revolver out of sight, I caught up my kit and quietly went up the uneven steps myself, prepared for anything.

My gaze was on the standing figure, trying to decide what to do if he turned this way. I couldn't just shoot him out of hand—

He turned. I dropped the kit and brought up the revolver.

Before I could say anything, Simon called to me, careful not to use my name. "Boy!"

There was urgency in his voice.

I felt a surge of relief as I reached down for my kit and ran forward.

He took my kit from me as I surveyed the scene.

Major Dawson lay quiet, not moving. One of his captors was rolling about, clutching a bleeding leg. And Terrence had his hand over a badly bleeding arm.

I looked at Simon.

"Knife," he said, gesturing toward Terrence, and I went to kneel by him as Simon checked on the Major, then went to deal with the third wounded man.

Kneeling by Terrence, I reached in my kit for scissors and began to cut away his jumper and the shirt beneath it.

The knife had gone deep into the flesh of his upper arm. I couldn't tell whether an artery had been nicked, but I saw him wince with the pain as I pressed on the wound to staunch the bleeding.

"How is the Major?" he was asking Simon.

"Unconscious." He was pulling a dressing from his pocket and applying it to the leg wound.

I began to bind Terrence's wound, but he pushed me away. "We need to go."

"And you can't row without a bandage," I told him in a low voice.

He let me finish, then got to his feet.

The man who had been helping to carry the Major to the edge of the precipice was quiet now, and I thought he believed we were going to kill him. But when Simon finished with his leg, he tied the man's hands and feet, blindfolded him, dragged him back to the wall, then went to attend to the Major.

I was sure I heard distant thunder.

"We've got to carry him," Simon was saying to Terrence, making sure he wasn't overheard. "He's not able to walk."

Terrence reached into his pack and pulled out a thin sheet. He and Simon together got the Major onto it and then tied knots into the four corners to ease the task of carrying it.

"Where's the other man?" Simon asked, kicking the small fire, to scatter it.

"He ran by me. I could have shot him, but thought better of it."

"He may have friends in the village. We ought to move."

Leaving the bound man where he was, they lifted the sheet with the Major on it, got him across the platform, but found it harder to get him down the steps to the lower enclosure. Lowering him to ground, Simon took the flask from Terrence, and lifting the Major's head, he poured a bit of the contents into the Major's mouth. He coughed, but it seemed to revive him just a little.

Simon told him, "It's going to be rough going. But you're safe. Just stay as quiet as possible." He pulled at the scarf covering his nose and mouth, then stuffed it in his pocket.

I couldn't tell if the Major was able to respond. They picked up the sheet again and we started back the way we'd come. I was grateful that it was downhill now, but in the dark, it was harder to tell just where we were putting our feet. I heard both Terrence and Simon swear under their breath as they slipped. And we hadn't even reached the path.

I was looking up at the distant sky, out over the Atlantic Ocean, and I could have sworn the lightning was much closer. Occasionally, as I followed the little party ahead of me, I also thought I could hear thunder.

We had finally moved out of the enclosures, we were on the path that led down the long slope of the land toward the village and the water, when I saw a flicker of light, like a torch, moving up the path toward us.

"Do you see those lights?" I asked. There was no place to hide, no cover at all.

Terrence said, his voice muffled. "Turn back—those sharp stones."

We turned, moving as quickly as we could, toward the cover of the stones. We followed them in the opposite direction from that of the path, tucked Major Dawson in behind several of the taller ones, and then the three of us lay flat in the prickly grass, hiding our faces.

We could hear the progress of whoever was coming toward us. They were moving fast, sweeping the torch from one side of the path to the other. I thought there were at least two people.

It was a long climb, and it was a while before they reached those defensive stones. I could hear them talking as they got closer, and I saw Simon reach out and put a hand over the Major's mouth.

Then they were even with us, and the sweep of the torch was coming too close. Squinting, my face in the dirt, I saw it come within inches of Terrence's foot. I held my breath. There were *three* of them . . .

And they moved on, concentrating on reaching the heart of the fortress as quickly as possible, staying with the path. I drew a breath.

They disappeared around the first wall, but we stayed where we were. Any movement was easy to see, even in the dark—just as we'd seen them, in time to hide. We'd been masked by the dark gray stone behind us, and we'd had no light.

I waited, but neither of the men in front of me stirred. When the men with the torch had disappeared behind the wall of the platform, Simon raised on one elbow.

"Sister?" he said, still avoiding my name. "If you hurry, and stay low, close by the field walls, you can make it to the currach."

"I'll stay," I said.

"No. We've already got the Major to watch. You'll be in the way."

"I can shoot—as well as you can," I retorted.

"That's not the point. We can hide Dawson here, and if we need to fight, we can. But I'd as soon get out of here without more bloodshed."

"What if they've already found the currach? And are guarding it? I'm safer with you."

"She's right," Terrence said. His voice was tight. I thought perhaps his arm was beginning to hurt him more than he was willing to admit. "If we separate, we'll end by leaving someone behind."

And so we waited. I lay there, looking toward the distant storm. Watching the play of lightning in the clouds. What was troubling, was seeing a few strikes out at sea. It was coming this way, the storm.

After what seemed an eternity, there was a flash of light as the men came out of the platform and started down. I couldn't see if they were bringing the injured man with them. Surely they wouldn't leave him there?

Beside Simon, the Major groaned. I had no idea what *his* injuries were, I hadn't had a chance to examine him. At least he was alive. But how much jarring could he take as we tried to get back down that long slope to where we'd hidden the boat?

Try as I would I couldn't tell if the escaping man had roused the village or just the two men he'd brought back with him. But the houses looked dark. I could only hope they were, that lamps I couldn't see were lit in windows turned toward the sea.

We lay there. An insect came crawling by, brushing past my chin. I clenched my teeth, hoping it wasn't intending to bite. Mercifully it moved on, not into the neck of my shirt or up a sleeve.

Progress was slow—I gathered that they had brought the injured man with them after all—compared to the pace they'd made going up. Soon we could hear voices, one of them angry, one whining, as if explaining how he and his companion had lost the Major. The torch was sporadic now, keeping to the path more than searching the ground on either side. But we couldn't be sure, and I had just moved a little as the insect came back, when the torch swept over us.

I didn't know how they could have missed seeing us. I tensed, wishing I'd taken my revolver out of my pocket when I had the chance.

But the four men, two of them supporting the wounded man, were demanding answers to questions.

And I heard one of them exclaim, "I tell you, they couldn't have vanished. Not with the Englishman in the state he was in. They must have tossed him into the sea. I think they wanted him dead—"

They were out of earshot, although I could hear their raised voices a bit longer.

We lay there. Time crept by. I closed my eyes, worrying about the Major, wondering if he needed help now, not later. My training told me to go to him, make certain he was able to breathe, that he wasn't dying.

Simon finally stirred. I heard him ask Terrence for the whiskey again, and I saw the faint light of the stars flash a little on the silver of the flask as Simon lifted the Major's head and offer him another drink.

I tried not to think how whiskey might hurt rather than help. But Simon had dealt with the wounded. He'd know what not to do.

Then he rose. "Let's go."

They took up the sheet and began to walk, as I brought up the rear.

It was a long, worrying walk down from the heights. Out in the open, nowhere to hide, and if there was a watcher, posted to keep an eye on the path, he would see us now, a quarter of the way down—then half. My ears were strained to catch any sound, and I wished we could use our own torch, to ease the way.

Simon said something to Terrence, and the reply was a shake of the head. I thought it was a question about his arm. He was using his right arm, but every step must surely have jolted the wound.

We were closer to civilization now, but we couldn't cut across the fields. Those low stone walls were everywhere, blocking off the land like a gray patchwork. We were all on edge, had been when we first started down.

And then we found the track that cut down to the boggy place where we'd left the boat.

I could smell rain, now. The storm was closer, the night sky split in half by sheets of lightning, but the thunder was slower in reaching us. There was still time—

It was impossible to see the currach until we were almost on it. I went ahead, stepping into the springy weeds and then into the water, holding the prow while they gently lifted the sheet into the bottom of the boat, then I followed, sitting in the bottom myself, next to the Major's head. Simon and Terrence took their places. We were just about to push off when we heard voices. Ducking our heads as low as we could, we waited. I couldn't be sure where they were coming from.

The sound of oars moving through water followed almost at once.

A boat had set out from the village and was heading back across the water to the mainland. It passed within twenty feet of us, its wake rocking us.

They were too busy pulling at the oars to see us. Peering over the gunwale, I counted two rowing and a third sitting lower in the boat, no doubt his wounded leg stretched out before him. And then they were gone, their voices floating back for a few seconds more, and then silence.

We waited a good quarter of an hour, and I watched the storm moving inexorably our way. The water was already getting rough. I didn't have any idea how good this wood-and-hide boat was in a storm.

Our oars went into the water, we backed out into the current, and Terrence guided us out into the sea, well offshore before turning toward Killeighbeg. *A dark boat on a dark sea,* I thought. Impossible to see the Major's face, but I could feel his breathing, ragged and painful.

Had they decided to drop him over the cliff because he'd told them what they wanted—or had they believed he would never tell them anything, and it was time to cut their losses? Up there on the cliffs' edge, his cries would have sounded like the gulls, and even a stray hare wandering into the enclosures would never have noticed it.

When we were well away from the island, Simon called over his shoulder, "How is he?"

"Alive," I answered.

Behind me Terrence grunted. Glancing back, I could only see the pale oval of his face as he bent over the oars. Several times he missed his stroke, recovered, and kept at it.

It was a long run back to the mainland. And the storm was moving faster. The lightning was lighting up the sea around us, the sea itself seeming to want to swamp us, and then the rain came rushing over us, pelting us with the first hard drops, then soaking us. I tried to protect the Major as best I could, but it was hopeless. The currach bobbed across the sea, and I found a pail near where Simon was kneeling, and tried to keep pace with the rain coming in.

Ellis stirred several times, as if in pain. I'd taken off my flat cap and put it over his face, to shield it a little, and I touched his shoulder from time to time, reassuring him that he was safe, not sure that he could hear me.

And then as quickly as the storm hit us, it had moved on. The rain was lighter, but the wind that had driven the storm was bringing cooler air behind it, and I was beginning to shiver in my wet clothes.

How on earth was I going to get back to Eileen's room, a bedraggled boy dripping puddles wherever he stepped? And what were we to do with the Major?

Finally the dark shape of land rose out of the storm, and I said quietly, "Si—" and stopped myself in time. "What are we to do? Terrence is wounded, you're being hunted, and the Major is going to need a great deal of care. Take him to the house? And how do we explain how he got there?"

I had to raise my voice to be heard.

Over his shoulder, he said, "We'll need some sort of distraction."

Ordinarily, I thought, the first glimmer of the summer dawn would be appearing anytime now. But the storm clouds were between us, still raging.

I could see the strand now, where we'd set out. A slim pale line against the seagrass and reeds that marked the land. Terrence had got us back safely.

Looking back at him, I was shocked to see how haggard he was, the line of his scars stark against the dark hair plastered over his forehead.

Simon looked no better. And I surely bore a resemblance to a drowned rat, with my hair every which way. No one would think I was a boy now.

And then we were running up on the strand and the currach stopped with a jolt that made Ellis cry out in pain.

Terrance was saying, "There's an empty croft not far from here. We'll take him there. Tomorrow is Sunday, they'll be in the church. We can carry him into my room, once they've left the house."

I said, "We can take him to Mrs. Flynn—your aunt. She has two rooms. No one will think to look in her bedroom. And no one will think twice about my coming and going from there. I can't visit your room."

Simon helped me out of the little craft, handed me my dripping kit, and then helped Terrence lift the Major out. When he was lying on the strand, they turned the currach over, then lifted him again and started through the high grass. I followed.

The croft was barely habitable. I could hear mice scurrying about in what was left of the thatching over our heads as we took the Major into the driest part. Terrence took a torch out of his sack, unwrapped the oiled cloth that had kept it dry, and turned it first on our surroundings—filled with windblown debris—and then on Ellis.

I knelt beside him. Like Michael, he'd taken a terrible beating. Both eyes were swollen closed, I thought his nose was broken, and his lips were twice their normal size. There were bruises and cuts, and that was just his head. God knew what else was wrong. Simon began to open his shirt. It was already torn in half a dozen places, and he had only to rip it a little more.

His body was dark with bruises and cuts. I thought he'd been kicked as well as beaten with fists. One hand was so badly swollen and dark that I knew it must be broken. There were burns on the underside of his arms, red and weeping. And I'd thought that fire was only for warmth and perhaps making tea!

"How bad is it?" Simon asked.

"He needs a doctor. If only we could get him into the cockpit, we could fly him out. But I don't think that's possible. I'm afraid of broken ribs—they could puncture a lung. Internal injuries—I honestly don't know how we managed to get him this far without killing him."

"Leave him here, with the Traveler to watch over him. I'll find blankets and a change of clothes. A Thermos of tea. You can come back in the light to see to him. Right now we must get into the house without waking anyone. We need to change."

He was right. But it went against my training to leave a wounded man untended.

I started to say something about that when I saw drops of blood on the floor by my knee. Fresh blood—

Looking up quickly, I saw that Terrence's arm was bleeding heavily. Not surprising after his exertion at the oars.

"I need to deal with that." Rising, I reached for his arm, but he stepped back. "Later."

"You'll drip your way through the kitchen and up the stairs," I told him, "if I don't do something."

Against his will, he held out his arm, and I did the best I could, cleaning it, then binding it well. I could tell it hurt like the devil, but he set his teeth and said only, "Hurry."

That done finally, I turned to Simon. "Will you stay with him? I'll speak to Maeve, I'll ask her please to help us."

"I'll stay," he said.

Gathering up my kit, I turned to Terrence. "The sooner we go, the sooner you can come back."

He left the torch with Simon and together we walked out of the croft—where the wall had tumbled in, a tree was growing out of the rubble. I hadn't even noticed it as we'd brought Ellis in.

Outside in the wind again, I could feel the chill in the air. Not unusual for June on this western coastline, open to the Atlantic storms. I was grateful that last night's storm had passed on, taking the rain with it, but banks of heavy clouds in the east promised a less than bright morning. Listening to the *squish* of wet stockings in wet shoes, the boy's shirt clinging to my back while the jumper smelled strongly of wet sheep, I couldn't imagine how we were going to dry our clothing.

We'd walked in silence, back through the high grass, over the slight rise, and were soon on Flynn land again. There Terrence said to me, "You know that man well. I heard you call him by name. And you work smoothly together. I noticed that too."

"I told you. I'd asked for his help, before I was taken into custody. He was willing."

"For a price? I know these Travelers."

"There hadn't been time to discuss a price," I said, evading the issue. "He can bargain with Ellis, if he wishes."

Terrence gave me a thoughtful glance. "Ellis."

"That's the Major's Christian name."

"I know. I'm surprised you do."

"We were English, we were outsiders. One can become friends in such circumstances."

"You have an odd way of collecting friends. Many of them male. The Major. The Traveler. The pilot who brought you here. Me."

I stopped. "I held the hands of men dying of terrible wounds. I listened to them in their delirium, calling for a wife or their mother. I wrote their last letters for them while they wept. And I wept too, when they couldn't see it. I've lived in a man's world for four long, terrible years. I couldn't save them all, but God knows I tried. I just wanted to save them. Even the Germans who were brought in bleeding and in need of care. I bound the wound in your arm, even though you once tried to rise up again my country. When someone is in pain, it doesn't matter who they are."

"You're a rare woman, Bess Crawford." And he turned to walk on.

When we reached the orchard, and could finally see the stables through the thinning trees, he stopped again.

"It's best if you go in alone. I can watch you as far as the door. When you signal me from your window that you're in and safe, I'll follow. We shouldn't be seen together."

I could understand that. Bloody, bedraggled, wet to the skin. God knows what Granny would have to say.

He stood in the deep shadows at the end of the stable block as I kept to the trees where Eileen's wedding breakfast had been set out. I was dressed in dark clothing, I hoped I blended in. But there was the open space between the last of the trees and the flower beds.

Holding my breath, I moved as quietly as I could to the side of the house. Only my windows and Maeve's looked down on this part of the gardens. And I devoutly hoped she was not a light sleeper.

I reached the kitchen door, stood there for a moment, listening. Then I opened it and slipped inside, and as quietly closed it again. I was just about to step into the back stairs when I heard someone else at the door into the kitchen hall.

I didn't stop to think—I simply opened the pantry door and stepped inside, praying that no one turned up the lamp and saw a wet footprint somewhere on the floor or at the door.

Footsteps came into the kitchen, then started toward the door to the back stairs.

Surely Terrence hadn't followed so soon? Unless there was a good reason?

I stayed where I was, the pantry door still open the barest crack because there hadn't been time to shut it properly.

There was a pause, and he crossed the kitchen, going to the pump, bending over and running the water over his head, then lifting it, reaching for the towel on the rack by the sink, rubbing his head briskly.

Tossing the towel on the floor, he turned back to the stairs.

Even in the dark kitchen, I recognized him. It was Niall. He wasn't as tall as his brother, and he was trailing a strong odor of whiskey behind him.

Listening to the footsteps climbing the stairs, I waited for the sound of his door to open and close.

Instead, I heard a voice call quietly, "Niall. The pub closed hours ago."

I didn't hear him answer.

"This must stop," his grandmother went on. "Now. Or you'll be of no use to us."

"I can hold my drink," he said, his words very slightly slurred. And defensive.

"You can. But people in the drink will talk. And talk will see you killed. You're not as clever as you think you are, boyo, and I'll have no more of it."

I expected him to tell her to mind her own business, but he cleared his throat, then said, "All right."

"Your brother is lost to us. You're the only one I can trust."

"He was there, in the thick of the killing. He says he hasn't the stomach for it now." There was scorn and disgust in his voice.

Mrs. Flynn said sharply, "Never think it. He's twice as clever as you are, and more of a man than you'll ever be, if you don't leave the drink alone."

"You're blind to him, that's what it is," he said, jealousy replacing the scorn.

"No. I'm a better judge of men than any of you. Go to bed. I only need to know, did you finish it?"

"No," he said, almost with a perverse pleasure. "He wasn't there. You'd said he would be."

"Then something came up. There's always tomorrow."

She must have turned away. I heard her door close, and then after several minutes, the door to Niall's room followed suit.

I waited a good ten minutes. Terrence must have seen his brother come into the house almost on my heels. He'd wait for my signal.

The dawn light was coming fast as I crept up the stairs and into my room. I went straight to the window, and pulled the curtains wide.

Only because I was looking, I saw him melt away around the corner and into the stable block itself.

And then I set about cleaning myself up, working in the dark until the sun was high enough to show me what I was doing. Stripping off the boy clothes—still wet and cold—bathing and putting on my night-gown, I washed my salt-caked hair, then sat by the window and dried it. But before I did, I took the wet clothes and hid them under the bed, where I hoped no one would accidentally come across them.

I was still at the window when Terrence came sauntering across the lawns, a bundle under his arm, and not a care in the world. Or so it appeared.

I ducked under the bed, pulled out my boy's clothing, and then waited for his footsteps on the stairs.

As he passed my door, I opened it, handed him the wet clothing, and shut it again as silently as I could. Never mind that my hair was down and I was in my nightgown.

If they were found in his room, it wouldn't matter. If they were dis-covered in mine, I could easily find myself in a cell once more.

Someone had been shot, up there at the prehistoric fort. Their pris-oner had gone missing.

They wouldn't rest, whoever they were, until they found him again and evened the score with whoever had taken him. They hadn't been able to touch Michael, because he'd reappeared in a church full of wit-nesses. The Major, hidden away in that deserted croft, would be a dif-ferent matter.

As long as I was free, I could take care of the Major until we could leave. The currach couldn't hold all of us—two wounded men, Eileen and her mother, Simon and Terrence to row.

We were going to need something larger . . .

I crawled into bed, pulled up the coverlet, and was asleep almost at once, worries notwithstanding.

At some point I heard my door quietly open, someone looked in and, when I didn't stir, shut the door again.

I hoped it was Eileen and not Niall. Or his grandmother.

When I came down to breakfast, it was nearly eight o'clock. Remembering my supposed headache the night before, I was prepared to play the invalid, then take a quiet stroll in the cool, fresh air, to clear my head.

I needn't have bothered.

Only Molly was there. She was red-eyed from crying. But when I tried to ask her what was wrong, she shook her head and turned away.

"Are the family going to church?" If so, they wouldn't be wanting breakfast. "Yes? Then go home," I told her firmly. "Whatever it is, you'll want to be over it before they come back, ready for their dinner."

"I daren't," she told me. "I must take out the roast in half an hour."

"I'll see to the roast. Go on, I won't tell on you."

With an anxious glance toward the stairs, as if expecting Granny to descend on her with fire and brimstone, she caught up her scarf and fled.

One less pair of eyes, I told myself. Looking in on the roast, I gave it ten minutes more, then set it on top of the cooker.

Next, I looked in on Eileen and Michael. She was dressing to attend Mass.

"I've much to be grateful for, Bess. I need to thank God for his mercies."

Michael, with more color in his face beside that of fading bruises, said, "I don't know that it's wise."

The church here was more involved in the lives of parishioners than the Church of England was at home. We went on special occasions, although others were far more regular in their attendance. We went to the spring fete or the Harvest Festival, and supported the campaign for a new roof or to stop the leaking pipes in the Rectory. We invited the Rector or the Vicar to Sunday dinner, and sometimes served as Wardens, and asked the church's blessings on our marriages and christenings and burials.

Here it was a depth of belief and a respect for the priest that went beyond Sunday dinner or a fete. He ruled lives in ways that we hadn't understood since the days of Henry VIII.

Still, I said to Eileen, "Perhaps Michael is right. Perhaps it's not a good idea to draw attention to how much he's improved. And there's confession, Eileen. To Father O'Halloran."

"I won't take the sacrament. I just—it may be the last time, Bess."

She hadn't asked about my headache. And so I said, "Be careful, that's all." Adding, "My headache is gone, but I need fresh air. I'm thinking of a little walk." Turning to Michael, I said, "I won't be long. If you need something."

He gazed at me, as if looking for hidden meaning behind my words. "Take your time," he said finally. "I'll be all right until she's home again."

CHAPTER TWENTY

I HAD TAPPED on Maeve's door before coming down, and when she answered, looking surprised—and very relieved—to see me there, I'd asked if I could speak to her.

She didn't appear to be dressing for early Mass. Moving to the window, well away from any ear pressed to the door, I said, quickly, "We've found Major Dawson. He's badly hurt. We need somewhere to keep him safe until he can travel—"

Surprised, she said, "How did you manage it, Bess—just the two of you? I didn't sleep all night, worrying."

"There—there were friends who helped." Even though I trusted her to keep the Major safe, I didn't think it wise to tell her everything. And it was true, in a way. "Now it's our turn."

"Terrence?"

"It's better if I don't tell you. When everyone has gone to morning Mass, can we bring him here, keep him in your room for a day—two—and prepare him to leave Ireland? There are people who want him dead."

"The same people who took Michael?"

"I must presume so. But he hasn't regained consciousness, he can't tell me who took him. Or why. It could simply be that he's English."

Again the less she knew—and thought I knew—the better. And he hadn't spoken while I was with him. I doubted that he had since then.

Maeve shook her head. "They'd have killed him outright, if it was only because he was English."

"Will you help us? It's a grave risk, you must understand that. But you'll be leaving with Eileen, you won't be here to answer for what you've done. It's just being discovered before we can go."

"Of course I will. Oh, Bess, I never thought I would have to flee my own country," Maeve said. "But my life here is untenable. Yes, I'll help the Major. I've liked him. I thought him quite brave to come here for Michael. He didn't have to, he could have made excuses." She gazed out the window. "It's interesting that Eileen and Michael turned to the enemy to support them in what should have been the happiest day of their lives. It says something about the upheaval in Ireland. And Terrence was going to give Eileen away in place of her father, even at risk to himself. That took courage as well." She looked at me again. "What will happen to him? I have always liked Terrence, you know. Eileen is quite fond of him as well."

But not in love with him. Still, I didn't think that Terrence would put her at risk by marrying her, even if she had loved him in return. Ireland had enough widows.

"Where is the Major? How will you bring him here?" she asked.

I didn't want her to know where he was at present. "I've left that to Terrence." Evading the question entirely.

"Well. It doesn't matter. I'll see that my bed is made ready." She smiled. "You're stronger than Eileen, you know. If someone threatened Michael, she would tell them whatever they wanted to know. And we can't blame her. Not after what she's endured."

It was a warning not to tell her daughter where the Major was.

We talked for several minutes about what the Major might need. As

I hadn't been able to do more than a cursory examination, I could only tell her what I believed he might require.

Crossing the room, she opened her door. There was no one there. "Go," she said softly.

With a smile, I slipped out of the room and made my way down the back stairs.

Free now to attend to the Major, I strolled among the gardens, then stopped by the stables. The epitome, I thought with amusement, of the English heretic endangering her soul while everyone else minded theirs.

Someone had already seen to the horses, and I strolled on to look in on the donkeys. No one was about and so I left my mug on a post and slipped into the orchard.

Finding my way back to the croft was no problem, but as I got closer, I began to whistle a tune, to let Simon know I was approaching.

He was standing by the tree in the opening, and he looked very tired.

"How are you? And how is the Major?" I asked quietly. "Has he been conscious?"

"Not completely. I think he knows he's safe. He's asleep now. Flynn brought what we needed earlier. Have you spoken to Mrs. Flynn?"

"Yes. She's agreeable. And she warned me not to confide in Eileen."

"I think that's best."

I followed Simon inside. Terrence had brought water, tea, blankets, and a change of clothing for the Major. And they had managed to bathe and dress him. I knelt by him and began my assessment. In the morning light coming through the broken walls and roof, he looked rather worse than he had by torchlight. And he was feverish.

The burns looked particularly bad, and I used the salve again. It had helped flyers rescued from burning aircraft, and I hoped it would help here. His eyes were still quite swollen, and I put ointment on them to help reduce the swelling, then used the same treatment for his broken hand.

Standing just behind me, Simon commented, "I don't think his arms or legs are broken. Ribs are another matter. He was savagely kicked as well as beaten."

"Yes, we must tape those. But first I need to treat the cuts. They must have used that knife repeatedly, the one that slashed Terrence's arm. Deep enough to cause pain, but not deep enough to kill. Rather savage of them."

"I don't know if they'd made him talk or not. From the look of his wounds, they hadn't. But they kept him tied."

He reached forward and indicated the lines on the Major's wrists and ankles.

I sighed. "I think I recognized one of those men—the one who ran past me. I'd seen him with the violinist. That tells me we were right when we thought we saw Padriac there at the edge of the wood."

"Yes, I think you're right. He's involved."

I worked for a good hour, cleaning and doing what I could to keep the wounds from getting infected. Then with Simon's help, I wrapped his ribs, using almost all of the bandaging in the kit.

There was a blow on his head that had crusted over. It must have been dealt when he was first taken, to subdue him. I couldn't imagine the Major going with anyone without a fight. Finally, I mixed aspirin with a little water, and Simon held the Major's head while I helped him swallow the draft.

His eyes opened—or attempted to—and he peered up at me over the rim of the cup.

"All is well," I said. "You need to rest now."

Obediently closing his eyes, he seemed to relax as Simon lowered him to the blankets again.

Simon had been quiet as I worked, helping where needed but saying very little. But as I was finishing, he asked, "Why is Flynn so willing to help you?"

I looked up at him. "Terrence? He's in love with Eileen. I think he'd do anything for her. And that includes helping me, if need be. Michael won't leave without the Major. Eileen won't leave without Michael. Therefore the Major had to be found. More importantly, I think, is the fact that Terrence wants to see her safely out of Ireland. As soon as possible."

Echoing my thoughts earlier, Simon commented, "Now that the war's over, I think England will deal harshly with any more upheavals. It's going to be far worse before it gets any better."

"The northern counties don't want to leave English rule. That's a sticking point. Irish leaders insist they must come out. And I don't believe there's a solution that will please anyone."

"I agree."

Finishing my work, I got to my feet.

As I did, Simon moved to the opening where we'd come in. He was standing there, his back to me, as I packed away the kit.

I walked over to where he was standing. "What's wrong, Simon?"

He turned to look at me. "Are you leaving the Queen Alexandra's?"

"I expect I shall have to. They're reducing the nursing staff rather drastically. I'd be teaching future Sisters. And I don't think that's something I want to do."

"What will you do then?"

"I truly don't know. I'm sure my parents would prefer to have me come home, at least for a little while." I took a deep breath. "I'm rather lost, Simon. The war filled my life so completely—my training, the need to keep men alive—that I never had time to consider my future. And now it's here, and I feel empty. I've wanted to talk to you about that, but you were off to Scotland while I was in Paris. And you've been rather—unapproachable—since you came home. I didn't know how to begin. I don't know what's wrong."

I hadn't intended to say anything to him. Much less this. I could have bit my tongue, but it came spilling out anyway.

He turned fully now, released the tree limb, and put his arm around my shoulders in the old way, and it was comforting. I leaned against him.

"It hasn't been easy for either of us," he said. "At least I know what I want, but it's not possible."

"I'm sorry. Can I help?"

He laughed then, that chuckle deep in his chest. "My dear girl—"

There was a sound nearby. Simon tensed, moved away from me, and reached for his revolver.

Terrence called, "I'm coming in."

And he joined us in the croft. "How is he?"

"I don't know for certain. You saw him earlier."

He grimaced. "God knows. He's alive. There's a chance. Has he come to his senses?"

"Briefly. He didn't speak, but I believe he recognized me. I spoke to Maeve. Mrs. Flynn. And the family is setting off to Mass."

"Yes, I watched them leave." Then he asked, "Why was Eileen with them?"

"She's grateful to God for saving Michael. She feels this is her last opportunity to show how grateful she is."

"There are times I'd like to shake her," he said grimly.

"I couldn't dissuade her. Neither could Michael."

"She should never have left him alone."

I agreed but I left it there. "Was Niall among them? He was the only person I couldn't account for."

Turning his attention to the problem at hand, he went on. "Yes. I made certain of that. I've brought one of the donkeys. I thought it might be simpler than dragging him about on that sheet again. Besides. It's beginning to tear."

I knew he was right.

It took us a quarter of an hour to wake the Major up enough to tell him what we were about to do. "It will be painful," I warned him truthfully. "But we need to put you in a clean bed where the chance for infection is less. Maeve—Mrs. Flynn—has agreed to take you in, and right now the family have gone to Sunday services. It's imperative that we move you quickly."

He said, "You—you put Mrs. Flynn—in danger." He seemed to lose his concentration for a moment, then added, "Stay here."

"You have too many open wounds. It's not safe," I replied, and he lay back, too weak to argue.

Terrence left to bring the donkey closer, and I said to Ellis, "We can't put you over his back. You must ride astride. Can you manage that?"

He nodded. The soldier, accepting necessity.

And he did manage. It must have been an agony to get him to his feet, then walk him as far as the opening. It took both men to put him on the donkey's back, while I held the reins.

"I'll come back for the rest," Terrance said, handing me my kit. "You take the lead, walk him slowly. We'll see that the Major stays on board."

He was already exhausted, his shoulders drooping. But his good hand was clenched in the donkey's mane.

I began what was to become a rather harrowing journey, as I watched a mental clock. How long would Mass be today? Was Father O'Halloran one who gave a long homily or a short one?

One of us needed to be at the house, watching. But all three of us were needed here.

It was so slow, our progress. I turned often to watch the Major's face, to make certain nothing was going wrong.

We left the sound of the sea and hungry gulls behind, close now to the orchard.

The donkey smelled his paddock and wanted to pick up his pace, and it was all I could do to slow him down.

Simon and Terrence were talking to the Major, encouraging him.

As we made our careful way among the gnarled trees, I nearly tripped over something hidden in the tall grass. *A broken bough,* I thought, thankful that St. Patrick had rid Ireland of snakes long ago. This was a perfect habitat for them.

We got through without too much fuss, then had to convince the donkey that he had a little farther to go before he could return to his usual home.

Terrence went ahead to be certain that the stable block was clear, and then we began the long stretch across the open lawn.

I stopped so short the donkey nearly pushed me over. *There was a face at the kitchen window.*

Keeping my head, I said, "Someone is in the kitchen."

Terrence swore under his breath. "Molly?"

"I sent her home. But she might have worried about the roast—"

The face vanished before I could be sure who had been there.

And then the door in the kitchen passage opened, and I saw Michael standing there, beckoning us forward. He was rather stooped, and I knew his ribs were still painful—and would be for weeks to come.

Smiling at him, I urged the reluctant donkey down the slight incline toward the house, carefully watching the Major. He was almost gray with pain and exhaustion but his fist still clutched a handful of the donkey's rough mane, and the slits that were all I could see of his eyes watched me. I smiled for him as well.

It seemed an eternity before we reached the door. And then Terrence and Simon were helping the Major down. I spared a moment's worry about those steep, narrow stairs, then said to Michael as I kept a firm grip on the reins, "How did you know?"

"Something in your eyes this morning. You didn't appear to be recovering from a headache. Where are you taking him?"

"Your mother-in-law's room." I moved the donkey out of the doorway so that the Major could be brought in. "She's agreed."

And then he too was stepping out of the way, back into the kitchen.

We got the Major into the house somehow. I thought it was as much his will as our help. In the end, we had to take him through the kitchen and front room to the wider front stairs, while Michael held on to the donkey. There, one step at a time, Simon and Terrence moved him up the flight.

Maeve was at the top. I heard her click her tongue as she looked down at the battered man making painful progress toward her, but she said nothing, except, "The room is ready."

I kept watch, staring down the lane. *Please, God, don't let them come now.*

Eight steps from the top—seven—six—

The lane was still empty.

I hurried back through the house, relieved Michael of the reins, and started leading the donkey back to his paddock.

"Watch the lane," I told Michael. "Give them a little warning."

The donkey, now that he was getting his way, was reluctant to come with me. I cajoled and pulled, wanting him out of sight and out of the way. I hadn't thought to ask Terrence if they'd walked to the church or taken the carriage—

Finally the stubborn little beast had had enough, and trotted beside me the rest of the way, and I had all I could do before opening the gate, to pull off his bridle. He was braying now, but I managed it at last. He went through the gate and into the pasture with a trot that took him across to the small shelter, and he began to eat.

I was just closing the gate and making certain it was latched, when I remembered my cup. Snatching it up, I ran back to the stable and shoved the reins on a hook in the tack room. Out of place they might be, but out of sight they most certainly were.

I started down to the house, scanning the ground for any droppings that would give us away, but thankfully there were none.

Michael was snatching up the bundle that Terrence had dropped by the door, and was waving frantically to me.

They were coming!

Lifting my skirts I ran for the house, cup in hand. Michael had already vanished.

Terrence was holding the door now, bundle in hand. I waved him off, and he disappeared.

I was in the kitchen when I heard voices coming toward the house. I could only hope that seeing Terrence on his own meant that Simon had got away.

My breathing had eased, though my heart rate hadn't, and I was washing out my teacup, the kettle already on the cooker, when Eileen came into the kitchen.

She said, "You look flushed."

I said, "I just had words with Michael. He wanted to walk outside, but I didn't think it was the best idea. Maybe in the cool of the evening you can take him for a brief stroll."

"You worry too much," she said lightly.

"How was the service?"

"All right. The homily was about the Israelites wanting to be free of Babylonian captivity. English captivity of course is what was meant. I just wanted to slip out, but I couldn't, I was under Granny's eye."

The kettle had come to a boil, and she busied herself with making tea. "I hope you didn't mind—I came in earlier, while you were still asleep, to collect my dress. You didn't stir."

"Once the headache started to fade, I went deeply asleep. You could have rearranged the room for all I knew."

Laughing, she said, "I told Michael we would be leaving this week."

I turned to her. "I don't know—"

"Of course he's ready. He says as much. And the Major is surely dead by now. We tried, we did our very best. I'm sad about that—he came here to support Michael, and it's horrible the way it's turned out. Still, we can't wait much longer."

"Yes, we must give leaving some thought," I said. "Take a cup of tea to Michael, and tell him I'm so sorry for forbidding him to go out. I meant it for the best."

And she did. I prepared a tray to take up to Maeve's room before Mrs. Flynn discovered that I'd sent Molly home.

There was the pot of tea, two cups, some little cakes, and the jug of milk.

I had just started to the stairs when Niall came clattering down them. "Is that for my grandmother?"

"No, I promised your aunt I'd bring her tea. And I felt like a cup myself. I'll be down shortly. Or you can make it yourself."

I was eager for an excuse to go up and see for myself what was happening.

"Let me have that one instead."

"No," I told him firmly. "You're perfectly capable of doing it."

"You don't care much for me, do you?" he asked.

"I'm not in the mood for a row, Niall."

"Granny told me Terrence had kissed you. Are you staying on after Eileen leaves?"

"I've no idea," I said. "Why don't you ask your brother?"

"I would. Only I don't think he's in his room. He comes and goes like a ghost in the house."

I walked past him, went up the stairs feeling relieved that we hadn't had real words. That would get back to his grandmother. When I reached the top of the stairs, I was braced to meet her and have *her* take the tray from me. I made it to Maeve's door and managed to tap lightly without spilling anything.

She opened her door a crack, then saw who it was and opened it wider.

"I thought you might care for tea," I said in a normal voice. "If you don't, just tell me."

"Oh, it's a lovely thought, Bess, thank you. Come in."

Shutting the door behind me, she laid a finger to her lips, then took the tray and set it on the little tea table by her chair.

She was chatting with me as if I'd really come for tea, as I moved toward the closed door to her bedroom. It wasn't completely shut, I had only to touch it for it to start to swing open.

The curtains had been drawn, leaving the room dimly lit. I could make out the bed and the figure lying still in the middle of it. I was about to step in when another figure moved into my line of sight and bent over the bed.

Thoughts flew through my mind—that Maeve had betrayed us, that someone had come to finish what had begun at Dún Aonghasa. And I had no weapon.

There was a tall, ornate candlestick on the chest by the door. I closed my fingers around it and started for the bed.

Maeve called my name, and in the same instant, the figure at the side of the bed turned.

I nearly dropped the candlestick.

It was Simon, wearing different clothes. I had the fleeting thought that Terrence was going to have an empty wardrobe very soon.

"I didn't know you'd stayed," I stammered. "No one told me."

"They were here before we'd got him fully settled," Maeve was whispering just behind me. "Terrence managed to reach his room while

Niall was with his grandmother. There was no time to find a safe place for Simon."

Simon? Not "the Traveler"?

He'd mended her chair . . .

Simon was grinning at me in the old, familiar way he had. I set the candlestick carefully back where I'd found it.

"No one told me," I said again, then walked to the handsome bedstead that must have been part of the master bedroom of the house, and looked down at our patient.

He was asleep.

"There was a little laudanum in your kit," Simon was saying. "He needed relief from the pain. Mrs. Flynn managed to find it."

I'd lost sight of it. Terrence must have taken it up when he collected his bundle. And then I saw it standing at the foot of the bed.

I nodded. "I'm glad." And gladder still that the Major appeared not to have opened any wounds, and he was sleeping well enough that I didn't wish to rouse him.

Maeve said, "If you can, look in on Terrence. I think his arm is bleeding again."

I wasn't surprised. It had needed stitching last night.

We had just returned to her sitting room when there was a knock at the door. Loud and imperative.

Maeve glanced at me uneasily as she crossed the room. By that time, I was seated next to the little table, teacup—empty—in hand.

She opened the door, and I saw Mrs. Flynn's angry face just beyond Maeve. Her gaze flew to me.

"Where is that lazy girl?" she demanded. "The roast is sitting there on the cooker, but there are no potatoes made, no other dishes prepared. You were the last down this morning. What did you do with her?"

"She wasn't feeling well. I sent her home."

"You had no authority to do that, young woman!"

"I feared it could be catching. There's a problem in the village with food that has gone off." I frowned. "Has there been any typhoid in the surrounding villages recently?"

She stared at me, her mouth open to rebuke me. Instead, she demanded, "Typhoid?"

I shrugged. "It's summer—it's possible."

She turned and stalked away.

Maeve closed the door.

"I ought to go and help with the meal," I said, rising.

"You haven't had your tea!" she scolded me. "And you're a guest in this house."

"Still. I brought it for you—and of course Simon." I made my way to the door as she said, frowning in concern, "What's the trouble with Molly? Is she really ill?"

"She was in tears when I came into the kitchen this morning. It was a good excuse to send her home. Fewer eyes—"

"Molly is only a child," she protested.

"Children can gossip," I said, and opened the door.

Molly was in the kitchen, the potatoes scrubbed and ready for the oven, with a vegetable and cheese dish waiting to be put together. She looked up in alarm as I stepped into the room.

"What did you tell her?" she whispered.

"That I was afraid you might be ill. I didn't think I ought to say you were crying."

"No—oh, no." She looked around, as if fearful that the very walls had ears. "I ought to warn you, Miss. English or not, you've been kind to me. The police are searching everywhere for an escaped prisoner. Just—just be very careful. The Constable had you once. Make certain—"

She broke off, terrified, as a heavy banging started on the front door of the house.

I said quietly, "You've done nothing wrong—stay here in the kitchen, go about your duties."

And I stepped through to the front room, saying to Michael, who was rising from a chair, "Lie down. Pull up the covers. If they question you, try to pretend you are still half out of your head—"

Eileen, shock in her face, said, "Dear God—" And she began to open up the covers she had tidily arranged on the bed, and helped him move into them.

Niall opened the door, I heard his voice asking what was happening.

I couldn't hear the response. I was already racing up the back stairs to warn Maeve.

Heavy boots invaded the front hall, and voices grew louder.

Maeve opened her door, I whispered the warning that they hadn't come for the Major—not directly—then slipped into my room.

And I stood there behind the door, listening as they began to search the house.

It was then I noticed a streak of mud on my boots. It clearly wasn't from the garden beds.

In a panic, I found a clean cloth, my little tin of polish, and got to work, praying they wouldn't come to my door next.

CHAPTER TWENTY-ONE

MY PRAYERS WERE answered. I heard the Constable and his men come tramping up the stairs knocking first on Mrs. Flynn's door.

She didn't take the intrusion well. Her voice carried as she said, "This house doesn't harbor runaway felons. And you shouldn't have lost him in the first place."

There was argument, negotiation, and then she agreed to the Constable himself searching her rooms while his companions cooled their heels in the passage.

I had just shoved the stained cloth into my pocket and the tin back into my valise when the pounding on my door began.

Opening it, my gaze met and held the Constable's. He hadn't got over the embarrassment of losing this prisoner, and his voice was cold as he demanded access to my room.

I didn't explain that it was Eileen's. I simply moved aside and let them in.

They poked and prodded, leaving the definite impression that what they were after must be a leprechaun. No reasonably sized man could hide in my valise or in the cabinet that held the washbasin and pitcher and matching chamber pot.

It occurred to me that they were punishing me for having evaded them.

With a grunt, the Constable nodded, and his men left the room.

I closed my door smartly but pressed my ear against it, because Maeve's rooms were next.

They knocked at her door, and politely asked to inspect her rooms.

I heard her reply, "I am so sorry, gentlemen. I don't feel well at all. I'm going back to my bed. Search as you like."

The Constable said, "It won't require more than a minute of your time."

"I'm sure. But if I stand here a moment longer—" There was the sound of retching.

She must have fled to her bed, leaving them to themselves, because I heard the Constable say "Be quick about it" to his men.

They were. I heard her door close quietly and they moved on to knock at Niall's door.

He had words with them. I couldn't hear what was said, but they must have searched his room thoroughly as well.

I worried about Terrence. His arm had been bleeding, according to Maeve. Were there bloody cloths or clothing in his room?

I heard them knock, then knock a second time. There was some discussion, before they called to the room's occupant that they were coming in.

No alarm went up. I breathed again.

When they had finished there, they went to the Major's door, and afterward began with the unoccupied part of the house, opening and closing doors as they went.

Finally they must have either run out of places to search or been satisfied that there was no "escaped felon" hiding in the house—nor a missing Major—was that the person they were actually hunting for? I heard them noisily descending the stairs, making some remark about the stable block.

They hadn't been gone more than a few minutes when there was a soft knock at my door. I expected it to be Maeve, and I stepped back to open it.

It was Terrence. His arms were full of bloody cloths and clothes, bundled into a blanket. His back and shoulders were covered with dust. I pulled him inside and shut the door quietly.

"Dear God—where were you?"

"In the back of the attics."

"Didn't they search there?"

"No, just the servants' quarters. Can you do something about this arm?"

"Yes, of course. But what will you do with those things?"

"Take them out to sea in the currach and drop them. If anyone finds them, I hope they think the Major drowned."

I'd left Eileen's kit in Maeve's room, and had to go fetch it.

She said, when I was inside, "Now I shan't be able to eat Molly's dinner. Or everyone will be suspicious. But it worked. They opened the cupboard, but they never looked under the bed."

"I'll slip something up to you. I've come for the medical kit."

"Of course."

I took it back to my room, and when Terrence had taken off his shirt, I cleaned and sewed up the wound in his arm. He took it well, grimacing as he asked how Simon and the Major had missed being caught. "There was nothing I could do—"

"Apparently your aunt managed quite well. I don't know the whole of it, but they didn't look under her bed. Or in it."

He smiled. "My grandmother has always underestimated Aunt Maeve."

I believed him. "I thought she might be—simple—when I first met her."

"She didn't know then if she would like you. Even to her, you're the enemy."

"And yet she took in the Major."

"More to spite her mother-in-law than to help him, I expect."

"There," I said, cutting the thread, then reaching for what was left of the bandages. "I need more supplies. Can you manage that too?"

"I'll find a way."

He'd just put his shirt on and was buttoning it when I heard Mrs. Flynn start down to her delayed dinner.

Terrence waited, then went down the front stairs, leaving his bundle under my bed until dark.

Shortly afterward I heard a soft whistle, and when I went to the window, I saw him quickly disappearing around the far corner of the house. It was taking a terrible risk, for the Constable and his men were in the stable block and the outbuildings, still searching. I found myself wishing he'd stayed in the attics. That wound was still too fresh, and whoever had been there in the fort last night would remember using his knife.

I raided the pantry after everyone had finished in the kitchen and Molly had washed the dishes.

As I was trying to decide how much of the roast I could take upstairs without having the household start to wonder at Maeve's sudden increase in appetite, I glanced out the tiny window. I could just see the stable block. Two men were coming from there and had stopped in the shadows of the arch. Apparently they had finished searching the outbuildings and were discussing their next stop.

The Major's bloody rags and Terrence's as well were under my bed.

Torn between guarding my door and needing to be certain where they were going next, I watched them converse, trying to gauge their mood. One was the Constable, and the other was one of the men who had searched my room.

Where was the other one? Had he been left to watch the horses or the house itself?

I frowned, trying to work it out. Just then the Constable turned, looking over his shoulder toward the stables, and a flash of memory came back to me.

I'd seen him before—but in the dark, only a silhouette talking to the tall man I'd called the singer, the violinist, from the pub, while Simon and I were hiding in the hawthorn clump.

And then he moved, and the similarity was lost. He was the familiar form of the Constable again.

Still, I was sure of what I'd seen. It literally opened my eyes.

All this time, when it appeared that he was enforcing the law as he saw it, he'd been one of the conspirators—he'd been a part of the circle of men who had taken Michael and then the Major.

I couldn't prove it. And I was English, it would be my word against his. No one would believe me.

But I had to warn Terrence. And Simon.

While that man had been taking me up for the murder of Fergus Kennedy, and hunting the countryside for Simon, he himself might well have ordered the artist's death. After all, he'd have been told that Fergus Kennedy had seen the boat setting out with an unconscious man aboard—Michael. His killers had even ransacked the studio for any sketch that might prove what had happened to the missing groom.

It explained so much of what had been happening. Two men who had served in the British Army had arrived for a wedding. And they must have become a target straightaway. An idea that had seemed impossible suddenly became possible. It explained why Padriac had arrived, the advance guard. Why Terrence was in their way, because this involved his own family, and he'd have wanted no part of it. And always, always, the Constable had turned a blind eye, because he was behind it all. No doubt pressure from above had forced him to take me into custody—an Englishwoman with no one to turn to—for the Kennedy murder, so that his superiors could see progress.

No wonder all the efforts to find Michael or the Major had failed. The only policeman we could turn to for official help knew where *not* to look.

I was angry—and worried. He had the authority of the Constabulary behind him. He could twist the truth, and he would be believed.

And we were a danger to him, Michael and Ellis and Terrence and I.

I heard horses, and there was the second man, bringing them around. I breathed a sigh of relief. The Constable and the other man had finished their conversation, were moving out toward the sound.

They were leaving.

In spite of my relief, I knew they could—would—come back anytime they wished. Or were ordered to.

I hastily made several sandwiches and took them up the back stairs. Knocking on Maeve's door, I started to say something, and something in her face warned me in time.

Her mother-in-law was sitting in the chair that Simon had mended.

"Mrs. Flynn has come to see if I was feeling a little better," Maeve told me.

I smiled, saying, "And I had brought up some sandwiches I thought you might feel like eating. How is your nausea? I'm sorry I had nothing to give you to help."

Mrs. Flynn was staring at the sandwiches. "That's heavy food for an ill woman."

"Well, they aren't all for her. I missed my dinner as well. And I'm trying to encourage Michael to eat. He must have lost a stone."

"I wish you would go and take the rubbish with you," she told me, and got out of the chair. I kept an eye on the cane.

"I am making arrangement to leave," I said. "As soon as that aircraft can come again, I'll be off. Perhaps Terrence or Niall can clear the meadow of horses?"

"I'd do it myself if it meant the last of you. I dislike forward women. It speaks poorly of your parents that you have no manners."

I thought I'd bite my tongue in two. It was one thing to make such remarks to me. But to speak ill of my parents went beyond the pale.

Instead I stood aside to let her pass out of the room.

When she was gone, and we were sure she wasn't listening at the door, Maeve smiled sympathetically. "I thought you might trip her up as she left."

"If I hadn't been brought up to respect my elders, I might have done just that."

She took one of the sandwiches. "This is heavenly."

"I must speak to Simon—"

"Yes, of course, please do. Take one of these to him. He must be starving, poor man. We haven't shown any of you proper Irish hospitality. I'm so sorry about that."

"Maeve. Begin to pack whatever you'll need. There won't be much room, but there will be essentials, things you can't leave without. We can't stay here any longer."

"The Major can't be moved—"

"We may not have much choice." I went to the inner door, tapped lightly. Simon came to answer it.

I handed him the plate of sandwiches and said, "I need to look in on the Major."

When the door was shut behind me, I put my hand on Simon's shoulder, and leaned up to whisper what I had seen.

He listened, nodded once, and when I'd finished, he said, "That makes him dangerous, the fact that he's part of the Constabulary. On the whole they're good men."

I said, moving away, "How is our patient?"

"Better, I think. He has had rough handling, but he's a strong man."

Walking to the bed, I felt his forehead, took his pulse, and checked the burns on his arms. They were still weeping. I was just started to rebandage them when he opened his eyes.

"I thought I was dreaming—delirious. I didn't believe I was safe." His voice was a thread. I had to lean closer to hear him.

"I'm glad you're awake," I said. "Did you recognize your captors?"

"No. There was someone they deferred to. I never saw him. But they were afraid of him, I think. They redoubled their efforts after he came and went."

He lay back, spent. "You must get out of here, Bess—"

"Not without you."

But he'd already begun to drift away.

Turning to Simon, I said, "If only we could get him aboard Arthur's aircraft. It's impossible, but it would be the best way out for him. And Michael as well."

"I could strap them to the wings. It would balance the weight. The problem is, he'd need a longer runway. And less fuel. I don't know if he could make it to Bristol with less."

"There must be somewhere in Wales where he could put down."

"You look very tired, Bess. This has been a heavy burden for you. Michael. The Major. And now this new problem. Go with Arthur when he comes. I'll see to Eileen and her mother. I want to know you're out of this, and safely home again."

Summoning a smile, I said, "Never tell a woman she looks tired. The thing is, I can't leave until I'm sure you're safe as well. And of course the parrot," I added lightly, preparing to leave.

"Terrence is wiring the owner of the caravan. He's to report it stolen, and then come and claim it. The parrot is safe."

His voice changed as he said my name. "Bess."

I turned.

And as I did, the door opened before he could tell me what he'd been about to say. Maeve came into the room.

After all, it was her bedroom. She had every right . . .

"Bess, it's best you go. I heard raised voices in the kitchen."

Indeed, as soon as I was close by the door in her sitting room, I could hear them as well.

It wasn't my place to sort out the problems of the Flynn household. Still, if we had any hope of getting out of here, the well-being of this family was very important. And so I hurried down the stairs.

When I stepped into the kitchen, the argument stopped at once.

Mrs. Flynn was there, Niall, and Molly. They turned as one to stare at me.

Molly had been crying again, but now her face was red and bruised. It looked as if someone had slapped her forcefully with the back of his or her hand.

Granny said sharply, "This is none of your affair."

I replied, "Who struck her?"

"I don't know," Niall retorted. "That's what we've been trying to discover."

"Yelling at the child isn't likely to help her confide in you." I turned to Molly, going over to the pump as I said, "Come, let's wet a clean cloth and put it on your face. It will feel better."

But she stared at me, too frightened to cross her employers. I remembered that her mother was ill, and Molly was the sole support of the family. It was the only reason she had stayed when the other staff went away in a huff over having English visitors in the house.

I smiled at her. "Come along," I said again. "They won't be angry with you if you let me help you."

If looks could kill, Granny had just reduced me to a bloody heap on the floor.

But Niall said, "Go on, let her help you."

I gave her the cool cloth to press against her face, then said, "Now then, is your mother all right? Is she hurt as well?"

She shook her head.

"Just you, then?"

She nodded.

"Who was it?" When she didn't answer, I went on. "Was it someone in this household?"

Glancing at Mrs. Flynn, she said quickly, "No, Miss."

Taking a chance, I said, "Is it someone we know? Does he have a name?"

Frightened again, she said, "Please, Miss. Don't ask me."

"Was it Padriac?" I remembered the fish dish I'd blamed for poisoning him. Had he in turn blamed Molly? "Was it about something he'd eaten?"

From fright, her reaction to his name went to outright fear. "N-no, Miss."

And suddenly I'd worked it out. A spy in our household. Molly, who needed the money . . . "Do you work for him, as well as for Mrs. Flynn?"

"I must go, Miss—please, let me go!" Dropping the cloth, she started for the door. Niall, interested now, quickly stepped in front of it, barring her escape.

I said, "Did he ask you to spy on this household?"

She began to cry again. "Please, Miss, don't make me tell you. He'll hurt my mother—please, sir?"

"Did he give you something to hide in my room?"

She didn't need to answer. There was guilt written in her face. "He said it was to make you laugh—"

"You help at the pub, sometimes. The man Padriac—was it you who gave him the fish that was off—to make him ill?"

"No, Miss—oh no! He'd have killed me for it!"

But I thought she had, for Eileen.

Looking at Niall, whose face was flushed with anger, I said, "Let her leave. She's terrified, we know what we need to know. It doesn't help to have her mistreated."

Reluctantly he moved aside, and she made her escape.

As soon as the outer door slammed behind her, Niall rounded on his grandmother, too angry to wait until I'd left them. "That lies at your door—you and your craving to see the end of anything English. To force them out of Ireland. Terrence is paying the price for it, and if you have your way it will destroy all of us."

"They killed your father, those English. *Killed him!* And I won't rest until not one is left on good Irish soil."

"Granny, it was an accident. I went to the barracks, I saw the report. I talked to people who were there."

"When did you do this?"

"Two years ago. I wanted to know, and what I learned was very different from what you'd told me all these years. I wanted to please you, Granny. I wanted to be the hero you wanted us to be, Terrence and me. But my heart wasn't in it. It never was."

"You're not your father's son. Get out of my house! I never want to see your face again."

"It isn't your house, Granny. It's Terrence's. Father left it to him." His voice was tired, now, his face drained of his anger. "God knows, we love you, Granny. We always will. But you must stay out of conspiracies. People like Padriac are hard and hungry for power. They aren't interested in freeing Ireland for us. They want it for themselves. You'll get us killed, Granny. Look what happened to Michael. And where's the Major? Or there's Bess, clapped up in jail on false evidence. She didn't kill Fergus any more than I did. This isn't the way to free this country. If it is, I'd rather leave, and remember it fondly from far away."

He turned and walked quietly out of the house.

I thought for a moment that she'd call him back. But her pride got in the way. Glaring at me, she thundered, "This is your doing, it was all going well, until you came. And that Major. Be damned to you both. If I never see you again, it will be soon enough."

Pounding the floor with her cane at every step, stiff-backed and head high, she walked to the door to the back stairs and began to climb them.

The door to the front room opened softly and Eileen, her eyes large with alarm, looked in.

"Bess?" she whispered. "Are you all right? Is Granny?"

"Yes, don't worry," I told her.

But I had to worry about getting us safely out of here.

When Terrence came back an hour later, he brought a sack of bandages and ointments and salves and little vials of everything he could think of, to replenish Eileen's medical kit.

Knocking at my door, he handed me the sack and said, "This should see you safely back to England."

"Come in, please. There's something you should know."

He did, shutting the door behind him. And I told him about Molly, Niall, and his grandmother. Not to be a tattletale but to let him know how things stood before he walked into the matter blind.

"I was afraid of this," he said when I'd finished. "Not about Molly, of course, that's news. Poor child, she ought never to have been caught in the middle of this. I'll speak to her. But I'd watched Niall's drinking, I suspected I knew why, but there was nothing I could do. Granny was driving him."

"What happened to your father? May I ask? She's so filled with bitterness."

"It was an accident. He'd gone to the barracks with my mother, they were to be guests at some function or other. There was a mishap with some ordnance—a shell had a bad fuse. At any rate it terrified the horses, and he was just about to step down and hand out my mother when they bolted. He was thrown from the carriage, and she was killed outright when it overturned. He lived a few hours, but it was hopeless— the doctor did everything he could, but the injury was to his spine."

He took a deep breath. "We were children, Niall and I. I remember the priest and someone from the barracks coming to the door, and then my grandmother screaming. The house was in turmoil. It was hours before someone came to tell the two of us that our parents had been killed. I'll never forget Niall asking, 'But they'll come home when they're better, won't they?' and later, when the coffins were brought into the main parlor—it's been closed off ever since—my grandmother took us to see them and told us the English had murdered them and we were never to forget that."

Dear God. It was a terrible burden to put on grieving children who barely comprehended death. I could understand why she'd become the vicious, bitter old woman she was. The tragedy was, she had carried her family into her own grief and shaped them through it.

I said—anything else would have been wrong—"I'm sorry. Eileen had never said anything."

"She didn't know. She and her parents were visiting Maeve's cousins in Dublin. It wasn't until her own husband died that Maeve became a recluse, having to live here without him to stand up to Granny." He looked down, his face sad. "It wasn't much of a life for my aunt. I did what I could to see that Eileen was happy."

"What will she do—your grandmother—when all of us have gone?"

"She'll have the house to herself. But it won't make her happy." He shrugged slightly. "She will never change, Bess. Even if—when—Ireland is free, it won't matter. I've a feeling she'll find a new crusade. And very likely it will be about the English who stole her family from her."

It was then I told him about the Constable.

He said, "Are you sure of this?" When I nodded, he went on thoughtfully, "It makes sense of course. It explains so much that we didn't understand. He covered his part very well, the bastard."

Clearing his throat, the closest he could come to apologizing for swearing, he added, "The sooner you're out of here, the better, given this news about Molly spying on us. But I can't fault her. She's caught up in something she doesn't understand."

"How involved is Granny with these people?"

"I expect they were happy to have her money and her open support. They have used her. And Niall. It gave them some respectability locally."

"Will they betray you, Terrence?"

"They won't have the opportunity. I've got a safe haven to go to, once Eileen and her mother are well clear of this place."

For an instant, something in his voice frightened me.

"Terrence—"

He smiled. "Not what you think. No, I'm stubborn enough to want to live to see Ireland free, and then to stand for office and be certain that it's done right. That between them the Church and the hotheads don't make a disaster of it, and bring the English back with 'I told you so.'" He turned toward the door. "I must look in on them." And then he turned back. "You know Simon, don't you? Who is he?"

"He's a friend of the family." I smiled. "I think he's spent a lifetime trying to keep me out of trouble for my father's sake. He borrowed the caravan from someone in Dublin."

"Along with the parrot, I presume." Terrence regarded me for a moment. Then he said, "Do you know that he's in love with you, Bess?"

I could feel myself blushing to the roots of my hair, my face suddenly quite warm.

"Thank you for the compliment, but he's like the son my father never had. An unofficially adopted brother."

Terrence shook his head. "I've seen the way he looks at you sometimes, when he thinks no one notices. I've had to hide my own feeling for Eileen for a very long time. I know what it's like. I know the signs. I know the ache when I see it."

I could only stare at him.

"Do you care for him at all?" he asked, curious now.

"I—" My voice failed me. I'd known it for some time. Only I hadn't been able to face it. Simon had been my friend for so long. I hadn't ever wanted to lose that. I'd wanted to stay with QAIMNS not only for the wounded, but also to save me from having to make any decisions about a future I couldn't have. My father cared for him like a son—how could I do anything that might interfere with that?

He smiled, and it was with warmth and understanding. And a longing for something he himself could never have.

"He's a damned lucky man."

And he was gone.

I stood there, facing the door, for the longest time. Unaware of the tears rolling down my cheeks until I could taste the salt on my lips.

Chapter Twenty-Two

I WISHED I'D had the forethought to hand the sack of medicines back to Terrence to be taken to Maeve. Simon would know what to do with them, and I wasn't quite ready to face anyone at the moment.

There was a very good reason for that, of course.

Terrence had been right about something else. We needed to leave. Whoever these people were behind what was happening in Killeigh-beg, they were dangerous. If they intended to blow up a British post, there would be all kinds of repercussions, and I didn't wish to see Michael or the Major caught up in that or any legal aftermath. I didn't want to see Niall caught up in this either. What I'd learned about him surprised me, but I didn't think he was lying to his grandmother. It was too deeply personal, what he'd said to her.

How to go about leaving? That was the problem. Could Terrence find a larger boat that would hold all of us until we were safely away? And how in heaven's name were we to get the Major to it? Michael would find it hard enough going, but his will would probably forbid him to admit to any weakness.

The donkeys again?

I needed to speak to Simon and to Ellis, to gauge just how serious his injuries were. We could kill him, if we weren't careful, even as we tried to save him.

Why did Terrence have to tell me that?

I dreaded going to Maeve's room, I dreaded having to face Simon until I had faced myself.

Eventually, the part of me that had come down from that many-greats-grandmother, the one who had danced the night away in Belgium, to keep the French from guessing that Wellington was marching to stop them at Waterloo, even when her own husband had slipped away to join his regiment, rose to scold me. She had put a good face on her personal pain and pretended that all was well. She had recognized her duty, and she'd carried it out with aplomb. My many-greats-grandfather had survived, although days had passed before she could be sure of that.

I collected the bundle that Terrence was to throw into the sea, opened my door, and looked both ways, then crossed the passage to tap at Maeve's door.

She had been talking to Terrence, and he looked grave as I walked in.

"These are yours," I said. "The sooner the better."

"Yes, right. Thanks."

"What's happened?"

"The Major doesn't look very well," he said.

"I've come to see how he's feeling. But it would help to know how soon do we hope to leave? I must prepare him." It was rather like having to move the wounded before a German push that was sure to overrun our sector. Ambulances lining up, doctors doing their best to stabilize the most seriously wounded, Sisters guiding the stretchers out of the tents and into the ambulance, and the fighting rushing closer to us. Only this time I had only two wounded, but no ambulance.

"Tomorrow night. I daren't leave it any longer."

I turned to Maeve. "In a bit, could you call Eileen to help you with something—something simple but necessary, so that she's not suspicious? I need to speak to Michael, to prepare him for what's to come." Frowning, I remembered something. "He was staying somewhere in the village, wasn't he? What's become of his things—valise, clothing, papers?"

"I brought them here and put them in my room to start, when he first went missing. Then I stowed them in the attic, not knowing what else to do with them. We hadn't told his family when he went missing. It seemed rather cruel to tell them anything until we had a body."

Relieved, I nodded.

"Bess—there won't be much room in the boat. You'll have to leave nearly everything behind. Put it in the attic, I'll send it later. Only what is absolutely necessary goes with you."

I hadn't considered that. "All right. I'll speak to Michael. He'll know if there are any papers he needs. But what about Eileen?"

"I'll see to her things," Maeve volunteered. "I know what matters to her—and what papers she'll want." She looked at Terrence. "That small portrait of her father. That must go. Whatever else stays."

"We'll put everything into a waterproof bag. All right." He picked up the bundle again. "I must go."

"Your arm?" I asked.

"It will do," he said, and then was gone.

He'd left his horse by the kitchen passage. Standing by Maeve's windows, I watched him mount and turn back toward the stables, as if taking the horse back there.

I went to the door, preparing to leave.

"You aren't looking in on the Major?"

"Oh—yes." I turned, and went to knock on the other door, before opening it.

Simon rose from a chair by the bed.

"Did you speak to Terrence?"

"Yes, I've come to see for myself."

But after examining Ellis, I stood there looking down at him, worried.

"What is it?"

"I think it's as much exhaustion as it is injury. They could have forced him to stay awake, no sleep, questioning him constantly." I reached down and touched Ellis's shoulder.

He flinched, jerking away from my touch. Saying his name, I said, "Can you hear me? Ellis, it's Bess."

It was several seconds before he opened his eyes. I could read the alarm in them. "Bess? For God's sake, get out of here—before they come back."

He'd been held by two men. And two men had been watching over him—Simon and Terrence. We'd kept the light in the room dim enough not to disturb him. With his bruised eyes, he must have seen only shadows moving about.

I said, "They're friends, Ellis. I trust them. You're safe now."

"This isn't my room—"

"No. We couldn't take you there, it wasn't safe. Maeve—the younger Mrs. Flynn—let us use her bedroom. Shall I call her? Let you see for yourself?"

There was a long sigh from the man in the bed. "Bess—are you certain—?"

I beckoned to Simon, who had moved back when I'd begun my examination.

"Major Dawson? May I present Sergeant-Major Brandon?" And I gave him the regiment.

"Hello, sir," Simon said, coming to the bed and reaching for Ellis's good hand. "Sorry to meet you in such circumstances. But they will be improving shortly. You can trust Sister Crawford. She's used to getting the wounded out of tight spots."

Ellis squinted to see him more clearly. "Thank you, Sergeant-Major. Happy to have you on my side. Now if you'll forgive me, I think I need to sleep." He closed his eyes and drifted away from us.

"Is he delirious?" Simon asked.

"He's not terribly feverish. But I think he held out through what must have been unrelenting pain. Not in expectation of rescue, but hoping they would kill him when they tired of trying to break him. It must be very difficult for his mind to accept that he doesn't have to fight any longer."

"He's been lucid before."

"Not with any consistency. Not enough to shock his mind into the present. He may have thought he was hallucinating."

"I don't like the idea of scuttling out of here, leaving those bas— men unpunished for what they've done."

"We can see to that once we're out of Ireland. Getting out is going to be difficult. Terrence says tomorrow night. We can only take what's important. Nothing more. I haven't been in the Major's room yet. To-night I'll try."

"Leave it to me when the house is asleep."

"Are you sure?"

"I'm going mad myself, shut up in here."

I couldn't help but smile. "Just don't run afoul of Granny. She's in a terrible mood."

He didn't return the smile. "Maeve told me there were angry words in the kitchen."

I gave him a brief account of what had happened.

"Terrence is right. The sooner you're out of this country, the better."

"I need to see if I can make a broth that he can drink. He's had no food, Simon. But I can never seem to find the kitchen empty. I'm going to tell them it's for Maeve. But what about you?"

"Terrence brought sandwiches from the village where he bought the bandages."

"Good."

I couldn't think of anything else to say or do, and so I left.

There was the bone from the roast, and I chopped the meat as finely as I could, then cooked them together with some vegetables from dinner as well.

I was just making sure it was fine enough to feed to him and not choke him when Eileen opened the door and asked, "That's a lovely smell. What is it?"

"Broth for your mother. She's not ready for a full meal."

"Oh, can I have a little for Michael?"

"He should have more than broth. Look in the pantry and make him a hearty sandwich."

I don't think she was best pleased, but she went in there, came back with bread and meat, made the sandwiches, then took them with a cup of tea back to her husband.

An hour later, I had what I needed, a broth that could be thinned with a little wine, or taken as it was.

Pouring it into a pitcher, I took it up the back stairs and gave it to Maeve.

"Simon can help you hold up his head. Only a little bit at a time, mind. And don't let him choke." I gave her a large spoon and several tea towels I'd taken from a drawer.

"Don't you want to help?"

"I have other things on my list," I told her, and left.

My opportunity to speak to Michael came an hour later. And it wasn't Maeve who drew Eileen away. I was in my room when I heard the familiar *thump!* of Mrs. Flynn's cane, pounding on the floor for someone to come at once.

I opened my door a little and finally heard Eileen running up the stairs as the pounding went on.

"Granny?" I heard her call as she went into her grandmother's rooms, and I took the chance to hurry down to speak to Michael.

"How is the Major?" he asked, one eye on the door to the foyer.

"He's not well, but we hope to leave tomorrow night and we'll have to find a way to get both of you out of the house."

"I can walk—"

"How far?" I shook my head. "You can't be sure?"

"I'll make it," he said with a fierce certainty, the same strength that had got him to the church to be married, whatever the cost.

I could hear Eileen on the stairs. "Say nothing to her—she's worried enough."

"Yes—"

I left and was just sitting at the kitchen table when Eileen came in. "She'd like tea and a sandwich. Is there any cake left?"

"I don't know. Let me help you."

We prepared a tray for her grandmother, and as we worked, Eileen asked, "How is my mother? There isn't anything really wrong, is there?"

"No. Just a little upset. I think she's been worried about you and about Michael."

"The Major is dead, isn't he? There's been no news—and I haven't seen anyone searching. Even Michael seems to have given up hope. Who are these people—what did they want with Michael or Ellis?"

"Heaven only knows," I replied.

"The only thing they have in common is the Army."

I dropped the knife I was using. "Oh, dear, I expect we're all out of sorts with worry. Both of them served in the English Army, remember? I expect that's the reason they were taken. It was the English Army that crushed the Rising."

Frowning, she said, "I'll be glad to leave Ireland. There's so much anger and heartbreak here. I thought I'd miss Granny, but she's been so cruel to Michael. I'll miss Terrence. He's always been there to look after me. Niall teased me, but Terrence protected me. He's a good man."

I said only, "My dear, it hasn't been the happiest wedding, has it? I am so sorry for that. You deserved better."

She started to cry. "You don't know how I felt when he came out of the shadows. I thought he was a ghost—I thought I'd conjured him up because I wanted so badly for him to be there, to marry me. Then I realized that everyone else had seen him too, and I touched him, and there was living flesh under my fingertips. Oh God, if I live to be as old as my grandmother, I won't forget how that felt. Now I just want to go, to break my ties with Ireland, and try to learn how to deal with the future."

We finished the tray, and then Eileen stopped, went out the kitchen door, and when she came back a few minutes later, she had a rose in her hands. "We'll add this to the tray. She'll like that. She's had a lot of sorrow in *her* life, hasn't she? I hope Niall and Terrence will remember that."

I hadn't seen Niall since the confrontation with Mrs. Flynn.

"I'm sure they will. They seem to care for her."

Picking up the tray, she carried it to the stairs. "It's funny about love, isn't it?" she said, before starting up. "There are those we care about because we're of the same blood. Whatever they are, they're our family. And then we meet someone and fall in love, and suddenly we're ready to leave that family behind and go anywhere with someone who isn't our blood at all. Why can't we all be happy together, why do we have to leave?"

And then she disappeared up the stairs.

I was on tenterhooks for the rest of the afternoon. I wasn't accustomed to being left out of the planning. Terrence hadn't come back, and neither had Niall. Twice I looked in on the Major, and he appeared to be resting now, not just sleeping in exhaustion. The broth was helping. But I couldn't be sure. He needed a doctor's care, and so did Michael, to be sure he was all right as well. And who would dress Terrence's wound? Impossible to do on his own, with only one hand . . .

Supper came, and it was only the two of us, Eileen and me. There was no sign of Molly. We made a toast, using whatever was in the pantry, and Eileen finished what was left in a wine bottle. I sipped mine, wanting a clear head. Finally, a little tired of each other's company, Eileen took a plate to Michael, and after she left, I went upstairs with another for Maeve and Simon. There was hardly anything now in the pantry.

But after tomorrow, that wouldn't be my problem.

Shutting myself in my room, I stood in the dark by the window and wondered if Terrence had told me the truth about Simon's feelings.

Iris, our housemaid in Somerset, had believed that Simon's journey to Scotland while I was in Paris had to do with someone he was in love with there. My mother hadn't believed that. But what if it *were* true? What if Terrence had been mistaken about what he claimed he'd seen? What he'd wanted to believe was Simon's feelings about me?

I'd be a fool, wouldn't I, to take that to heart, however well-meaning Terrence had been? I would only embarrass both of us, Simon and me, by saying something . . .

The thoughts went round and round in my head, as if the darkness in the room let me feel, then doubt, then question, then wonder, in circles. Where no one could see and I could even hide from myself.

At last, knowing I ought to rest, I changed and went to bed, only to stare at the ceiling for hours. It was close on three when I heard a horse trotting across the lawn. I didn't know whether it was Niall or Terrence. I wanted to stand by the door and see which one came up the stairs. If it was Terrence, I could ask if he'd found a boat.

But that was foolishness. After all, we weren't leaving tonight.

Whether he'd found a boat or not. There wasn't time now to get everyone out of the house, all the way to the strand, and into a boat under
cover of darkness. Not with summer's early sunrises. We'd be here one
more day.

I'd know in the morning. Either way there was nothing more I
could do tonight.

Still, dawn was just breaking when I fell into a restless sleep.

There was no opportunity to speak to Terrence—I only saw him at a
distance, working in the stables, and I couldn't very well walk out there
for a friendly chat.

Niall was morose, wandering about the house, uncertain what to do
with himself. He had words with Michael and then Eileen, went for a
long walk, and came back in no better frame of mind.

I was beginning to wonder if we should have called in the Army,
and let them sort it all out. But the village would suffer, and there was
Molly as well. I couldn't have her taken up just because she feared for
her mother. But when I was back in Somerset, I was going to find a way
to see that the Constable paid for all he'd done, and the singer with
him. I was certain the Colonel Sahib knew someone who could deal
with it quietly.

That was, if there was time, if they hadn't put off their plans—if it
wasn't too late.

There were eggs and bread and some bacon for breakfast, as well as
porridge, and Niall brought a box of food from the pub for our dinner.
I could hardly swallow food, wishing I knew what lay ahead. But I told
myself sternly that I would have need of it later, and so I ate what was
in front of me, not tasting much of it as it went down.

We took plates to Maeve, and I made certain it was a generous
amount.

And then I went to my room, sorted my belongings, laid out warm clothes for the boat, and put the things I must carry with me in the inner pocket of my coat.

After that, I could only hold on to my patience and wait. It was hard to leave everything to Terrence. I was used to having a part in things, not sitting quietly until I was told what to do. A nurse has to use her wits, her training, her eyes, and even her nose. Matron expected her to know the file for every patient, what had been done, how much medication he'd been given and when, what doctors had seen him, what their diagnosis was, and what their prognosis might be. How much he'd eaten, what fluids he'd had and when, and whether his body's functions were working. Dehydration could kill as well as shrapnel and bullets. Missing a piece of the puzzle could mean the difference between survival and losing him.

And here I sat, the afternoon breeze lifting the curtain slightly. And tried not to think about Simon.

The hours passed. The sun seemed to linger in the sky forever, as if we lived at the Pole and it only had to dip below the horizon.

I went down to supper, talking to Eileen as we washed the dishes— Molly hadn't come back, and I was glad.

It was dark outside at last. Niall came in from tending the horses, and went up to his room without a word to anyone. I wondered if he guessed that we'd be gone soon, now that Michael was slowly improving.

Terrence came into kitchen just as I was going upstairs to change.

"Keep Eileen busy. We're bringing the Major down, Simon and I."

The waiting was over . . .

I made a pretense of examining Michael's leg. There had been deep bruising, down to the bone. But as I moved it in different positions, he winced but stopped himself from swearing or crying out.

Finishing my work I noted that he'd changed into dark trousers and shirt, teasing Eileen about the fact that she hadn't washed his clothes.

I noticed too that a heavy coat lay over the back of a chair, within easy reach.

I counted the minutes as I asked Eileen to tell me about Dublin. But she barely remembered it. "I was taken for walks, and I attended Mass with my parents, but I never really saw the town. Terrence had been there, of course, and he told me about the river and the docks and all the sights."

And then Terrence came in, knelt on the floor beside Michael, and said, "We must go. I've got everything you need. Maeve has Eileen's things. There's no time to lose."

Eileen opened her mouth to argue, and he stopped her with a raised hand.

"No. If we don't leave now, tonight, and quietly, we may not have another chance."

"But Granny—"

"You can write to her later. Let's go." He took Michael's arm to help him stand, and Eileen, frowning with worry, fussed over him until he ordered her to stop.

I left them, ran upstairs, changed my clothes, and caught up my coat. Maeve was coming out her door, the medical kit and a small box in her hands. She smiled nervously at me but said nothing.

We were the last to leave the house. And just as we walked out the kitchen door and turned to shut it softly, I heard the thumping of Granny's cane on the floor.

We made it across the lawns and past the dark stables, and then we were in the orchard. I thought, with all this passing back and forth, flattening the grasses, it won't be difficult to discover how we had left.

That caused me to wonder uneasily where Niall was.

We got through the orchard without any problem, then started toward the high ground from which I'd first seen the sea. Ahead of us, Eileen was leading Michael's donkey. I couldn't see Simon and Terrence.

Another fifty yards and we were on the strand where the boat was waiting.

It was another currach, larger than the other one, but we were going to be rather crowded, I thought. *Still,* I told myself, *one can't go about stealing a large enough boat without announcing the reason for taking it.*

A donkey was standing quietly, inspecting the seagrasses, and that meant the Major was already in the currach. Terrence was helping Michael dismount and walk out to the boat. Then he came back for Eileen.

As we came down to the water's edge, Terrence was standing in the surf, waiting to hand us in. Simon was already manning the oars, holding the boat steady. I took Maeve's packets while Terrence lifted her, carried her the few feet, and deposited her in the currach.

It was my turn, and I started forward, but Terrence lifted me as well and easily carried me out. I took my place, noticing that Michael was in the bottom of the boat and Eileen was cushioning Ellis's head.

I asked Terrence, "What about the donkeys?"

"I left the gate open. They'll find their way back."

Turning, I caught Simon's gaze, and he smiled. I smiled too, and then Terrence was leaping in behind me, and I handed him his oars. The surf was taking us now, and I drew a long breath of relief.

We were going to make it.

Chapter Twenty-Three

WITHOUT ANY WARNING, there was shouting as two men came running over the hill, racing down toward the strand.

The surf still had us, Simon and Terrence were pulling at the oars to take us over the incoming waves.

The two men didn't stop at the waterline. They kept coming, out into the surf. And the larger man of the two lifted his weapon to fire. It was the Constable.

Terrence's back was to him—a perfect target. I reached into my pocket, pulled out my revolver, and without taking proper aim, fired. A spray of water spurted up close by the Constable's feet.

That spoiled his shot. But the other man had a shotgun, and he was taking aim now. Behind me, Eileen was crying, and I heard Maeve gasp.

Terrence called, "If they hit the currach, it will sink us."

He dropped the oars, took my revolver from my hand, firing almost as it came to bear.

I caught up the oars, and then quickly looked back toward the beach. The taller man—the singer—pulled the trigger but the shotgun was pointed to the sky as he went down and didn't move again.

I could hear the pellets coming down into the water.

Terrence fired again, and the Constable fell backward. The tide pulled out, leaving him half in the water, half on the strand. And then it came rushing back again.

Neither man tried to get up and fire again.

Terrence shouted, "We'll have to go back. We can't leave them there. It will fall on Niall and Granny, this close to the house."

Simon called, "There isn't time. They may not be alone—someone will have heard those shots."

"No—I can't leave until we dispose of them—"

Just then another man came running over the hill, stopping short for an instant as he saw what was in the water. He ran on, coming toward us.

Terrence was bringing the revolver up again, ready to fire, but I said, "No—I think—*that looks like Niall.*"

He didn't lower the revolver, watching as his brother came within hailing distance.

"Go on—" he shouted. "I'll pull them out into the sea—"

"I'm coming in—"

"No, I tell you. I'll see to it."

And he began to drag the first body deeper into the water, pulling it until it began to move with the surf, and then he pulled it farther, almost chest deep in the sea, so that the tide wouldn't bring it in again—where the current could carry it well away.

Then he went back for the other body and was pulling it out as well.

Simon called, "Terrence. We need to go."

Terrence couldn't seem to take his eyes off his brother. And then he turned and I handed him the oars as he dropped the revolver into my lap. I was near enough to see his face, and the pain in it.

Beneath his breath, I heard him say, "Mary Mother of God keep him!"

And then he began to pull hard on the oars, sweeping us out into the current as Simon turned the little craft toward the north.

I tried to comfort Maeve and Eileen, both of them distraught, holding each other as they wept, and all the while I too was still seeing those two men drop into the sea.

I had wanted to punish them for what they'd done, I had wanted to see them stand trial and pay for their crimes. I hadn't expected it to end like this.

But they'd made the choices that had led to their own deaths. They had seen us there in the currach, they had known how easy it would be to sink it, and they had no idea how many of us could swim, could make it back to shore. For all I knew, they'd have shot anyone who tried. I didn't think they'd have waded out for any of us, unless they'd wanted Terrence alive for reasons of their own.

I took a deep breath. "It had to be done," I told Terrence. "It was a choice—our lives or theirs."

"I'm not used to shooting Irishmen," he said, and then fell silent, intent on the oars.

We had a very long way to go. I had no idea where we were heading, but I didn't think we could make it around the northern tip of Ireland and as far as the safety of the Welsh coast.

For a time there was only silence, the sound of the oars sweeping rhythmically, and the sea lapping the side of the little boat. I saw Maeve lean forward to be sure Ellis was covered by the blanket wrapped round him. We must have been an hour out at sea, moving steadily, no storm on the horizon to worry us, just the night. I knew Simon could navigate by the stars, but there were fishing boats that traveled these waters. I tried to keep watch for one.

We were well into our second hour when I heard a sound I recognized.

An aircraft. I looked up, searching the night sky for it, but I couldn't find it, even when it was nearly overhead. Had an alert gone out already? Surely not!

A light flashed as it began to circle. Simon, shipping his oars, pulled out his torch and signaled back. *It must be Arthur,* I thought, watching the aircraft moving in graceful loops.

There was a series of flashes then—code, I realized—and Simon shouted, "The patrol boat is only a mile away."

I too could read code, but the message was terse. I called anxiously, "Ours? Or theirs?"

"Ours."

A final exchange of flashes, and the little aircraft moved off.

Very soon thereafter, we saw the distant running lights of a much larger boat. Faint at first, and then growing brighter.

Simon signaled it, and it was very soon alongside.

It was difficult to get the Major aboard. They had to send down a sling. Simon called it back for Michael, who protested that he could climb the rope ladder. Simon said something to him that I didn't hear, and Michael subsided, climbing carefully into the sling when it came down again.

We sent our possessions up with him.

Maeve to my astonishment went up the ladder they sent down next with the ease of a girl, but Eileen was uncertain about her legs, and Terrence had to help her climb.

Simon was behind me when I started up, the empty currach, tied as it was, bobbing in the sea, so that I had to step wide to catch the bottom rung. I started to climb. And then I was on board the patrol boat and Simon followed.

Terrence was shaking hands with Michael, then giving his aunt a hug. He turned then to Eileen, and if that embrace lasted a little longer than the others, I wasn't surprised.

Turning to me, he kissed me on the cheek. "Well, me darlin'," he said in a stage Irish accent, "what am I going to do without you?"

I said, "You aren't going back—Terrence, they'll find out—they'll take you and hang you."

"No, they won't. And who is there to keep Niall in hand, and Granny from finding herself in more trouble?"

"You don't think she sent them after us?"

"No. How? And she's my grandmother. I have to take care of her," he said in a serious voice now. "Goodbye, Bess Crawford. Come back to Ireland when she's free." And he put his arms around me in a friendly embrace before turning to shake Simon's hand, finally waving to the officer on the bridge.

Then he was over the side, one last long look at his cousin, and down the ladder, picking up the oars before casting off the rope. I was closest to the side. He waved, then took the oars in hand.

"I don't know where you got that revolver," he shouted to me. "But bless you for it."

And he began to row back the way we'd come.

I watched him out of sight as the others were being taken below, where Ellis was waiting.

Simon came to stand behind me.

"It was your father who remembered that there were sea patrols. Ever since the Germans tried to send arms for the Rising. The war is over, but you know how it is. Easier to start a campaign than to end it."

I was very tired. But we'd got everyone out. The Major would have proper medical care very soon. Under my feet, I could feel the engines come to life as the patrol boat began a wide turn to go back the way it had come.

"Do you think they'll blame Terrence for the murders?"

"No. The ringleaders will have seemed to disappear. The rest won't hang about. They'll scatter and try again another day."

"*Were* they going to attack the Army?"

"Terrence believed they were planning to blow up Richmond Barracks in Dublin. It was where some of the leaders were court-martialed, then taken the short distance to Kilmainham Gaol, to be shot. That's why they needed the Major and Sullivan, to learn how to pose as soldiers long enough to lay charges. The Major murmured something about Richmond there in the ruined cottage, while he was half conscious, and that gave Terrence what he needed to know. Murphy and his lot probably saw the act as avenging those men. Instead it would have brought the wrath of London down on Ireland again. I just don't see why a Royal Constabulary man would risk his career working with the likes of Padriac Murphy and his friends."

"I believe I do. I don't think it really mattered to him whether their plan was successful or not. The Constable must have hoped to put the blame on Terrence as their leader. There were rumors he might be in Galway, but there was an even better chance that he'd be seen at his cousin's wedding. Think what it would do for that career if the Constable brought in the man everyone has been searching for?"

"You could be right, Bess." He paused. "Your father thinks that the Government is going to crack down on the Irish Problem, as they call it, and soon. To stop the mounting unrest. Harsh measures to stamp out rebellion altogether. I'd have said it would work before coming here. Now I have my doubts."

I shivered. It wasn't from the cold. I looked once more out at the empty sea where a little currach was moving steadily back to Killeighbeg. I owed him so much . . .

"There's tea below. There's nothing more you can do, Bess. Try to put it behind you."

"I was thinking how beautiful Ireland looked, flying over the countryside as I came in."

As I turned back to the man standing so close to me, I added, because I thought it might matter, "I've finally made a decision, Simon. When I'm back in Somerset, I'm going to send my resignation to London." But I intended to keep my flat in London. At least for a while.

There was silence for a moment.

"And then?" he asked.

Before I could answer, an officer was coming down from the bridge to speak to us, hailing us as the engines began to pick up speed, a low rumble that made talking more like shouting.

The officer greeted us, asking if I was Sister Crawford.

"A pleasure to meet you, Sister. Glad to have you safely aboard."

"Thank you, sir. I can't tell you how happy we were to see you."

"I've sent a message to your father, letting him know that everyone was safe."

"That's very kind of you. May I present Simon Brandon?"

"A pleasure as well, Brandon. The Colonel ordered us to see you both back to Somerset. And any of your party who cares to come with you." They shook hands, and then the officer said, "Do come down. The wind is picking up as we add speed. It will be cold out here."

I started forward, but Simon answered, "I think I'll stay on deck a little longer."

"Whatever you prefer. Sister? This way."

There was nothing to do but follow him below.

Ever since that moment in the orchard when I'd realized just how much he meant to me, I'd been afraid that Simon might not feel the same way. There was Scotland to consider. And my parents. I *wanted* to believe that Terrence was right—but I still didn't know how I'd hurt Simon, that day on the strand, when he'd walked away from me. If he'd even forgiven me.

What if he hadn't?

I'd always tried to find answers to problems—that was why I'd been such a good nurse. But this was different. This was my future. The future I'd tried so hard *not* to think about.

And I wasn't sure how reach for it.

I dared not make a mistake . . .

ACKNOWLEDGMENTS

To Ruth Dudley Edwards, our thanks for her talks in Indiana about the Rising. They helped us understand the personal feelings of the people involved on both sides, not just what the history books had to say about 1916. It was a much better story because of that.

And our thanks also to Lindblad Special Expeditions, and the Endeavour, which got us to Inishmore and Dun Aonghasa, the Aran Islands, and a pub in Galway where the music was wonderful.

And finally our thanks to our agent, Lisa Gallagher, who took photographs of the places in Dublin where the fighting took place during the Rising, to be sure we remembered it all aright.

ABOUT THE AUTHOR

CHARLES TODD is the author of the Bess Crawford mysteries, the Inspector Ian Rutledge mysteries, and two stand-alone novels. A mother-and-son writing team, they live on the East Coast.